# SWEET LOVE, SURVIVE

## Susan Johnson

BANTAM BOOKS

New York • Toronto • London • Sydney • Auckland

Sweet Love, Survive

A Bantam Fanfare Book/published by arrangement
with the author

PUBLISHING HISTORY
Charter edition published July 1985
Bantam Fanfare edition/June 1996

ISBN 0-553-56329-7

*Published simultaneously in the United States and Canada*

Bantam Books are published by Bantam Books, a division of Bantam
Doubleday Dell Publishing Group, Inc. Its trademark, consisting of the
words "Bantam Books" and the portrayal of a rooster, is Registered in
U.S. Patent and Trademark Office and in other countries. Marca
Registrada. Bantam Books, 1540 Broadway, New York, New York 10036.

PRINTED IN THE UNITED STATES OF AMERICA

RAD    0   9   8   7   6   5   4   3   2   1

*Dear Reader,*

SWEET LOVE, SURVIVE is the third book in my Kuzan trilogy. Written fourteen years ago, it's been long out of print and I'm pleased Bantam is re-issuing it. I was much enamored of the Kuzan family at the time and as I finished each book, another seemed to spring to mind. Apollo's story takes place in the closing days of the Russian Civil War.

The internecine warfare convulsing Russia at the time was so bloody and brutal, the scale of human cruelty so unimaginable, the images still haunt me today. Much like the aristocrats during the French Revolution, Russian nobles often escaped their homes literally seconds before the Bolsheviks arrived.

Fifteen thousand works of émigré literature have been documented so an enormous number of books are devoted to this apocalyptic period. I read extensively from this vast body of material. And from that research, Apollo and Kitty's story slowly evolved. The Caucausus cavalry troops fascinated me, the tribal customs undimmed by the progress of time intrigued me, as did the vast scope of human tragedy played out against the upheavals of war. SWEET LOVE, SURVIVE focuses on just one small part of the conflagration that swept Russia and on two people who find each other amidst the chaos.

It's a story of hope in a hopeless time.

And of the power of love.

*Best wishes,*

*Susan Johnson*

# SWEET
# LOVE,
# SURVIVE

# 1

"Almost there."

"I need a drink."

"And a bed—preferably with someone soft and warm in it."

"Jesus, Mahomet, don't you ever think of anything else?"

"What else is there?"

"Right now I'll settle for a fire to thaw my frozen feet."

An affirmative murmur of deep male voices whispered through the score of riders like a light wind through dry leaves, followed by another silence born of exhaustion.

The weary cavalry troop cantered up the linden-lined driveway; elongated shadows cast by the flanking trees sketched inky patterns on the snowy sweep of open field on their right. At the end of the long drive, a three-story manor house sprawled along the crest of a rise, its bulk shining white in the clear winter moonlight, its numerous Palladian windows darkly shrouded except for two golden, lamplit casements on the main floor. From the base of the hill, stretching as far as the eye could see, fertile wheatfields lay dormant under a deep blanket of drifted snow. Dark fringes of forest rimmed the remote horizon of frozen steppe, and silhouettes of weeping willows bowed languidly over the icebound river cutting through the frosty, moon-drenched fields. All was crisp and still in the bitter December night.

1

The clinking of mouthpieces and the faint jingle of spurs sounded softly as the horsemen moved up the avenue. Each man rode by instinct, half-asleep, exerting a knee pressure only sufficient to keep him in the saddle with the least effort. Heavy shubas of marten, sealskin, and beaver were crisscrossed with cartridge bandoleers and belted with double-holstered Mausers. Wolfskin or astrakhan *papakhas*, pulled low against the raw air, framed youthful faces and tired, cynical eyes which had seen savagery and bloodshed on an epic scale. Held slack in leather-gloved hands, reins slapped gently against sweat-streaked horseflesh. Half a verst back the thoroughbreds had smelled the stables, snorted, lifted their elegant noses, and of their own accord broken into a canter. Food and rest were near; the fatigued animals could sense it.

"Damned late to be bringing home twenty houseguests, Peotr," noted the young coronet keeping pace with the officer in the lead.

"Kitty's used to it," his companion grunted laconically.

"We're not in Piter[1] anymore, Aliosha, and concerned with manners," someone behind them commented dryly. "There's a war on, remember?"

"As if one could forget," a low-pitched murmur halfway down the ranks lamented. "Bloody, depressing war."

"But not in the last few weeks!" cried a triumphant voice. "We whipped their asses, by Christ! Two thousand roubles says those munitions depots we blew are still burning!"

"And five hundred more says Budenny's cavalry are still running toward Kamishin. Hip, hip—"

"Hurrah!" Twenty strong voices rose in exultant chorus to rousingly finish the cheer.

Seldom in the last months had they been able to rejoice so roundly. Since mid-October, Denikin's over-extended White Army had been in full retreat. Kolchak's Siberian armies were finished, and General Yudenich and his small body of volunteers from Estonia had been defeated at the gates of Petrograd. On October 20, the Reds had retaken Orel, the Ukraine had fallen, and now Kharlov was threatened. The Bolsheviks were proving to be formidable opponents.

In spite of the recent disastrous reverses, General Mamontov had undertaken a deep raid behind Red lines. His cavalry mass, or koulak (fist), had smashed through the left flank of the Red Army and had reached Tambov, some 140 miles from where he had first broken through, then had turned westward and had moved along a zigzag route, dodging large Red troop concentrations for well over a hundred miles before turning back south and rejoining the main lines of the White armies. In the course of his daring raid, Mamontov had completely disrupted the rear of a wide sector of the Red front. He burned army supplies and depots, blew up bridges, destroyed locomotives and rolling stock, and executed captured Bolshevik commissars.[2] Cheerful jubilation in the South Russian newspapers noted there hadn't been anything remotely like it since the cavalry raids during the American Civil War half a century earlier.

The officers cantering up the snow-covered driveway had been part of that roving cavalry under Mamontov. They were one of the special cavalry units from Turkestan and the Caucasus incorporated into Mamontov's IV Cavalry Corps; members of the Touzémnaya (Native) Division, unofficially known throughout Russia as the Dikaya (Savage) Division. They were regarded, by others as well as themselves, as the elite of the White Army divisions. Their outward appearance was at best irregular. Flamboyant riffraff of every race and creed was the polite description. Some called them a pack of killers. Whatever the definition, all acknowledged their incredible skill and bravery, as well as their remarkable loyalty to each other, which went well beyond the usual standards of courage. They never left their dead or wounded on the battlefield but brought them out regardless of the circumstances.

Although young, all had served a bloody apprenticeship in the Great War and there had learned to cast aside everything not essential to battle: idealism, military discipline, regulation equipment, tack, and polish. They were unorthodox in every way—even to a completely different style of riding. It was a style more sporting than military, for they all rode thoroughbreds on short stirrups with a long rein and no bits, enabling them to keep up a pace that no one else could rival.[3] The riders had a variety of *nagaikis* (whips) and *kinjals* (knives) tucked into their boots which they used with a kind of effective carelessness that earned them their reputation for savageness.

"That Balashov arsenal was sheer beauty, Apollo," said a hawk-faced Kurdistan dressed in sheepskin, leather, and silver-embroidered breeches to the tall, well-built rider slouched in the saddle of the magnificent Karabagh mare cantering alongside him. "But crazy, definitely crazy."

"I can count on Leda to get me out of any tight spot," the large man impassively replied. "A mullah once told me Leda and I were both touched by the sun . . . some mystical sort of thing. Not that I believe it, particularly, but it doesn't hurt. I'll take all the luck I can get." Mystical or not, it was an apt description, for the spectacular golden color of the mare and her master's pale yellow hair—unseen at the moment, beneath the wolfskin *papakha* pulled down over his forehead—was a superb match.

"Touched is right," his companion remarked facetiously, referring neither to mysticism nor coloring. "You're a damned maniac, Apollo, going in to blow up that guarded arsenal smack in the middle of Budenny's army."

"Hell, I couldn't let an opportunity like that pass. Damn nice fireworks—good for night riding." An inner smile briefly lit hooded eyes.

"It was like a full moon over the Erivan plateau. . . ."

"I thought you'd appreciate it, Sinko, brigandism being in your soul and all. Reminded you of the night raids so dear to your heart, eh?" There was a teasing mockery in the timbre of the deep voice.

"Nostalgic as mother's milk, my friend."

"As you damn well know"—the muscle in one lean cheek clenched momentarily—"it doesn't hurt to be a maniac, fighting this war. All the truly rational men were done in long ago. And as for dealing with unpredictable situations and explosives . . ." Throwing off the brief melancholy, the negligent drawl was restored: "Dare I make the cliché comparison to women? Handle them with a delicate touch and they'll all make you feel good in the end." Turning his head slightly, he smiled at Sinko in that lazy, faintly ironic way that was so much a part of his character.

"You should know, Apollo," the dark-skinned, showily dressed Kurd replied with a flash of white teeth. "Wherever we stop there's some woman giving you the eye and more than willing to make room for you in her bed that night."

"War's like that, Sinko. Take it while you can. Who knows if you'll live to see morning."

Sinko glanced at the man riding next to him, expecting to see the familiar teasing smile. The well-favored face was dead serious.

Even now, regardless of their recent successful raid, everyone in the cavalry troop knew the White armies were fighting a losing battle. Every week, every day and hour, the Red armies were becoming better organized and better equipped. They outnumbered the Whites by almost two to one, had vast reserves to cover their casualties, and had supplies vastly in excess of those of their adversaries.[4] It was only a matter of time until the Whites were defeated, unless new Allied aid arrived—and since the French had evacuated Odessa and the Hampshires had sailed from Vladivostok for home in September, the promised support didn't appear very likely.

Among the Whites, Alexeiev was dead. Kornilov was dead. Kaledin had committed suicide. Kolchak had been shot. Everyone gone after two years of war except Denikin and Wrangel. The end was near. But no one ever admitted the fact aloud. It was understood they were all committed to fight to the very last.

Every officer in the group on that chill December night had his own reasons for fighting, for staying when every practical consideration screamed its dissent. The reasons were as many and varied as the men riding together in this cavalry troop, the scions of aristocratic, leisured families who had ruled Russia unchallenged for a thousand years. Although the troop was highly irregular on the surface—a cross section of mountain tribes: Circassian, Kabardin, Ingushian, Chechen, Dagestan, and Tartar—each man had been trained in one of the empire's elite Guard regiments, and all were superb horsemen, crack shots, skilled tacticians—and, by repute, the most wanted group of men in Russia. Each officer carried a price on his head guaranteeing its recipient a comfortable retirement. The Central Executive Committee in Moscow, as well as the General Staff of the Red Army, would breathe a collective sigh of relief if this renegade remnant of the dreaded Savage Division were ever captured.

Skirting the darkened west wing of the manor house, the men rode around to the stables and wearily dismounted. They had been in the saddle almost continuously for days, in bitter cold, moving through war-torn country where there was very little food or shelter. Back in safe territory now, the troop had been granted four days of rest before resuming the campaign. The *koulak*'s raid had been a very satisfying maneuver—well conceived, well executed, successful. A cavalry corps against an entire field army, and . . . a glowing success. They were all in a mood to celebrate, despite their fatigue.

Leaving the horses in the grooms' care, the men strolled around to the main house, now laughing and joking, their guard down, the nervous tension so much in evidence during the last weeks had instantly dissipated once their feet had felt firm ground again, and gratifying thoughts of warm food and drink replaced the ruthless, bloody images of war.

"Welcome! Welcome home, Your Honor," the old retainer, opening the door, happily greeted his master.

"Thank you, Pavel. It's good to be back." Colonel Peotr Radachek smiled, pulling off his stained leather gloves. "Some champagne and vodka, eh, Pavel?" he remarked, shrugging out of his heavy fur coat. "We've some celebrating to do!" Tossing aside his *papakha*, he sauntered down the darkened hallway, flicking lightly with his ever-present *nagaiki* at the caked-on mud gracing his boots, followed by the affectionate, voluble Pavel and a dusty, dirty group of suddenly loquacious cavalrymen.

Minutes later they were sprawled around the table in the

hastily opened dining room. An enormous crystal chandelier dispelled the room's midnight gloom and cast a brilliant glitter over a lengthy mahogany table, which was covered immediately by busy servants with a clutter of wine bottles, vodka decanters, *zakuski*, caviar, glasses, and cigar and cigarette boxes. A meal was being prepared belowstairs, the mistress of the house had been informed of their arrival, and the officers were counteracting the chill and rigors of the journey with generous draughts of Khahetian champagne and local vodka. Most of the men had cast off their tunics and now lounged in shirt-sleeves. Boisterous, joyful masculine voices rang out in toasts: to their cavalry division, to the White Army, to General Mamontov, to General Wrangel, to the success of their raid. They stood each time, as was the custom; tall, young, trim, their muscles honed to steel by years of warfare, their faces bronzed by the wind and sun of long months in the saddle. They stood proud and triumphant as they threw back their heads and tossed off the vodka for each toast in a single gulp. Servants quickly refilled the glasses; as soon as one toast was completed another raucous slur on the enemy would follow, or a pledge to honor and to country would be celebrated. In very short order, each member of the troop had jubilantly saluted his companions and the brilliant triumph over the formidable Budenny. After the fifth or sixth round, a great deal of grandiloquence and merriment accompanied the speeches.

A scant half hour later, Countess Radachek appeared in the doorway.

"Good evening, gentlemen." Kitty Radachek was the kind of woman whose breathtaking beauty could silence a room—and very briefly it did.

The countess blushed.

The men jumped up.

Rosy-cheeked, she smiled diffidently. "Please, make yourselves at home. Supper will be served soon."

The amenities observed, the men all resumed their comfortable sprawls, the buzz of conversation began again, and the young pretty countess quietly greeted each man as she walked the length of the room to welcome her husband home. Having dressed hurriedly when the servants woke her, she wore a simple but elegant, unornamented lilac-colored frock by Vorobiev and no jewelry. Her honey-gilt hair, catching the sparkle and glimmer of the chandelier, was undressed, simply pulled back with an embroidered ribbon to fall in silken waves down her back, giving her the appearance of a dainty schoolgirl.

"What a nice surprise. Welcome home, Peotr." She smiled shyly at her husband. "Everyone's so cheerful, you must have been victorious."

"We ran Budenny's First Cavalry Army back to Kamishin." Peotr grinned, casually draping his arm around Kitty's small shoulder and at the same time raising his glass to his companions.

They were an incongruous pair standing at the head of the table, for Count Radachek was as tall and swarthily dark as his wife was diminutive and fair. Leaning her head against her husband's great bearlike chest, the countess half closed her sea-green eyes and murmured, "I'm happy you're safe."

Peotr had turned to respond to some bantering remark concerning the merits of horses and women and failed to hear his wife. Patting her shoulder carelessly, he turned back to her briefly to suggest, "Sit down, Kitty. Have some champagne with us," and then his voice rose in jesting comment, shouting across the table in reply to some vulgar inquiry.

Kitty sat down with a soft whisper of lavender wool and was gallantly handed a glass of champagne by a smiling lieutenant who bowed, clicking his heels together very smartly. Unfortunately, he was not exactly sober; having accomplished the adroit maneuver, he fell facedown on the table.

"Hey, hey, Sandy," someone yelled. "Damn good form. Didn't spill a drop." And indeed he hadn't; infinitely polite, the lieutenant had landed eight inches to the south of Kitty's glass. Efficient servants restored him to his chair and the countess quietly sipped from her glass while joking repartee, noisy songs, and shouts of laughter passed back and forth, and as high spirits riotously escalated.

"To Apollo!" someone shouted. "And to his devilish cool hand with dynamite!"

"Hear, hear!" The chorus stood and refilled glasses were tossed down once again.

"There was a little bet concerning the possibility of infiltrating the arsenal at Balashov," Peotr explained to Kitty. "Apollo took up the challenge and somehow managed to get in. That munitions dump rose sky high. It lit up the heavens clear to Kabul. Apollo won himself a roan stallion—which he doesn't need, since he's enamored of that Karabagh mare he rides. We were all watching from the bluffs south of town, and when Apollo came racing out of that depot area riding hell-bent for leather, we knew the fireworks were about to—"

"Hey, Apollo!" Peotr's narrative was interrupted by a booming voice. "Where'd you learn the technique? Some bloody anarchists in your family tree we don't know about?"

A lazy drawl replied, "It helps, Azof, to have owned a munitions factory or two." Apollo was now elegantly disheveled and more than a trifle drunk. His clear, golden eyes glittered brilliantly. "Learned the finer points of blowing up the world at my papa's knee," he added with a flash of a grin, his fine white teeth shining against his deeply bronzed skin. There was something demonic in his expression—the smile with the mouth alone, perhaps. The captain had the look of a great tawny mountain cat, sleek, powerful, lean. His eyes were cat eyes, sparkling and yellow, their corners lifted high in a bold, sensual slant beneath heavy brows many shades darker than his blond, sun-streaked hair, which was long and carelessly brushed back like some rough lion's mane. He had the reputation of having the best hands in the world—an instinct he had been born with, and one which allowed him to deal gracefully and flawlessly with horses, cards, firearms, explosives, and . . . women.

"He's so wild tonight," a sandy-haired corporal said *sotto voce* to his table companion.

"As usual" was the dry retort. They both watched as Apollo carefully emptied a sizable portion of a bottle of vodka into his glass. Unaware of the scrutiny, and satisfied his task was accomplished when the clear liquid rinsed the rim, Apollo leaned back in his chair, one long-fingered hand curled around the perfectly filled glass. Abruptly, as an afterthought, he lifted the bottle to his mouth and drained the few remaining inches. Waving a servant aside, he very carefully placed the empty bottle at the end of a neat row arranged before him.

"Holds his liquor like a Siberian peasant," the corporal said with a certain awe.

"A pity at times," declared his more worldly companion. "Might save himself a lot of trouble if he'd pass out occasionally. Remember the time when, after two solid days of drinking, he set out for Moscow to assassinate Lenin? Got there, too. Amazing. Only Lenin was in Petrograd at the time, and Apollo was beginning to sober up by then so he came home. He said it was hair-raising, coming back through enemy territory stone-cold sober."

Apollo was known to favor a mode of life wilder than most, and this predilection for dangerous play and drunken adventuring often required a nimble use of his wits, an instinct to survive, and occasional assistance from his two personal bodyguards, Karaim and Sahin.

Like noiseless shadows, these two mountain men guarded the Young Falcon—or As-saqr As-saghir, as Apollo was familiarly known in their mountain aul—at the request of Alex, Apollo's father, and of Iskender-Khan, their leader and Apollo's great-grandfather. In the course of battle one took one's chances, but at least in the extraneous turmoil of civil war Apollo would be relatively safe from other forms of treachery—Karaim and Sahin would give their lives to protect their ward.

Now they sat impassively watching their handsome charge, who for some time had seemed detached from the raucous hum of conversation buffeting to and fro across the table. Suddenly his animal eyes came to life and a white blaze of vitality lit the golden depths.

Rising from his slouching sprawl in a deceptively fluid motion for one so inebriated, Captain Prince Apollo Kuzan lifted his glass to the table at large and, a malicious glitter now evident in the pale eyes, indolently saluted, "To the Bolskis."

A stunned silence greeted his toast.

One dark brow rose sardonically at the sudden hush. "May they all be blown to kingdom come," he softly finished with a slow grin. Apollo's yellow eyes were suddenly bland, his expression one of celestial affability. Raising the brimming glass to his lips without spilling a drop, he proceeded to pour the vodka down his throat.

"To kingdom come!" twenty rollicking voices shouted in unison and twenty throats were washed with fiery alcohol.

And so the celebration went its clamorous way in a surge of masculine bonhomie.

Forty minutes later, the countess excused herself to check on the preparations in the kitchen. The door had scarcely closed on her back when the count inquired of the table in general, "What say to a couple of days at Zadia's little nest in Niiji? Ilya says she's brought in six new girls from Georgia." He looked around questioningly.

A drunken roar of approval greeted his suggestion.

"After we eat, then—off to Niiji," Kitty's husband declared emphatically.

"I'll drink to that," decreed a slurred, sibilant Petersburg accent, perfectly on cue. "A woman, a meal, and a streak of luck—what else does a soldier need?" And all glasses were emptied again in roguish agreement, anticipation of Zadia's special brand of comfort running high.

After dinner, when port and cigars had been passed around, Peotr blandly announced to his wife, "We've a scouting mission beginning in the morning. Have my orderly pack some clean clothes for me. We're off within the hour."

"Oh, Peotr, I thought you were staying for a few days." Kitty's disappointment was obvious.

The count's shoulders lifted in a Gallic shrug as he gazed at his pretty little wife, deciding absently she was not a pleasure he would ever appreciate. "Sorry, pet, we're expected at Wrangel's headquarters in the morning." The lie came easily. Zadia was one of Peotr's favorite paramours. "I'll be back in two or three weeks if all goes well. You'll take care of things for me while I'm gone?" He bent to brush his wife's cheek with a kiss. A detached, obligatory kiss.

Kitty lowered her heavy lashes. "Of course, Peotr; you know I will," she answered dutifully, but her heart lost its warmth. What did she expect, anyway? she asked herself with sad frustration. Why had she thought it would be any different this time? She knew full well why Peotr had married her. Rationally, she understood the arrangement. She always had. A marriage of convenience, contracted by their parents years ago. The estates were adjacent; it was a profitable marriage for both parties—but Kitty, innocently shunning logic, had hoped and dreamed her dark, handsome husband with those beautiful gypsy eyes would come to love her. It hadn't worked out that way. After three years of marriage she should have known better, should have learned the futility of romantic yearnings, been immune to disappointment.

Peotr always treated her with courtesy and a careless affection, much as one would treat a friend's sister or a relative. Theirs wasn't a conjugal relationship so much as a lack of a relationship altogether, a polite fiction of a marriage. Kitty had been orphaned while still in her teens, and during the remaining two years of her minority she'd been chaperoned by a paternal aunt reluctantly dragged away from Petrograd and brought south to "do her family duty." Kitty and her aunt had never more than courteously tolerated each other, unfamiliar as Kitty was with all the feminine graces, pastimes, and idle amusements so dear to her aunt—so dearly missed by her aunt. Kitty had been reared to take an interest in the estate and trained by her father in all aspects of stewardship; when her parents died in an accident on the Volga it was both natural and necessary for Kitty to take over management of Kuchin. As natural as becoming engaged to Peotr, whom she had known all her life.

Shortly after Kitty's eighteenth birthday, on one of Peotr's leaves from the western front, they had married. Immediately after the ceremony, Kitty's aunt, her duty discharged, had climbed into a carriage loaded with her trunks and left for Petrograd. Two days later, Peotr had returned to the war, leaving Kitty alone, responsible for running both estates.

Peotr genuinely appreciated Kitty's administrative abilities and often praised her competence and proficiency. But neither his careless, brotherly affection nor his compliments on her management acumen were what Kitty craved from her husband. She wanted his love. Sighing quietly, Kitty gazed at her raffish, ebullient mate—who was intent at the moment on emptying a decanter of vodka—and advised herself against such folly. After all, she understood the ways of the world as well as any other gently reared female. She understood the position of women in her class. Husbands loved and adored their mistresses but they didn't marry them; they took chaste, respectable, fresh young girls for their wives. But the converse was depressingly true . . . they didn't love them.

Several more bottles were emptied and another hour elapsed before chairs scraped back and the young cavalry officers rose to their feet, bid the countess a polite, if drunken, good night, and somewhat unsteadily mounted their horses for the twelve-verst ride to Niiji.

Morosely returning to the house after seeing her husband off, Kitty dismissed the servants. It was late, almost three o'clock; the cleaning-up could wait until morning. After one last look about to see that no lamps or cigarettes were left burning, Kitty started upstairs.

She felt very much alone. Unhappy feelings resisted all practical attempts at composure. Prospects for the future with Peotr seemed bleak. Such reflections smacked of self-pity, Kitty realized, perturbed with herself, and she chastised herself for such selfish thoughts. It was mean and ungenerous to fret about her future when Peotr's life was in mortal danger every day. In any event, with the war progressing as it was, what future did any of them have? Death, exile, servitude were the specters of the future—ominous thought. But for the moment, their district was still secure, and by busying herself with the supervision of the estate and trying to remain optimistic her mind would be distracted from the ghastly war, from her terrible fears for Peotr's safety. In these awful times, she could be of service to her husband at least as an estate steward if not as a wife and lover.

Then the haunting dread, which managed to slip around the most meticulously constructed mental barricades, reappeared. Dear Lord, Kitty thought helplessly, what would ultimately come of them? The area under White control diminished each month despite the summer victories of Wrangel and cavalry units such as Peotr's. The Red armies, well supplied, freshly reinforced, were tightening the ring each day. How much longer could they be beaten back? Kitty attempted to dismiss these morbid apprehensions, not wishing to contemplate the devastation of their estates or the fearful consequences of defeat any more than she cared to recall Peotr's instructions to her when he'd left to fight with the White Guard at the very beginning, in 1918.

"I've written everything down. Instructions are in a sealed folder in the study safe. Money's deposited for you in Paris. If I'm killed and defeat appears imminent, promise me you'll leave in time." He had looked at her very somberly, his gypsy eyes full of sadness, and had repeated, "Promise you'll leave."

Kitty had nodded, forcing herself to reply, "I will," although she had died a little then at the thought of losing Peotr and of leaving the land that had been her family's for a thousand years.

"And just in case . . ." Peotr had added, leaving the sentence unfinished, handing her a vial of morphine. Stories of atrocities, of torture and rape practiced by the Red Army, hung malevolently in the silence like a gruesome corpse on a gibbet. Neither could bring themselves to comment further. Kitty had nervously taken the vial from Peotr, burying it in the depths of her vanity case. It had never been mentioned again.

All the memories and daunting anxieties for the future, freshly recalled, served to further depress Kitty's spirit. Very near tears, she tightened her grip on the stair railing and steadied herself by sheer willpower against the coming attack of weeping. Damn the war, she swore silently. Damn all the senseless slaughter and misery. And damn, too, all the Zadias of the world, offering their kind of shameless, unconventional love, irresistible to husbands like Peotr.

Kitty knew very well where her husband and his friends had gone. Peotr's voice had carried quite clearly through the dining room door. At the thought of Peotr's indifference, Kitty's long suppressed tears suddenly spilled over, like a quicksilver break in a weakened dike. Determinedly, she dashed them away with a tiny closed fist, sniffling and blinking in a resolute effort to regain composure. Not too long ago, Kitty had promised herself never to cry again over Peotr's inconstancy—and damn, she didn't intend to so easily forget her resolve and become a watering pot tonight. Three years of shedding tears over the impossible dream of a loving husband were enough. Kitty had pragmatically jettisoned all but logical considerations regarding love and loving; for the future, she had intrepidly determined, all romantic illusion was to be summarily quashed.

# 2

Kitty walked into her dressing room and discarded the lilac frock, slipping back into the white, lace-trimmed batiste gown she'd so hastily discarded when Peotr and his troop had arrived. Untying the ribbon binding her hair, she padded barefoot into the adjoining bedroom and began extinguishing the lamps left burning in the large, pine-paneled room. The pungent fragrance of sweet peas wafted through the air, their redolent perfume rising like whispers of summer from several large *famille verte* bowls filled with massive bouquets of the delicate pastel blooms replenished daily from Aladino's hothouses.

But another faint, disparate aroma drifted indistinctly to Kitty's senses as she moved to dim the lamps. A scent not vivid enough to enter her consciousness; an odor only vaguely noted. Approaching the bed, the elusive, earthy essence, previously indistinguishable, became remarkably clear—faintly leather, vaguely horsey, and . . . decidedly alcoholic.

In the shadowy glow of the small brass bedside lamp Kitty saw a man sprawled facedown on her pristine white coverlet. A tunic jacket lay in a heap on her carpet, along with a glistening cartridge belt, holster, and sword strap. The officer slept with his face buried in the pillow, clad in a shirt, elkskin breeches, boots, and spurs. His tall, powerfully muscled body, revealed so blatantly beneath close-fitting elkskin and white silk, took up a great deal of space on the birchwood bed. Although most of his face was concealed in the pillow, the long, sun-streaked hair and the portion of dark, winged brow and stark cheekbone verified the usurper as Prince Apollo Ku-

16

zan, one of her husband's young captains. Kitty glanced quickly around the bedroom, half expecting to find Karaim and Sahin hovering in the shadows, but Apollo was alone.

It looked as if she'd be sleeping in another bedroom to-night, Kitty rapidly decided. The prince was much too large for her to move, and it was senseless to wake him simply to ask him to transfer to another room. The cavalry troop would still be at Zadia's in the morning. Apollo could rejoin his companions after a good night's rest. However, consideration for the delicate, embroidered counterpane Apollo was lying on induced Kitty to conclude that pulling off his boots before she left might be wise. Those wicked spurs would wreak havoc with the padded silk if he tossed and turned during the night.

One moment Kitty's hands were grasping a grimy cavalry boot, and the following moment she was lying on her back in the center of the bed, her hips straddled by muscular, leather-clad thighs. A lifetime of training in the Caucasus Mountains, as well as the last few years of war, had instilled a finely tuned sense of survival in Apollo. He was a *very* light sleeper.

"Ah-h-h." He relaxed the harsh grip of his fingers around Kitty's slender throat and smiled warmly at the soft female beneath him. No enemy. The adrenaline ceased its furious pumping through his nervous system. "Forgive me, *dushka*," he said, exhaling softly, soothing the angry red marks his fingers had left. The lean, brown hands massaged her neck lightly with apologetic caresses.

Apollo looked down on the beautiful perfumed woman ly-ing under him, felt a fleshy female body between his legs, and the familiar scene stimulated reflexes schooled to perfect re-sponse by countless incidents in the past. To wake after drink-ing and find a woman in bed with him was no novelty—and his need for a woman's warmth was achingly real after weeks of campaigning in the unpopulated steppes.

Without a word he bent to kiss her, not a gentle caress, but a barbaric kiss that shook Kitty's spine, a dangerous kiss that ate at her lips, her tongue; teased the soft interior of her mouth; suffocated the cry of alarm which died in her throat.

His hands moved up swiftly, lost themselves in her golden tresses, and held her captive as he lowered his body. Kitty couldn't move, couldn't cry out; she was trapped beneath Apollo's powerful frame while he savored her mouth with a greedy, sharp-set passion—savored her with the avid hunger of two weeks' abstinence, his lips warm and soft, his tongue languidly probing, his sensitive hands leaving their indelible imprint, until a small flame of response, unwonted and disturbing, began to smolder in Kitty. Apollo felt it, the infinitesimal acquiescence, and he lifted his mouth to trace a path downward, lowering his head to kiss the crest of a pale, rounded breast.

Released from those dangerous, encroaching lips, Kitty cried, "Apollo! No! Please stop! Apollo . . . you mustn't—" She ended in a wail, struggling to push the heavy body away.

There was amusement in his voice. "Why did you tumble into bed with me, little Marousia, if I *mustn't*? Ah, *dushka*, hush. Hush, you always say no, at first; I know you." He laughed softly. "No games tonight, *ma petite*, not tonight," he murmured into the hollow beneath her ear while his hands played down her waist and over her slender hips. His fingers slid under her. Large hands grasped firm buttocks, pressing her fiercely, impatiently, against his body. Kitty gasped at the imprint of his hands burning through the sheer material of her nightdress and inadvertently whimpered in response to the urgent hardness pressing into her belly.

Catching her breath, she frantically whispered, "Apollo! Please! I implore you!" But her agitated request was strangely breathy.

Raising his head, Apollo smiled teasingly and laughed again. "You needn't beg, little Marousia. I'm more than willing."

Kitty was seized with both outrage and a terrible excitement. What was he talking about? Who was Marousia? Kitty nervously searched the amused face so close to hers and looked into half-closed, tawny eyes; eyes strangely opaque, dimmed by alcohol. She realized with a sudden sinking feeling that Apollo didn't know who she was. Good God, he didn't know!

The tearful "No!" the gentle resistance, like a scented gauntlet thrown down in the game of love, was a piquant challenge to the prince, whose brain was being forcefully guided by the tightness of his breeches. His head dipped to kiss his little Marousia again, and while his lips stifled a muffled protest, his hand slipped beneath her nightdress, gently touching the smooth flesh inside her thighs. Kitty pressed her legs together, but one strong, bronzed hand, remorseless as a steel wedge, nudged them apart and the light strokes resumed, moving slowly upward. Apollo was enjoying the feel of velvety skin, taking his time, touching, rubbing, his lean, experienced fingers fondly playing with the sensitive fragrant flesh; wooing the lady. Kitty's brain was reeling uncontrollably; she was incapable of protest as inexplicable emotions terrifyingly mingled with guilt and common sense all cascaded headlong down a turbulent whitewater of desire while those questing hands took liberties, leisurely explored.

Apollo's tongue claimed her mouth without haste, alternately demanding and cajoling, lingering to experience the sweet pleasure it gave him. Then his fingers encountered damp silken hair and a great heat. Kitty moaned, a shattering surge of passion and soaring pleasure burning through her trembling body.

It appeared—the prince's inebriated brain registered from vast experience in these matters—it appeared the lady was ready. Rolling over, he sat up to pull off his boots and breeches.

When Apollo moved away from her, Kitty was left breathless, feeling strangely bereft. But freed as she was from his disturbing embrace, in a few cool moments, commanding purpose was restored to her fevered mind.

"I'll scream," Kitty hissed in a stage whisper. "Every servant will be here in a minute!"

Apollo looked over his shoulder at her briefly and considered the threat for a moment. His sense of situation in these boudoir encounters flawless, he resumed unbuckling his spurs.

"So help me, I swear I'll scream," Kitty continued lamely, but even as she threatened, she knew she wouldn't scream.

How could this scene possibly be explained to the servants who would come running to her rescue?

And Apollo also knew, however drunk he was, however vague and hazy his senses, that the threat was quite empty. He had divined the lady's desires with a sure libertine's expertise. He recognized the signs—could feel, taste, smell that delicious stirring of female response. He knew it from one end of Russia to the other. Yes, the lady was ready. No, the lady wouldn't scream.

Apollo stood for a moment or so unbuttoning his shirt and breeches, then, discarding his clothes, moved back to the waiting woman. Broad-shouldered, lean-hipped, he displayed an arousal so blatant the sight sent a quiver melting down Kitty's spine, half fear, half anticipation. The illumination from the bedside lamp played over bronzed skin and rippling muscles as he came toward her, splendid as a half-tamed leopard.

Kitty had known Apollo casually for years, but Captain Prince Apollo Kuzan asserting his full powers at close range she had never known. He was so near she could feel the warmth of his skin; his hair seemed in the fragmented light like spun gold. Without touching her, he swept his gaze over her body, his pale eyes attentive, flaming with gathering violence. She was held fast by those heated eyes, by his physical magnificence, by the sight of him naked and aroused, and a sudden turbulence exploded quietly within her like a blaze on a cool autumn night.

The silence of the room, breathlessly still, remained unbroken except for the faint whisper of the bed dipping under its new weight. Apollo's hands reached out to deftly untie the ribbon on the neckline of the white batiste gown. He opened the lacy décolletage, smoothing laces and ribbons aside with a sensuous brushing motion, soft as a held breath, and smiled in a lazy, leisurely way, his untamed, smoldering eyes sweeping the full gleaming ivory curves now rising and falling in breathy agitation. His dark fingers slid peacefully inside to gently cup the heavy breasts, his gilded head bending toward her upturned face.

Kitty's lips opened submissively and Apollo Kuzan found warm haven after weeks of war.

With teasing lightness he nibbled at the fullness of her lower lip, slid the tip of his tongue over the fleshy moist verge, ran tantalizingly over Kitty's small white teeth, across the delicate arch of her upper lip, teasing, tempting her, his smell of alcohol pungent and sweet, close enough to taste. The devastating tongue danced and incited and asked for more, but still his mouth remained a millimeter away, only brushing her lips occasionally with a touch light as dandelion down in the wind.

Then his intent, busy hands released her nipples, now taut and achingly erect, and slid up over the flushed fullness of her breasts, squeezing gently, listening to her breathing, pausing to hold the weight of each breast in each of his hands, moving to drift up to the smooth whiteness of her neck, lean, splayed fingers softly gripping her small chin. Kitty, warming, breathlessly yearning for the feel of his kiss, twisted upward. With her small movement his grip tightened almost fiercely and suddenly his mouth moved swiftly down, fastening over hers like an animal with its prey. Kitty cried softly in surrender, overwhelmed by the burning contact, her lips crushed by the hunger of a man who has waited too long. Apollo's golden eyes closed for a moment in homecoming before he stretched his long body over hers. Supporting himself on his elbows, Apollo rained little kisses of welcome, thanksgiving, and ungentle desire on Kitty's eyes, forehead, cheeks, ears, always returning lingeringly to her achingly eager lips, taking her breath away with his searing kiss.

Kitty responded with an unexpected hunger previously unknown to her, and while it excited and tantalized, it also shamed. She tried then, in a fit of conscience, to stop, to pull away . . . anything but give in to this madness. But when she struggled briefly, saying, "No, no," in a despairing whisper, turning her mouth away, twisting beneath him, pushing at his muscular torso, Apollo took one of the hands beating at his chest and pulled it slowly down until it touched his rampant hardness. He drew in his breath sharply, his own hand shaking on hers.

"Yes," he said in a soft, ragged voice, knowing nothing could stop him from possessing her now—not the threat of hell itself. Then his mouth closed over one nipple, biting softly, tugging gently with teasing teeth, and Kitty, almost paralyzed by the electric flashes of desire tearing through her body, stopped her ineffectual struggles. For dazed, breathless moments Kitty was lost to everything but the glorious heat stealing over her.

Apollo lifted his mouth when she whimpered a little, and when he moved to recapture her mouth her moans were lost in his breath. "So quiet tonight, Marousia," he whispered. "Unlike you." He laughed softly, possessively, assured. "Soon you'll be screaming, *dushka*, soon." His knee buried itself between Kitty's legs, his aroused male force beyond further waiting. She was hot-blooded and ready, and he *needed* to bury himself into her, feel her close around him.

All Kitty could think of was the enormous size of him, the hardness and length she felt under her fingers. "It's too big . . . I can't," she faltered, a little frightened.

Oblivious to her hesitant murmurs, Apollo swung over her and positioned himself. "You know very well you can, Marousia, my pet. You've been abstinent too long, that's all." He smiled faintly. "And I as well."

"No . . . I can't. I mustn't . . . I don't want to."

"You want to, darling. It's very clear," he said softly, probing the opening that lured him, touching hot, sticky dampness. "Now there." Apollo sighed softly, feeling the velvety-smooth tightness. "I'll go slowly . . . only a little at a time," he soothed, having learned while still very young to use care in order not to hurt. His hands moved under Kitty's hips and he lifted her. "Welcome me home, Marousia," he whispered, "as only you can." As her thighs parted to make way for him, he began sliding into Kitty's slick wetness and warmth. "See," he said hoarsely, "how easy it is"—with melting skill he drove himself deeply into her—"to take it . . . all."

Kitty's breath suddenly lapsed as he buried himself, and a long denied blazing sensuality opened, exploded, flamed into ravenous need. With a plaintive whimper she threw her arms around his neck and, arching high, held him with all her strength, drawing in the exquisite pleasure. Her eyes, dark with desire, saw nothing, her ears were only tuned to his low, murmured lovewords, and the sense of ecstasy beginning to overwhelm her throbbed like a raging storm out of control.

Once he was completely fitted into the shape and feel and contour of her body, driving upward Apollo nudged gently, a delicate skilled little nudge, meant to give pleasure, *guaranteed* to give pleasure, and Kitty's world exploded, every excruciatingly tingling nerve, all sensation trembled on the edge. She reached for him countless times to pull him deeper, wanting the blissful oblivion, whimpering for the tantalizing delight she felt so near. But he broke gently away each time, withdrawing slightly, forcing the disciplined pauses, whispering as softly and quietly as a northern landscape at dawn, "Wait, Marousia. Don't rush, little kitten . . . I'll make it better." And while her mind was screaming, No, I can't wait another minute, not another angel breath of a second, he made her wait, knowing from long practice the importance of patience, knowing that the quivering holding back only made the eagerness peak more acutely.

Each time he moved back on the withdrawal stroke, small fingers dug into his back, trying to hold him close, not wanting to lose the pleasure, and the clawing, passionate female desire triggered his own ardor, sending new blood into the engorged maleness, swelling him larger and longer. With only a slight pause on the brink of withdrawal to savor the frantic woman whimpering, moaning, clawing at his back, he sank in once again, hard, rigid, penetrating deeply. She was tight, silky as rose petals, and he drove home with a soft sigh of pleasure. His hands slid lower on her hips, he nudged her thighs slightly wider and, bracing himself, settled into a familiar rhythm of thrust and withdrawal that brought them both insensate enchantment. And he was right, of course. He did make it better. Much, much better.

Abruptly, for their own private reasons of urgency, neither was interested in further delay, only in flesh-to-flesh convulsive need, raging passion, surge and countersurge. When Apollo's breath broke against her cheek, Kitty, reaching her own rapturous paradise, sobbed quietly and opened wide to receive his seed pouring into her. Then, from a great distance, as if muffled through mountains of cotton wool, Kitty heard a panting scream. Too lost to everything but the pleasure searing the whole of her being, she never knew the unprecedented cry was hers.

Apollo gazed down at the ripe lips half-open in ecstasy and, well pleased, afforded himself the smallest smile. There. He knew Marousia always screamed. Gratified with her obvious satisfaction, he tipped his head down to draw in the last dying sigh and, pulsing out his own profound release, spilled into the quivering, luxurious woman.

With Apollo still inside her, Kitty, all warmth and contentment, lazily drifted away from a pleasure unlike any she had ever felt; and when, only moments later, Apollo, growing again, thrust delicately against the exact tingling focus of her bliss, shocked and surprised, she whispered a protest. "No . . ." She couldn't again; she was too drowsy, too sore. But Apollo didn't listen to her, as he hadn't before, and within a quiveringly short time the building carnal sensations caught Kitty's breath in her throat. Several careful, skillfully proficient movements later, maddened by long, slow strokes that teased and caressed, Kitty, astonished, unbelieving, with a low, keening cry experienced another violent climax.

Swollen with blood, Apollo rode her still, bringing her up again and again, slowly, leisurely, exquisitely, until finally Kitty sank into a trembling exhaustion. Only then did Captain Prince Apollo Kusan, having politely pleased the lady, decide it was his turn again, and with a shuddering groan he ground into her, filling and filling and filling the lovely countess with a long suppressed orgasm so intense his hands shook.

Neither spoke as they both lay there, momentarily overwhelmed with a delicious lassitude. Only the fire crackled in the ornate porcelain stove. The soft light from the small lamp played gently over the entwined figures on the rumpled bed; the long-limbed, bronzed male form almost completely covering the small, white woman. The embroidered counterpane Kitty had been so concerned about lay crushed under their feet. Kitty's nightgown trailed forgotten, half-on and half-off the bed. Her delicate face, eyes closed, lay framed by gilded waves, and her tiny feet were dwarfed by muscular, tanned calves. The scent of sweet peas floated like a serene goddess over all.

Apollo's sweat-sheened body lay sprawled over Kitty, pinning her beneath him, throbbing and diminishing within her. His face was buried in her throat. After long, awkward moments, Kitty moved a little, but he didn't stir except for a soft exhalation warm against her neck, the tiny motion rasping his stubble across her skin. She tried to ease away, murmuring softly, and only then realized Apollo had fallen asleep. His weight was heavy on her, his hands in sleep gripping involuntarily. Even the slightest movement brought a tightening of those sun-dark fingers. He could not be wakened, moved, or dislodged. And very soon, because she had no choice and it was very late and she was very tired, Kitty drifted into sleep, thoroughly astonished at what had taken place, but pleasurably, contentedly satisfied, Apollo's sperm warm between her thighs.

She woke to the feel of him swelling, an infinitely languid sensation that slowly filled her. And when he woke, too, to the realization that the warming flesh, the gentle urgency, was not a dream, his half-lidded eyes gazed indolently for a moment and then closed again as he concentrated on the rhythm set by the moist, tight sheath enfolding him. Small hands came up to pull his face down, and Apollo felt only the deprivation of a long starved man. Later she touched him and he touched her in every delicate, succulent, shameless way possible, and far into the night they explored the depth, height, and breadth of conventional and unconventional lovemaking. It was close to dawn in the dim grayness of the room before Apollo rolled away, flooded with a luscious, ringing weariness, and even then the delicate, soft woman nestled near into the curve of his arm. With the casual familiarity of well-versed practice, he gathered her close and peacefully fell asleep.

# 3

The bright winter morning insinuated itself through triple-paned windows into the master bedroom on the second floor; the late morning sun, creeping in all golden and scintillating past the lace curtains, cast a wayward beam across Apollo's face. Like an unwelcome visitor the light woke him, and Apollo slowly became aware of two unpleasant facts: he had a violent headache, and his right arm was stiff and cramped. Opening his eyes with a certain reluctance, he glanced down at the small woman cradled in the crook of his arm and became aware of a third slightly staggering fact. He swore softly under his breath.

My God! *Bozhe moi!* It was Peotr's wife! The dainty honey-blonde with a face of jewel-like purity, breathing gently in his arms, was none other than his superior's wife. Wonderingly and half-dismayed, he said "Christ" quietly several times. He knew he shouldn't have had that last bottle of champagne. Then, like genial Mediterranean breezes, the events of the past night swam pleasurably into his brain and voluptuary memory warmed him. Christ, he breathed again, why had Peotr always talked of his Kitty in wifely terms, describing her as chaste and uninspiring? Were they talking about the same woman? A pensive frown creased his brow, adding to the pounding in his head. Maybe, he speculated with a neutral dispassion, she'd had some instructors since Peotr rode her last, for *Sacristi*, the countess he had reveled in bed with last night had been as uninhibited and passionately spontaneous as the most practiced whore. But whatever the circumstances, he acknowledged ruefully, he shouldn't have bedded Peotr's wife. It wasn't good form. Actually, it was frightfully *bad* form. In the cold soberness of morning, several hours too late, he reminded himself reprovingly of the requirements of civility and good manners.

Kitty woke at that moment, her lashes feathering open, and gazed into cool, golden Tartar eyes, scrutinizing her thoughtfully. The keen examination was sufficient to render the countess very uncomfortable.

There was a long moment's silence.

But even in this most unusual of situations, the prince's exquisite good breeding did not desert him, although he did look a slight bit disconcerted. "Accept my apologies, madame," Apollo offered pleasantly in the sibilant French of the Petersburg aristocracy. "I had too much to drink." She at least didn't look surprised, he thought, which meant one of them anyway must have been sober.

Kitty's cheeks blushed rosy at the bland, dégagé apology. Did he think . . . ? Oh, Lord. Stammering in embarrassment, she said, "I'm not in the habit . . . I mean . . . I usually don't . . . I mean, I never—" She didn't know how to continue. The entire episode, the whole night, her incredible behavior, was unbelievable.

"Nor I, madame," the young captain murmured politely. Contemplating the arresting, widely spaced emerald eyes, the gentle grace of her shapely mouth, he found himself enchanted. A small voice reminded him pertinently that one of the few rules he had chosen to observe was that of staying out of any superior's wife's bed. It had always seemed a sensible maxim, a small enough concession to society's conventions by a man otherwise distinguished for his unorthodoxy, and one likely to guarantee the least possible trouble in the long run— but then Apollo looked once more into those marvelous green eyes, as deep and clear as a tropical lagoon, and the sensible precepts began to lose their grip. Prudence was slipping out the door without so much as a backward glance while hot blood started pulsing through his veins, irresponsibly, iniquitously, with a completely unprincipled disrespect for good manners.

His body was beginning to respond in defiance of his mind's command. Jesus, why did she have to be so beautiful? And married? Then his focus drifted onto dangerous ground—so warm . . . and soft . . . and enticingly . . . sensual. He tried briefly to order his vagrant libido, and failed. The taboo on commanders' wives suddenly seemed inconvenient.

In the space of a few seconds and rather to his own surprise, Apollo's mind was made up. Zadia's could wait.

Kitty found herself unable to resist the penetrating attraction of those pale golden eyes, primitive in their need, tentative and suggestive, probing to her very soul. It was those eyes particularly—in all that golden, bronzed, supplely muscled perfection—that drew her. Luminous, vital eyes like those of a nervously elegant, gold-encrusted icon; bold, dramatic, dark-centered eyes pervaded by an underlying extraordinary sensuality. Then Kitty felt Apollo's newly aroused body stir and come to life against her warm thigh, and an answering heat, wayward and inexplicable by any previous standards of her circumspect life, coursed through her senses. She shivered slightly from fear, helplessness, and a piercing sense of susceptibility.

Apollo, feeling her tremble, drew her closer into the circle of his arms, very gently, so she could stop him if she wished. His muscles tensed as their bodies touched, but she didn't move. His heart beat faster.

His nearness, the heat from his body, the intimacy of expert fingertips tracing a delicate pattern down her spine, intensified the discomposure Kitty was experiencing. Apollo was holding her so close she could feel the pounding of his heart through the musculature of his chest. "This is . . . all quite ridiculous," Kitty whispered nervously, trying desperately to overcome her mindless, melting physical reaction to this virtual stranger.

"Yes . . . quite ridiculous," Apollo softly agreed, his eyes caressing her face, coming to dwell on her inviting pink mouth, knowing, in defiance of what was right, that he could not stop himself from what he was about to do. Lowering his

golden head to kiss those full, cherry lips, he murmured very,
very gently, "Absolutely . . . ridiculous."

Kitty tried to pull away but it was already too late. She felt
the sudden springing surge of his body and her senses reeled
beyond caution, reminded of all she had discovered in the long
night hours. Strong brown hands slid down to her hips and
crushed her tightly against a pulsing hardness. Kitty heard
faintly a groan of pleasure against her hair, and from that
moment she could not have obeyed her fleeting instinct to
escape had she even wished. And when his mouth crushed
down recklessly over hers, she no longer cared. Apollo's lips
and tongue pillaged and despoiled, greedy for a renewed taste
of her, for the woman taste, sweet, pungently libidinous.
While their mouths clung and tongues intertwined, his hands
lingeringly explored the curves and contours of her body, savagely efficient, sparing nothing. With a quicksilver shiver
Kitty responded, the memories of last night provocatively
lush, all Apollo had taught her of audacious, delectable passion between a man and a woman still piercingly fresh. Before
the kiss was over, inescapable, perfect, unutterably disturbing,
she let him know without speaking that what he wanted, he
could have.

In an incredibly short time, Apollo was delighted to enjoy—perfectly sober—all that he had only vague recollections
of having enjoyed the previous night. The countess had enormous proclivities as a courtesan, he thought pleasantly, adjusting her legs on his shoulders. His headache was quite
forgotten.

An hour later they lay content, wrapped in each other's
arms. Kitty was feeling a compelling need to say something
about her behavior, her mind a shambles of conflicting emotions. Stumbling skittishly over the words, she said, "Apollo,
I want to explain. That is . . . well, I've never behaved—you
must believe me . . . I don't know what came over me!" she
ended plaintively.

The prince, who had been dozing lightly after his latest
exertion, slowly eased his eyelids open and regarded the lovely,

flushed countess whose glorious cloud of buttercup curls was bewitchingly tousled from hours in bed. Just basic sexual desire, my pet, Apollo thought to himself, amused at Kitty's sudden restoration of modesty. But his bland social mask, schooled to perfection in drawing rooms and boudoirs across Russia and Europe, betrayed none of his reflections. "No need for hysterics, Kitty," he soothed comfortingly, his voice still drowsy. "It happens to everyone."

"But not to me, Apollo! Don't you see? I'm so ashamed! What will the servants think? What if Peotr finds out? Oh-h-h . . . it's terrible!" Kitty's lush lower lip began to tremble, and her fingers brushed nervous patterns over his ribs.

Pulling the distressed woman onto his chest, Apollo gently took her fine-boned face between his hands and, gazing kindly into huge, panic-stricken eyes the color of medieval jade, quietly said, "*Dushka*, relax. The servants can think what they will, it doesn't signify. Peotr will never know. And . . . little kitten," he murmured, drawing her closer, his eyes sparkling as he touched her lips lightly, "it was *not* terrible."

On that point alone, Kitty could not demur.

Lifting his head a fraction, Apollo brushed his mouth across the tip of her nose, then, dropping back onto the pillow, disarmed the countess with a reassuring smile. "Now be a brave soul," he said mildly, "and ring for some breakfast. I'm starving."

He sat across from her at the small table in the bedroom, washed and shaved, wearing Peotr's navy silk dressing gown edged in red cord, looking superbly handsome, all golden hair and bronzed skin. Kitty found herself drawn by his strength and beauty, at once attracted and ashamed. Despite the degree of familiarity they had shared, she felt herself on very uncertain ground with Prince Kuzan in the clear light of day. The prince for his part appeared undisturbed, only concentrating on his food until Kitty, stricken by remorse, began speaking again of the strange circumstances of the past night.

With color flooding her fair skin, she said, "I'm really not in the habit of doing this."

"It's not a bad habit at all, pet," Apollo said, smiling, "if you ask me." Levity was the worst possible posture he could have taken, he recognized instantly. Kitty's mouth went hard, her body stiffened. Immediately putting aside his knife and fork, Apollo spent the next several minutes apologizing. Having won his way, with some trouble and much soothing, back into the lady's good graces, he then thoughtfully let her talk, listening calmly to all the protestations, the explanations. It was a woman's way. He understood. She had been taught to guard her virtue and felt she had to account for her conduct. Tinged as he was with slight failings as both a voluptuary and debauchee, he could have told her he was immune to all the prohibitions of traditional society and had in fact been intimate with too many women to be astonished at any female's actions in bed; but the declaration would have sounded too callous and brusque. Instead, well mannered when it suited him, he diplomatically expressed all the courteous rejoinders, responding politely as was required by social custom.

He accepted complete blame, thus absolving the countess from any suggestion of having harbored inappropriate intentions. Well-brought-up young women didn't engage in such indecent conduct, Kitty's utter confusion conveyed, and they certainly should experience an abashed, ladylike reaction to their absolute disgrace, her blushes and stammering comments implied.

So, in a reasonable, temperate tone, Apollo insisted he had quite brashly been the aggressor; it was his fault entirely—his drunkenness; his ignorance of her identity; his improper abuse. "You see, Kitty," he indulgently declared, "I basely forced myself on you." He deliberately neglected to mention their most recent want of principle and its attendant rapture, consummated in the morning light. The lady, also, chose to ignore that particular episode.

His self-reproach seemed to soothe her. The countess appeared relieved, less agitated.

"I am," he said, placidly agreeable, "sensible in the bright light of midmorning, sober, and"—a faint smile effaced the lie—"have no designs on your virtue. *Paix*, then, and friends?" His face was innocently clear.

Kitty's reserve broke and vanished. Smiling in return, she said simply, "Friends."

Apollo, about to return to his eating, was arrested—a hand midway to his tea glass—by Kitty's quiet question. "Who's Marousia?"

He laid his hand on the creamy damask before answering.

"Sorry about that," he said, his eyes holding Kitty's for a moment.

"It's perfectly all right, I understand," Kitty replied complaisantly, her expression placid. "Only a natural curiosity—"

Apollo's mouth quirked wryly. "I deplore excuses, but . . . the last two weeks *were* wearing. Normally liquor doesn't make me that befogged. Marousia's an old friend of mine from Yalta. Small, blonde, er—nicely shaped. Quite like you." Then his smile flashed and one brow lifted idly. "Actually," he said softly, "not like you at all." Kitty flushed at the meaning, quite clear although unspoken. "And if I hadn't been so drunk," Apollo continued teasingly, "I would have noticed sooner. You are, my little kitten"—his finger brushed slowly over her lips—"very *unlike* Marousia."

Kitty, unused to flirtatious sensual banter, pulled back and blushed an even more rosy hue, further heightening the distinction between herself and Marousia. What a marvelous naiveté, Apollo thought, slowly letting his arm fall and wondering if Marousia had ever blushed in her life. Reflecting pensively that some of their sexual adventuring certainly could have induced even him to an occasional blush, he could not, to the best of his recollection, recall Marousia ever having been so inclined. Kitty was quite a darling, he decided, settling back into his chair with a charming smile for his companion.

They continued with breakfast then, conversing civilly and coolly like any well-mannered society husband and wife, avoiding any further mention of the previous hours, lightly touching on general topics, trading innocuous chatter. On that bright December morning, in the interests of the countess's peace of mind, Apollo uttered all the inconsequential social banalities he had learned so effortlessly years ago.

"This strawberry jam is delicious," the gentleman offered in lieu of mentioning the weather.

"I picked the berries myself."

The golden-haired captain responded with unimpeachable politeness, "How nice," and continued spreading the scarlet preserves on his toast.

A few moments later when Apollo paused briefly between forkfuls of country ham, Kitty inquired in a pretty wifely fashion, "Would you like your uniform cleaned this morning?"

"I'd appreciate that. I've lived in it for two weeks." He smiled pleasantly at the ravishing woman with cornsilk hair and amended courteously, "*If* you don't mind the bother."

"No, it's no trouble at all. Are you sure the toast is warm enough?" The countess nibbled at her luscious lower lip in absurdly enchanting concern.

He nodded.

There was a brief silence across the blue forget-me-not Limoges porcelain and sterling cutlery, during which Apollo helped himself to more smoked sterlet and Kitty appeared to scrutinize the appliqué work on the placemats. Suddenly her heavy lashes lifted and she asked bluntly, "Why haven't you married?"

He looked startled and then amused. "No one has proposed to me, I suppose."

Kitty smiled lightly. "Be serious, Apollo."

"I am serious," he replied, looking entertained, "and if I ever receive a proposal"—his brows lifted—"of *any* kind, you can be sure I'll give it careful consideration."

Kitty chose to ignore the innuendo. "In other words, you're not inclined to marry."

"So far I haven't."

"Surely someday?"

He stared at her. "I expect so, but right now it scares the hell out of me." He added a question she didn't care to hear. "Have *you* found marriage satisfying?" He was looking at her, his face a perfect mask—not a wink, not a smile, not a frown, just one eyebrow seeming slightly higher than the other.

Countess Radachek's large green eyes became studiously blank. "Point taken," Kitty replied with dainty precision. She readjusted the embroidered napkin in her lap and said mildly, "So tell me, how does your sister like the Loire valley?"

Apollo, courteous to a fault if the mood moved him, responded gracefully to Kitty's conversational shift away from an unpalatable subject. "Ninia's happy wherever there's a stable. She's at the age to be horse-mad."

"More tea? And your mother—what historical research project is she working on now?"

"A new one, last I heard," Apollo replied, holding out his glass. "Apparently there's a remnant of some ice age migration locked into a valley somewhere in the mountains of Hungary."

"Your father?"

"Devoted as ever to polo. Only Maman can get him off the field."

And thusly the patois of mannerly discourse went on. Everything was so ordinary they could have been married twenty years. But during the course of that very polite breakfast, so circumspect and correct, Apollo noted the quick little glances of shy admiration Kitty flashed at him when he appeared to be absorbed in his food. He saw that beneath her charm and graciousness she was tremblingly aware of him and thought to himself—with the arrogance born of perpetual success with women—that he'd further their acquaintance and have her again just as soon as the meal was over. Once the lady's inhibitions had been overcome, she was quite insatiable and much better, he decided, than what he could have found at Zadia's. Intercepting another surreptitious glance, he smiled warmly at the lovely countess, who flushed and looked away.

Twenty minutes later, Apollo's healthy appetite appeased,

he set his tea glass down. Breakfast had been superb and he said so, particularly praising the Kyakhta tea. It was the best tea in the world, fragrant and heavy as alcohol.

"Would you like more Kyakhta?" Kitty asked.

"Later." He smiled affably, stretching lazily before catching his hands behind his head.

"I'll ring for it now," Kitty said. "It'll take some time to prepare and bring upstairs." One beautiful breast was partially revealed by the deep cleavage of her white eyelet robe as she rose from the table. Turning toward the bellpull, she inquired, "Would you like anything else?"

Apollo's eyes narrowed, his gaze raking her slowly as he unlaced his fingers. "Perhaps one thing," he murmured, reaching out to catch her wrist. The strong grip arrested her progress and Kitty turned to look questioningly at him. He smiled then, a brilliant, flashing smile of mischief and friendship. "Ring for tea later," he suggested gently, drawing her close, holding her immobile.

Glancing down, Kitty flushed crimson, feeling breathless, flustered, embarrassed. The navy silk dressing gown was lifted in a very obvious way. Apollo had been erect from the first intercepted, tremblingly aware glance over the breakfast table, but he had known enough to let the lady's desire grow, one tiny reluctant glance at a time, before alarming her with his rigid maleness. Her passion needed time to stir and blossom, and, over the leisurely, intimate breakfast, it had. Need for him shone in the quiet mossy pools of her eyes.

"Come, Kitty," Apollo coaxed huskily, totally relaxed and unashamed of his arousal. "Come sit on my lap. The tea can wait." Disregarding Kitty's irresolution, he reached up for her, lifting her effortlessly onto his knees. The silk robe fell open and Kitty, seeing the extent of his arousal, shivered uncontrollably. Gently Apollo took her hand, guiding it to him, running her fingertips up the sensitive underside of the engorged shaft, rubbing them delicately in a slow circle around the quivering crest, bringing fresh blood to swell the starkly prominent veins.

"Dear Kitty," Apollo breathed softly and he flexed his spine languidly in an unabashedly sensual way. His eyes closed, long dark lashes resting briefly on prominent cheekbones as all sensation centered on the countess's delicate touch. He sighed deeply in blissful appreciation. Moments later when his golden eyes slowly reopened, genial amusement blended with smoldering passion in their tawny depths. "See what you do to me?" he said in a light tone, then his slender fingers closed entirely over Kitty's small hand and he moved it down to the base of the swollen maleness pulsing in her grip. "Sweet, sweet Kitty," he murmured, his smiling lips in her hair, his free hand untying the belt of her ruffled wrapper.

Kitty tensed when her robe fell open, felt her heart give a sudden, nervous jolt. "Apollo, wait," she gasped uneasily, fearful and alarmed at the sudden heedless flame he so easily provoked in her. Ignoring her admonition and her rather feeble attempt to push him away, he raised his fingers to her exposed neckline and slid his hands under the lace gown, knowing only that her skin was like silk and that a devouring need raged within him. Kitty sat quietly beneath his hands, conscience-stricken at the almost unbearable, searing desire kindling like wildfire at his slightest touch. She should resist. He had said only friends . . . no designs . . . what was he doing to her? Why was she allowing it? Gentle fingers were forcing the fine fabric from her shoulders, gliding the material down her arms, lifting her to pull the wrapper free. Impatiently, Apollo tossed the garment to the carpet.

"The servants . . . might walk in—" Kitty protested weakly. She had forgotten how quickly he moved.

Holding her lightly, he parted her legs, intent on fondling the silken triangle between her thighs. "They wouldn't dare," he replied helpfully without looking up. Those incredibly adept, lean fingers that had explored every inch of Kitty's body now found the soft, pouting flesh they had sought and slipped very gently past the entrance swollen from the night's pleasure. Feeling the distended tissue, Apollo whispered an apology. "I'm sorry. Used you too hard . . . I'll be gentle, *dushka*." And he soothed, caressed, comforted, his gentle touch slowly stretching, entering, penetrating the moist inner warmth, drowning any discomfort in the tender flesh with new humid fires.

The countess knew that propriety required she repulse him, but Apollo knew exactly where to touch her. His lightly brushing movements found the secret lodestone of her womanhood, and try as she did to persuade herself of the monstrous folly of her conduct, Kitty could not deny the surge of wild excitement, the shiver of agonizing need induced by those fingers which stroked her as a connoisseur would gently fondle the last Tanagra figurine in the world.

With a soft moan she collapsed against him, blotting out all thought, abandoning herself to the exquisite chaos of sexual greed and desire. Kitty's head fell back on his shoulder, a flood of honey-peach hair whispering across navy silk, and once again swelling passion exploded into flame deep inside her. Lying back against the powerfully muscled chest, solid as primordial nature, she gloried in the feel of hard, strong fingers sliding in and out, sometimes only an inch or two up, sometimes reaching as far as they could go, sometimes teasing until she restlessly arched upward, seeking the withheld delight.

How many times in the last few hours had she felt this intoxication, the diabolical sensuality? She who had always only mildly enjoyed the marriage bed; she who had shyly understood the duties of wife but had never relished them; the same woman who only yesterday had considered herself content as estate manager and helpmate to her husband, ignorant of what passion was, how shameless she could feel. How could she be so wanton, hungering for this stranger as much and as often as he wanted her? Yearning, like the most depraved addict, to indulge once again in delicious excess? Then small explosions began building where the prince's obliging massage penetrated so exquisitely, and awareness of the depths of her folly faded. She reached for him, whimpering soft little cries, overwhelmed by a blazing heat which rose from her parted thighs. "Apollo," she sobbed quietly, "Apollo—"

He'd only been waiting for her to ask this time. Satisfied

the countess was ready to accommodate him, his hand wet with the evidence of her urgent need, he caught her around the waist and lifted.

"Here?" Kitty was shocked.

"Here," Apollo murmured huskily, the roughness of his shaven cheek against the curve of her jaw, his lips brushing one soft, pink earlobe. Kitty's exclamation which had begun on a whisper of dismay ended on a transported sigh, for strong hands slid her slim body very slowly, very carefully down the full, hard length of him.

No sooner did he enter her than a wild and desperate passion conquered Kitty; in two strokes, with a shuddering sob and a cry, she blissfully succumbed. She clung to him, lying limp in his arms, her breath coming in gentle ebbing sighs. Apollo ran his hands leisurely up her naked back and smiled knowingly, his pleasure infinitely enhanced by hers, pleasantly envisioning many more panting orgasmic cries before he brought himself to climax. This wife of the leader of his troop was most delightfully eager—and surely one of the more voluptuous, greedy little vixens he'd seen. His hands glided to her narrow waist, lean fingers splayed over her reed-slim slenderness and gently rounded hips. He filled her still, his hardness undiminished; she was impaled on him like a willing sacrifice, her ivory arms, pale against the dark silk of his robe twined around his neck, her head nestled into the hollow of his shoulder. The hands lying on her hips tightened and pressed down, and Kitty tensed her arms around Apollo's neck, her fingernails digging into his shoulders. Both moaned very softly. Apollo's heavy pectorals and biceps rippled and coiled as he raised Kitty then eased her back down by deliberate degrees. It can't be happening again . . . so soon, she thought in a haze of spreading sensual languor. Surely . . . no. . . . But he was murmuring lovewords, suggestive, delicious words, very low in a rough-soft voice, telling her what he was going to do to her, telling her to look down and watch—*making* her look down and watch—and at the sight, at the enormous, terrifyingly delectable sight, she collapsed, tiny convulsive tremors rolling up the sensitized hardness buried deep inside her. She cried out and the sound of her surrender, her helplessness, triggered a primitive sense of triumph in him. He rested, brushing the long golden waves away from her flushed cheeks, kissing her face lightly, aware of the sounds of her breathing. Then he began again.

Captain Prince Apollo Kuzan, as it turned out, had the Countess Kitty Radachek not only after breakfast, but after lunch and dinner as well. In fact, she was his constant, luscious, inexhaustible diet for the next three days. Thoughts of Kyakhta tea were quite forgotten that morning, lunch was very late, dinner later still. Indeed, the conventional routines of dining were completely abandoned for the following few days.

And once, very late one night, the prince, taken by surprise, was heard to remark with mocking gruffness, "Hasn't anyone explained to you, darling, that making advances is unladylike and wholly a man's prerogative?" At which point he laughed softly at the lady's muffled reply, reached down to run his fingers lightly over tousled honey-rose curls, and said with a teasing smile, "Well . . . as long as I'm awake now . . ."

There was something of triumph in that lazy smile, for the lady's burgeoning sensuality was in part a tribute to his talents. Where at first she had been only eager, now she was demanding of her own pleasure, craving him, wanting to possess him, joyfully squandering all her silky treasures on him. And soon, very soon, he was as ravenous as she. He groaned softly, his fingers tightening in the gilt strands of hair, and he murmured pleasantly into the darkness, "Darling, if this is going to be another sleepless night, I'll have to pray to God for strength. . . ."

He interpreted her "Umm-m-m" as an affirmative response. His smile flashed in the dark, and he settled back to enjoy himself.

# 4

Very early on the morning of the fourth day, before the sun was more than a mellow gray light on the distant horizon, Apollo was on the road to Niiji, Karaim and Sahin once more by his side. There was no other sign of life on the vast, empty steppe, only drifted snow and utter silence. At a signal from Apollo, the three powerful thoroughbreds broke into a loping gallop.

He had left Kitty asleep. Apollo had been touched by her beauty, grateful for her company, enchanted with the blazing excitement of her passion, but there would have been nothing to say this morning except good-bye. He didn't know where the war would take him; with the boiling caldron of civil war engulfing Russia there was no guarantee he would ever see Kitty again. Conversing around that kind of uncertainty would have been awkward, even painful. Capricious fate would determine the direction of all their lives in the next few months; capricious fate and the bloody buildup of Red Army forces in the north. He hoped she'd understand. He had said his good-byes in bed last night.

During their three days together, Kitty had talked of her marriage, about Peotr, trying to comprehend what had shockingly come over her with Apollo. Peotr was never home, Apollo had wanted to say; it was understandable, her need for a man. And such great loneliness as Kitty's was no protection against a cajoling, determined man like Apollo, used to having his way with women and intent on shutting out the war for a brief time.

Kitty's softly spoken, unreserved comments concerning

41

Peotr and their marriage were by way of thinking aloud, a mental catharsis to which Apollo quietly listened. If he had chosen, he could have told her he knew more about her marriage and about her husband than she did. He and Peotr had served in the Corps de Pages together, had campaigned for two years on the western front together, had practically lived within sight of each other for twenty months in Mamontov's renegade unit.

Apollo knew all about Peotr's marriage and was acquainted, as well, with Peotr's mistress and two children in Baku (of whom Kitty was ignorant). He had companioned Peotr in scores of revels in scores of brothels from Petrograd to Kabul. He even knew exactly why Peotr had married Kitty (the land—marriages of convenience were still the norm in the aristocracy) and exactly why they didn't get along (Peotr found chaste, young girls for company and apparently had never sought to know the woman).

Granted, Apollo's information had been primarily one-sided, but at least he was familiar with the arrangement—although he had never intended to become *this* familiar with the wife. As graphic memories of Kitty surfaced, of her captivating innocence and shy boldness, his hand inadvertently tightened on the reins and his splendid horse fidgeted nervously. Apollo was startled from his musing. "Sorry, Leda," he apologized, stroking the carefully groomed golden-chestnut neck.

Hell, he thought reasonably, it wasn't so uncommon. Many wives had lovers of their own, and in a sense Peotr and Kitty's arrangement had never been a marriage. In any event, Apollo decided sensibly, it was nothing to lose sleep over. He had wanted her, he had taken her, he had found her company enjoyable and felt no regrets over the enjoyment. In these uncertain times, one took one's pleasure where one could. It had been a pleasant, very charming three days, that was all. Now back to the war. Back to the damn war they were losing inch by inch, mile by mile.

•     •     •

Kitty stood at the bedroom window watching Apollo ride away. He sat on his horse with a careless arrogance, broad-shouldered under the heavy marten officer's coat, all the accoutrements of war buckled and belted on once again. Apollo was riding hatless in the chill December morning, and his long, golden hair shone like a saintly aureole in the blue-gray light preceding the dawn. She had curled her fingers in those golden waves, Kitty recalled vividly; had been lured into the smiling depths of Apollo's great tawny eyes.

Pensively, she wished she were a gypsy or peasant girl or one of the new Cossack women who fought as soldiers, so she would have dared to ride away with Apollo. It would have been joy to travel by his side, sharing the pleasure of his presence; she envied Karaim and Sahin. But it didn't really matter, any of her wishes . . . because Apollo hadn't asked her to come with him. Hadn't mentioned anything about seeing her again. Of course he hadn't, she quickly told herself. Even if he had wanted to . . . And a hundred excuses for his reticence poured into her brain.

In any event, she wasn't a gypsy or peasant or Cossack girl. No matter what happened, she still remained Princess Kurminen and Countess Radachek, was very much married, and carried sole responsibility for the land that had passed unaltered in these adjoining estates through fifty generations. No, she couldn't leave, no matter how pleasing the dream. Her audible sigh broke the stillness of the room.

Kitty's small hand let the lace curtain drop back into place, obscuring the distant figure of Apollo behind the delicate filigree. She turned away from the window and turned away from the man who had given her warmth and laughter, had taught her the vital spirit of passion. A man who smiled easily, charmed irresistibly, emanated the very essence of life. Kitty looked at the white birchwood bed where she had learned to love and knew she would never be the same again.

In little more than an hour Leda covered the short distance to Zadia's, and Apollo dismounted before an elegant marble pavilion, architecturally derived from Madame Pompadour's Petit Trianon, the dalliance ground of an earlier courtesan of splendid taste—and in those opulent terms Zadia styled herself, despite the remote geographic situation of Niiji. Wild and uncivilized the terrain might be at the base of the savage Caucasus foothills, thousands of miles from the leading cities, but Zadia's was not even marginally provincial. It had the advantage of being scant hours from Besh-Tau and Kislovodsk, the richest spas in the world.

Apollo turned to whisper briefly into the mare's ear, soothed the long, silky mane with a leather-gloved hand, then handed the reins to Karaim. The two bodyguards remained behind as Apollo strode up the gentle rise of marble stairs, slightly numbed from an hour's ride in the arctic temperatures. Heavy wooden doors opened at his approach—Zadia prided herself on her liveried staff of servants—and Prince Apollo walked into the familiar travertine-floored foyer. Hovering footmen divested him of his weapons, coat, *papakha*, and gloves, and at his request ushered him into the small breakfast parlor in the east wing.

Moments later, as Apollo was contemplating a serving of curried eggs, his solitude was broken by several companions of his cavalry unit. His cheerful greeting was met by a variety of responses, individually dependent on the exact nature of the addressee's alcohol consumption the previous night. Some were genial, others slightly subdued, a few merely acknowledged Apollo with a short nod of recognition—verbal exercise, at the moment, being beyond their capabilities.

When Prince Kadar Guirey sat down at the linen-covered breakfast table, his thin Tartar lips drew into an assessing smile. Slowly stirring his glass of tea, he said, "Lost your way, eh, Apollo? Knowing you, we didn't send out a search party. She must have been superior to interest you for the entire three days. Anyone I know? But then, you've always been a shade careless where you've slept, haven't you?" The leer was almost too obvious.

Fitting his shoulders comfortably into the curve of the Chippendale chair, Apollo leaned back in an elegant sprawl.

Smiling pleasantly, he merely said in a noncommittal way, "She's shy."

"I didn't think you liked them shy."

Apollo's mouth twitched. "I like 'em any way."

"Regardless of age—right, Apollo?"

"Leave off, Kadar. That was a bet. Anyway, Helene wasn't that old—in her forties, probably."

"Try fifties!" his mirthful interrogator genially replied.

Apollo digested this. "Really?" he said, amazed for a moment. "Well, regardless, it turned out rather nicely. In fact, I had lunch with her a few months ago, before she closed up her house and left for Europe."

"*Just* lunch?" Kadar was in waggish good humor.

Apollo shrugged. "What can I say—Helene's in marvelous shape. And—" his eyelids lowered suggestively—"there's something to be said for years of experience."

"You're incorrigible, Kuzan." There was more than a hint of disapprobation in the languid drawl.

"Hell, no. Just willing to taste indiscriminately from the, er, 'smorgasbord' of life." Apollo's face was bland.

Prince Guirey drew in his breath sharply. Flushing under his swarthy skin he hissed, "Apollo! You promised not to mention that!"

"Relax, Kadar, my lips are sealed." A slow smile creased Apollo's sardonic face. "By the way, how is your sister?"

"Fine!" Prince Guirey snapped, his face reddened.

"Good. Happy to hear it," Apollo lazily drawled. "It's not often brother and sister get along so famously."

A party several years ago had gotten out of hand, and when someone drunkenly suggested the lights be turned out and partners picked in the dark from a smorgasbord of willing, unclad females, a roar of young voices riotously agreed. When the lights were restored hours later, Kadar was aghast to find the young lady he had been making love to so long and so blissfully was none other than his sister.

"So then," Apollo went on convivially, his teasing tormentor neatly set down, "it looks as though everyone had an entertaining time without me." His smile widened as his clear, alert, golden eyes regarded the variously slouched and sprawled officers. Only a few were eating breakfast; most chose to cradle their heads in their hands and stare at their coffee or tea. Moans and groans greeted his remark.

"Christ, Apollo," exclaimed one extremely young coronet. "How the hell do you always look so goddamn fresh?" The speaker's face was pale and of a distinctly greenish cast. Apollo threw him a commiserating look.

"Mostly, Kolya, because I love the ladies, and it, ah, works out better if I pass out *after* the tumble in bed rather than before—so I pace my liquor. When you get older, *mon pauvre*, you'll iron out the sequence." Suddenly a small smile tugged at his mouth. "Although"—Apollo's mind drifted back to his initial encounter with Kitty—"the sequence of events is not necessarily inflexibly rigid."

Another officer, arriving in time to see the roguish grin play across Apollo's face, asked, "So who is she? I see that pleasingly smug smile. Don't be selfish now, Apollo. You know how things are—here today, gone tomorrow. Give us a name, anyway, so we can warm her bed if you're blown off your horse." It was a sentiment silently entertained by more than one man there that morning, for Apollo's standards concerning women were deliciously diverse, and always high.

Apollo shrugged eloquently. "Sorry, Mahomet. Courtesy forbids me." He arched one brow, the pleasant smile still in place.

"Damn. So you found a high-class whore. Some people have all the luck!" Mahomet Shamkhal was a Baku Moslem, and in his culture, harems protected refined females. He didn't understand the western distinctions regarding upper-class women and love affairs—the distinction that protected a lady's name, but not a peasant girl's. In Mahomet's milieu, any female allowing herself to be touched by anyone but her husband was a whore.

"Mahomet, you have no delicacy in matters of the heart."

"Since when does heart have anything to do with it, Apollo? You know damn well it's a different piece of female anatomy that you're interested in. So tell us the name of your society hussy in case you reach Paradise before us."

"The lady's name," said Apollo in an unmistakably honeyed voice that did nothing to hide his lethal thoughts, "is not open to comment." He fixed a cool eye on the Baku Moslem who had offended him.

Never in anyone's experience had Apollo been so discreet. His reticence suggested someone's protected daughter, at the very least, was the cause of his absence—a delicious virgin, no doubt. Formerly, of course. With those sorts of deductions racing through everyone's minds, Apollo's response was a foregone conclusion. A dozen pairs of eyes rested on him.

"I would appreciate a retraction of your remarks, Shamkhal." The smile suddenly vanished from Apollo's face, and with it all his cultivated graces. Skull, flesh, and muscle, every fluent line and stark shade of Apollo's face betrayed the mountain savage. There was a cruel edge to his voice in the formal use of surname enunciated in frigid accents. Damn Moslems, anyway, Apollo thought irritably, keeping their women in cages like dumb animals. A lady who enjoyed lovemaking had never seemed less of a lady in Apollo's opinion, and he was quite ready to defend his convictions with his *kinjal*.

Apollo's reputation with *kinjal*, the prescribed weapon for duels in the Caucasus, was formidable. Mahomet Shamkhal, brave against ordinary standards, wasn't foolhardy. He'd rather die in a cavalry charge or expire worn out by his harem than be cut to pieces with Apollo's mountain dagger. Mountain duels were to the death, there were no half measures.[5] But more than anything else, more even than Apollo's notorious reputation as a dueling opponent, the supreme confidence in his voice convinced Mahomet. There were flashes of unguarded violence in Apollo that it didn't pay to provoke. Mahomet decided the name of the aristocratic whore wasn't worth his life.

Having withstood the pale gaze for as long as self-respect demanded, Mahomet shrugged and said smoothly, "Of course. Retracted, by all means."

"Thank you," said Apollo with simplicity, quite calmly and quite unlike his habitual response to a challenge. More than one mind decided that whoever the aristocratic tart was, she certainly had a soothing effect on their quick-tempered friend.

A blood-letting had been only narrowly averted. A quiet sigh wafted around the table; tempers were always short the morning after a carouse, and one never knew how far the demands of honor would go. The irregular troop was diverse in religion, culture, and language, but all the men were warriors, imbued with a warrior's sense of affront.

Apollo, stretching casually, broke the uneasy silence, inquiring in a once again pleasant tone, "Is Peotr up yet?"

A curly-haired subaltern found his tongue first. "Breakfasting with Zadia."

"You know how possessive Zadia is with him," declared someone halfway down the table.

"Haven't seen him since we arrived," a third voice added.

Apollo had considered himself beyond conscience after so many years of taking his pleasure with a great variety of women, but it pleased him momentarily not to have cuckolded a faithful husband. To view Peotr as even passingly faithful was ludicrous, but with Kitty, somehow, it had seemed different. Apollo didn't want his thoughts of her tangled up with disturbing implications of ruining some happy marriage. Peotr obviously had enjoyed himself outside the conjugal bonds in his usual manner these last three days; Apollo need have no fear of having pleasured himself with someone's dearly beloved wife. In fact, if his conscience needed salving—and it bothered him briefly that the notion even crossed his mind—it was perfectly clear the pleasuring had been mutual. There. That neatly disposed of any faint stirrings of scruples. He closed his mind to the issue.

So a half hour later, when Peotr finally came down from Zadia's boudoir, Apollo had no problem at all looking him straight in the eye.

"Good morning, Peotr."

"Apollo!" Peotr smiled warmly. "So you're back. Found a friendly bed en route to Zadia's, eh? Was she good?" Peotr winked cheerfully, his spirits ebulliently refreshed after three days of Zadia's sympathetic expertise.

"Of course." Apollo smiled. "Would I stay so long if she wasn't?"

"So. Recuperated, then?"

"Admirably."

"Unlike some of this troop, I see." Colonel Radachek's splendid dark eyes swept the room, taking in the full array of health and vigor—or lack thereof. "I suggest extra coffee or tea, gentlemen, for those whose heads or stomachs rebel at the thought of hours in the saddle. It's only eight o'clock, and I know the war shouldn't start before ten, but unfortunately Wrangel's a purist, not a sybarite. We leave in an hour. First to the depot at Divnoie. From there we entrain for Kharkov. The Savage Division is being used to guard the troop trains retreating south, since the Green guerilla bands are becoming bolder and attacking troop and Red Cross trains. It's up to us to serve as rearguard. In an hour, men." Turning to Apollo, he said, "Come into the library. We'll check the newest front on the maps. I talked to headquarters earlier this morning."

Minutes later Zadia joined them in the library, gliding in gracefully in a familiar cloud of jasmine scent, a pretty diversion in peach organdy and silk. She was tall, auburn-haired, fair-skinned, and although in her thirties had preserved the vivid, arresting sparkle of her youth. Ever since Apollo could remember she had reminded him of a glittering butterfly.

"Ah, Apollo. We missed you." The warmth in her voice was that of an old friend.

"And I missed you, Zadia," Apollo replied, moving forward to greet her with a kiss. "Forgive me for not arriving sooner, but, unfortunately, events—"

"Apollo has an uncanny ability when it comes to the comforts of home," Peotr cut in teasingly from the Chinese lacquered desk where he was unrolling a much used map. "I swear, if there's a pretty woman anywhere in the vicinity, he'll find her."

"I have constantly to fight for my reputation," Apollo mockingly retorted, his smile angelic.

"He does have a way about him," Zadia agreed with a sunny glance, her arms linked comfortably in Apollo's.

"Thanks to you, Zadia, my sweet," Apollo observed sportively. "You taught me everything I know."

Zadia looked at him fondly, reaching up in a motherly gesture to push aside a wave of sun-streaked hair falling low on his forehead. "I had a very good teacher myself, years ago." She smiled knowingly. "By the way . . . how's your father?"

"Well. Safe in France, working out his excess energy on the polo fields. Which reminds me. I've instructions to urge you to leave soon, and I am also commissioned to reextend Papa's offer for assistance. Old friends are the best friends, Papa says, and you're always welcome at Chambord."

"Soon, Apollo. I'm—"

"If you two can break away from family nostalgia," Peotr interrupted, "we've a war to fight. Come here, Apollo, and look at the advances Budenny's been making near Manych."

# 5

The next two weeks were a nightmare. The unit had just disembarked at Kharkov when the entire front crumbled. The Whites were evacuating the town immediately; the Savage Division was to cover the retreat. The Greens, increasing like mildew with the imminence of the White collapse, kept up steady pressure on the trains, attacking nightly with their guerilla bands that swept down in large masses, harassing, devastating, blowing up track, their machine guns and field artillery mounted on small gerrymandered *tachankas*[6] lethal to anything in their way. They would send up flares and then in rushing waves ride alongside the tracks, firing into the trains—hospital trains, troop trains, civilian carriages, none were immune. Night after night the attacks continued, the guerillas relentless in their hatred of Red and White alike, interested only in plunder and personal gain. The officers of the Savage Division took turns snatching sleep when they could in the daytime, but no one had had more than three hours of rest at a stretch for a fortnight now.

The double track was completely blocked with southbound trains moving at a snail's pace, locomotive to caboose, extending the entire two hundred miles from Kharkov to Rostov. On the route south were constant reminders of less fortunate southbound trains: trains tipped over, looted, burned, with charred corpses showing the success of a guerilla raid.

Human misery was everywhere, so prevalent, so awful and tragic that one became anesthetized as a survival mechanism. Dead bodies littered the sidings and roadways—civilian ref-

51

ugees, women, and children dead by the hundreds; soldiers crippled, maimed, dead; all broken by the weapons of war, by starvation, by sub-zero temperatures, but most of all by the typhus epidemic that raged throughout war-torn Russia. The unsanitary conditions in the ravaged land were especially conducive to the disease-carrying louse. Bathing was difficult—there was no wood to heat water, even if one could find the time to indulge in the luxury—but primarily the typhus virus had been spread like wildfire by the crowded conditions in the refugee-and troop-packed trains and the hopelessly overrun seaport towns.

Just two days ago Apollo had seen an entire hospital train sitting silently on a siding outside Debaltsevo. The patients, lying on the stacked bunks, were visible through the windows but not a sound issued from the line of thirty carriages. He found out later from a doctor at Kupyansk that everyone on that hospital train had died—patients, nurses, doctors. That evening, at a small depot north of Taganrog, they had seen what looked to be a pack of gray wolves slowly approaching the train, only to discover, as the shadow materialized through the blowing snow and gloom, that it was a group of soldiers in their gray hospital gowns crawling toward the train. Victims of wounds and typhus, they had been left behind in the retreat, believed to be too ill to survive the journey. With their last ounce of strength, on hands and knees, they had crawled from the hospital to the depot.

With the retreat it seemed as if mercy had left and the heavens had crashed.

What ate at one's soul in lucid moments was the unutterable calmness with which such horror was accepted by the mind. In the five and a half years since Russia had entered the Great War, Apollo's life had been so inundated by gruesomeness—by battle, by tales and eyewitness accounts of death, bestiality, massacre—that another death, a hundred deaths, even a thousand, scarcely caused a ripple in his mental receptors. Perhaps it was an act of God, for certainly there was going to be no hiatus in death before Rostov.

By the time they reached Taganrog, the railway depot for

Rostov, everyone was exhausted by days of steady skirmishes and sleeplessness. Several of the cavalry officers were wounded, but none seriously, a telling enough indication of their skill in the hard-fought retreat. Everyone was looking forward to Christmas in Taganrog; a time to rest, recoup, and mostly drink to forget.

No sooner did they reach the northern suburbs than Peotr bid adieu, his heavy saddlebags slung over one shoulder. "I've hitched a ride with Sergei to Baku. He managed to requisition some gas for his Niewport." When Apollo's eyebrows lifted, Peotr added, "Don't ask me where. *Bon Noël, mon ami.* I've two full days with Suata and the children."

"I see," Apollo said slowly, digesting this remarkable turn of events and realizing upon further contemplation that he didn't see at all. Leaving one's wife alone at Christmastime was a bit too blasé even for his hardened conscience—but it was none of his business, Apollo decided with his usual cool pragmatism. Wishing Peotr a *Joyeux Noël* in return, he refrained from asking the obvious question about Kitty. "My best to Suata," he added, pouring himself another drink from the cognac bottle he'd been saving since Niiji. Everyone had taken to their habitual form of relaxation since Taganrog had been sighted, and several groups of men were at ease on the banquettes that had so often served as beds on the journey south from Kharkov.

Peotr nodded happily. "Thanks, I'll relay the message."

"And to Mirza and Alina, too, of course."

Peotr's mouth widened into a beaming smile. "You should see Mirza, Apollo. He's almost six now and rides a horse like he was born in the saddle. Since you saw him last year he's grown another three inches."

"And Alina," Apollo teased, "does she ride like an Amazon?" Alina was only five, but on Apollo's visit to Baku a year ago, little Alina, darkly beautiful and dainty as a Dresden doll, was determined to keep up with her older brother.

Peotr laughed aloud. "Damned if she doesn't. On that point Suata and I have finally agreed. Suata, as you know, was raised in the Moslem ways, but I won't allow my daughter to be reared in that restricted fashion. Alina does exactly what Mirza does, causing Suata to frequently throw up her hands in dismay at such unladylike behavior."

"Sensible of you to insist, Peotr," Apollo said. "That sort of harem training has to be a thing of the past. Good God, it's the twentieth century."

"That's what I said to Suata." Peotr grinned. "She finally came 'round to my way of thinking."

Like any well-trained, harem-raised wife, Apollo thought. That precise lack of independence Peotr deplored for his daughter, that harem-schooled acquiescence and emphasis on male-pleasing, was exactly what he found gratifying and lovable in Suata. Evidently Peotr had never seen the discrepancy, too heedlessly self-centered to perceive the incongruity. Although Apollo and Peotr had been friends for years, Apollo recognized that Peotr generally put his own pleasure and comfort first, though in a blithely innocent way, like an unassuming child, egotistically certain that the world centered on him.

Through the window Apollo caught sight of a frantically waving aviator across the snow-covered railway tracks. "There's Sergei, waving at you to hurry."

Peotr shifted his saddlebags. "Right. I'm off, then. I see the Red Cross nurses are here in force. I'll leave you to your life of depravity, and with your recent boudoir history common gossip—Apollo's eyes came up in a startled action, and then he realized Peotr was speaking only in general terms—"the Red Crosses are probably drawing lots for you already." Peotr smiled at Apollo amiably.

His composure restored, Apollo quipped, "And you're leaving them all to me?"

"This time, *mon ami*. This time, they're all yours. I suggest you take a break in your drinking and eat a hearty meal. You'll need your strength. See you in four days." A smile spread across his swarthy face. "Provided there's anything left of you."

Apollo looked squarely at Peotr, his expression pure as a nun at prayer. "Don't worry about me. I'll probably spend the holiday alone with a good book."

Peotr's brows lifted dramatically. "Ha!" he said succinctly. Halfway out the train door he paused, turned, and said, "Let's hope they don't evacuate Taganrog before I get back." Then, shrugging, he added, "Although, come to think of it, maybe that wouldn't be so bad either."

Everyone knew by now that Red victory was imminent. A sense of impending doom had settled upon the retreating army and refugees alike. As officers, though, both Apollo and Peotr, along with the entire division, would follow orders until there were no more issued. All the years of military training in the elite Guard regiments had left their mark. No one would desert the cause, no matter how hopeless it was, but just the same, everyone knew it was only a matter of time now. The front was dangerously close to Ekaterinodar and Rostov. If they could not be held, it would be full-scale panic to the seaports. Already the six-hour train journey to Novorossiisk took over four days. What would happen when all of South Russia tried to retreat via the southbound train?

After Peotr left, Apollo stood in the doorway of the railway carriage, his thoughts alive to an intoxicating situation: Peotr's wife was spending Christmas alone. Very tempting, he mused, his eyes ranging over the hundreds of railway cars drawn up in the snowy yards north of the depot.[7] Damnably tempting. He could talk one of his pilot friends into lending him a plane for a day or so. Apollo had learned to fly at fourteen, while other boys his age were learning to drive their first motor cars, and soon after that he'd driven his parents to near apoplexy by insisting on flying his own plane in the treacherous cross-currents of the Caucasus mountain valleys near their aul. In less than two hours, he thought with a spoiled child's relish for excitement, he could be at Aladino. That would give him almost four days—provided he could keep the plane that long—to be with Kitty. They were both alone for Christmas. Why not?

Apollo turned from the doorway and was halfway down the corridor to his compartment to pack before the unpleasant answer materialized. For a long moment he stood arrested in the corridor, then swinging around with an exasperated ges-

ture he struck both fists on the inlaid mahogany paneling.
"Damn." What sort of explanation could he give for Peotr's
absence when the unit was obviously on Christmas leave? The
truth, of course, was out of the question. Your husband has a
mistress plus a family. Always unpleasant news to a wife.

Pushing away from the wall, he thought, Oh, hell. He'd
make up some kind of story. He resumed his long-legged
stride down the corridor. Some plausible explanation could be
fabricated before he reached Astrakhan. Wartime was chaos
at best, anyway.

Apollo paused, his hand on the doorlatch, contemplating a
facile lie, and in that brief moment hardheaded pragmatism
began reversing his spontaneous decision to see Kitty. All the
unwonted practical considerations flooded into his mind. Remember, she's your best friend's wife. Regardless of Peotr's
behavior, there is no excuse for you to become even more
ungentlemanly than you already are. Perhaps more pertinent,
why renew a relationship with no future? It would be even
harder this time to say good-bye. God knows it was hard
enough—for some unknown reason—last time.

Much as Apollo wanted to see Kitty, he realized, with a
grimace of astonishment, that he found the thought of treat-
ing her with the careless expediency of an erotic interlude
distasteful. For a man who prided himself on the laudable
merit of erotic interludes, this was a staggering conclusion.
And what settled the issue in the end was not the moral or
ethical considerations, but the uneasy recognition that Countess Kitty Radachek had become a constant image in his mind
of late, a disturbing, devouring, never-diminishing focus of
desire. This preoccupation, this *decided preference* for a specific
woman—there were no reference points in his previous experience to explain it. He didn't know what love was. He
certainly didn't admit to himself he could be in love.

Under the circumstances—Kitty being his best friend's
wife, and the certainty of losing the campaign ominously
real—that sort of intemperate desire should be repressed
rather than encouraged. In the desperate, frantic hedonism
prevailing in the wartime atmosphere of South Russia, Apollo

decided pragmatically, if disgruntledly, that if he was going to eat, drink, and be merry, he'd damn well better pick some female who could be easily forgotten.

Consequently, on the afternoon Peotr went off to spend Christmas with his mistress, Apollo, very begrudgingly, for reasons not altogether familiar to him, gave up the idea of passing the holidays in bed with Kitty. It was, as a matter of fact, the first action in his life concerning a woman that was undertaken with prudence, and, had he known it, the most useless.

With sensible concepts now perfectly balanced against flighty hedonism, Apollo was easily persuaded by several of his fellow officers to join them at a party in the Red Cross train parked four tracks east of them. The nurses had several gallons of high-quality alcohol, transformed into vodka, while Prince Ghivi, resourceful soul that he was, had managed to trade his diamond watch to some profiteer for eight cases of champagne. There was enough liquor, Apollo was assured, to keep everyone drunk for the entire four days of Christmas furlough.

To Apollo, four days of drunken oblivion sounded decidedly appealing. As it turned out, he managed to reach that stage very rapidly and maintain it for the prescribed period— although the pretty young Red Cross nurse who marked him out as hers the minute his tall frame crossed the threshold of their lounge car with that careful, indolent tread produced by consuming half a bottle of cognac never realized her companion was quite so inebriated. When drunk, Apollo neither staggered nor slurred his words; the only indication was the vaguely abstracted way he exercised his charm, and none but his closest friends could recognize the subtlety. How was Sophia Feodovna to know that the soft-spoken, casually teasing young prince who drank with her, called her "my darling," "my angel," and made love to her for four days was so into his cups that he wouldn't recognize her if he ever met her again?

Someone had found two gypsies to play, and the sound of music and laughter cascaded through the parlor car. Dinner had been formal that evening in honor of the Christmas season, so the carriage sparkled with jewels and decorations, saber hilts, gilded epaulets, shimmering silk, and painted mouths. Later, a balalaika playing Russian folksongs, its softly strummed chords joined by voices here and there, wove music and memories through the dim, candlelit car. Heavy with food and wine, warm and weakened by the season's nostalgia, the hour advanced, conversation and laughter fell to a mellow buzz.

Much later, when even the balalaika had ceased, Apollo eased his long, lean body over the nurse whose name he couldn't remember and thought of Kitty. Much to Sophia's sensual pleasure, she was made love to with infinite care and patience because Apollo in his drunkenness was intent on pleasing a golden-haired countess with laughing eyes the color of spring.

The next morning when slivers of sun filtered through the slats in the blinds of the sleeping compartment, Apollo lazily turned his head, glanced down at the girl in his arms, and felt a brief moment of melancholy when he beheld dark curls resting on his shoulder. His next movement remained fairly constant in the following three days. He reached for the vodka bottle resting on the frosty windowsill.

In the closing days of the White Army's defeat, the population of South Russia was not just living for the day and disregarding tomorrow, they were living for the moment . . . only the moment.[8] When the tide of Bolshevism washed over the land, no one's future was assured for longer than it took a bullet to snuff out the breath of life. Of course, that was assuming you were fortunate enough to be shot rather than bludgeoned to death, hung to expire in a slow gasping death on some makeshift gallows, or doomed to die agonizingly at the hands of some psychotic Cheka interrogator.

So while Apollo saw Christmas through an alcohol haze, Kitty spent the holidays quietly. Many of the neighbors had emigrated over the course of the last two years and those who remained were too disheartened to celebrate. There wasn't a home, whether aristocratic or peasant, that hadn't lost at least one son, husband, father, or brother in the last five years, and there were many that had lost all the male members of their family. Princess Davidov had been especially hard hit when her last son had been killed in the summer campaigning. Kitty tried to visit her regularly, making a special effort to be with her on Christmas Day, but only a shell of the woman remained. The princess still held herself ramrod straight and spoke in the same quiet, refined way, but her spirit had deserted her body, drained away by a torrent of tears.

The silence of the house was oppressive, and one's nostrils were immediately struck by the musty smell of patchouli, dust, old age, and death. The princess's plain black dress, with the deep mourning white *pleureuses* around neck and cuffs, seemed to hang on nothing. All the clocks in the house were stopped; the princess had never again wound them after her last and favorite son Ghigi had died last August 18 at Tsaritsyn. She had lighted candles framing a large photo of him on the north wall of the drawing room, and Maria Alexandrovna spent most of her time before this memorial to her son, talking to him. When Kitty came for tea, the princess would, out of courtesy, attempt to respond, but before long her eyes would stray to the dark brooding glance of her son in the candlelit portrait and Kitty would be forgotten.

Many of the Davidov servants had fled, superstitious of the lonely old woman who spoke to her son although he had been dead since August. A few remained out of loyalty and love, caring for the bereft mother.

If Christmas hadn't been disheartening enough, Kitty's call on Princess Davidov dampened her mood beyond redemption. Maria Alexandrovna had insisted that Kitty visit Ghigi's room, where all was exactly as he had left it. The princess had pointed to the narrow campbed and said, "Ghigi liked the austerity of the campaign bed. Now I sleep here and imagine I sleep with him as I used to when he was a baby and felt sick in the middle of the night." Princess Davidov had sunk to her knees before a lighted icon near the bed and had begun talking in soft tones to "*mon enfant*," once again oblivious to her guest.

Kitty had slipped away and returned home. After a solitary supper in her room that evening, she'd cried herself to sleep.

Life had been lonely before, but with Apollo's departure the word had taken on new meaning. Before, she had been ignorant of her deprivation. Now, she attacked the problem in the only way she knew: by throwing herself into the routine duties of Aladino with intemperate fury, hoping to distract her thoughts from the all-too-frequent images of Apollo.

The servants passed knowing glances behind her back. The countess was driving herself mercilessly, and they were all close enough to the earth to know why.

Late one afternoon, after totaling a column of numbers in the estate ledger for the third time and arriving at the third different sum, Kitty threw the pen in her hand clear across the room, then burst into tears.

Once her composure was restored she decided perhaps she should slacken her pace a bit. Her determined efforts to over-work must be causing these frequent bouts of weeping, and the depressing reports of the war didn't help, either. Whatever the cause, it was distracting. Never prone to tears in the past, she, of late, had been curiously inclined to cry at the smallest provocation.

The instability of her temperament was not helped, either, by the astonishingly persistent thoughts of Apollo. Kitty chastised herself not only for her inexcusable behavior on those days almost three weeks ago now, but also for the unfaithfulness of her mind, which dwelt with increasing frequency on vivid recollections of an elegant young captain with gilded hair and a tongue like sweet nectar. And hands . . . such perfect hands, her body would sigh, hands that stroked with the delicacy of baby's breath. The yearning sensations were so real that at times Kitty found herself crying aloud in her sleep. In the light of day, she rigorously forced herself to dismiss such disturbing dreams, forced herself to remember she was a married woman, tried to recall Peotr with the same blaze of reality, the same stark hunger that memories of Apollo engendered.

Peotr refused to appear on cue, refused to be drawn into

the center of her consciousness, and the terrible recollection of her willing tumble from faithfulness haunted her, confused her, tumultuously perplexed a straightforward innocence that had, until three weeks ago, never even contemplated infidelity. Now she not only contemplated it subconsciously, if her dreams were any indication, but, she had to admit, consciously as well. Quite often she longed to be held in Apollo's arms once again. Like a trickle of water sliding over a flooding reservoir, the memory of him invaded her, and like the merciless slippery liquid she could not push it back. Somewhere deep in her heart, she had been keeping alive a small hope . . . that he would come again when he could. At Christmas that small hope had become something more; somehow, someway, she'd felt he'd appear.

What had happened, she had asked herself a hundred times, in only three short days? How could one's life be changed so incredibly by the passing of a few transient hours? The full effects of those three days were disturbing, incalculable and . . . irrevocable. Somehow her life *had* changed, and Apollo had been the catalyst.

Not that it mattered now in the least. In this bloody caldron of war neither wishes nor dreams and hopes counted as much as two candles in the fires of hell. Not even Kitty's blind, eager longing for Apollo could change the hundreds of miles and unknown days, weeks—perhaps a lifetime—that separated them. There was no guarantee, either, that her chrysalis loving of him, if she dare put a name to her fledgling feeling, would be reciprocated even if the distance could be broached. Perhaps that explained her tears. She had had no experience in seduction, while Apollo, she knew, was a favorite of the ladies, and men like Apollo, with their capacity for pleasing women, never put the same emphasis on pleasant bedtime diversions as did the recipients of their wooing. Apollo was, in fact, according to Peotr, notorious for a kind of warding-off politeness which prevented the long and lovely parade of women in his life from detaining him when he no longer cared to be detained. The dreary speculation served to further lower Kitty's spirits.

Her dream that Apollo would come at Christmas proved to be another stupid illusion. What with her solitude, the disheartening news of the war, and her trembling new, terribly wicked heartache over Apollo, Kitty gave in to her depression, feeling she had a right to cry. With desolation washing over her, she did, with fresh hot tears.

# 6

Peotr returned to Taganrog on schedule four days later, bursting with happiness and glowing reports of his lovely mistress and children.

For some reason this *joie de vivre* caused an unfavorable reaction in Apollo. Certainly not prudishness at this late stage, Apollo decided. Probably resentment that Peotr had done as he'd pleased without regard for practicality or decorum, while he himself had decided against pursuing his desire for what now appeared totally incomprehensible reasons. The last four days of continuous drinking and mouthing insincere pleasantries had done nothing to improve his disposition. The net result had made him extremely touchy.

"Tone it down, will you," Apollo sullenly retorted as Peotr unpacked his saddlebag in the compartment they shared.

No rude retort could dispel Peotr's ebullient mood. He only turned and grinned at his roommate sprawled on the opposite sofa. "Sore head, Apollo?" Peotr commiserated. "Too much wine, women, and song?" Every line of Apollo spoke of dissipation. The black mountain clothes he preferred, oriental and rich, were vaguely slovenly; his skin seemed pallid under the sun-glazed surface; his fine eyes were half-lidded over a world-weary ennui; his mouth insolent and self-indulgent. And, Peotr observed, the captain had less than steady hands. He'd been drinking seriously for a long time.

"Maybe not enough," Apollo grumpily replied. Damn Peotr's soul. Why did he deserve to be so happy when Apollo's Christmas had been so wretchedly dismal? Since those days with Kitty, making love to other women had become a perfunctory performance, physically orgasmic but for the first time in his life unsatisfying. He had only made love with his nerve endings. All the time his brain had been scheming, planning, analyzing, drunkenly fantasizing about Kitty.

Perhaps because of his huge burden of resentment, Apollo snappishly inquired, "Ever think of your wife at Christmas?"

Peotr turned from the closet where he was tossing in his boots. Standing there in stocking feet, he searched his friend's face with bewildered eyes. Sullen contempt met his reflective stare. "Kitty?" he said slowly. Scanning his friend spread across the sofabed, he decided Apollo was magnificently drunk. Lifting his broad shoulders in a shrug, he said evenly, "Don't worry about Kitty. She always manages just fine. Competent woman, there."

"And how," said Apollo precisely, "do you know whether Kitty's competent or not? You haven't spent more than four consecutive days at Aladino since your marriage." Apollo instantly muzzled his white-hot flash of resentment. Drunk he may be, but not about to become ingenuous.

Peotr, buttressed within by the potent happiness of his own contentment, failed to see the brief blaze of Apollo's anger. He gave another lithe, indifferent shrug. "She *seems* to manage on her own well enough."

Staunchly in control once again, Apollo muttered, "Amen to that."

"What?"

"I said, I hope you're right."

There was a pause and Peotr's blue eyes narrowed, but Apollo's face was closed, offering nothing to Peotr's scrutiny.

"Say . . . didn't things go well here?" Peotr's voice expressed genuine concern, for Apollo was rarely churlish.

Apollo gave a hoot of derisive laughter and, stretching like a cat, reached for the vodka bottle resting on the sill above his head. "Of course things went well. I hardly left my bed. The Red Crosses were entertaining. Mostly a black-haired one. Occasionally someone different slipped in, I think. It's not entirely clear, actually."

"And that wasn't to your liking?" Peotr was vaguely bemused, since this pattern had been common for years without any apparent distaste on Apollo's part.

Apollo replied without emotion. "Why was I born? To eat, sleep, fight, make love, spend money. What else does anyone do?" Saluting Peotr with the bottle, Apollo raised it to his mouth and drained a large draught. "I wish to God, though," he went on suddenly with mild exasperation, suddenly bored with the self-indulgence of casual bedpartners, "that just once I could remember their names." A disgruntled edge was undisguised in his velvet voice.

It startled and confounded Peotr momentarily, since Apollo's practice had always been to indiscriminately refer to all women as "darling." Then Peotr's face brightened perceptibly as an idea formed in his mind. "*Merde*," he said. "Do you know what we should have done? We should have gone to Aladino first. You could have come along."

"Now *that* shows a little more concern," Apollo said, relenting somewhat in his opinion of Peotr's treatment of Kitty.

"Christ, yes," Peotr emphatically declared. "That's what we should have done. Since there was nothing going on here you cared about, I could have dropped you off at the village and you could have entertained Kitty over Christmas. Could have picked you up again on my way back from Baku. Kitty wouldn't have ever known I was anywhere in the vicinity."

Apollo's mollification changed instantly. Astonishment and anger at Peotr's casual offer of his wife's company mingled with seething rage at the opportunity missed.

Peotr's mouth pursed under his black cavalry mustache. "How irritating not to have considered the possibility sooner. You would have been perfect company for Kitty."

Apollo responded in a casual drawl tinged with disdain, "Aren't you concerned about your wife alone with me—well schooled as I am in all manner of vice?"

"*Kitty?*" Peotr's brows raised in surprise. "Are you serious?" Peotr now appeared as astonished as Apollo had been earlier. "She wouldn't even know what you were after if you tried to make love to her."

"So sure, Peotr?" The drawl was insolently bland.

Peotr's image of his wife was quite fixed, and Apollo's hidden sarcasm escaped him. He laughed a short, gruff bark. "Positive, *mon ami*, absolutely positive. Look, I've been married to her for three years. She has nothing but farm accounts and crop production on her mind. Passion, sensuality, romance?" He snorted in disbelief. "Not my Kitty. On second thought, you probably would have been quite as bored there as here. Just as well you didn't go."

And at that remark, if it was possible, Apollo sank even deeper into gloomy brooding. Contrary to her husband's perception, Apollo knew very well exactly how damnably sensual Countess Kitty could be. A surge of desire burned through him at the memory. Damn and bloody blast! Not only could he have avoided this misery and spent Christmas with Kitty, he could have done so with her husband's blessing. Fresh resentment and frustration swept through Apollo's mind, his ready temper mounting dangerously. "Don't say another word, Peotr," he snapped, justifiably riled, feeling like the man bluffed out of straight flush by two pair. His deep, resonant voice was stripped—as was his whole bearing—of his customary pleasant negligence.

Peotr looked both pained and inexpressibly sympathetic. "*Sacristi, mon ami.* Has some woman put you out of sorts?" This behavior was quite unlike Apollo, who rarely indulged in fits of temper.

"You might say so," Apollo answered tightly.

"My God, is it possible? Is there a woman you fancy whom you can't have? I didn't think I'd live to see the day." After a moment of icy silence, he added, "Care to talk about—"

"No."

Persevering, Peotr asked, "One of the Red Crosses?" and watched for some observable reaction. He was disappointed. Apollo simply shook his head. No impulse there for disclosures, Peotr decided. "Well, in that case, I'll take myself out of your brooding presence"—Peotr's good humor was still unimpaired, his mood quite unaffected by Apollo's sulkiness—"and see if I can join the baccarat game in the lounge. We don't move out 'til tomorrow morning." With a casual

wave of his hand he walked out of the compartment and padded down the corridor in his stocking feet.

The vodka bottle Apollo had been nursing hit the wall.
*Merde*, he thought morosely, focusing with a frown on the
shattered glass and rapidly expanding stain on the royal-blue
carpet. He could have had Kitty in his arms the last few days
instead of . . . whatever her name was. The next time he was
tempted to see Kitty, by God, he was going to go. He should
have known better. What a fool to have equivocated at all.
Damned shoddy thinking! Wasn't the war all the more reason
to seize whatever opportunities life presented? And hadn't he
lived well enough all these years disregarding damn near every
social convention? It was a family trait, Apollo had discovered
as he grew older, implicit in the Kuzan lineage. Beginning
with the first Kuzan, who had aided Michael Romanov in
wresting control of the Duchy of Moscow from a multitude
of warring boyars, each subsequent Kuzan, in his privileged
position as an intimate of the crown, had done exactly as he'd
pleased.

Still, there was the matter of Kitty's feelings—and then
Peotr's friendship, of course. . . .

With an exasperated sigh, Apollo rolled over restlessly. Lying quietly for a moment, his face on his wrists, he studied
the damp carpet and, drunk and fatigued, made one of those
irrational decisions that was to change the course of his life.
He had denied himself Kitty, he who had never denied himself
anything. He told himself it wouldn't happen again: the next
time he wanted her, he'd have her, by Christ.

Unfortunately, from that day on, there was no other opportunity to see Kitty, scarcely time to *think* of her; for the
following morning their division was shipped out to Tsaritsyn
in hopes of protecting the front, which was inching disastrously near the city. Hardly had their unit been deployed
near the west bank of the Volga than the order to retreat was
received. Tsaritsyn fell January 3. Taganrog, where Apollo had
passed the holidays, fell January 6. In a matter of three days
the Reds had marched into Novocherkassk and the capital of
the Don Cossacks was in Bolshevik hands. By January 11,

Rostov was captured, forcing the White General Headquarters back to Ekaterinodar, where they had begun two long years ago.

Even in the midst of a massive retreat, Wrangel and Denikin were still carping at each other by letter and telegram like jealous prima donnas, the two generals symptomatic of the lack of *entendre* and common purpose that proved to be so debilitating throughout the war. Since Kornilov had been killed, no general had been charismatic or powerful enough to attach the loyalties of all the disparate elements making up the White Army.

The jealousies persisted, worsened. Denikin, an able administrator, was no tactician; Wrangel, though brilliant, offended many with his arrogance. Their subordinates often indulged excessively in heroin, cocaine, drinking, orgies, and plunder, and didn't listen to either general. The White command was a hotbed of sedition, suspicion, and rivalry, with every regimental commander feeling the fewer wires between himself and divisional HQ the better.

The intercommand feuding wasn't so different in the Red Army. Policy making and execution were unwieldingly undertaken by politbureau, and the bane of "discussion" was further muddied by Stalin and Trotsky jockeying for supreme control. Budenny and other field generals were forced to follow orders from HQ that were suicidal, and often only survived by "not receiving" them. Moreover, the Red Army command was no more immune to the indulgences of alcohol, women, and drugs than the Whites. The vast majority of participants saw this civil war in terms of personal survival, and an all-pervading sense of insecurity encouraged any means to alleviate the nervous tension and forget the slaughter for a moment.

Meanwhile Lenin was exhorting each and all "to win without fail and regardless of cost," to "fight to the death." By telephone, letter, telegram, the "inspiring" messages came.

In the midst of all this squabbling and histrionics, Apollo, Peotr, and the Savage Division were slogging through the bitter cold, trying to stay alive, trying to win battles without supplies, munitions, or fodder, trying to keep Budenny and the Red Army at bay, and . . . losing.

In mid-January, some of Wrangel's Caucasian Army cavalry units were transferred to General Pavlov. Apollo and Peotr spent the next month campaigning under Pavlov on the Manych front. The newly formed regiments—consisting of Don Cossacks, Kuban Cossacks, and mountain men—fought against Dumenko and won several victories. General Pavlov's 12,000 men were horsemen, bred to the saddle and the soldier's life. They functioned as shock troops and were disastrously effective against the Red Army.

As White victories escalated, Budenny's Konarmia was quickly brought to the Manych area, and on February 16 Budenny and Pavlov confronted each other across ten miles of snowbound steppe. Pavlov, now commanding the IV Cavalry Corps, knew the coming battle would be decisive. Budenny also understood the significance of the engagement. A defeat for the Reds would effectively arrest the impetus of their advance, giving the White Army valuable time to rest and regroup. Lenin's persistent telegrams to HQ at the front were screaming for victory "at all costs," a dire, imperative necessity considering the waning vigor of the Red Army and their enormously long supply lines, which were beginning to break down. A Red loss could conceivably turn into a rout toward Moscow.

On February 25, Pavlov reached Torgovaia, but of the reinforced White cavalry of 20,000 beginning the march, only 11,000 were fit for combat after moving for three days through severe blizzards and the intense cold of the steppe. Food, fodder, and shelter were unavailable on the unpopulated left bank of the Manych; the toll in both casualties and diminished fighting strength of those remaining was enormous. Peotr and Apollo—stoically accompanied by Karaim and Sahin—had survived the death march by riding for a half hour and then walking for a half hour all the way to Torgovaia. They were near exhaustion, but alive. Budenny's 20,000 men, although harassed by the weather conditions, were virtually intact, having had the advantage of hugging the railway lines and supply depots.

Pavlov and Budenny stood facing each other at a distance of only a few versts, neither trusting the ability of their forces and both afraid of tempting fortune in a decisive encounter. Pavlov knew he had to attack soon; his corps became weaker by the day.

It was below zero the next morning, and when Pavlov's orders—"To horse!" and "Mount!"—were given, only slightly more than half the original corps was able to comply. Scouts cantered off but almost immediately turned back to the commander, who in turn rode up the gentle rise. Budenny's army was poised for attack in the shallow valley below. Pavlov immediately shouted out the order, "Sabers—lances!" accompanied by his familiar battle cry of "Come on, boys, get those sons of bitches!"

The White cavalry set off in slightly loose order at a trot—most were unable to force their exhausted horses into a canter. As soon as they reached the top of the rise the first thick wave of Red cavalry was almost on them. Behind could be seen the broad valley and thousands more cavalrymen advancing in waves.

Raising their sabers, Pavlov's men charged. The melee ebbed and flowed like a tide. Both sides advanced and retreated countless times, producing a constantly changing pattern.

They fought on the frosty gray steppe, in a strange silence only occasionally punctuated by a pistol shot or scream. Every time a squadron was thrown back, it would halt, about-turn, and then charge again. The waves swept backward and forward; no mercy was shown. Minds ceased to react to the danger, became oblivious to the moans of the dying and to the wounded being trampled under the hooves; soldiers just numbly continued spiking and hacking and occasionally firing their pistols.

By midday Pavlov, his men and animals suffering from fatigue and exhaustion, had lost the initiative. The situation was fast deteriorating. By afternoon, numbers alone determined the outcome.

Budenny's Konarmia won. The Whites lost not only the battle but the war.

Now nothing could stop the Red drive to sweep into the sea the Whites and all they stood for. Denikin ordered all officers and their families to evacuate via Novorossiisk, leaving the Don Cossacks under General Kutepov to serve as rear guard.

Apollo and Peotr, fighting knee to knee with a kind of insane inspiration, somehow survived Pavlov's defeat on February 26, battering and hacking their way to freedom late that afternoon through a screen put up by Kotovsky's brigade. But more than half of their unit was lost in the tragic battle—dead of the cold, killed in the fighting, or captured and executed.

Peotr and Apollo stayed in Kutepov's Cossack brigade, protecting the retreating column of the White Army until March 17, when Ekaterinodar fell. As of that day, there was no more South Russian Government. The fighting was over. Denikin was already on board an evacuation ship in Novorossiisk. There was not the scantest hope for a reversal of fortunes.

Mounted, their tired bodies propped on their pommels, Apollo and Peotr rested on a stark hillside overlooking Ekaterinodar, the first and now final capital of the South Russian Government. So far their small group had evaded Budenny's scouts, but it was time to split up and go their separate ways. Apollo and Peotr were at a distance from the others as they surveyed the grim landscape.

Peotr was the first to speak. "It's over," he said in a low voice, hoarse with fatigue. "No more Allied aid. No more government. Christ, I've only a few score cartridges left. I hope it's enough to get me to Baku."

At the mention of Baku, Apollo turned from the view of Ekaterinodar below and cast cool golden eyes on his friend's face.

"I know. I know," Peotr expostulated wearily. "You think I'm a bastard about Kitty. But, God Almighty, I don't have time to go to Aladino and Baku both. And they're my *children*, Apollo. Am I supposed to abandon them to these bloody beasts?" His voice had risen. Peotr flicked his trouser leg nervously with his *nagaiki*. He'd witnessed too many scenes of

slaughter, torture, and unholy massacre in the last two years
to expect any quarter from the victorious Red Army.

Neither spoke for a moment. They were both tired, their
nerves lacerated from the strain of the last few weeks. Apollo's
gaze silently returned to the scene of defeat two short miles
away. He ran a weary hand over the gold stubble of his beard.

He understood Peotr's dilemma, but it didn't change the
shocking callousness of his decision. God knows Apollo himself had committed his share of crimes over the past few years,
and nasty habits had become a way of life, but . . . to leave
your own wife to the invading Red Army?

Peotr made a jerky, troubled movement. "If the Reds
weren't advancing so rapidly to Baku for those bloody oil
fields," he said hurriedly, "I might have had time to see Kitty
to Novorossiisk on my way to Suata—but under the circumstances it's impossible. Kutepov said yesterday the Eighth
Army had reached Derbent already. If I don't leave now, it'll
be too late. Suata and the children mean a great deal to me—
and they're totally dependent on me. You see, don't you,
Apollo?" Peotr's tone desperately asked for understanding
from his best friend.

Apollo, leaning on his pommel, the short fur blowing on
his hat, stirred, then glanced back to Peotr. He regarded his
unshaven, tired friend, and noticed the skin drawn tightly
against his cheekbones. No one had had much food or sleep
the last two months. "Of course, Peotr, I understand," Apollo
said in a quiet, steady voice. Who was he to pass judgment?
Peotr had fought tirelessly for the cause, bravely willing to
give his life. He had honorably performed his duty and had
upheld his commitment, as he saw it, to country, wife, and
mistress, but now time was running out. Choices had to be
made . . . and Kitty was the least dear of his obligations. Peotr
was only human, like the rest of them; no paragon of virtue—
and after four years of villainy, what possible capacity did any
man have for judging right and wrong? Years of filthy habits,
slaughter, blood, and death had changed them all. Their finer
sensibilities had been forsaken long ago.

"Apollo?" Peotr's query was one of entreaty, and it brought

Apollo's unpalatable musing to a halt. Peotr's large, dark eyes anxiously searched the clear, golden depths of his companion's.

Apollo, who in the chaotic last few weeks had mentally made numerous and what he considered highly practical plans to avoid seeing Kitty again, changed his mind. "You don't have to ask. I would have done it anyway." Apollo's softly spoken words were reasonable, casual; a friend helping a friend.

A deep sigh signaled Peotr's relief. Quickly reaching over, he grabbed Apollo's hand and pumped it vigorously. "You don't know what a comfort that is. A thousand thanks. Sincerely, a thousand!" Still gripping Apollo's hand, Peotr said, "I hope you don't think me too coldhearted. Christ, I even prayed last night for the first time in years for some solution to the problem—but logistically it wouldn't work out, no matter what I tried."

"Lord, Peotr, don't agonize. Suata and the children need you. I'll take care of Kitty." And with that simple statement Apollo's spirits soared. Even in the midst of an absolute, bloody defeat, his mood altered felicitously, unbelievably. He'd see Kitty soon!

Peotr managed a small smile now, only a thin reminder of his usual buoyant *joie de vivre*. He released Apollo's hand. "It may not be as bad as it appears. There's a possibility Kitty emigrated already. I left instructions with her to leave when conditions became dangerous. We're so out of touch with the eastern front, I'm not sure how far the Red advance has progressed. Communication has been erratic for the last month."

"Kitty gone?" Apollo found it difficult to restrain the despondent feeling that overcame him. Immediately he took himself to task for the utter selfishness of that response. Good God, the best thing would be for Kitty to be halfway to Constantinople right now. He was an unfeeling monster to want her still in the midst of this war simply so he could see her again.

"She could be. I've no way of knowing."

"I'll check," Apollo said in a quiet, determined voice. "Rest assured, if Kitty's there, I'll see she embarks for Constantinople."

"How can I ever repay you?" Tears shone in Peotr's eyes.

"No need." Apollo swallowed hard. In all the years of their friendship he had never seen Peotr cry. "Now," he said with bluff briskness, "we'd better get going or neither of us will outdistance the scouts. I see a patrol starting to move south out of Ekaterinodar already. Is Tolia going with you?" Peotr's orderly was originally from Petrograd, and many soldiers were attempting to return home.

Peotr nodded. "Between the Cheka and starvation, his family's all gone. He's alone now."

Apollo raised his hand and laid it, gloved and familiar, on Peotr's broad shoulder. "Better go. See to Suata and the children, and leave Kitty to me. *Bonne chance.*"

"*Au revoir,*" Peotr replied. "I won't wish you luck. You don't need it. I only pity any enemy crossing your path."

Leda stirred a bit and was quiet. Apollo flashed a warm smile and saluted Peotr casually. "See you in Paris this summer."

Peotr's face broke into a wide grin. "It's a date. Stay in happiness, Apollo Alexandrovich," he said in the old way, then, snapping a salute, he wheeled his mount and struck off to the southeast, Tolia following.

Apollo, Karaim, and Sahin wasted no time in leaving the rise. The Red patrol had spotted them through their field glasses and were breaking cross-country toward the low foothills. The Dagestani thoroughbreds broke into the easy lope they could sustain for hours at a time, and by late afternoon the three men had traveled sufficiently east to be out of the area of Red Army movement. That night they wrapped themselves in their *burkhas*, tethered their mounts in the lee side of a haystack, and burrowed into the sweet-smelling hay to sleep. The poignant promise of possibly seeing Kitty soon lulled Apollo into a peaceful slumber. Two more days to Aladino, he thought pleasantly just before dozing off.

# 7

Unconcerned with the personal daydreams of Captain Prince Apollo Kuzan, General Beriozov's Sixth Division had advanced eastward and, in an unexpected offensive three weeks earlier, had launched a rapid flanking drive into Astrakhan. General Erdeli's inadequate defenses had been badly mauled, and the Whites had retreated south in disorder. Several flying units were spearheading the Red drive, outdistancing the main army by twenty miles a day, pillaging, burning, and raping as they overran the district.

After Christmas the number of refugees streaming through Astrakhan, pushed down after Kolchak's defeat on the eastern front, increased steadily. At first Kitty helped with food and clothing on a haphazard basis, but by February the teeming influx of refugees stopping by the estate had reached such proportions that the gatehouse and two large stables had been transformed into a kitchen, infirmary, and barracks. Several hundred émigrés a week stopped to rest, eat, and warm their chilled bodies for a brief time. They stayed a few hours or overnight, occasionally a day or so, but no one tarried long with the Red Army pressing ever closer. The refugees were headed for the Black Sea ports, and Kitty knew she, too, must depart for the safety of those ports. But she kept putting off the decision.

Every cavalry officer coming down the road caused a sudden lurch in her heart, until, her eyes straining, the image at closer range became clear. Not Apollo this time either, she would quietly sigh. Maybe tomorrow. And she waited.

Occasionally an optimistic report would be passed along. Erdeli had won a major battle; he was holding the Reds back; there was even talk of a counterattack.

One evening in February after a long, tiring day at the infirmary, Kitty ate two bites of supper and immediately had to dash upstairs to throw up. She had been feeling strangely languid in the morning, not inclined to touch food until near midday, but had dismissed the odd new symptoms as the result of her heavy schedule at the refugee barracks.

Minutes later, lying pale and exhausted on her bed, a memory spread poignantly along the corridors of her mind, and with hope and apprehension she knew. It wasn't hard work and long hours that accounted for the absence of her monthly cycles. She was going to have a child.

Kitty tried to conjure up some feelings of shame and remorse as she lay curled in the pillows, but inexplicably she couldn't. With a curious sense of elation she now knew quite conclusively that she was carrying Apollo's child. Placing her hands on her flat stomach, she visualized the new life growing inside her, imagined the young child who had sprung from the joyous passion of those three days in December, and she whispered softly, "I will love you . . . as I love your father."

It was the worst of times in the eye of a hurricane devastating her only known world, but for a brief moment it was the best of times for her, and nothing mattered but the love child she carried.

Two days later the stream of refugees diminished to a trickle, then abruptly ceased. Pavel, sent into the nearby town with a note to Kitty's grain dealer, had returned with no reply. Eschlov and Sons was closed. They had left for Constantinople.

Kitty should have realized then that the Red troops were near, and in the back of her mind she did know. But if she acknowledged that fact she would have to leave, and that meant coming face to face with the very real possibility of never seeing Apollo again. It was unsafe to stay, but she was ruled by her heart and by the life growing within her. It was a silly romantic dream, but she desperately hoped it would come true, hoped that Apollo would return to her and to his child. Just a few more days, she told herself, holding on to a scrap of a dream in the face of logic, only a few more days . . . then she'd leave.

In retrospect, it was a very foolish thing to do, and after years of being practical, dutiful, and reasonable, it was a very bad time to become foolish.

Late that night Kitty's frantic maid wakened her. Anna was hysterical and Kitty felt a flash of panic at the first stir of disaster. In the space of a heartbeat Kitty knew the worst had finally befallen them.

"The Bolotokov and Nikitin estates are afire!!!"

Kitty ran to the window, hoping the young girl was somehow mistaken. No mistake. The flames of both properties blazed blood red on the horizon.

"Mistress, what will we do? Everyone has fled!"

Kitty's mind was rapidly gauging the time and distance from the Bolotokov estate, which was nearest, as she threw off her nightgown and tossed a woolen gown over her head. "Anna, don't panic," she said as calmly as her own frantically pulsing heart would allow. "We've still about fifteen minutes at least. Put on your coat and boots and run home to your grandmother. The Bolsheviks are friends of the peasants. They shouldn't hurt you." Kitty knew the Reds were no champions of any person or class who stood in their way, but it wouldn't serve to alarm the girl further. "Now, run. Go! And God go with you."

The young maid hesitated for a fraction of a second, but fear overcame her sense of loyalty even as Kitty said, "Don't die because of me, Anna. Think of your grandmother. She needs you."

The girl stuffed her fist into her mouth to stifle a sob, then turned abruptly and vanished down the long hallway. Kitty followed closely behind, only taking time to gather her jewels into a leather vanity case and pull a warm fur from the armoire. Running down the long curved stairway, she dashed into Peotr's study. With trembling fingers she unlocked the safe, snatched his directions from the strongbox, and——hearing rifle shots terrifyingly close—fled through the ominously empty house out the terrace door to the stable.

The first armored cars were screaming up the long driveway when Kitty exited Aladino for the last time.

With only moments to spare, the young groom who had always cared personally for Peotr's mount tossed Kitty up onto her favorite mare and whipped her on her way. She rocketed out the wide wooden doorway, her horse breaking across the frozen fields behind the stable just as the first members of the Red patrol broke down the front door of Aladino.

The cold stinging her face, her body trembling in nervous reaction to the narrowness of her escape, Kitty bent low over the mare's neck, alternately shivering and inhaling long, calming breaths. She had to remain sensible. The countryside was alive with marauding Bolsheviks. How to find the safest way south to Batum, Sochi, Novorossiisk? Lord, give her courage! Angling west through the fields, staying well away from the manor house and buildings, Kitty reached the concealing shadows of the willows lining the river. She clung to the dim anonymity of the gray murkiness, following the river's course for several versts, heading in a rough southwesterly direction toward Stavropol. If she could reach the city, perhaps it would be possible to purchase a rail ticket south. Moving slowly through the snow-covered landscape, careful not to leave the protective darkness of the drooping willows, Kitty gained a minor byway which eventually widened into one of the country roads to Stavropol. She was several versts from Aladino and the fires glowing well east of her were now only a minor radiance on the horizon. She allowed herself a brief prayer of thanksgiving, profound relief coursing through her ravaged nerves as she gazed at the distant fires. Striking out for Stavropol, she congratulated herself on her hairbreadth escape.

Riding down the deserted road, Kitty straightened her shoulders, drew in a deep draught of the frosty night air, and crooned encouragement to her mare. With a bit of good fortune, she speculated optimistically, she'd be in Stavropol tomorrow.

As it was, her current streak of luck was scheduled to run out.

Scarcely ten minutes later, just as Kitty's mount settled into a comfortable canter, the tranquil darkness of the star-strewn sky was broken by twin beams of vivid yellow light. Seemingly out of nowhere, double streaks from incandescent mercury lamps shone heavenward, ahead of the rider on the empty road. A startling second later a large touring car followed, hurtling out of one of the ravines that cut through the steppe and roared down the road directly toward Kitty.

The mare reared in terror at the sudden light and noise. Kitty lost the stirrups and felt herself falling. There was only time to breathe one soft, exasperated curse, before Lady Luck deserted Countess Radachek and her head struck the ground.

The Russo-Baltic motor car, flying the fanion of the Sixth Division, quietly slid to a halt. From the backseat, a strongly built, well-preserved officer stepped out. Dressed by the best Petrograd tailor, his greatcoat thrown over his shoulders in a manner copied from the old imperial generals, the officer walked slowly over to the crumpled form in the middle of the snow-packed road. With the toe of one splendid riding boot, he rolled the unconscious female over. Snapping his fingers, he barked, "A torch!" A beam of light immediately shone on Kitty's body. A slow smile creased the general's[9] tanned, leathery face. "Put the, ah . . ."—he glanced at Kitty's rich sable and expensive gown—"lady into the backseat." Aristocratic ladies were much to his taste, and such a pretty piece, he decided, should amuse him for quite some time. To the victor, et cetera . . . The Revolution had pleasantly expanded the circle of women available to the son of a poor Siberian peasant.

Surveying the newest plunder of his pillaging troops would wait until later. Reversing his previous order, General Beriozov instructed his driver to return to Stavropol.

Several times on the return journey, the general switched on the interior lights and examined, with the eye of a connoisseur, the very latest—and to date, the most beautiful—of his acquisitions.

• • • •

Kitty woke the following morning in an unfamiliar feather bed in an unfamiliar room, albeit an opulent one. Her dark green eyes scanned the brocaded walls, the gilt-embellished sculpted ceiling, the heavily swagged windows and Second Empire furniture. The sweep of her gaze returning to the bed, Kitty was startled to see an old woman seated directly beside her.

"Where am I?" Kitty asked, wincing slightly. The back of her head was tender and her neck felt stiff as she struggled into a seated position.

"Stavropol, Excellency." Evidently the elderly nursemaid left to watch over Kitty had not completely embraced the new egalitarian form of address in which no classes existed and everyone was "comrade."

"Where in Stavropol?"

"The Hotel Russia, Excellency."

"Who brought me here?" Kitty now recalled the car bearing down on her.

"General Beriozov, mistress."

"How kind of him."

The last Kitty had heard, Stavropol was still in the hands of the Whites. How fortunate that her savior was with the White Army.

The old woman's eyes slid away from Kitty's. "Yes, Excellency. Would you like a glass of tea and a headache powder?"

"Oh, yes, thank you. That would be marvelous. My head's pounding dreadfully."

From a samovar bubbling in the corner, atop a monstrous inlaid table, the woman brought Kitty tea, a packet of powder, and a plate of beautifully decorated cakes.

Kitty swallowed the medicine with her tea and was nibbling on a delicious brioche when the door opened and a large man in the uniform of a general of the Red Army entered. He gave one curt nod, and the old nurse scurried out. Drawing a comfortable armchair near the bed, he dropped into the down-cushioned seat, crossed a leg clothed in superbly tailored wool twill, and lounged casually against the embroidered back of the chair. His thick neck was strapped with muscle, his eyes like sea pebbles, unreadable. He gave the impression of brute force overlaid by years of merciless experience, but he was handsome in a cold, ruthless way.

From the moment he had appeared in the doorway, Kitty's heart had begun to hammer so loudly she was certain it was audible. The brilliant, blood red epaulets gracing the general's shoulders were terrifying to behold. She sat white-faced and unbreathing, sensing the final closing of a trap, horror beating at her paralyzed senses. A tiny shiver traveled over her skin, responding to the danger in the general's cold-eyed appraisal.

What to do? What to do! Whispers of reason attempted to catch at the panic numbing her mind. He apparently didn't plan to kill her immediately, the tiny, reasonable voice hinted, or she wouldn't be ensconced in this flamboyant room. As soon as that thought crossed her mind, the obvious alternative presented itself, and Kitty silently cursed herself for waiting so long—waiting *too* long—to flee Aladino. Useless, romantic hopes had kept her there. Ridiculous, irrational hopes of seeing Apollo again—and for that idiocy she might very well now die, caught in the Red trap. She had had some news to impart to Apollo. How quaint. It appeared now as if that information would never be transmitted. Briefly, Kitty wondered how Apollo would have reacted to the announcement that he was about to become a father.

Never to know now, in any event—and if the tales of cruelties perpetrated by the Red Army were indeed true, perhaps the child would never be born. At that staggering thought, some maternal instinct flamed deep inside and Kitty instantly resolved—as many had before her throughout this war-ravaged land—to survive, whatever the cost. She wanted Apollo's child, *her* child, to know the glory of life.

While these tumultuous thoughts raced and tumbled through Kitty's fearful brain, the general calmly steepled his fingers under his chin and surveyed the most striking woman he had ever seen: slender, fair, with a precious beauty that shocked the senses—translucent white skin like pearls in moonlight; luxurious tangles of sun-kissed hair; finely

sculpted aristocratic bones; a classic nose any goddess on
Olympus would envy; enormous, heavily lashed eyes the color
of an Irish landscape on a misty morning; and, most tantalizing, full, sensuous lips, unmistakably ripe cherry in hue. It
was an overall effect no man would ever forget, and a far cry
from the coarse peasant women previously available to him in
his former station, who'd been modeled more like pack animals than females.

The general's eyes silently took in the full scope of Kitty's
extraordinary lushness. He still hadn't spoken. In no hurry,
he was rather relishing the hunted terror in her expression and
was contemplating with delectable fondness the ultimate ca-
pitulation of this gorgeous woman.

Kitty's nerves were stretched taut. The general's eyes continued their slow perusal. Finally, no longer able to withstand
the oppressive silence, she said in a deliberately calm voice,
white-lipped but composed, "What do you want of me, General Beriozov?"

There was something new in her manner—a decisiveness
and resolve that hadn't been there before. The panic-stricken
fear had been quelled, but with what? Aristocratic backbone,
fortitude? That self-reliant confidence that centuries of wealth
nurtured? In addition to the heavenly gift of her looks, apparently she had character. It should prove amusing, the general thought, to toy with such a strong-minded woman.

General Beriozov carefully recrossed his muscular legs and
tapped his fingertips together gently before answering pleasantly, "Whatever you care to offer me, Countess Radachek."
He'd become familiar with her name after perusing her single
piece of luggage.

"And if I choose not to offer you anything, General?" The
question was couched in a mild, courteous tone as if she had
queried, "One lump or two?"

"I am almost certain, madame," said the general dryly,
"you'll reconsider in the end." He stood in one swift movement, phenomenally graceful for a man of his bulk, and, leaning over, took Kitty's small hand. He stroked the back of it
very gently with his powerful tanned fingers, almost as though

he were gentling a foal. "I have no intention of hurting you, my dear," he explained with fine courtesy. "On the contrary." Kitty attempted to pull away. His fingers tightened their grip. "You will be my hostess tonight at dinner." The general's pale gray eyes held no warmth now. The flinty coldness that had allowed his swift climb to the top of the Red Army trapped Kitty's horrified gaze. His fingers constricted further on Kitty's hand until she winced. "I suggest you say yes," he continued with unruffled persistence.

She paused for half a heartbeat, her hand captured in a viselike grip that could cripple if it chose. "Yes," she whispered.

"Good girl." He released her hand and the briefest smile passed over his face. Turning on his heel with a sharp military precision indicative of training in the tsar's army, General Beriozov strode from the bed. Pausing at the door, he lingered, hand on the latch, and added mildly, "Agrafena will bring you gowns. Take any you like. I prefer red or black velvet if it suits you." Opaque eyes of gunpowder gray rested reflectively on the small woman seated stiffly in the enormous bed, her long golden hair cascading over her satiny shoulders. Receiving no answer, he walked out, the door closing on his blood red epaulets.

When Kitty entered the drawing room that evening, the general's brows lifted the merest fraction; otherwise his expression remained unaltered. He crossed the luxuriously carpeted floor with the stride of a cavalryman and bowed smartly to the perfectly groomed, golden-haired woman who stood just inside the room as if contemplating a rapid retreat. If, in fact, Kitty had envisioned any hope of successfully ignoring the general's command, she would have defied him; as it was, however, compliance seemed the only option, and here she stood. Her spine stiff, her head high, the smallest affordable act of defiance now covered her slender form.

"Blue silk is most becoming to you, madame. May I offer my compliments on your toilette." The tone was perfectly modulated, slightly bemused, and Kitty wondered for a mo-

ment whether she had imagined the general's expressed preference for red or black velvet.

She murmured a commonplace in return, determined to be
as unsociable as circumstances permitted. No martyr, though,
and youthful enough to desire life above all, Kitty realized
that total indifference was out of the question. The short conversation earlier that day in her bedroom left little doubt of
the general's plans for her immediate future, so within reason
she would remain aloof until such a time as even that prerogative was denied her.

The general's next comment put to rest Kitty's reservations
concerning her hearing. Sliding his arm around Kitty's bare
shoulders, he drew her near, at the same time gently propel-
ling her toward the archway leading into the dining room. "I
hope," he said softly, very near her ear, "that you will attempt
to please me better tonight. While I admit you are exquisite
in this shade of blue, I must warn you, my dear, I will not
tolerate defiance in my bed. Understood?"

Two steps more and they were in the dining room. Receiving no answer, he stopped and spun Kitty to face him, his
arm remaining around her shoulder. "Understood?" he repeated. His cold, gray eyes, short inches from hers, held a
distinct hint of menace. General Beriozov, commanding the
entire Sixth Division, was unaccustomed to insubordination.
Indeed, since the first days of the Revolution, he had been
intolerant of refusal. His life of late had been peerlessly, ruthlessly self-indulgent.

There was a short, tortured silence. Against such an
adversary, Kitty's answer—short of suicide—was predeter-
mined. Dropping her lashes, she nodded mutely, sick with
fear and loathing.

A short bark of laughter broke from the general and a satisfied smile followed. "You well-born ladies know the art of
pleasing a man." His eyes raked Kitty insolently. "What else
did you ever have to do? Never any work to dirty your dainty
pink hands . . . plenty of time to primp and perfume yourself
for men and to practice accommodation."

Kitty's eyes snapped indignantly at this grossly unfair assessment of her life, which had been almost totally devoted to running the estate. Her all-too-ready temper outweighed any discretionary caution. Pale and trembling, she enunciated in formal tones, "May I inform you, General, that your image of ladies is profoundly mistaken!"

The general found Kitty's quick anger appealing; it indicated some spirit—a characteristic he much preferred to mute and passionless acquiescence. So he baited her, his eyes narrowed appraisingly. "In what way, madame? Do they *not* know how to please a man?"

"No more, I expect," Kitty hotly replied, "than women of any class!"

"Since you have had little experience in comparing the, ah, female expertise of each class," the general murmured, "let me stand authority on that subject. Aristocratic ladies are, madame, a damn sight better in bed than any Siberian peasant girl or scrawny factory drudge from Moscow."

Seething inwardly—but, as the general pointed out, unable to speak with any great authority—Kitty snapped, "Well, in any case, we don't all sit before our mirrors and primp. Many work!"

The general brushed this aside. "Not the ones I've seen."

"And your experience is so wide?" she sarcastically inquired.

"Actually, quite varied. Particularly, you understand," he replied softly, "in the last two years."

Kitty's heart sank at the quietly deliberate reply. What did he do with women like herself once he was through with them? Just how short a future did she have? Damn him and damn his arrogance! With a fresh surge of resentment she thought, whatever her future, she'd not collapse at his feet in a display of trembling fear. Let him bully some more timid soul. Looking directly into those steely gray eyes—which appeared slightly amused at the moment—Kitty said with a cool detachment she was far from feeling, "As you say, General, the last two years have immeasurably altered our lives."

"How true . . . and because of the Revolution," General Beriozov said with mocking amusement, "I now have the opportunity of making your acquaintance, Countess."

"And I, sir, have the opportunity of viewing the inside of this delightfully garish hotel." While the timbre of her voice was spun sugar soft, Kitty's sarcasm was bluntly pointed. If her future was indeed as short as circumstances suggested, at least she was going out of this world with courage.

Kitty's jibe struck General Beriozov where he was most vulnerable. However successful he was as a professional soldier, in matters of style and taste he was most insecure. He was dressed by the best tailors, insisted on the services of a French chef, furiously cultivated the manners of his former commanding officers, but his lack of sophistication could not be easily altered with a veneer of culture. It galled him that that inferiority remained despite the upheavals of the Revolution. Refinement had been bred into the aristocrats over the centuries; they had breathed the atmosphere of wealth and privilege from their earliest days in the cradle. They were cultured; he was not. They knew music; he did not. They could discuss the paintings hanging on their palatial walls; he could not. They'd all been raised in elegant, tasteful surroundings and knew how to behave. They could be amusing, insouciant, intensely interested in the newest exhibition or ballet. They laughed mildly, lounged negligently, were intricate and graceful as snowflakes—and what the general felt he most severely lacked, they possessed in abundance, attuned with an almost casual indifference to aesthetics that would take him decades to attain.

He had too much self-control—an asset, by the way, that had stood him in good stead in the acrimonious jealousies and bitter rivalries constantly compromising the effective operation of the Red Army General Staff—to show his annoyance, but the general resolved to punish the countess for her impertinence later, in the privacy of his bedchamber. A certain amount of spirit was desirable in a woman, but ridicule was unacceptable. This fair-haired female must be made to understand the permissible limits of expression. Her position within his household was to favor his whims and afford him pleasure. Tonight he would begin to teach her. He was looking forward to the schooling.

"Madame, my apologies for housing you in such mediocre lodgings. Alas," he continued with cool mockery, "the viceroy's palace is out of reach until we take Tiflis."

When Kitty's face paled at the certain confidence in his declaration, General Beriozov drawled with lazy cruelty, "No more than a month, Countess, and you will be living in the elegant luxury to which you're accustomed."

Kitty shivered involuntarily at the prospect of the entire south of Russia conquered. Peotr gone—dead, wounded, buried somewhere. And Apollo. She almost wept at the prospect of so vital a man, obliterated from the world and from her life. Only superhuman resolution kept the tears from falling. Kitty's wet, shiny eyes did not go unnoticed by the acutely perceptive general. Satisfied his cutting remarks had struck home, he said with renewed amiability, "But enough of the future, Countess. Glorious as the prospects are, one must not lose sight of the prosaic present. Come now, my dear, as my hostess tonight, I have need of your finesse in some matters. Tell me. May a colonel be seated on my right or must a major general take precedent?" Switching from his menacing manner to his affable personality, the general was all goodwill and warm solicitude in an irreverent sort of way as he pulled Kitty, pale and numb, around the lavishly appointed table which gleamed with gold, crystal, and fine china.

The seating cards were exchanged, although Kitty's instructions were barely audible. All she could think of was the end of everyone and everything she had ever known.

"And about the soup course . . . May I call you Katherine?" the general inquired in a dangerously smooth tone. "After all, we shall soon be, er, intimate friends."

Kitty flushed at the sarcasm and frantically assessed her chances of escaping the room, the hotel, Stavropol. Cold resignation soon replaced the momentary impulse to flight. She would be recaptured before reaching the door of the suite. "Yes," she said, yielding to his position of strength.

"In that case, call me Dmitri."

I'd choke on the word, Kitty thought.

"Now then," the general continued blandly, ignoring her silence. "There seem to be two approaches to the soup course. Shall we serve it first, in the French fashion, or as a third course in the Russian style? And the salad—should it be separate in the French manner?"

"Third for the soup, and no, not separate for the salad."

"So positive?"

"We've always served them that way."

The general put two fingers to his brow and closed his eyes briefly. "Of course, I should have known." We *always* have. His already fragile equanimity was goaded by a flash of pique at the inimitable tone of assurance exhibited by the dainty lady at his side, whom he could break with his bare hands if he cared to.

An extra measure of discipline tonight, he promised himself. No cowering creature here at all. For the first time in his life he considered a woman as something other than mindless chattel. This comely young woman refused to fit into any of the usual female categories. An interesting challenge, he mused with a certain dispassionate fairness; no previous female had ever provoked such anticipatory interest. Let no one mistake the extent of the general's sense of fair play, however. Mysterious and piquant the challenge may be, but in his world only one winner was allowed—and General Beriozov hadn't shouldered his way to the command of an army division by turning the other cheek. He achieved what he sought at all costs. No scruples stood in his way, and many anonymous graves marked the path of his ascent to power.

"And the flowers?" he continued pleasantly, years of military discipline restraining the niggling impulse to strike out at someone.

"White would be better. The red of the roses clashes terribly with the wallcovering." Kitty's eyes swept the overdecorated room. "And the velvet cover of the mantelpiece should be removed. It's quite bourgeois." Glancing at the ladened zakuski table, she added, "I hope the chocolates are from Ballet."

The general searched Kitty's face for a brief moment, trying to decide if she was deliberately nettling him. Kitty only shrugged her lovely white shoulders and returned his stare. "You asked me," she said. The countess looked, the general thought with a pang of fury, roughly as humble as Catherine the Great; Queen Tamara of the Georgians discarding a tiresome lover might have worn such a look. Even their goddamn chocolates had to be from the right store. She'll pay tonight, by God, he silently vowed.

"Ivan!" the general bellowed in a voice that had no doubt been used above the roar of battle on many occasions.

In seconds a servant came running into the room. "Get rid of all these red roses," Beriozov snapped, jerking a finger toward the table. "Immediately! Bring white ones! And that velvet cover over there—take it away. Hurry!" he shouted to the sprinting servant who was already halfway out the door carrying two vases of crimson roses.

Moving to a sideboard that held several bottles of champagne cooling in a magnificent silver monteith, the general carefully opened a bottle and filled two glasses. Kitty stood near the long dining table set for a score of guests and wondered if it might be better to die after all than survive under these conditions. Later, after the dinner party was over—she cringed at the sordid image of what might follow, then continued her train of thought—after the general was asleep, it would be very simple to swallow the morphine in her traveling bag. To go to sleep and never wake . . . mightn't that be easier? Only the physical reality of Apollo's child, the very real presence of a part of him beneath her heart, tempered the overwhelming desire to simply give up.

Could she really contemplate killing his child? Even if Apollo didn't survive the war, a child of his to hold and love would be a reminder of the happiest days of her life—days and memories given to her by a warm, loving, tumultuously sensual man who had made her smile and laugh and had taught her to love. Merely thinking of his child made her yearn to hold it close. And if it was any consolation, she wasn't alone in her misery. All across Russia millions of people were doing what they had to do to survive. All the polite rules and courtesies had fallen by the wayside, bludgeoned to death, torn apart by the bestial wave of revolution. She could and would join the ranks of the survivors, if for no other reason than for Apollo's child. In her musing she could almost picture Apollo's languid smile, lighting up his eyes, fine teeth shining white against his sun-bronzed face as he laughingly said, "Live, sweet *dushka*, to love me another day. Live, come what may, with or without me, for there's pleasure in life and none in dying."

Reality reintroduced itself. The general was handing her a glass of champagne. Kitty shook her head. "No, thank you."

"I'd like you to join me." Although the words were pleasant, his chill voice was not.

Kitty's hand accepted the glass. Lesson number one, she thought, in the new primer of survival.

"To us, Katherine," the general proposed. Kitty hesitated, unnerved by the prospect of responding to such a toast. She had never been coerced in her life, and each new devastating discovery was appalling.

"To us," she finally managed to whisper, lifting the glass to her mouth, and lesson two was shakily concluded.

Powerful fingers stayed the glass short of her lips. "To us . . . who?" Beriozov softly demanded.

Their gaze held for a full five seconds and Kitty contemplated the vicious gleam deep within the general's narrowed eyes. "To us . . . Dmitri," Kitty quietly capitulated, and lesson three was accomplished.

And so the evening went, the general gently forcing, the lady reluctantly complying—an amusing sparring match for the former, and a grim education in survival for the latter.

All too soon the last course was served, the last jest, compliment, tactical strategy bandied about. At opposite ends of the table the general and his new hostess had superintended a faultless dinner party.

The guests were an assortment of officers and their companions from various ranks of society, ranging from well-bred ex-army officers who had joined the Red Army for a variety of reasons[10] to those from the coarsest of peasant backgrounds. Occasionally Kitty detected a note of sadness in the eyes of some from the old regime, but after several bottles of champagne had been broached, a certain degree of gaiety prevailed amongst all. In truth, Kitty felt herself the least able to condemn those officers who had changed their allegiance and now wore Red Army uniforms. Wasn't she doing the same? Capitulating to stay alive?

As the evening wore on, Kitty drank more champagne than she was used to, for the general signaled the footman to replenish her glass whenever a toast was concluded. At heart, she wasn't particularly averse to overimbibing—the liquor would dull her senses for the inevitable conclusion of the evening. Merely the thought of having Beriozov touch her intimately drove her hand frequently to the stem of her champagne flute, and a great deal of bubbly wine passed down her throat. While her senses numbed, however, her foreboding became if anything more acute.

By two in the morning the general had waited quite long enough to try out his new paramour and he curtly bade good night to his guests. Within minutes the apartment was empty, the servants dismissed as well.

"Now, my dear," General Beriozov said, lounging at his ease on a large brocade-covered sofa, "perhaps you would undress for me."

Kitty stood very still, steadying herself with one hand on a small tea table. "I'd rather not," she said with the flatness of apprehension.

His cool gray eyes were unmoved. "But I want you to," he said without emotion.

Oh, God, now what, Kitty fearfully thought. After a pause, she said, "Could I at least have some privacy?" Her knuckles were white on the applewood tea table.

"It's perfectly private. I've dismissed everyone."

She still hesitated, then whispered, "Must I?"

"Don't be a fool, my dear," he said acidly. "Your choices are limited. Either you undress yourself or I'll undress you, and I'm much more pleasant if my orders are followed. You haven't seen my collection of silk whips. They're quite elegant, and rarely leave a mark."

Swallowing the lump in her throat, Kitty forced her hand up to the tiny sapphire studs, arranged diagonally down the bias-cut bodice of the blue dress.

General Beriozov leaned his head back and unhooked the collar of his uniform. "Go slowly, Katherine," he ordered quietly. "Very slowly."

Her fingers were trembling so much that it was simple enough to obey that command. Minutes passed before all the buttons were properly unfastened. Neither spoke. The ticking of the mantel clock sounded unduly loud in the hushed stillness of the room. Kitty proceeded as if hypnotized by the general's pale, piercing eyes, shocked at what she was forced to do but obligated by the requirements of survival. Her mind seemed to divide from her actions, as if her dignity could retreat unviolated to an innermost part of her being.

When all the studs were undone, Kitty slipped her arms out and the blue dress dropped down her slim hips and swished in a soft, silky breath to the deep pile of the Tabriz carpet.

The general caught his breath involuntarily. Kitty's shoulders were bare and white; wisps and ringlets of her pale gold hair floated free of the heavy coils pinned high on her head and lay in arabesques on the ivory velvet of her shoulders.

She wore a thin lace chemise, delicate and ephemeral. Looking straight ahead, her deep green eyes unfocused, she deliberately raised her shaking hands and pushed down both shoulder straps. As the front of the chemise slipped lower, more and more of the soft slope of her breasts became visible, the deep cleft between them widening as the lace fabric eased itself almost to each nipple.

She held her head high, but about her eyes was a sadness and resignation, like a captive from an age long ago. She was indeed captive, although, astonishingly, it was the twentieth century; she was undressing under duress, dropping one by one the prerogatives of her independence. But her brooding resignation and sullen beauty challenged the general more acutely than the most avid, wanton response. Beriozov sat transfixed by the lady's instinctual grace and pride, her deliberate, resigned movements. A powerful, pleasurable surge of feeling swept through him. In all his variety he had never possessed such beauty.

Kitty's hands returned to her chemise, holding it up in a gesture of modesty. Her eyes begged the general to call a halt to this agony.

Without taking his chill, smoky eyes off Kitty, the general raised his hand in the gesture of a man accustomed to total obedience and pointed his finger down, firmly and deliberately.

Kitty loosened her grip and the filmy chemise dropped around her waist. Her breasts were completely exposed, full, firm, splendid, the large round aureoles rising audaciously like rose-tinted buds on ivory sculpture. The general's gaze slid downward to her bare breasts and lingered in rapt attention. His lust licked out and touched Kitty like a living carnivore.

A frozen moment passed and suddenly the general's anticipatory waiting ended. Rising swiftly, he strode to her and, facing her, cupped his hands under her breasts; with his thumbs he caressed her nipples. Kitty shuddered and closed her eyes. His touch was repellent. The caresses moved from her nipples to the entire breasts, the general's large, coarse hands kneading and stroking. Kitty submitted silently although her senses let out an inner scream of torment.

When his fingers moved to her waist, she whispered, "Please . . . let me get dressed. Please."

"Don't be absurd," Beriozov muttered, deaf to her pleas, his fingers already unfastening the hooks on her slip. When it, too, fell to the floor, the smooth white flesh of Kitty's thighs was exposed above her gartered stockings. In a carnal frenzy the general dropped to his knees and buried his face between the cool whiteness of her legs.

The contact chilled her with icy horror. "Don't . . . don't, my God, no!" Kitty begged in a moment of uncontrollable panic. She pushed against him, hopelessly twisting, but he held her mercilessly. To a man who could ruthlessly massacre entire villages and then sit down to an evening meal, Kitty's protests were quite futile.

"No . . . please! No!" Kitty cried again, trying to draw away from the brute holding her prisoner.

Quickly losing patience, the general reached up and slapped her sharply into silence. With the countess once again submissive, he pushed the lace of her panties past her hips and with a final deft flick they dropped to the floor. With the final rampart broached, the general's rapacity could no longer be contained.

Pulling Kitty down onto the carpet, ignoring her crying, shaking sobs, his face cruel with lust, the general fell on her like a mighty bull, only taking time to unbutton his trousers before plunging in desperately, deeply, causing Kitty to cry out in pain. The chestful of medals on his tunic jacket bruised Kitty's soft skin and breasts as each powerful surge drove brutally into her. Thankfully, the general's spasms quickly overtook him. Immediately rolling away, he dozed off in drunken satiation.

Kitty lay inert, huddled in misery on the floor, tears rolling silently down her cheeks. Filled with horror and loathing, she felt stunned and almost unbelieving of what had happened— was happening—to her. Some minutes later, painfully, resolutely, avoiding the sight of the man who had humiliated and tormented her, she stumbled to her feet and crept into the bedroom, her whole mind and body and spirit drowning in a murky pool of shame, resentment, and physical revulsion.

After this devastating initiation into her new role of paramour, Kitty collapsed on the bed and retreated from the horror of the real world by seeking refuge in an exhausted sleep.

The next morning, screaming in startled fright, she woke

to feel the general's hands on her body. He slapped her hard twice, and in the future Kitty forced herself to wake in silence, silently making the abysmal adjustment from dreams to harsh reality. It wasn't Apollo at her side, as in her dreams, but the ruthless Beriozov.

The pattern of Kitty's life settled into a familiar if harrowing routine. The general, with his simple peasant openness, treated Kitty with a naive, deferential courtesy when sober. He was extremely conscious of the exquisite beauty fallen prize to him, but when he was drunk, he was a malignant animal. These spells occurred with great regularity, and at those times he abused and tormented her, satisfying his sadistic personality, taking physical and psychological revenge for all the inequities he felt he had suffered under the tsar's regime.

"It has been declared that noble women are common property," he once pronounced brusquely. "I understand Bolshevism," he continued with the particular bias that suited his political theories. "It is the realization of one's will." At those times, Kitty would feel the brutal results of his hatred, and while the general was correct in declaring silk whips left no marks, they did hurt dreadfully.

As the most prized of Beriozov's possessions, Kitty was guarded diligently.

Despite the wretchedness of her captivity, there were no opportunities of escape. Although she was allowed outside the hotel for carriage rides, she was never unattended by fewer than two guards. Only at night were servants and guards dismissed; the general was quite confident in his ability to guard his paramour, and ill disposed to anyone listening to the occasional cries coming from the bedchamber. He hadn't yet acquired the aristocrat's disdain for the world's opinion.

Often in those weeks, during the dark hours before dawn, Kitty would take out the vial of morphine and sit, desperate and filled with self-loathing, listening to the drunken snores of Beriozov, wishing for nothing more than oblivion, trying to find the courage to end her life. The thought of Apollo's child within her stayed her from the deed, but she often wondered if death wouldn't be a solution for them both. Sometimes she despaired how she could bring a child into a world like the present; a world painted red with the blood of innocent men, women, and children; a world of famine and pestilence. Then she would remember three days in the snowy depths of winter, and a warm, isolated bedroom with Apollo's teasing smile against her lips and his clever hands cool on her skin. His memory, which returned to warm her a hundred times a day, kept her alive. *Was* he alive somewhere? Was it possible he still lived? Would she ever see him again? At times, in the deepest depths of despondency, Kitty realized that only the slim hope that Apollo lived kept her on this earth—and that if, in this maelstrom of revolution, she heard otherwise, she would gladly join him in death.

# 8

Apollo arrived at Aladino with Karaim and Sahin three days after leaving Ekaterinodar. The countryside was in turmoil; the roads clogged with refugees, everyone moving south toward the Black Sea ports. In certain areas Apollo and his companions had to avoid Red patrols, and on the last day of their journey into Astrakhan the Red Army activity was so intense they decided to sleep in the daytime and travel the last forty versts at night.

Inwardly, Apollo was alarmed. Obviously the country had been overrun by the Bolsheviks; troops were numerous on the roads and bivouacked in many of the villages. Had Kitty escaped? Was it possible she was still safe at Aladino? That likelihood appeared remote with the current state of the war, but it was the hope Apollo liked least to relinquish.

When the Revolution first began, Apollo had entered the conflict with the cold facts of warfare neatly arranged in logical compartments in his mind. He knew after serving on the western front that he might die, and friends could be lost, but he faced these consequences with the military discipline of an officer. How could he have known that the merest chance— one bottle of champagne too many, a few brief days with Kitty—would scatter those neat compartments into irrevocable disarray? Since those days in December, not an hour of his life had he escaped being touched by the glorious memory. Now, when he had finally decided he *must* see her again, and fate—in the guise of her husband—had practically handed Kitty over to him, the grim fortunes of war might have snatched her away. Apollo was no longer able to view the consequences of war with his former dispassion.

In the pink haze of a March dawn, Apollo rode up the familiar linden-lined driveway, his heart filled with dread. Even from this distance he could see that the Red Army had preceded him. Remnants and odd pieces of clothing were scattered along the driveway and on the snow-covered verges. Fragments of furniture, ruined tapestries, torn and half-burned books lay helter-skelter where the plunderers had tossed them. With the evidence of wholesale pillage before his eyes, Apollo now hoped, despite his need of her, that Kitty was far and safely removed from this blackened wreck of Aladino.

Riding into the graveled courtyard, Apollo caught sight of the charred remains of the stables and outbuildings. The huge three-story limestone manor house had survived the torches only because of its construction—the pale stone had refused to burn, and the marauders had had to content themselves with destroying the interior and gutting the home of its furnishings and treasures.

All the windows had been broken and hammers and sickles smeared in blood decorated the walls as well as the front door, which now hung on one hinge. The three men dismounted before the deserted house, then slowly climbed the marble stairway, crossed the colonnaded portico, and went in through the broken doorway.

Machine-gun bullets had riddled the fine paneling of the entrance hall. In the drawing room the hangings, saber-slashed, hung in shreds. Red cavalrymen had used the Venetian mirrors for pistol practice, and the Canaletto at the top of the stairs was slashed through. Apollo closed his eyes for a moment, saddened and repelled by the sight, although he had seen hundreds of similar scenes in the last few years.

He hesitated briefly before ascending the stairs to the second floor, afraid of what bloody evidence he might find in Kitty's bedroom suite. He mounted each step slowly, paused at the top, then continued down the hallway, bracing himself for the worst.

The door to Kitty's room was gone. Apollo stood in the doorway, his pale golden eyes swiftly scanning the room. Every detail of the pine-paneled bedchamber had been etched in his mind during the course of the days he and Kitty had secluded themselves from the outside world. He remembered the large soft bed, the glowing porcelain stove, the small dining table set before the arched Palladian windows that overlooked the sweep of snow-drifted field. The pungent fragrance of sweet peas flooded the air. Kitty's favorite flowers. The images, the words, sounds, textures, had all been filed and folded away to be summoned countless times since then.

Nothing remained now of that idyllic retreat. All the furniture had been carried off, the curtains ripped down, even the carpet had been torn from the floor. Only a few shreds of pale green Kirman still remained tacked in the corners, mute evidence of the haste with which several centuries of a family's accumulated treasures had been violated.

A faint glimmer on the floor near the dressing room door caught Apollo's eye and he walked over to pick up the object. It was one of Kitty's gilt hairpins. He touched it to his lips before placing it in his tunic pocket. At least there were no bloodstains visible in the room. Whether Kitty had escaped or not, was dead or alive, it appeared quite certain she hadn't been surprised in her bed and killed in *this* room. That single positive fact, however, did not alter the multitude of disastrous fates that may have overtaken Kitty. If not already dead, she was vulnerable to all the rest of the apocalyptical horrors. Would he be able to find her in time? Would he be able to find her at all? Was he too late—did she already lie dead in some unmarked grave.

He started his search. For the remainder of the day the three men scoured the neighborhood for clues to Kitty's fate. All the peasant cottages were locked tightly. The army that had ravaged the area had moved on only a week previously; no one wished to open his door to an officer, regardless of the intent. The peasants, having suffered from both armies requisitioning food, horses, and supplies, were justifiably suspicious of any soldier.

Determined to find some clue, however small, to Kitty's disappearance, Apollo refused to be deterred by the silent huts and closed shutters. He pounded on doors, pleading and threatening until someone would timidly open the door a crack, and in this fashion each peasant in the neighborhood was interrogated. By late afternoon Apollo had tenaciously pieced together the events of the sudden arrival of the Sixth Division's shock troops, but no one had any specific details about the Countess Radachek. Apollo traced Kitty's maid Anna to her grandmother's home, but Anna could tell him nothing of Kitty's actions after her own flight. Anna suggested Apollo talk to the groom, Boris—as she had fled that night, she had seen him in the stables. If the Reds hadn't killed him, he might be able to tell Apollo something.

Apollo was becoming more and more depressed with each interview. In these brutal times, no one had any inclination to do more than save his own skin. It was understandable, of course, but it frustrated Apollo's quest ruinously, for everyone had been so intent on self-preservation when the Reds had come that no one had given any thought to Kitty.

Although Apollo wasn't optimistic, he traveled with Karaim and Sahin to a solitary hut hidden by a deep curve of the river. Approaching the remote farmstead, Apollo recognized two of Peotr's mounts left behind during their last visit. His heart leaped for joy at the familiar sight, but as he dismounted cold practicality cautioned restraint. The fact that the groom had taken some of the horses from Aladino did not indicate he knew anything about Kitty. Even so, Apollo felt elation at seeing something that had belonged to her.

The groom answered Apollo's initial questions with native peasant reticence. The presence of Karaim and Sahin, garbed like mountain savages, did little to loosen his tongue. They both looked as if there weren't a crime they wouldn't commit, and they presented a vicious appearance, dressed in their black *burkhas*, crossed with bandoliers, with *kinjals* thrust into their belts and Lebel rifles slung on their backs.

"So you don't know where Countess Radachek went?"

"No, Your Excellency." It was the same, almost mute disclaimer Apollo had been hearing all day. No expression was on the groom's face, no understanding in his eyes—the mask of ignorance that had protected the peasant for thousands of years. Distrust of authority of whatever political persuasion was as deep-seated as peasant fatalism.

"Did you see the countess at all that night?"

"No, Your Excellency."

"Well, did you see Anna? She said she saw you."

"No, Excellency."

"The horses—they're from Aladino."

"Yes, Excellency. They're too good for the Red Army." There was an infinitesimal change in expression; a barely perceptible disparagement when he mentioned the Bolsheviks.

"You don't want the Bolshis to have Peotr's horses?"

"No, Excellency, the count would never allow it."

Apollo smiled at the groom's stubborn loyalty. Here he was, still preserving the count's wishes when the entire south of Russia was rushing toward an unknown fate.

"Peotr would be pleased that you have his horses."

"Thank you, Excellency." The groom briefly relinquished his suspicion at the smile Apollo bestowed on him and asked hesitantly, "Will the count be back?"

Apollo's face became grave. "No, he won't be back."

"Not ever, Your Honor?"

"No," Apollo said in an exhausted voice, "not ever." All the despair at having reached a dead end washed over Apollo. Suddenly he looked miserably tired, heartsick. Several weeks had passed since the Red invasion. Even if they tried to track Kitty, the odds against success were practically insurmountable. He'd been totally unrealistic. There was no hope.

Apollo straightened a twisted saddle mount with his gloved fingers, put his foot in the stirrup, and vaulted into the saddle. Gathering the reins, he looked for a moment at Peotr's horses. What now? Kitty could be anywhere in the teeming refugee population of South Russia, or in the Middle East, or Europe. And he couldn't find her. Tears wet his eyes, startling and embarrassing him. Good Lord, he hadn't cried since he was eight. His mind quickly flashed through the rationalizations as he surreptitiously raised his gloved hand to brush away the wetness. It was the frustration, the sense of defeat, the last three weeks of snatched sleep and heavy riding. Everything was taking its toll. He could have withstood everything else, he knew . . . and, indeed, he had for four long years. It was losing Kitty that was destroying his self-control.

Karaim and Sahin respectfully looked the other way, allowing the Young Falcon some privacy in his sorrow. If sheer bravado could have produced the young lady, they would have gladly given their lives for their master, but as it was, they both resolved to attempt to track her at first light tomorrow, no matter the overwhelming odds. Neither contemplated failure. They would succeed for As-saqr As-saghir, however long it took.

Boris, too, noted the shiny gleam of moisture in the young officer's eyes and quickly reconsidered his position. After all, the count was not returning. All the servants had been aware of the blond officer's intimate visit with the countess. From the look of it, he cared very much.

Apollo was wheeling his horse when he heard Boris say, "She went to Stavropol."

Apollo jerked Leda around. "*What?*"

"She went to Stavropol. I saw her off just as the first armored cars were coming up the driveway."

"Why didn't you tell me before?"

"I didn't know *why* you wanted to know."

"I promised Peotr I'd see her to safety."

"It may be too late. Stavropol is in Red hands now."

"You actually saw her get away?" Apollo's voice was sharp and excited.

Boris nodded. "She rode toward the river."

"If she's still in Stavropol, I'll find her." Apollo spoke softly, more to himself than to the others. His mouth widened into a broad smile. He looked at Karaim and Sahin.

Answering smiles appeared on their dark faces.

Apollo leaned down and put out his hand to Boris. "Thank you," he said. "Thank you very much."

•   •   •

They slept in the plundered house that night. Apollo curled up in his *burkha* on the floor in Kitty's bedroom and felt more cheerful than he had in days—weeks, in fact. To Stavropol tomorrow. If Kitty were still alive, he'd find her!

Before Apollo and the mountain warriors could enter Stavropol, it was necessary for them to acquire some identity papers and at least a partial Red Army uniform. By and large the Red Army suffered from a lack of uniforms, so hybrid attire was acceptable; a tunic or two would serve. Beginning early the next morning, all three men shrouded themselves in their black *burkhas*, packed their *papakhas*—which bore the green crescent and half-moon insignia of the Savage Division—and, looking as anonymous as possible, set to stalking some suitable victims of sizes and shapes to accommodate them. A certain finesse was essential in requisitioning the uniforms, since bulletholes and bloodstains should be kept to a minimum.

After midday they came on a small troop escorting an officer into Stavropol. The troop's horses were tied outside a roadside cafe, and judging from the sounds of laughter coming from inside, the men had been drinking for some time. There were six mounts in all, one with an officer's holster for pistols.

"If it looks as if the uniforms will fit, we'll stay and drink with them," Apollo stated. "If they're insistent about our papers, shoot first. Six against three—the best odds we've had in two years. Ready?"

Karaim and Sahin nodded once, never requiring lengthy explanations when it came to killing. They performed extemporaneously with considerable expertise.

Dismounting, they tied their horses loosely to a rickety wooden fence and walked bareheaded into the dim interior. The soldiers were all grouped around one table, while several peasants sat on a bench against the wall. Apollo strolled over to the group at the table, Karaim and Sahin flanking him two steps back. "Mind if we join you?" he drawled ingenuously.

The officer looked them over suspiciously and asked who they were.

"On our way to Stavropol. Reassigned from the Eighth Army to the Sixth Division." Apollo's face was friendly and bland.

"Papers," demanded the officer. At his harsh tone the others interrupted their card game long enough to cast another glance at the trio.

"Left behind when Mamontov surprised us at Manyich two weeks ago. Attacked us while we slept in the village. We retreated in our underwear that day. Had to scavenge some clothes after that." Apollo gestured at their *burkhas* and mountain trousers.

The officer scrutinized them carefully, and then the one whom Apollo had already measured by eye as the owner of his new uniform snapped, "What did Comrade Lenin say about the right of self-government of the peoples?"

"Self-government until independence!" Apollo answered earnestly.

"What does communism lead to, economically speaking?"

"From the domain of temporary economical anarchy to that of systematic production," Apollo continued fluently, thanks to the barrage of leaflets the Reds were constantly dropping from their few aircraft. The Bolshevist dogma had been perfect for starting fires.

Apparently Apollo passed the interrogation, for the officer beamed with satisfaction at his own cleverness and poured him a glass of vodka. "Have a drink, comrade."

Apollo took the glass and sat down, motioning for Karaim and Sahin to do the same.

"Do *they* have papers?" the Red officer inquired, nodding toward the mountain men.

"No, theirs are gone, too. We'll get new ones in Stavropol."

"Are they Bolsheviks like you, comrade?" The officer knew the Caucasians were irregulars for both armies, fighting generally not for political principles but for plunder.

"They barely speak Russian, comrade," Apollo replied. "Lenin's ideology, even if they could understand it, would concern them little." He smiled faintly. "They kill for the joy of killing; their allegiances are purely personal."[11]

The Red officer was an ex-peasant from the Don region, one of the *inogorodnie*[12] who had lived under Cossack rule all of his life. He was familiar with blood-thirsty warriors and had a healthy respect for them. Leaning over, he whispered out of the corner of his mouth, "Will they obey you?"

"Absolutely." Apollo nodded solemnly. "We're blood brothers."

The Red officer's eyes widened in alarm. He had heard of the ceremony in which warriors cut deeply into their forearms and then mingled their blood. For a simple peasant from the Don, such exotic barbarism was threatening. It wasn't that he, as a peasant, was particularly benign, but he preferred beating someone to death or shooting them. The various forms of torture practiced by the mountain tribes had been conveyed in terrified whispers by the peasants of his region. With another apprehensive glance at the two hawk-visaged, dark-skinned warriors in black, their arsenals on their persons, he hastily decided it was time to leave.

"Going so soon?" Apollo affably inquired when the officer rose.

"We're on our way to Stavropol, too—and behind schedule." His eyes flicked nervously.

"Let me buy you a drink. Surely you can stay a bit longer?" Apollo pushed the vodka bottle toward him.

"No, no, we must be on our way." The officer was moving away from the table. Two of his men came to their feet as well, but the other three eyed the vodka bottle longingly. Apollo refilled their glasses.

"One quick swallow, comrades." He winked, his manner sympathetically friendly. The three men tossed the liquor down as the officer and two soldiers were leaving. "One for the road," Apollo said, shoving the bottle toward them. He gave one swift glance to the door. The officer and soldiers had reached the outside. Looking at Karaim and Sahin, Apollo nodded once. Before the three Red soldiers could react, Apollo, Karaim, and Sahin were on their feet, *kinjals* slashing. The drunken soldiers died in their chairs.

"The others will be back in a second," Apollo tersely said. "The door."

Karaim had no more than run to the door and flattened himself beside it when one soldier reappeared. He walked one pace into the room, his eyes sweeping the interior. Recognition dawned. He opened his mouth to scream but the sound never came. Dark hands moved with flashing speed and the soldier's head jerked before he slid to the floor. Four down, two to go. Apollo smiled grimly. Karaim flexed his long fingers.

By this time the two remaining outside had decided all was not right. The sound of horses galloping away indicated their flight.

"Damn," Apollo swore. "Strip two of these for yourself. I want the officer." While Karaim and Sahin turned to their task, Apollo strode toward the door. "Catch up with me," he tossed over his shoulder. Passing the bar, he laid three gold roubles on the countertop. The proprietor and local customers had silently disappeared at the first sign of violence, but Apollo knew they'd be back soon to strip the remaining corpses.

Leaping onto Leda, Apollo coaxed her into a racing gallop through the dingy streets of the village. Bending low over her neck, he crooned gentle, cajoling words and Leda responded with more speed. Within a verst he caught a glimpse of his prey; he knew Leda could overtake them. Members of the Red Army were not known for their equestrian prowess.

The officer was slightly in the lead of the twosome, which suited Apollo perfectly. When he was within twenty yards of the soldier in the rear, he drew his *kinjal* from its sheath at his belt, stood in his stirrups, balanced the knife, judged, and threw. It was a difficult target with both horses going full out. The blade hurtled straight through the air, its Dagestani steel penetrating the back of the fleeing soldier clean on target. The man gave a brief cry and slumped over his horse's mane. A mountain maxim passed briefly through Apollo's mind: A rifle may miss, a pistol may jam, but the dagger is always true. His expression altered infinitesimally in agreement.

Apollo leaned over to retrieve his dagger. The soldier's body fell to the ground as Apollo galloped after the officer. Casually he wiped the bloody blade on the black sweep of his *burkha* and sheathed it. No blood on this next one. He wanted the uniform.

As Leda closed the gap, the officer drew his pistol and fired at Apollo. Not wanting to return the fire, Apollo counted the shots and stayed out of range. A pistol wasn't accurate unless steadied and fired at fairly close distance. If the Red officer hit him, it would be a miracle.

When the last chamber was empty, Apollo gave Leda her head and the margin narrowed. Leaning out on one stirrup for the required leverage, Apollo measured the span with one practice arc of his saber, and as the two horses drew close Apollo swung the blade with all the power of his strong right arm. With skill, grace, and flawless coordination of horse and rider, the blunt edge of Apollo's gold-hilted saber caught the Red officer somewhere between the ear and the collarbone and cracked his neck. The man was dead before he lost his stirrups and fell to the snow-covered road.

Apollo pulled Leda up and jumped off immediately. Within seconds he had stripped off the officer's tunic and slit his throat for good measure. Now there was one less Bolshevik left to kill and torture in the name of progress.

Short minutes later, Karaim and Sahin came pounding down the road, their saddlebags bulging with army uniforms and hardware and extra horses on long leads behind them. They helped pull the dead men off the road, covered them with snow (the wolves would get them soon enough), and then the three men set out for Stavropol.

"Picked up a few horses, I see," Apollo remarked conversationally.

"A pity to leave them behind," Sahin said in Dagestani.

"A pity," Apollo agreed.

"We can sell them in Stavropol," Karaim said. Karaim always was in need of money since he was one of the more eligible bachelors in the mountain aul. Gifts for the ladies were expensive.

"Let's stop soon, then, and discard their army bridles and tack. We should get into our uniforms pretty damn soon, too, and check out our new identity papers. And I suppose I'd better take a knife to this hair, what with the Red Army regulations. No reason to take any risks." It was the understatement of the week, since they were about to ride into Stavropol and into the midst of ten thousand Red Army troops.

When the Red officer with newly trimmed hair and his accompanying mountain irregulars—all dressed in hybrid uniforms, part Red army, part Caucasian warrior—rode into Stavropol late that afternoon, they found themselves surrounded by the press and throng of General Beriozov's Sixth Division. The city was bustling with activity, crowded with soldiers as Beriozov regrouped his division before making the last push to the Black Sea.

The three horsemen leading the string of extra mounts rode slowly through the muddy streets. On every side were Red soldiers: lounging against the buildings, walking the streets, riding by on wagons, horses, gun *tachankas*. Even an armored car with Cheka markings was loaded with extra troops clinging to the wide runningboards. None of the trio wondered, as perhaps more practical men might, how exactly they were going to extract themselves from this enemy stronghold.

As Leda picked her way daintily around the worst of the mud, Apollo did, however, speculate fleetingly on the unique impulses that had driven him into the center of the enemy camp. He could say he was simply performing a favor for a friend—honorbound, et cetera. It *could be* he was simply curious—in a slightly suicidal way, one might add—to discover the countess's fate. While both explanations were reasonably credible in their own right, they accounted for but a minimum of the real truth. Apollo was, in fact, hoping—more than hoping; desiring desperately—to find Kitty for reasons of his own, reasons that centered around vividly palpable memories of lush Kitty, flushed from lovemaking, her laughing, sensuous, full-lipped mouth bending to caress his, or her soft voluptuous body arched beneath him. The memories, like some sweet torture, had been recurrent since December.

Apollo's search was in fact inexplicable in terms of success and logic, unorthodox in every sense of the word, but, like the quest for the Holy Grail, it was unshakable in its conviction, spiritually necessary, and sectarian only in the passion of its goal. Even that passion, powerful and unassailably determined, had antecedents in the knightly tradition.

Over several glasses of liquor in one of the local cafes the question was where the devil to begin searching for the countess in a city this size. In the event that Kitty *had* managed to reach Stavropol, *and* in the event she had money, *and* in the event she wasn't murdered for it, they decided she may have stayed at one of the hotels. When Aladino had been overrun almost four weeks ago, Stavropol had still been under White control. It was natural for Kitty to first seek refuge here. Unfortunately, it appeared that the city had fallen along with the districts near Aladino, and Beriozov and his Sixth Division had been ensconced here ever since.

Apollo left to survey the hotels, leaving the Dagestanis at the Georgian Cafe drinking the *aracq* they favored. It was the strongest liquor in the world, especially when heated, and they were quite content. While nominally Moslem, the mountain men subscribed to a religious expediency; they understood the Prophet frowned on liquor, but they believed in his mercy, and man is weak. . . . In any case, they might as well relax and enjoy themselves. Neither would have been much help with Apollo's inquiries anyway, since both spoke only limited Russian, and that with such cavalier inflections as to be practically unintelligible.

Selecting the Hotel Russia—the most exclusive establishment—as a starting point, Apollo inadvertently saved himself considerable time. Approaching a small, freckle-faced youth who apparently helped with guests' luggage, Apollo slipped a gold rouble into his grimy hand, saying, "I'm looking for a young lady with long blond hair, about this tall." He drew his hand to one shoulder. "She has green eyes and may or may not call herself Radachek. Have you seen her in this hotel anytime in the last few weeks?"

For the extravagant gesture of a gold rouble the boy would have scoured the town for a woman of that description, but as it turned out, Apollo's question was quite commonplace. The young boy had inquiries concerning the lady several times a day. *All* the officers were interested in the pretty countess who shared General Beriozov's suite. When did she go out for her carriage rides? Had she returned yet from either the morning or afternoon excursion? Was the general in or out at the moment? Answers regarding the lady's whereabouts augmented his pittance of a salary enough to feed his mother and younger brothers and sisters.

So the boy affably answered Apollo's query. Had the lady been in the hotel recently? Certainly. She was upstairs in suite 17 right now. General Beriozov's suite. "And comrade"—the boy was careful to use the correct form of address since a new clientele had taken over the hotel—"for a gold rouble, I'll find out anything else you want to know." He winked conspiratorially.

Apollo nodded in an abstract way, comprehension scorching his brain, like a branding iron on tender flesh. "Perhaps later," he said quietly, retracing his steps to the entrance, trying to deal with the shock. *Upstairs? General Beriozov's suite?*

The stunning news affected Apollo in a sudden, strange, and sharply antithetical way. He wanted to murder Kitty . . . and he wanted to rescue her. Pushing through the crowd of officers near the door, he discourteously shouldered his way outside, not caring whom he buffeted. Heads turned and mouths were about to offer complaint, but the sight of the tall, tawny-haired man, powerfully built and definitely angry, deterred the impulse.

Adrenaline was pumping through Apollo's nervous system. His first impulse was to kill both the lady and her lover. Don't ask for reason. He had never been a reasonable man.

All his former anxieties turned to acid in his mind. He had been a fool, he thought grimly, risking his life—and those of

Karaim and Sahin as well—for some elusive dream, for some sensual memories of a golden-haired beauty, memories he had half-convinced himself were some kind of love.

He walked the streets, not taking the news at all well, oblivious to everything but the tormented chaos in his mind. How *could* she? How the *hell* could she? He wasn't thinking very clearly, at first, but time and the chill March winds eventually calmed his initial fury over unreliable women, and common sense ultimately prevailed over baser masculine concerns such as territorial rights, outrage, and something very close to covetousness.

There was no reason to immediately think the worst. There was a possibility, a good possibility, Kitty was no more than a captive. The young boy seemed to know her well enough, though. She must be seen outside the suite. Not too much of a captive, apparently.

"*Merde*," Apollo swore darkly. Capricious bitch, changing allegiances as swiftly as dressing for dinner. Still, he realized he could never rest until he knew for certain. Well . . . only one way to find out. A plan was set in motion. Not much of a plan, actually—more like barging into the lion's den and then winging it.

# 9

That evening as General Beriozov and the countess were entertaining several guests at dinner, a servant announced a caller. "Colonel Zveguintzev to see General Beriozov," he said.

The general, his hostess, and guests all turned; eighteen pairs of eyes slewed round to the open door.

Lean and striking, the visitor entered with the lithe, supple stride of a mountain cat. He stopped abruptly just within the room, his tall form and sensationally cropped silky head framed by the delicately gilded doorjamb, an image of raw masculine power limned within borders of cavorting putti. The intruder's pale eyes surveyed the group quite at random and he spoke first in a quiet, deep voice, "Good evening, General; ladies and gentlemen."

One could not mistake Apollo, the figure or the face. From the first moment, Kitty had been struck dumb, immobilized and incredulous, but at the sound of the so-familiar voice, the stillness in the room was broken as the fork she had been holding clattered noisily onto the Sèvres porcelain. The general, exceedingly jealous, darted a dangerous glance at her while a murmur and rustle of shock flowed around the table.

Apollo, who had excellent control of his facial muscles, stepped in quickly to cover the gaffe, saying in an indolent drawl, "How awkward. Countess Radachek, no doubt, has heard the greatly exaggerated accounts of my death on the western front. I assure you, madame," he said, bowing slightly toward Kitty, his tawny eyes expressionless and smooth, "no apparition here. The reports were highly inaccurate."

Kitty wore cream moiré silk accenting the pallor of her

skin, but the brilliant, blood red rubies on her white throat and at her ears drew Apollo's gaze for a fleeting moment. (He knew it was one of those vignettes frozen in time, destined to be etched permanently in his mind, the sensation of large drops of blood on pure white flesh.)

The startling pallor of Kitty's face was duly noted by the general as well, and he viewed with instant displeasure the naked longing in her wide emerald eyes. The expression was gone in a moment, for Kitty, quickly collecting her wits, composed her features and attempted to hide the violent beating of her heart, the ecstatic joy flooding through her.

The general's pale gray eyes directed another searching look at both Kitty and the newcomer. "You know the countess?" Beriozov's angry glance flicked over Apollo's lean figure.

Apollo received the harsh challenge tranquilly. "Years ago, we had mutual friends in Petrograd, sir," he murmured politely. "Her husband, actually." He leered slightly, hoping to convey just the right tone of derision.

A kindred smirk appeared on the general's face. "So . . . that accounts for the reaction."

"I believe so, sir. Fortunes change, so rapidly," he said pleasantly. "And some, ah, adjust better than others," he finished with a disarming smile.

"Oh, Countess Radachek has adapted quite well, haven't you, my dear?" The general patted her hand and Kitty controlled the impulse to snatch it away. Her face stiffened into a mask, behind which her eyes gave away nothing.

"Why not be sensible?" she said in a light, dispassionate voice. Smiling thinly, she took a sip from her champagne glass.

Apollo had purposely abstained from contemplating Kitty too much, uncertain of his reaction. If his vague plan hoped to work at all, it was going to be a long night. Avoiding the general's remark, Apollo drew himself up and said, "The past is dead. The corrupt tsarist regime has been smashed and the glory of the Revolution is the future." Then, snapping a smart salute—catching himself just in time before his spurs clicked together in the tradition of the Guard regiment—Apollo declared, "Colonel Zveguintzev reporting from the Kiev front, sir. Sent by General Bogdan to instruct the pilots with the captured Camels, sir."

"Ah, yes." General Beriozov relaxed, his favorite topic having been broached. And apparently the colonel was merely an acquaintance of the countess—no lover. It never hurt to be suspicious, though. One never knew with those damn aristos and the scandalous ways they had lived their lives. Fortunately the Revolution had changed all that, and finally the proletariat had a chance to revel in some of the decadence. About time, too, the general reflected, casting an appreciative eye over the sumptuous elegance at his disposal. Leaning back, he waved his hand expansively. "Sit down, Colonel. Have you eaten?" At Apollo's affirmative nod, he snapped his fingers. "Champagne for the colonel! Now then," Beriozov said, lighting a Cuban cigar, confiscated from the humidor of a Russian noble who had hastily departed the country, "the Camels, eh? You can handle them, Colonel?"

"Yes, sir," Apollo replied with a broad smile. Raising his eyebrows for leave, he settled into a red plush chair for a long night of drinking. "A little hard to handle, but worth it in maneuverability. And on the turn, the Camel can beat anything in the air." He seemed at leisure from gilded head to polished boots. "Don't you think?" he asked comfortably.

From that point on, all the other guests died of boredom. Flying was a passion of General Beriozov's. Luckily it was equally so for Apollo. The rest of the guests politely hid their yawns and excused themselves early. Every plane that had been flown in the Great War was discussed: Nieuports, DH-9 bombers, Spads, Fokkers, Camels, Albatrosses, Sopwiths. A glow of triumph and success enveloped the general that night as the liquor warmed his blood, the reminiscing of his early days flying aerial reconnaissance in North Manchuria satisfying in retrospective. The Civil War was now gearing down; the Whites were about to be driven into the sea: the advance was scheduled to begin in a fortnight. A luxurious apartment to live in, good food, bountiful liquor, and a beautiful Russian countess to pleasure him. A smug contentment warmed the general. "What do you think of her, Colonel? The rewards of the victors, eh?" He chuckled.

Only the three of them were left seated in the drawing room, the general and Kitty side by side on the gold brocade sofa, Apollo lounging in an imitation-bamboo armchair nearby. The general was quite drunk, his tunic partially loosened, his arm flung around Kitty's shoulder, his leathery fingers idly fondling the pure white flesh of her upper arm.

Apollo looked away, fury overwhelming him momentarily. He fought the impulse to shoot the general on the spot. "A very pretty reward, I'll agree," he said, the timbre of his voice slightly hoarse from his effort at control.

Kitty lowered her eyes in shame that Apollo should witness her degradation, but she dared not antagonize the general; his temper was unpredictable and savage.

Just how unwilling a captive was Kitty, Apollo wondered, vicious resentment clouding his mind, his eyes drawn to the blunt fingers carelessly roving. She appeared passive enough. Had he wasted his time and taken unnecessary risks to appear here tonight? Did the lady even wish to be rescued? Apollo recognized Poiret's touch in Kitty's gown. Just how accommodating did one have to be for *that*, or for the rubies around her neck? Nothing seemed to make much sense right now, and the vodka he and the general were consuming further served to undermine any objective detachment he may have possessed.

Then the general casually slipped down the narrow shoulder strap of Kitty's evening gown, and her breast sprang out from the confining silk. Beriozov's dark hand ran slowly over the curving mound of exposed satiny flesh, then cupped its sumptuous heaviness briefly. Moving upward, one finger slid into the blue shadow between her breasts.

Sweat broke out on Apollo's brow; an unwanted swelling began to rise inside his trousers, and his hand, pouring more vodka into the general's glass, shook. Maybe he *should* kill the bastard here and now. Damn dog dared to touch Kitty's naked skin, dared to stroke *his* Kitty's breast. He noted in passing that Kitty's breasts were fuller, softly engorged, but there was no time to speculate on this subtle change. Stronger, fiercer emotions very close to sheer primitive sensation were at the forefront of Apollo's brain.

The atavistic impulse for possession took over in a blaze. No longer wondering whether the lady was willing or unwilling, Apollo vowed to take her out of here whatever her inclination. He wanted her, dammit, and—having seldom denied himself anything in his young, indulged life—it was now simply a matter of abducting the lady, with or without her consent.

Any doubt in Apollo's mind had been wiped away by a primordial impulse stronger than civilization's niceties. His plan—formed by his temper and helped along by the quantity of liquor he'd consumed—now seemed perfectly clear.

Apollo glanced at his watch, refilled the general's glass, and proposed another toast. The bastard would have to pass out eventually, he thought grimly. "To the lady's, er, obvious charms," Apollo said suavely, raising his glass and smiling wolfishly.

Giving the breast he was fondling a squeeze, Beriozov looked squarely at Apollo as if to say, Remember, this is mine; I own it. Then the general laughed aloud and tossed down his vodka. Wiping his mouth with the back of his hand, he said in a softly slurred voice, "A fancy lady, eh, Colonel? Care to touch her and see what real aristocratic flesh feels like? Until the Revolution I never touched any. Now we can feel all we want." He winked heavily, "And do anything else we want."

Kitty flushed deep rose in an agony of humiliation at the indignity of her position. Frantically she wondered how much more of this she could take. She longed for nothing more than to say, "Kill him, kill him, Apollo!" but she knew a valet always readied the general for bed, and even if she wanted to, she couldn't end this charade without calling down every soldier and guard on the floor. Escape would be impossible then.

Apollo did not know the exact schedule of the general's life, but he knew that if Beriozov were found by his valet in the morning sleeping off the night's imbibing—rather than dead—they would have several extra hours before the alarm was raised. So he only smiled politely, pretending to ignore Kitty's soft breast and the general's invitation to touch it. Apollo's nerves were strung out, the vodka firing his blood, but he forced himself with every ounce of will in his body to remain lounging casually in his chair.

"Come," the general insisted, motioning somewhat drunkenly with his glass, splashing droplets of liquor over himself and the sofa. "Come. Put your hands on her." He laughed indulgently. "A little treat for you, Colonel, with my compliments."

Apollo didn't move. "No, thank you," he replied in a strained, quiet voice.

The general's heavy brows met in the center of his forehead. "You prefer boys?" Chortling roughly at his cleverness, he continued with a keen-eyed look. "That's why so timid?"

"No, not boys," Apollo said flatly.

"If not boys . . ." The general's pale gray eyes gleamed, and an instant distrustful anger put high color in his cheeks. Beriogov's mood switched abruptly from benign good humor to brooding enmity. Five decades of bitterness now surfaced. He searched the fine-boned features of the young colonel opposite him, whose lean face seemed to take on an aristocratic cast. "Don't you like her?" he asked belligerently. "Isn't she *good* enough for you?" he continued with the oversensitive touchiness of the newly arrived. Drawing himself up somewhat unsteadily into a stiffly seated posture, he commanded in a voice like the crack of a whip, "Put your hands on her!"

The general's mood was dangerous. Apollo sucked in his breath, and his knuckles tightened involuntarily on the painted bamboo of the chair. Then, leaning forward, he reached out slowly. "My apologies, General," he said with a lazy agreeableness he hoped concealed the effort it took to voice. "The invitation was not unattractive. I was only concerned with encroaching on your property—otherwise I would have responded immediately. The beauty of the countess, sir, is above reproach." Apollo found himself sweating as he placed his long fingers gingerly on Kitty's bare shoulders, letting his hands rest lightly on the warm, pale skin.

The general relaxed instantly, his erratic goodwill immediately restored. Appraising Apollo's tentatively disposed hands, he laughed. "She won't break, Colonel." He gave another guffaw and then cast a significant glance at Kitty. "We know that, don't we, Countess?" Kitty shivered slightly, memories of the general's silken whips uncomfortably vivid. Apollo's eyes jumped to her face at the tiny shudder, but he learned nothing; her downcast lashes effectively shielded any expression. The general, however, had seen her quickly concealed fear, and it only encouraged a further round of chuckles from him. "No, Colonel," he continued, his face creased into a leering smile, "she don't break at all."

Taking Apollo's hands, he cupped them directly over Kitty's breasts. The Red commander was obviously enjoying himself, enjoying the blush of shamed embarrassment on Kitty's face, and sportive over the colonel's unease.

Reaching over, he pulled Kitty's dress down to her waist in one swift movement and Apollo saw the week-old bruises faded yellow on the white skin. Beriozov paid no attention to the marks of his temper. Repositioning Apollo's hands, he jovially said, "Now you can really feel. Rub her, Colonel. An aristocratic countess. Like fine silk, isn't it?"

Apollo responded with difficulty, for the instant his hands had touched Kitty's breasts, had cupped themselves over the pliant mounds, her nipples had risen solidly against his palms.

"Rub them some more, Colonel. Soft and warm, eh?" the drunken voice intoned. The general was gratified by the other man's appreciation of his prized possession. And Apollo's traitorous hands obeyed the general's order, brushing lightly over the tips of Kitty's nipples again and again. Not soft at all, Apollo thought inadvisedly, the reflection further swelling his already throbbing masculinity. Searching Kitty's flushed face, he knew he could bend his head and suck on them, and knew she would open for him. With a violent summoning of restraint he forced his mind back to the present situation.

Looking up, he replied with what he hoped was equanimity, "Very fine, indeed, sir." But he was struggling with his self-control. Her breasts were so smooth, the points so hard.

"Kiss her," the general insisted, delighting in his voyeurism, delighting in the discomfort of both parties. A peal of laughter followed.

Glancing at Beriozov, Apollo attempted to demur. How much self-discipline did he have? "General Beriozov, sir," he began, clearing his throat, Kitty's nipples burning into his palms.

Paying not the slightest heed to his guest's wishes, the general pursued his idea. "Kiss her, I say," he snapped viciously.

Apollo bent to do his bidding, daring not look into Kitty's eyes. As their mouths were about to meet, the general curtly declared, "Not on her mouth."

Apollo's head came up sharply. "Good Lord, sir!" he exclaimed.

At which point, the general laughed uproariously.

Taking the opportunity to remove his hands from Kitty, Apollo leaned back in his chair.

In between chuckles, Beriozov gasped cheerfully, "Such . . . manners . . . my boy. Was your mama a schoolteacher? No more manners now! Gone, gone. If you could see your face!" He jovially beamed. "So you like my little countess after all." He struggled upright to refill Apollo's glass, saying in a thick-tongued rumble, "A toast to the comforts of the Revolution." He winked heavily before draining his glass.

Kitty moved slightly to restore the bodice of her dress, tugging gently at the heavy silk. She had lifted the cream moiré to half cover her breasts when the general noticed her actions and roughly brushed her hands aside. "No!" he barked in an unmistakable voice of command. "Leave it down. I like the sight of a bare-breasted woman—and what other use do you have, Countess," he said with an insulting sneer, "except to entertain us?"

Kitty prayed the humiliation would end soon. With increasing despair she wondered if she and Apollo really had any chance of escaping, knowing even while the speculation flowed through her mind that any chance at all was worth taking. If she was obliged to remain with the general much longer, she would take his life herself, or die trying. She rallied to hold out a few hours more. Surely Beriozov must pass out soon; he was so terribly drunk already—but then she remembered the times he had lasted until dawn, and those memories forced her deeper into desolation.

The general, sinking further into inebriation, was in the mood to taunt the young colonel. Zveguintzev seemed so reluctant to touch or even look at the countess that the baiting was amusing. Perhaps he really did like boys after all. It wasn't so unusual in this part of the world, what with the centuries of Persian, Turkoman, and Ottoman rule. And if it were not a question of preference, then this was a young man with too many scruples. In either case, the general always enjoyed exerting his power and authority.

In a deceptively amiable voice, but with eyes like flint, Beriozov said, "Get up, Katherine. Go and sit on the colonel's lap. I want to see if he *does* like women."

There was a crisp silence. The demand was deliberately perverse. It was catastrophic. Kitty froze, her face reddening. Apollo hardly breathed.

Their reluctance only encouraged the general. In fact, their shocked response to the depravity quite appealed to him.

Since neither stirred, Beriozov took matters into his own hands. Rising somewhat clumsily from his seat, he dragged Kitty up from the sofa and he pulled her forcefully over to Apollo, pushing her into his lap. "There now," he pronounced, a proprietary hand on Kitty's bare shoulder, "we'll see if the colonel likes boys. Although," he continued, chuckling roguishly, "the countess, I think, could induce even a eunuch to try." Weaving back and dropping heavily onto the brocade sofa, the general said blandly, "And what does your manhood suggest now, Colonel, with the countess so close?"

"My manhood suggests the obvious," Apollo replied dryly, "but not necessarily with you watching."

"Nothing to be squeamish about, my boy. We're all friends here. Isn't that right?" Behind the piercing gray eyes was not a hint of friendship, only sadistic amusement and anticipation. "Hold her, Colonel," Beriozov said comfortably, watching him. "Kiss her. Fondle those big, naked breasts. Come now, we're all friends." His voice was heavy with overplayed camaraderie and underplayed authority.

Reluctantly, Apollo's hands moved slowly up to Kitty's shoulders; his touch was light, tentative, restrained.

"The breasts, the breasts, Colonel. For God's sake. *Radi Boga*! Do I have to tell you everything?" Beriozov's voice was snappish now, the abrupt and mercurial switch typical of his drinking mood.

Apollo exhaled quietly, his fingers obeying, slipping down over the high fullness of Kitty's magnificent thrusting breasts, and when his thumb and forefinger, quite by reflex, closed gently over one rosy nipple, the general was pleased to see the reaction he'd been waiting for. Although Apollo's teeth were clenched, Beriozov heard a strangled moan.

"Ah . . . you *do* like my pretty little pigeon."

"She's very nice," Apollo managed to say with some semblance of calm. His erection, hard and insistent, ground into Kitty's soft buttocks.

"Kiss her, Colonel. I haven't seen you kiss her yet. I think I'd like that." Apollo's gaze slowly locked with the general's. Beriozov smiled. "Kiss those breasts." There was a short silence. Not a muscle moved in Apollo's face. And then he complied. This was a command performance in every sense of the word.

Lowering his head, his lips brushed Kitty's tantalizing nipple. A searing sensation burned through Kitty and she was terrified. Her body was betraying her, as it always did at Apollo's touch.

"Come, Colonel, you can do better than that. Make the countess feel more than that. Take one of those hard, pointed nipples in your mouth."

Apollo's mouth closed over one peaked tip and very delicately his tongue, seemingly of its own accord, traced a silky pattern that warmed and aroused.

No! Kitty thought frantically, I must resist! I can't let this happen! But heated blood was already racing to her tingling erect nipples, stirring, agonizing, gradually spreading an unwonted arousal through her body. Tears of shame and frustration sprang to her eyes.

The general chuckled then, reminding them both of where they were. He gave a low, satisfied laugh. "Oh, yes, you're making real progress, Colonel. I can see the countess is quite taken with you. Such hard nipples, dear Katherine—a tantalizing sight. And you who are usually cold as ice. Do you like an audience? Is that it? I'll have to keep it in mind. And now, my boy, I think it would be amusing to have you kiss her on the mouth. Such a full, succulent mouth," he mused almost to himself, and then, jerking back from a drunken reverie, he abruptly snapped—suddenly vicious—"Kiss her!"

Apollo glanced at the general, then bowed his head faintly, acknowledging the command. Both his hands gripped Kitty's shoulders and slowly, very slowly, he drew her to him, her eyes closed now, her breathing rapid. Near her lips, his voice was no more than a warm murmur. "When he passes out, we'll leave."

Kitty's eyes clenched tighter. Fear and tremulous desire paralyzed her. She could do nothing but play out the game and hope desperately they gained their freedom.

"What was that?" Beriozov grunted.

"I said the countess has a lovely mouth."

"She does, doesn't she?" the general lazily agreed, an audacious light kindling in the flat gray eyes. "And you've just given me an idea." He laughed crudely, having a cheerfully perverted mind. "Never mind the kiss. Lift up her skirts, Colonel," he ordered.

Apollo looked once briefly at the general, met a hard, uncompromising stare, and pushed aside Kitty's full moiré skirts.

His breathing stopped.

Under Kitty's voluminous taffeta skirts, welded tight, barbarously golden, medievally anachronistic, girdling her creamy flesh, was a chastity belt.

The general's smooth voice broke through Apollo's stupor. At the sound Apollo dropped the skirt back into place, and then, because he was near suffocation, he refilled his lungs.

Outrage filled his brain. He wanted to kill the general at once, and if it were only his life he was risking, he would have. He had nerveless confidence in his ability to extradite himself from any tight situation, but he couldn't risk it with Kitty. If he had to travel fast and brutally, she'd never be able to keep up. So, with roaring affront echoing like the wails of whirling dervishes, he said with rigid, icy calm, "Interesting."

"I thought so." The general was smug.

Apollo thought himself sophisticated enough to have seen about everything in the unblushing, flourishing world of erotica, but until now this little subtlety had escaped him. "Yes, very clever," he said. His golden eyes swept Kitty's body with deliberate slowness, and then a hint of malice crept into his deliberately bland voice. "Is it really necessary?" he asked gently, and saw Kitty crimson from breast to brow.

"She only wears it when she goes out of the suite or when we have guests," Beriozov explained, smiling thinly. "It's the only way to ensure fidelity with such faithless creatures. So you see," he continued agreeably, "it's not *such* a monstrous thing. A temporary safeguard occasionally, nothing more."

All this time Kitty sat quietly rigid, trying to ignore, to black out the pleasantly deriding voice discussing her. She had learned over the past weeks to put up outer defenses which couldn't be breached. That ability to withdraw within herself was all that saved her sanity.

But Apollo's presence, his touch, his voice, every vital nerve in his body was disastrously affecting her, and no matter how she tried, her heart beat violently when he was near.

"The belt," the general went on pleasantly, "you understand, limits the lady's availability, but that's not to say she can't pleasure you in other ways." His eyebrows rose with a clumsy heaviness. "Her mouth." He laughed. "Such a pretty mouth . . . what a marvelous idea, Colonel." Beriozov's hand was shaking but he managed to pour himself a half glass of liquor. "I feel in a generous mood, my boy. I think we'll let the countess express her thanks for your company this evening." He smiled a faint, chill smile. "You aristocratic ladies have been taught your manners, haven't you—and know how

to be pleasant to a guest? Get down, Countess. Hurry. Hurry!"
His chiding voice was cruel now, his eyes like chips of ice.
"Pleasure our guest with that pretty mouth."

Kitty caught her breath. Without moving, she softly said,
"No."

Apollo began to add his protest. Midword he stopped, seeing the general's pearl-handled pistol languidly waving in
their direction. "I say yes, Countess, and I'm the one with the
weapon." Kitty's heart sank.

Apollo tried again. "General, the countess has been gracious enough. Further diversion is not necessary." The barrel
of the pistol wavered back and forth. From such a short distance there would be no hope of saving Kitty if he aimed at
her. She'd be blown into the wall.

"Your modesty does you credit, Colonel, but in truth, it's
*my* pleasure being served. The countess is so . . . reluctant. She
must be taught a lesson." The pistol steadied suddenly, the
drunken eyes sharpened briefly. "Down, Countess Radachek,
if you know what's good for you."

Silently Kitty slid from Apollo's lap to the floor, forcing
herself to keep from crying, from screaming and breaking
down completely. Tortured in countless trivial ways over the
last few weeks, this was heartbreakingly the very worst—but
escape . . . freedom . . . so very near this time. She knelt between Apollo's legs.

Apollo gripped the arms of the chair with both hands, the
triphammer of his heart beating against the framework of his
ribs. He felt Kitty unbuckle his belt and unbutton his trousers, her fingers brushing like gossamer over the stiffness of
his arousal. He inhaled quietly, immobile except for the thick,
jutting shaft which strained upward. Kitty's body touched
the inside of his legs, her sumptuously heavy breasts, free of
the confining dress, were warm against his thighs. Her elaborate upswept coiffure had fallen loose from some of its
jeweled pins; gilt tendrils framed her face and rested on the
bareness of her shoulders. Her large eyes, not quite daring to
meet his, were agonized.

"Touch him, Countess," the general ordered. Her lashes

fell, and after only the briefest hesitation, her hand moved. Very delicately, with the lightest possible touch, her fingers strayed over the pulsing organ and freed it from the confines of his uniform.

The Red commander's heavy lids rose fractionally at the sight. "You must please the ladies, Colonel. Katherine won't be able to take it all. Do your best, dear. I know you aristocratic *belles* can be accommodating." He laughed crudely, infinitely cynical, drunk as a peasant on feast day.

Kitty hadn't moved.

"Such timidity, Countess." The general chuckled maliciously. "One would think you didn't know what to do—but we know better, don't we?" And he guffawed uproariously at his own heavyhanded humor, his pistol glinting ominously in the artificial light.

Apollo's fists clenched and he ground his teeth in frustration. Kitty was distracting in all the worst ways for clear thinking; that damn handgun could go off any minute in that drunken sot's grasp—and the urge to kill was pressing hard on the limits of Apollo's self-control.

Beriozov's drunken laughter ceased as quickly as it had begun. "I'm bored with your false modesty, Katherine. You know what to do," the general barked, the veins throbbing in his thick neck. "Do it!"

Kitty shuddered, then took the swollen shaft in her hand. It was so hard she had to hold it back firmly. Moving her mouth down, she hovered over it for a long moment while Apollo held his breath, despising himself for wanting her anywhere, anytime, anyplace, detesting what she had become under the general's tutelage. Then, gradually, Kitty lowered her lips onto the pulsing tip. Apollo couldn't prevent a groan from escaping his throat.

He tried everything while she ministered to him. He counted the crystals in the chandelier, tried to concentrate on the frigid temperatures outside, silently recited the German alphabet backward, anything to force his mind from Kitty's persistent, excruciating touch. But the flicking tongue didn't stop, nor could he ignore the soft, pliant lips wrapped around him. No matter how he tried to distract himself, the blond head between his legs kept moving gently up and down, and the aching, agonizing pleasure screamed through his body, building and racing to an inevitable conclusion. With a tortured gasp, he gave up; his arms swooped down. Capturing her head between his urgent hands and cursing his weakness, he thrust upward violently.

When it was over, a deep exhalation of regret quietly broke from him. Reaching down, he lifted Kitty's face, but she averted her eyes. Gruffly he offered her a half-empty bottle of wine.

Kitty accepted the bottle, her eyes evasive as she raised the wine to her lips.

"Bravo, Countess. Your performance was superb. Don't you agree, Colonel?" Tossing aside the pistol, the general's blunt, powerful hands mockingly applauded.

"Indeed," Apollo replied, but the cynical drawl didn't quite take. Quickly rearranging his clothes, Apollo tossed down half a glass of vodka to wash away the bitter feeling of disgust—disgust with himself for succumbing and irrational disgust with Kitty for her expert touch.

The general's sturdy arms pulled Kitty upright and back onto the sofa. His cool gray eyes swept her with casual indifference, taking in the half-nude, flushed, moody beauty as one would check a minor possession lent to a friend. "Smile, Countess," he chastised flippantly. "You were very good. Smile." He snapped his fingers.

All Kitty could think of was Apollo's eyes condemning her. Why did Beriozov have to insist on offering her to Apollo, of all people? He had never done that before. In fact, he had always been particularly possessive. Oh, damn! Did it really matter anymore—all these subtleties of captivity in this horror of what Russia had become? Tonight had been the final humiliation; this time she hadn't been able to withdraw, detach herself, pretend, as she had for weeks, that it was happening to someone else. "I can't," she said in a low voice.

The general looked at her closely, not sure he had heard

properly. He thought rebellion had been whipped out of her long ago.

Suddenly Kitty's eyes came up with a defiant snap and met his directly. "I won't." She sat disheveled, dishonored, half-naked, yet beautiful in her stiffly upright posture, obdurate in all the pride and dignity of her spirit. For a long moment their glances held, and then General Beriozov guffawed drunkenly.

"The countess is pouting." Another burst of laughter broke from him and, quirking his brow in a parody of insouciance, he addressed Apollo. "A woman's temperamental way, eh, Colonel? For all their favors, they must be humored occasionally." He lifted his glass in toast. "To the fair sex, Colonel. Countess"—he turned his glass to Kitty—"to the gentle sex. May the gates of paradise be always open."

"To women," Apollo growled, his voice tense with distaste. He, too, emptied his glass.

# 10

When Apollo had devised the scheme of drinking the general under the table and stealing Kitty away, he hadn't reckoned with the hard head of a Siberian peasant, weaned on cheap, government-monopoly vodka and raised in a climate where one was forced to stay inside nine months of the year, partaking of the one available amusement—the vodka bottle.

It was touch and go near the end. Apollo, his eyes lifting to gauge the distance to the sofa, decided he might have to slit the bastard's throat after all, orderly or no orderly, if Beriozov didn't pass out soon. But blood will tell, and a thousand-year tradition of hard-drinking Kuzan males rose to the occasion. Where a Siberian peasant might have perseverance and bulldog tenacity, a Kuzan had positive genius when it came to drinking more than anyone else.

The general finally slid quietly to the floor right in the middle of an argument over the Fokker's and Camel's maneuverability in an Immelmann.

Apollo came to his feet in a movement so swift Kitty was startled. Bending over the bulky form, he hissed, "Where's the orderly?" Apollo knew that, whether Red Army or White, there wasn't a general who readied himself for bed.

"In the dressing room," Kitty whispered, still shaky.

"Call him," he said quietly, moving from the inert body of the general to face Kitty. He reached over to pull up her dress, murmuring, "After the general's put to bed, I'm going to dismiss the orderly for the night. Think he'll leave?" he questioned, helping Kitty slip the straps over her shoulders.

Somehow a clothed woman made it easier to think, even if his head wasn't at its clearest.

"I hope so."

"Doesn't matter. I can always slit his throat."

Unprepared for that response, Kitty looked at Apollo wide-eyed and gasped, "Oh, no—must you?"

His answer was perfectly matter-of-fact. "Killed six already today on this 'mission of mercy.' Surely one more can't signify."

Kitty's hand went to her mouth and she breathed, "Six?"

"Jesus Christ Almighty," he snarled softly, "do you want to *stay* here?"

"No, no," Kitty hurriedly replied, pushing aside any misgivings she might have about murder.

"Call him, then."

After Apollo and the orderly had settled the general into bed, Apollo drew three gold roubles from his pocket. Handing them to the general's batman, he said, "Countess Radachek and I thought we might have a nightcap. I'm sure the general won't be needing you anymore tonight. Do you think you could find somewhere else to sleep?" Apollo lifted his dark brows suggestively. "Just until morning, you understand."

The batman recognized lust when he saw it and while his nature wasn't particularly benign, the three gold roubles were more than sufficient to make him temporarily kind. He immediately thought of the little chambermaid down the hall and only hesitated a second to pose the query: "If the general should call out for me—?"

Apollo looked at him speculatively from under half-lowered lids. "I'm *sure* Countess Radachek can handle it."

In two seconds the door to the servants' entrance closed on the orderly's back.

Kitty slumped into Apollo's arms and collapsed against his strength, shuddering convulsively. The harrowing tension of the last few hours, the shameful humiliation, the fear, the terrible despair that all would fail through some awful quirk of fate, was suddenly released and a pouring surge of tears swam over her rigid restraint of the last hours, days, weeks, washing unchecked down her pale cheeks.

"Oh, Apollo . . ." she whimpered brokenly, quiet sobs making a staccato of her anguished cry. "Thank God you're here. Thank God, thank God—"

"There, there. . . ." Apollo soothed, holding the weeping woman gently. "You're safe . . . everything's fine." And although he intended to be comforting, the words came out a shade stiffly. Niggling doubts remained. How *had* she come to this? Just how adaptable had Kitty been in her new position? Had it been simply a way station until something different came along—in this case, himself, but, perhaps, anyone?

Kitty's sensuality those days in December—her unique, open, ardent sensuality—made Apollo skeptical. She had warmed his bed willingly enough those days he was a guest in her home. How many like him had there been before or after? How opportune had the general's offer been to a refugee with nowhere to go? How ill disposed was the lady to her current situation—or how eager? She had performed tonight despite the general's presence—was she a devotee of sex with danger? Was that kind of titillating sensation now her specialty?

He could still imagine the sharp, hard feel of her nipples in his palms; tonight, and when she had been seated on his lap, her moistness had dampened them both. How many times had she and the general . . . He wrenched his mind from his heinous thoughts, but a whisper within him persisted, a small bitter flame of accusation and jealousy. He meant to deal with this calmly, but, irrationally, he could not. "Why did you stay here?" he asked abruptly in a tight voice, his reproach evident even in the lowness of his tones.

Kitty looked up in astonishment and met Apollo's somewhat grim golden eyes. Sadly she thought how easy it was to be a man and only have yourself to consider. I wanted to make sure your child lived, she wished to say, but something in the disapproving line of his jaw held her back.

"I couldn't get away," she said simply.

"Surely sometime you might have. He's drunk every night." A mild rebuke, distaste evident in every syllable.

Kitty drew away and Apollo let his arms drop. Right now, Kitty thought with a kind of numbness, she was tired unto death. Taking a small breath, she said, "Save me your piety."

"Why the *hell*," said Apollo with fury, "why the *hell* couldn't you get away? You had your freedom of the city!"

"My suicidal impulse isn't very strong."

"Or," he retorted harshly, "you *preferred* staying."

"No!" Kitty hurled back angrily, and then almost instantly she shrugged resignedly, her gaze going opaquely closed. Is this what she had hoped and dreamed for, is this what rescue meant after all she had gone through—another opinionated, arbitrary male?

"Damn you to hell," Apollo growled, his eyes bitter. "You have no better explanation?"

"You're drunk," Kitty replied, lifting her eyes suddenly. "And you've already made up your mind. Leave it, can't you?" she said softly.

"Why should I?" Apollo demanded in a clear, forbidding voice. "I want—"

She interrupted him, her eyes dark and angry. "I know what you want. You want me to apologize for wanting to live. You want to goad me into making admissions about my faint courage. If I won't do that, you want some excuse—any plausible, tenuous excuse—to salve your affronted masculine honor. I'm quite conscious of what I did and how I've lived these last few weeks, of all my misdemeanors and impieties—but I'm traveling light now. No principles, no philosophy; only survival. You and I disagree about the means of survival, that's all."

"Life at any price," Apollo said dryly.

"More or less," Kitty returned steadily.

"Just like a woman," he snorted dismissively.

Just like a woman carrying a baby in her womb, Kitty thought, but pride kept her silent. "Think what you will," she said to the steely, restless warrior now assessing her with a world of malice in his pale eyes. "I at least claim the right to make up my own mind." She stopped and shrugged wearily again, her own nerves betraying her. Suddenly she was too tired and too dispirited to argue over priorities, or to debate further the nuances of male and female attitudes toward survival. She'd concede him his victory; he could think anything he pleased if they could only escape from this prison, now, tonight. Shaking a little from fear and fatigue, Kitty drew herself straighter and said as calmly as possible, "Could we go? I'll get ready." She didn't wait for an answer but turned to enter the general's bedroom.

Before she reached the door, Apollo's arm shot out, bringing her back by a painful grip digging into her wrist and jerking her hard against the muscular length of him. "What do you need in there?" His voice was unduly harsh. Its anger chilled her.

The tremulous sensations that always accompanied close contact with Apollo shuddered down Kitty's spine, even as she recoiled from the ice-cold rage in his expression. "The key on his wrist," she replied rigidly. "Now let me go; you're hurting me."

The fingers that manacled her wrist remained firm; the heat and power of his body was searing her, discomfiting her. She could feel him rising into the softness of her hip. "Please, Apollo, don't," she whispered, trying to pull away. All she saw in his face was aggression, a madness composed of anger as well as hunger.

"Please—"

"Why not?" he said grimly, a need for conquest thundering through him. "You've been whoring for the general," he said with exaggerated reasonableness. "Why not for me?"

"If you want to rape me, feel free," Kitty hissed indignantly. "But rest assured, that's what it'll be."

Apollo laughed softly. "I don't think you've changed that much." His tawny, half-lidded eyes assessed her with a slow, intimate appraisal, and an insolent smile twitched on his lips. "I'm sure it won't be rape," he said quietly.

All the joy of rescue, all Kitty's happiness at having found Apollo in the mass hysteria of full retreat, now disappeared before the angry resentment of his accusations. Was self-preservation so terrible? Was she supposed to drink hemlock rather than be dishonored? If that was the case, every man in Russia would be obliged to self-destruct. Stiffening her spine, Kitty lifted her chin and glared at Apollo, hating him for his accusations, hating him for not even knowing or caring that scarcely a single decision in her life had been made since those three days in December without her measuring it against the yardstick of his wishes—as if her life hardly belonged to her any longer. Breathing deeply to steady her fury, Kitty replied with fiercely acid sweetness, "You might as well do whatever you want." Her voice quivered with venom as she added, "*Don't all men?*"

Green eyes battled gold for a long moment and then abruptly Apollo pushed her away. "*I'll* get the key," he spat, the declaration short, curt, chill, the voice of a stranger— quite unlike the laughing, loving, obliging Apollo of several months past.

"Very well," Kitty replied, indifferent. She had learned to make adjustments. It had been unrealistic to expect their relationship to remain immutable. Apollo had come into her life briefly, dazzlingly relighting the dying embers of lost illusions, but the last few weeks with General Beriozov had explicitly reiterated the bald facts concerning the ubiquitous double standard as well as the importance of women in the new revolutionary society. And on occasion, if she had momentarily forgotten her place, the general's pretty whips were quick to refresh her memory. Apollo now was making the identical affronted male noises she had grown to despise.

She had decided, a few weeks ago, to survive in this tidal wave of blood, and survive she would, for herself and for her child—and if Apollo or anyone else took issue with her methods . . . too damn bad!

Now all she had to do was get this hideous indication of male possessiveness and insecurity unlocked from around her hips and she'd be on her way.

Apollo came out of the bedroom with the small golden key in his hand, his face a grim mask. Meeting the rock of his anger, Kitty was in no mood to renew the flaming row. With an economy of movement she turned, her back stiff with icy mortification, and lifted the skirt of her gown.

When Apollo saw again the intricate bands of chased gold shackling Kitty's hips, he let out a stream of cool, sarcastic invective.

Kitty was impervious. Let him vent his anger any way he pleased, just so long as she was freed from this bondage and mark of male monopoly. And then her heart froze—for Apollo was making no move to unfasten the lock.

Why not, he thought, eyeing the delicate medieval device. It was the ultimate symbol of ownership, after all. No one could touch her. He had the key. And wasn't she his now? A prize of war, as it were.

Oh, no, not you too, Kitty silently pleaded. Why was it masculine sexual jealousy so naturally turned to constraint and coercion? But she would not beg, never again. Kitty refused to submit to a continuation of the old tyranny. Without turning around, she said simply, "I can't ride with this on."

Her words broke through Apollo's mesmerized, irrational state. His hand moved silently and swiftly. The girdle of precious metal fell open and dropped to the carpet. Stepping over it without a glance, Kitty walked toward her bedroom. "I'll be back in a minute," she said impassively, trying to quell the hysteria that was building inside her. "This dress will never do for winter riding."

Apollo's tanned face was lightly sheened with perspiration, but there was no tremor of emotion in it. He didn't seem to hear her. Standing where she'd left him, Apollo retrieved the cage of gold from the floor and balanced it for a moment between his strong hands. All padded silk inside. Considerate bastard. What's this? Sliding latches . . . ingenious. Apollo's slender fingers expanded the gilded bands experimentally. The casual slavery of it left a foul taste in his mouth, while the possible need for it made him feel suddenly physically ill. Try as he might, he was far from being detached. For a long moment, thin-skinned and resentful, he did not stir, reason battling violence, then abruptly his powerful fingers convulsed, brutally crushing the expensive trinket in his grip.

Stripping off her evening gown, Kitty let it fall to the floor. Rummaging through her armoire, she had her hand on a red dress when a deep voice, just a little hoarse with drink, said, "I like the green."

Kitty spun around.

In the doorway, swaying gently, his pale eyes sparkling, stood Apollo. "Just looking," he observed lazily. "And I must say the view is fine."

Kitty naked—all curves, white skin, and slender long legs—was doing dangerous things to Apollo's ready appetite as well as to his sense of restraint.

"Do you mind," Kitty spat, her jaw obstinately set, her full, rounded breasts raised high from the stiffness of her spine.

"I don't mind, if you don't mind," Apollo drawled, still hanging in the doorway. His voice, amiable in its sarcastic fashion, went on softly. "Is it an invitation you're giving?"

"*Get out of here!*" Kitty cried, stricken and heartsick at Apollo's callous drawl. "Don't you dare touch me!" Undone by the events of the horrendous evening, aglow with incredulous fury, and trapped like a cornered animal, she stood erect and furious, gloriously nude, staring at her tormentor. "Don't you dare!"

"If you knew me better," he said in that same lazy way, unabashed, "you'd know I always pick up a challenge." His voice fell to a hushed resonance. "Always." His braced arms fell and in one purposeful stride he was on her. His right hand closed like steel on her wrist, and he said with mocking softness, "I dare *anything*, Katherine." Her proper name, pronounced as the general had, with a brutal courtesy, conveyed Apollo's long evening's worth of frustrated outrage.

To Kitty, already sensitized by the indignity of a brutal captivity, the words were like a pricking goad. Eyes blazing, she jerked back and with a sweeping movement snatched up with one hand the heavy silver mirror from the boudoir table. She aimed for Apollo's face just as he reached for her other arm. Miraculously, he twisted out of the way, but barely in time—inebriation slowing his normally fine-tuned reflexes.

He dodged again to avoid the mirror's returning swing, but the blunt edge grazed the top of his head. Kitty was like a sea storm out of control, and it went on for a long while—lunge, feint, thrust, twist, his cruel fingers never relinquishing their harsh grip on her wrist—until finally he was able to tear the mirror from her hand. But he bore more than one bruise from the struggle.

All the crystal toilette objects went next, hurled with more fury than success, until Apollo's free hand swept the marble tabletop clean with one mighty stroke. Undeterred, near hysteria, Kitty began striking out blindly. Her hand closed on a lizard belt tossed carelessly over a chair back. In her grasp it became a formidable weapon: the snaking metal buckle cut sharply over Apollo's shoulder and his grip on her wrist tightened just short of breaking bones. She was splendid in her naked fury but dangerous as hell, and up until the belt laid open his cheekbone, Apollo had constrained himself admirably.

That was the end for him.

The belt was ripped from her hands and landed across the room. "That's enough," he said sharply, capturing her other hand, "or I'll have to hurt you." Blood was already tracing a path down his lean cheek.

Flushed, trembling, Kitty stood captive in his steely grip, breathing hard, her eyes flashing fire. "You've got your bloody nerve!" she screamed, her breasts heaving from the exertion. "How can you *possibly* hurt me more than you already have!"

For a moment Apollo was taken aback by her unexpected violence. Even the distasteful events of the past hours couldn't provoke that degree of sheer, undisguised hatred. And, discounting this evening—impossible, he knew, until the day he died, but—*theoretically* discounting it, their previous acquaintance accounted even less for this bitter animosity.

"At the moment," he stated matter-of-factly, "I think I have more battle damage than you." He stood looking at her, his gaze traveling down her gleaming body and lingering in an intimate appraisal that caused her to tremble even more.

With apparent effort his glance returned to her face. "What do you mean, hurt?" he asked, smiling a little.

She glared at him. "How typically male," she said hotly. "Don't let me overtax your imagination." Her eyes and her chin defied him and she tried to jerk her hands free. Apollo's slender brown fingers tightened, but his expression remained equable, only an eyebrow faintly mocked.

Kitty felt at a distinct disadvantage standing naked before Apollo. He was calm, fully clothed, in control as usual, and that damnable unshaken arrogance only added fuel to her already blazing temper. But her breath felt constricted—and it wasn't exclusively from the fury inside her. "You come barging in here like Saint George," she hissed, "doing your knightly duty—saving the lady. It's all in a day's work—the big, strong mountain warrior knocking off another little adventure. And, since you're three parts drunk, why not seduce the lady, too. *That* role's second nature to a Kuzan, born to charm women, raised to please them in a hundred ways. You're just living up to the legend."

Apollo's eyes crinkled. "Thank you," he said agreeably.

"It's not a compliment," Kitty retorted coldly.

He tried to look mollified but only managed to look amused.

"And now that the maiden is rescued I'm supposed to fall gratefully into your arms, is that it? After all your accusations I'm supposed to capitulate cheerfully at the merest glance from your all-too-suggestive eyes?" Even as she spoke, self-hatred fed the flames of her wrath—because that was exactly what she wanted to do.

Apollo regarded her for a moment, then said lightly, "For my part, the proposal's tempting. And if you can't bring yourself to be exactly cheerful, I'll settle for anything this side of murder." He smiled this time with his eyes, long-lashed, sensuous, and those pale Eastern eyes—taking her already in their lazy possessive way—reminded her of what he could do to her without half trying; reminded her of a rumpled bed in a flower-filled room, of masculine power and erotic passion.

No, she wouldn't give in, wouldn't allow those thoughts to take over. Damn his arrogance. Damn that confidence he was exuding even now of his power to arouse her. Fighting him, fighting herself, she shouted, "You want a proposal? Rape me then! After the last few weeks I know exactly how it goes." Her lips curled into a bitter sneer. "You might as well get in line."

Each stood quietly taut for a moment, both consumed by self-righteous indignation. Then Apollo's fingers uncurled from Kitty's wrists. Smiling thinly, he lifted a hand—ripped by Kitty's fingernails—to wipe away the blood dripping from his jaw.

"Sorry," he growled, her taunting invitation goading his own cold fury. "You'll have to wait if you want to be raped. Today's Monday. Tuesday's my day for rape. On Monday it's murder. Six this morning, if you recall. Come to think of it, tomorrow may not work out, either. It's been such an exhausting night—" the tone was recognizably a hundred shades too sweet—"what with all the drinking and . . ." Apollo looked at Kitty pointedly. "Other things. I don't know if I can even guarantee you tomorrow. So you're quite safe. By the way"—Apollo's eyes raked her insultingly—"I prefer my rape victims quieter. Screams are so distracting. Keep it in mind." And because Apollo still retained some semblance of decency even under his drunkenness and outrage, he turned and quietly left.

While Kitty dressed, Apollo entertained himself with the vodka bottle. Sprawled deep in a plush, cushioned chair, he speculated in a very subjective way on the vagaries of females.

Some minutes later, Kitty walked into the drawing room and Apollo looked up. "Very chic," he said, his narrowed eyes sweeping her with something very like scorn.

"It's warm," Kitty replied tersely.

"Sable and purple cashmere is always *très élégant*," he went on as if she hadn't spoken. "So sorry, Countess, I've no violets tonight. Sables positively cry for violets. The war *has* brought its privations, alas." The golden eyes were half-lidded in vexatious irony.

"I'm not used to violet corsages, anyway." Kitty nervously watched him refill his glass.

"Ah, yes, I forgot," he drawled, "you're a simple innocent, rusticating in the country." On the word *innocent*, his gaze swung up from the task of pouring and waited for her reaction.

Kitty refused to respond, so he merely lifted the glass in salute, smiled dazzlingly with his easy, self-assured charm, and tipped the liquid into his mouth. With the carelessness of the inebriated, Apollo set the glass down casually in the vague direction of the table, then heaved himself out of the comfortable armchair and started for the back door in a lazy, rolling stride.

Having fortified himself with the additional liquor, Apollo's equanimity was now restored—or if not restored, suitably cozened by alcohol. He had made himself a promise while slouched in the general's chair, drinking the general's vodka, and waiting for the general's paramour. He'd kill him. Not tonight. Not now. But he'd kill Beriozov. And with that comforting thought, Apollo's mood had mercurially swung to the tinsel light mockery, which Kitty was finding as difficult to deal with as the cool anger. Following him silently, she retreated into muteness and prayed they reached safety. Using the servants' rear staircase, they left the general's suite.

Karaim and Sahin were waiting, saddled and ready in a stable three blocks away.

"What took so long?" Karaim asked shortly, stamping his feet to restore the circulation, silently taking in Apollo's cut face and the fingermarks on his hands. Marks of a woman—and in Apollo's present mood, prudent to disregard.

"The general's hospitality was most pressing," Apollo replied lightly. "I don't think he likes to drink alone."

Karaim could see the brilliant drunken glitter in Apollo's eyes and, knowing his temper, wondered academically how fast they must ride to stay ahead of pursuit. Apollo sober was someone to be reckoned with; Apollo sodden was a child of danger immune to caution, flirting with death.

"Did you kill him, then?" Karaim inquired quickly, for if that was the case, their hunters would be unrestrained.

Dark straight brows were raised and a golden gaze sorrowed. "Do I look that drunk?" a slurred voice said, mildly chagrined. "The day I can't drink a Siberian peasant under—"

Karaim didn't think he had time to hear the entire story. He kept to the point. "Did you kill the general?"

"He was in the best of health when I left," Apollo said in an obliging, slurred tone, rocking slightly on his heels. "In fact, I tucked him in myself. Save a roaring headache, and—" a note of contempt crept into his voice and this time he spoke with no slur—"a missing bedpartner, come morning all will be identical in his life."

At Apollo's last, rather rude remark, Karaim's eyes swung to the lady. Her spine stiffened. Kitty spoke, staring straight at Apollo, cold outrage in her eyes. "Suppose we drop that subject."

"The general's bedpartner, you mean?" Apollo asked tauntingly.

"That, and the general, and everything to do with him." It was so quiet her breathing was audible.

"Wouldn't that be convenient?" His level denunciation rolled through the silence like a tornado through a ripe wheatfield.

Kitty's face burned, but during the last few weeks she had learned to stomach humiliation. Besides, her freedom was worth any price. "If not convenient," she replied with a terrible smile, "at least it will make our journey bloodless."

Knowing Apollo's unpredictability when drunk, Karaim interrupted before his master could reply. "The sooner we leave—"

About to say something, Apollo apparently curbed the impulse. "Good idea, Karaim," he grunted. "I've been indecently reasonable all evening, but my control doesn't last forever in this state. And we must be into Tuesday by now," he finished nastily. His own dark thoughts obsessed him for a moment; images of Beriozov with Kitty tore at his composure. Stalking toward Leda, he consoled himself with his earlier murderous promise.

Extending a hand to Kitty, Karaim helped her into her saddle, and the trio followed Apollo out of the stable.

He rode far ahead of the others, bareheaded, stiffbacked, in a murderous mood. His hair seemed paler than ever in the eerie gray predawn light, and Kitty's eyes were drawn repeatedly to his rigid shoulders. By the time the first pink streaks of morning sun were lighting the horizon they were twenty miles from Stavropol. By midmorning they were in White territory, so they stopped to rest in the shelter of a deserted barn.

Karaim and Sahin guarded the entrance, keeping watch on the distant ribbon of road which disappeared into the dip of a river valley. Several miles beyond the point where the road dropped out of sight rose a small plume of smoke—and one never knew if a Red patrol, having broken through the lines, would suddenly appear.

Kitty was exhausted. They'd been on the road for almost seven hours, and they had stopped now only because the animals needed rest. In the short break before they set off again, Kitty dropped to the ground, leaned against an unused grain storage bin, and looked out at the winter landscape with unseeing eyes.

After talking briefly with his two bodyguards, Apollo came into the barn, discarding the tunic of his Red Army uniform. Rummaging through his saddlebags, he slipped into the black *beshmet* and tight-fitting, leather-seamed *cherkesska* he preferred, enveloping himself once more in the shaggy black *burkha* that served as cloak, blanket, and bedroll.

He had a violent pounding headache from the heavy drinking of the previous night and even seen through taut nerves and blood-veined eyes Kitty was looking much too desirable. Golden curls, tinseled with moisture, peeked from beneath her fur hat; her nose and cheeks were prettily tinged with pink, her long-lashed eyes dark in the dimness of the barn. The immediate arousal he experienced annoyed him.

Exhausted, bleakly resentful, and lamentably sober, he sank to his haunches near Kitty and addressed her gruffly. "Are you warm enough?" While the sentiment was one of concern, the voice was cool almost to the point of discourtesy.

Kitty, responding to the tone, disregarded the fact she was thoroughly chilled and said, "Yes, fine."

A floor-length sable *should* keep one warm, Apollo thought caustically, taking in the sumptuous, long-haired, saffron fur engulfing Kitty. Where did the general steal that? he wondered. "Good," he replied brusquely, and, the social niceties briskly concluded went on to explain in a formal tone how he happened to appear in Stavropol.

"I promised Peotr I'd see you safely to Novorossiisk."

"Peotr! Is he . . . ?" Kitty's white teeth unconsciously bit into her soft, crimson upper lip, and her eyes, dark-lashed absinthe, seemed to fill her face.

"He's fine," Apollo quickly interjected. "Not wounded, the last I saw him. And . . . fine," he finished lamely, no glib excuses ready on his tongue. It had been a long night.

"Where is he, then?"

"Well . . ." Apollo's mind was racing as fast as his excruciating headache would allow. "The last I saw him was at Ekaterinodar. We separated there, both starting east. One of us would get through, we figured." Peotr was heading east, although it was to Baku, not Aladino. "Aladino was practically on my way." *Merde*, he hated to lie, but none of that was *exactly* a lie.

"Do you think Peotr was hurt or captured?" Kitty asked anxiously.

"No," he answered a little too fast.

"Oh," was all Kitty said, but her overquiet reponse indicated full understanding. More misplaced anxiety for the same indifferent husband, she ruefully acknowledged. And Peotr may not be quite as callous as it appeared; after all, he had left instructions for her to leave at the first sign of trouble. It was her own fault she hadn't followed his suggestion. "We're on our way to Novorossiisk, then?" she inquired into the uncomfortable silence.

Apollo paused briefly before answering. "That's what I promised Peotr." His voice was flat, colorless.

So. He'd come only out of duty to an old friend, Kitty unhappily reflected. He had risked his life to save her—but for Peotr. She had hoped in some ridiculous, illogical way that he cared for *her*—that wanting to find and save *her* had been his motive. That silliness could now be summarily dismissed. It had all been simply another of Apollo's dangerous games, played out for its own pleasure. Winning was the prize; not her. Suddenly, for a moment, her will to live waned to a whisper. Her last desperate illusion—the talisman that had kept her dream alive, had sustained her through long, dreadful nights—lay in shattered fragments at her feet.

She really must try to control this terrible inclination to fantasize, she decided, very near tears. All that romanticism should have been left behind with childish games and what by now must be the ruins of Aladino.

As Apollo balanced before her on his powerful legs—all force and lean masculinity, his hair, as usual, a ruffled, wild mane, his yellow cat eyes assessing her with a guarded look—she wanted to say, despite all she knew and understood now, despite all that had been revealed to her of Apollo's motives: I've missed you. But the cool restraint in his glance, the grim line of his mouth, curtailed the impulse.

"It's the most sensible course," he went on slowly. "All of South Russia will be overrun in a matter of weeks, maybe less. The best thing is to get you on a ship to Constantinople." His tone was logical and detached. While jealousy gnawed at his innards and misplaced pride goaded his resentment, Apollo was still sensible enough to realize, regardless of his own whims, that the wisest course *was* for Kitty to leave Russia.

He scarcely knew how he felt or *what* he felt, or, for Christ's sake, what *Peotr* intended to do once everyone was safely in Europe. This ruined barn a few versts within the White lines wasn't the place to make lengthy decisions about anyone's future. Even if a more amenable environ could be found, none of them had the time. Simply to stay ahead of the Red advance would probably tax everyone's endurance.

Be practical, he told himself. The sorting out can come later—if they all lived through the next few weeks.

"Aren't you evacuating with the rest of the troops?" Kitty asked.

Apollo said briefly, "No. Later, maybe."

"What are you going to do?" If she had any pride she wouldn't even ask, but, unfortunately, she wanted to know. And when it came to Apollo, all her bridges were burned. At the thought of never seeing him again she had no pride, no conscience, no scruples. If she thought those chill golden eyes would relent, she'd throw herself at him and say, "Take me with you! Anywhere—I'll go anywhere at all." But there were degrees of foolishness even she wouldn't approach, and throwing herself at such uncompromising aloofness was one of them.

"I'll go back to the mountain aul—that is, if Karaim, Sahin, and I can find our way through the Red Army."

"It's suicide," she breathed, and a bit of her died at the thought of his proud young life thrown away.

"Everything's suicide nowadays." Apollo's soft, even voice paused a moment as he thought of all the useless waste, and the prospects for his future, then resolutely went on unaltered. "I can't guarantee your ship will be much better. Typhus is epidemic."

There was a long silence, but in the end she couldn't resist; her control was weaker than his. "Let me stay with you, then," she blurted out. There. Her defenses, pride, all put aside. Almost immediately she wished she could have cut out her tongue.

Excruciating seconds passed. His lack of response was an insult in itself. Apollo's closed expression hid any clue to the impulses of his mind, and if he wavered for a moment, he quickly firmed his resolve. At last he said with a small sigh, "I can't."

Ignored by a husband and now rejected by a lover. It was worse than Kitty expected, although she had cautioned herself often enough about the "lasting affections" of men like Apollo. The resulting humiliation was more painful than she thought possible. Don't cry, she cautioned herself inwardly, Don't . . . you . . . dare . . . cry! And only a long, drawn-out breath gave indication of her tremendous effort to overcome the most terrible urge to weep.

Any inclination she'd had to disclose Apollo's imminent fatherhood was effectively crushed by that short, curt, "I can't."

"Well, off to Novorossiisk, it seems," she said with brittle élan, curtailing the conversation by rising from the ground and moving toward her horse. Apollo uncurled without comment to let her pass. "Have we rested long enough?" she asked casually, adjusting the girth on her saddle.

"Long enough," Apollo replied, grasping her around the waist and lifting her into the saddle. Adjusting Kitty's booted feet into the wooden stirrups, he said, "We'll be in Novorossiisk tomorrow morning."

Kitty swayed slightly atop her mount. Tomorrow morning was long hours away.

Catching the bridle, Apollo reached out a hand to steady her. "Are you all right?" he asked, seeing her face pale visibly. Suddenly she looked very small, despite the long fur coat and high peaked hat.

No, I'm not, Kitty thought, staring at him. I'm cold. I'm tired. I'm hungry. Every bone and muscle in my body aches from the last seven hours of riding. My husband has left me. My lover doesn't want me. My mind and body are soiled from tortured weeks with General Beriozov. My nerves are shattered, my hopes are crushed. I'm carrying my lover's child and am about to be put on a boat for Constantinople to make a life for myself in a new land, alone.

Fortunately the years after her parents' deaths and the years of her joyless marriage had fortified her defenses; she had also found the strength to survive General Beriozov. The future required she garner the necessary strength once again. She had done it before, she could do it again. She must; there was no other way.

Whipping the reins free, she said stiffly, "Thank you, I'm perfectly fine."

"Would—" It was too late. With a whirl of cold air Kitty put her horse into a canter. Dammit, Apollo thought angrily, running toward Leda, she didn't look *fine* at all, but what the hell could he do about it now? No one in this hellish war-torn land was fine anymore. Not a man or woman, not a child or beast, so why in God's name should they be any different? "Fine" had suffocated in the bloodbath of the Revolution long ago. Don't think, just do what you have to. Novorossiisk. That was the goal. Maybe Kitty at least would be saved. He had Leda into a gallop before she had left the barnyard.

# 11

A thin winter sunlight shone on Novorossiisk when Kitty and
Apollo reached it the next morning. The weak rays glanced
off the dirty ice in the gutters and shimmered on the hardened, slick surface of old snow, littered with paper, blood,
refuse. The icy *nord-ost* wind tore at their clothes and chilled
skin. Owing to the White Army's rolling back too rapidly,
the city had become a madhouse in the last three weeks as
every refugee rushing before the lethal Bolshevik sickle fun-
neled into the last free seaport in Russia. Typhus was rampant—the deadly louse-carried virus had already killed more
than two million people in the last three years. Dead bodies
were everywhere, lying stripped of their clothing by those so
desperate for warmth against the subzero cold that they took
their chances with contaminated garments. The naked bodies
lay in the streets, on the sidewalks, piled in mounds of frozen
flesh.

The horses shied nervously, tossing their heads, snorting
with fear at the scent of death, sidestepping the corpses as the
group picked its way slowly through the littered streets. Most
of the restaurants were closed; storefronts were boarded up.
Lines before the shops that remained open were blocks long.
Nearing the quays with the steamship offices, they could see
mountains of luggage and furniture waiting to be loaded or
left behind by refugees unable to pay the freight charges. The
quays were also stacked with row upon row of field guns and
towers of ammunition, supplies, equipment methodically being pushed into the icy waters of the bay rather than have
them fall into Bolshevik hands.

Kitty tried to avoid the sight of the dead bodies, training her gaze at a point several feet above the street, but turning the last corner to dockside, the sound of dogs snarling drew her eye.

She reeled in the saddle. Three starving dogs were fighting over a small child's frozen body.

Snatching at the bridle, Apollo twisted Kitty's horse around and supported her, pinning his own horse hard to keep Kitty from falling. "Jesus Christ," he muttered, "this is impossible." After the merest hint of a pause, strong arms lifted Kitty. Curt orders were thrown to Karaim. Kitty's horse was put on a lead. She felt the warmth of Apollo's *burkha* close over her and leaned gratefully against his muscled chest.

Holding Kitty firmly, left-handed, the reins in his right, Apollo wheeled Leda and viciously spurred her. Answering his heels, she spun around and then raced through the polluted city, not slowing until they reached the foothills surrounding the harbor.

In the shelter of a small grove of cypress and leafless olives, the party dismounted. Feeling her feet touch ground, Kitty attempted to steady her trembling legs.

Apollo was genuinely worried at her weakness. She was pale as a wraith leaning against him. Lifting her away to more closely scrutinize her, he held her gently by the shoulders. Kitty swayed uncertainly.

Bending down, he looked at her closely. "Do you feel sick?" He put a hand to her forehead.

"I don't think so," Kitty whispered, her eyes only half-open. "Just all that . . . death. I think I fainted."

At least she wasn't hot. Burning with fever was a sure sign of typhus. Dropping his hand from her chalky face, he looked at her for a long time, then turned his eyes to the contaminated city. "You can't sail out of Novorossiisk, that's certain," he stated firmly. "It's too damn dangerous with all the tif."

"What else can I do?" Kitty asked wearily, leaning her head into Apollo's shoulder to keep herself upright. "If Peotr wants me to emigrate, I'd better," she murmured into his *burkha*. "I'm supposed to meet him in Paris."

Holding Kitty lightly in his arms, Apollo wondered moodily how the devil that little triangle in Paris was going to work out. Jesus, everything was becoming complicated.

Ever since leaving Stavropol—actually, ever since Kitty's whereabouts had been ascertained—Apollo had been sulky. And with good reason. He wanted Kitty, damned if he didn't, and it annoyed him. It annoyed him that he thought of her constantly. It annoyed him that she was so close and he wouldn't let himself touch her, really touch her. She was someone else's wife. She had been the general's playmate for several weeks. Had she been coerced, or had she decided the exchange was profitable—her passion for a pampered existence? The sable, the rubies, the Poiret gown . . . Was she available to the highest bidder? Suddenly it mattered that he know—and *that* annoyed the hell out of him, too. Being the highest bidder didn't present a problem; he had plenty of money, but whether he wanted someone for sale—that was the predicament.

Unfortunately, in the weeks since December Kitty had become his devil, his princess of desire, his glimpse of heaven as well as his burning fires of hell. Emotions pulled and tugged his feelings and desire around like playful gods of Olympus while logic stood aside from the melee and cautioned restraint. Apollo clenched his teeth in bitter irritation, the muscles high over his cheekbones twitching convulsively. Some decision had to be made, and rapidly.

Male pride and anger dictated it.

"We'll try Tuapse," he said flatly. "Maybe it's not so goddamned squalid. Some ships there should be standing by."

After a brief rest for tea they pushed on. On sheer willpower alone, Kitty mustered the energy to mount her own horse, but she no longer had the stamina to keep up. Several times in the next hours she fell behind, forcing the men to slow their pace. It didn't help that food had been minimal and that she'd been cold for two days.

With the March sun well past its zenith, shining red across the low foothills bordering the Black Sea, they stopped again to rest. When Kitty dismounted, her numbed feet and legs held her up only briefly before she fainted.

For a long time she heard distant voices, swinging to and fro like sunlight on quaking aspen, but they didn't affect her, crushed as she was in the misery and chill of her own blackness. Low voices spoke in the vernacular; she recognized the word for fire . . . food . . . and her name. Her name? She tried to draw herself away from the darkness but all her energy had been drained. Reviving at last when the aching chill began to leave her blood, Kitty found herself in Apollo's arms wrapped in his *burkha* and a fur robe, seated close to a fire Karaim and Sahin were briskly building up.

"What's wrong, *dushka*? Tired? Is the pace too hard? Hungry?" Apollo quietly asked. For the first time since her rescue his tone was warm and concerned. Kitty looked up into his golden eyes, filled suddenly with tenderness, and decided to tell him the truth. If this was a dogged test of endurance, Apollo had resoundingly won. She would never be able to keep up on the journey to Tuapse—sooner or later some explanation would be necessary. Taking a deep breath for courage, Kitty said, "I'm pregnant." Braced, she waited, apprehension filling her mind.

Pale eyes stared unmoving at Kitty. So *that's* why there were adjustable latches, his mind declared. It was his very first thought. Then some very rapid calculations snapped through his brain, digesting, evaluating. She didn't show any indications . . . the early months yet. "Will Peotr be pleased?" he inquired.

"I don't think so," she answered.

Well . . . that's pretty clear, Apollo thought. "The general?" He quirked a brow.

"No," Kitty said softly.

"No?" He seemed surprised. "Whose?" he asked quietly, more casually than he felt.

"Yours." She had never before seen the blood drain from a man's face. The sharp planes of Apollo's skin became startlingly pale and his eyes, surprised and shimmering, turned disconcertingly blank. He continued to stare at her and she was frightened.

Finally he took a whistling lungful of winter air, swallowed, and inquired gently, "Mine? Are you sure?" At which point all kinds of unflattering jealous suppositions came to his mind. How many other men had there been before and after him?

"I'm sure."

His effort at self-control was apparent, but Apollo's hands were trembling as he gripped Kitty's face between his large palms. His voice, when he spoke, was forced. "Say it again," he said in a queer sort of whisper. "Tell me again." And in the ensuing silence he didn't move, waiting for her answer, taut, expectant, his eyes no longer blank but piercingly alert.

Kitty was paralyzed by his behavior, shaken by his reaction; a reaction so much worse than her most morbid fears. Woodenly she repeated, "I'm sure."

His hands fell away from her face. No equivocation, he mused. Give her credit for audacity. "The contest for your child's paternity has been brisk, I'd say, these last few months. It's friendly of you to declare me the winner. And *you* no doubt"—his mouth tightened into a lazy smile—"are the prize." Abruptly his dark brows drew into a scowl. "God Almighty!" he growled. "What a damnable mess!!"

Kitty's composure, already slim and fragile after weeks with the general and the long hours of the previous night, could carry no more pressure. With a brief, uncontrollable shudder, it snapped. Her lips quivered and a flood of tears burst forth. She was freezing. Exhausted. Lonely. Abandoned by her husband and now the recipient of the least comforting words a pregnant woman could hear: "What a mess." Fresh tears sprang into her eyes and Kitty sobbed her heart out, dripping rivulets down her frigid cheeks.

Apollo gazed at her for a long moment. Why hadn't she terminated her pregnancy? he wondered, his mind turning to the private hospital in Petersburg where society ladies used to have their abortions before the war. The last time he'd been in Petersburg he'd noticed their retreat had been turned into a hospital for soldiers, and he had wondered where they went now—knowing that with so many embattled males around there must be quite a demand for that sort of thing. Slaughter and procreation are blood kin. He supposed in the turmoil of the White rout Kitty hadn't known where to go for an abortion. It never occurred to him she would have chosen to keep the child. Bringing himself back from his musings, he reminded himself since she *was* going to have the child, the problem must be dealt with. He refocused on the woman in his arms.

Her sad eyes were enormous, her face as white as chalk, two dark half arcs of sleeplessness were like bookmarks on satin beneath her eyes. Yet despite the high tempered strain, her face was still beautiful, framed with heavy honey-rose waves of hair, her pale pink lips accenting her pallor. A beautiful Astrakhan princess. She shouldn't cry, he decided. It wasn't her fault he wanted her more than he should. He was no different from the general. They both wanted to own her, and now she was his for the asking. Was pride going to deny him his desire?

The question staring at him defied his impulses for thirty seconds. And then it occurred to him—the first positive thought in a snakepit of heinous emotions—that, outside of pride, there was nothing to stop him from going home . . . and taking Kitty with him. No husband to care, no Aladino to return to, no Russia left for them, only the mountains and . . . his home. He had, after all, lived most of his young life purely on impulse, bereft of a delicacy of morals, and on thinking it over, he decided, Why stop now?

His cool, golden stare softened and his face came to life despite the bitter cold and the exhaustion he was feeling. His hands moved tentatively, brushing Kitty's face lightly, then suddenly his fingers sank into the gilded rivers of her hair. Bending, he kissed her fully on her cold mouth, and her rose lips opened slowly, softly, bewitching him with their promise.

She wept then in painful memory and thankfulness, her glossy pale hair streaming over his arm, the pulse of his breathing warm and quiet against her cheek. He hugged her to him, cuddling her to his chest, murmuring endearments. As he clasped her with all his strength, Kitty pressed into him as if he were the only refuge in the world, and in the shelter of his big body, she could feel the shattering misery in her heart begin to thaw, melting from the warmth of his comforting arms and soft lovewords.

After long, breathless moments, Apollo's arms released her and his tanned fingers caressed Kitty's cheek tenderly. "We're going home. Can you stand the trip into the mountains?"

Her big, moist emerald eyes mirrored her joy. She nodded.

"Good," Apollo said—and he knew he had agreed to be the father of her child, whosoever it was.

The following week they traveled only by night, resting in deserted peasant huts, cellars, remote caravanserai, even caves—any shelter offering concealment from Red patrols. Since current news rarely penetrated to the rocky trails of the Caucasus foothills, they weren't aware of the Red Army capture of Novorossiisk three days after their departure, no more than they knew that behind them by only days were sixty thousand Cossack troops of the Don and Terek. Left behind by the last ship in the bay, these scattered units of the White Army were attempting to break their way south and east to the tenuous freedom still available in Georgia. From their vantage point high on the mountain trails the small party could view the rapid massing and transport of thousands of Red troops westward along the north coast of the Black Sea, but they had no way of knowing the reasons for the vast deployments. They simply counted their blessings. With some urgent campaign drawing so many troops westward, their journey east would be that much safer. Living on wild game and nourishing Kalmuk tea, they traveled slowly over precarious mountain terrain.

Apollo was solicitous on the hard trek; helpful during Kitty's bouts with nausea; attentive to her delicate stamina, carrying her with him on Leda more often than not. He kept the pace to one Kitty could manage, making sure she always had the best of their food, the warmest position by the fire, all of the fur robe and *burkha* when they curled up together to sleep.

After the first week a certain sense of security prevailed, for no one but a mountain man could navigate the perilous tracks fringing the deep and seemingly bottomless chasms. Although it was March, the temperatures at the higher mountain elevations were chill; none of the party had been thoroughly warm for many days. Each night, however, they came closer to the mountain aul ruled by Apollo's great-grandfather, Iskender-Khan.

On the last days of the trek, Karaim and Sahin dared to enter local villages for food and supplies, since the Red Army had scarcely penetrated into those areas of the Caucasus. Still, they avoided the main roads, for an armored car or cavalry troop would occasionally be sighted. Although the mountain villages were largely removed from the political schisms disrupting the mighty Russian empire, there were instances, even in the remote mountains, where a native, having left to join the army or work in the cities, brought back the credos of Bolshevism.

Kitty noted, on the long journey, that she was often the recipient of Karaim's and Sahin's cool, watchful gaze. She remarked upon their careful scrutiny to Apollo and was placidly told, "They disapprove of my taking you for my woman because you've been dishonored by the general. With due consideration for both my honor *and* my desires, they have expressed their conclusions on the subject. They said, 'She is yours. Her life belongs to you. You can take it or spare it. The Adat permits either.' They expect you're only a passing whim of mine, and when you disappoint me or begin to bore me, they'll be happy to kill you."

Kitty's eyes widened in astonishment.

"Don't worry," Apollo teased, his eyes alight with amusement. "I'm very hard to disappoint."

Two days later the four riders reached Apollo's home and were welcomed into the prosperous mountain valley by volleys of rifle shot echoing from all the sentry posts encircling the fortified aul.

"That's Pushka's palace over there," Apollo said, pointing out his great-grandfather's square-towered fortress, crenellated and medieval in character, situated at the end of a narrow, winding trail halfway up the valley wall.

"And there's ours," he continued, his arm sweeping to the opposite end of the valley. The elaborate fortress-villa built by Apollo's father Prince Alex some twenty years before was perched on a rocky escarpment overlooking a breathtaking view of the entire area. Now its hundreds of windows were twinkling in the rays of the afternoon sun. The white marble of its exterior, brought up laboriously from the coast, glistened like snow in the moonlight; the whole structure, with its numerous terraces, wings, towers, and colonnaded porches, was a masterful combination of elegance and utility, designed to function as both keep and home.

"It's magnificent," Kitty whispered, reining in her horse. The very prosaic manor house of Aladino paled in comparison; like a working member of the corps de ballet next to the prima ballerina. Apollo's home would have housed any of the imperial Caesars with luxury and ease.

Apollo's mouth quirked into a fond smile. "Papa, I'm told, was out to dazzle Maman."

"And succeeded admirably, I expect," Kitty replied, smiling back.

"Papa has always been extravagant with Maman. He dotes on her. As a matter of fact, that's why they're in France now. Maman wanted to leave—so we children would have a future, she said. Papa would have preferred to stay, but he couldn't stand to see Maman unhappy. When I refused to leave Papa took my side; he understood, even if Maman couldn't. I send cables whenever I can to let them know I'm still alive. Papa made me promise to do that much, at least, to save Maman from worrying. He protects her from every discomfort. He says it's to save himself from her fiery temper, but it's really for love."

"How lucky they are," Kitty said, and a sense of melancholy struck her at the memory of her own disastrous marriage. But that was all in the past, she reminded herself, and she loved Apollo with a totality of feeling never experienced before. Could their life together hold on to such happiness, even in these troubled times? Before the morbid thoughts of war intruded any further she quickly asked, "Did your father build it before you were born?"

"No, after. But I was too young to remember." Apollo, too, recognized the difference between the peaceful married years of his parents and the uncertain future he and Kitty faced. That he wanted her he didn't doubt, but how much a husband, the war, and a stranger's child would challenge that certainty he had no way of knowing. As resolutely as Kitty, Apollo pushed aside the pessimistic musing, continuing his narrative in a voice unrevealing of his inner doubts. "I was two," he went on pleasantly, "when it was completed, so Papa's aerie is the only home I've ever known. And now, sweet *dushka*," he said gently, his pale eyes filled with love, "it's yours as well. Welcome home." Leaning over, he slipped an arm around Kitty's shoulders and kissed her softly on the cheek.

Tears sprang to Kitty's eyes; tears of happiness, relief, but tears of sadness, too, for all that had been lost in her young life. "Thank you," she said simply, lifting her face toward Apollo to offer the softness of her lips, hoping with all her heart they had reached safe haven at last. Kneeing Leda closer to Kitty's mount, Apollo kissed Kitty's full, pink mouth with almost hesitant care. They had gone through so much to find each other—but from this moment she was his, and they were secure in his home valley. Remote from any villages and roads, accessible by only the most tortuous, perilous mountain trails, and protected by a single pass so narrow two men could hold off an army indefinitely, the valley of Dargo was safe from the outside world.

At a discreet cough from Karaim, Apollo resumed his seat in the saddle, his mouth curling into a boyish grin "See what decadent civilization does to one's morals?" he said to Kitty sportively. "Mountain warriors with their oriental restraint don't approve of overt signs of affection to females in public."

Kitty raised one eyebrow impishly. "Do I run any risk of violence from your two bodyguards over this breach of etiquette?"

"No, rest assured, kitten. You're my chattel," he went on with bland geniality, his mocking tone disguising the very real truth from a countess unfamiliar with mountain ways and much used to living her own life. "They won't raise a hand to you unless I sanction it."

"It seems, then, that if I value a long life, I must gratify you at all costs." Her soft, feminine voice was husky with suggestion.

"I look forward to the experience," Apollo said, a teasing light in his yellow cat eyes, "with bated breath."

Their gaze held for one lush, expectant moment before Kitty, her glance swiveling in Karaim and Sahin's direction, inquired, "How close are they going to stay around—as bodyguards, I mean? Forgive me for asking, but I'm new to these quaint ways."

"Quite close, actually."

"Not in the bedroom, though, if I remember."

"Well . . . not always."

"Apollo!" Kitty cried.

"Never with you, love," he quickly acceded, flashing a grin. "*Those* days are past."

"Are you sure?" Kitty asked, suddenly plaintive, her memories of Peotr's infidelity creating a need for reassurance.

"Very sure, *dushka*." Apollo's hand went out and his fingers lightly glided over the curve of Kitty's cheek. As if reading her mind, he said quietly, "Everyone isn't like Peotr." Wanting to erase the unhappiness and anxiety from her face, he added, "I won't hurt you, little kitten, I promise."

Then, since Karaim's and Sahin's horses were restlessly pawing the ground, Apollo—with a degree of confidence he was far from feeling—declared, "But now we must see my great-grandfather, Iskender-Khan. I'm sure he was informed of our approach many hours ago when the first glimpse of us was reported by the lookouts. Karaim, Sahin, and I were recognized, but I know he's anxious to meet the lady accompanying us. Don't worry; although he appears formidable, Pushka rarely disapproves of anything I do."

"That sounds ominous. What does he do when he disapproves?"

"Never mind."

"What do you mean, never mind?" Kitty was looking at him with that narrow-eyed look he had first seen at the general's apartment.

"There's nothing to worry about," he replied, evading her question. "He'll fall in love with you the minute he sees you."

"What if he doesn't?"

"Would you please not argue with me, chattel of mine, in front of Karaim and Sahin?" he said teasingly. His voice took on a mock plaintiveness. "I'm losing face by the second. Just be pleasant to Pushka—as pleasant as you always are," he added, forestalling the retort coming to Kitty's lips, "and all will be well. Later this evening, after dinner with Iskender, we'll be in our own home. Now be a dear and follow me." Kitty was silenced by Apollo's hand. "Not another word now. We can fight tonight, if you wish, in the privacy of my bedroom." His lids half-lowered over speculative yellow eyes, taking in the mildly affronted beauty beside him. "As a matter of fact, the idea's damn enticing. It's been weeks since I've seen you in bed."

"Months."

"And you missed me," he said with all the old arrogance.

"Not really," Kitty lied.

"I missed *you* like hell." His voice dropped to a scarcely audible murmur. "I missed every delectable part of you."

"Lecher," she whispered.

"You noticed."

And they both laughed with the gaiety of adolescents.

Scaling the steep streets to his great-grandpapa's palace citadel, Apollo hoped with a certain degree of nervous apprehension that Iskender-Khan did, indeed, take to his newest paramour. He was unable to marry Kitty, since she was already married, so that was exactly the position she would hold in his life as far as his great-grandfather was concerned. Apollo recalled with an inner wince of dismay the occasion, several years ago, when a lady love of his hadn't met Pushka's approval. After a very few days she had . . . disappeared. He must make it absolutely clear to his great-grandfather—a private talk was imperative—that under no circumstances was Countess Radachek to . . . "disappear."

Hurrying down the imposing bank of granite stairs, Iskender-Khan greeted Apollo in the courtyard of his fortress home. Although over eighty, Iskender was tall, vigorous, and still mighty in sinew and limb, carrying about him the splendid authoritarian air of a king. He embraced Apollo heartily, kissing him on both cheeks, then gripping him by his hands and holding him at arm's length to survey him.

"We've been worried," he said in a bass rumble. "Word reached us a week ago that all of Russia has been overrun by these Bolsheviks. I sent scouts out looking for you at Ekaterinodar."

"We came from Stavropol and traveled by night."

"Sensible, very sensible." The old man patted Apollo's shoulder fondly. "Come in, come in. The women have been scurrying around for hours preparing food for you. Word came from the guards at the pass."

Kitty was still seated on her horse, watching the warm welcome being given Apollo. "The Falcon is back!" Kitty heard on all sides. "As-saqr As-saghir is home." It had been known soon after the first sentry's sighting; word had been passed along and voices had been busy since then rejoicing at the news. "Have you heard? As-saqr As-saghir is back!" And sometimes when a woman said it, her voice would be different and she'd laugh gaily. Side-slipping looks had been directed at Kitty all through the long meandering ride through the village toward the citadel, and everyone wondered what part she played in their Falcon's life.

A beaming, chatting host of warriors and retainers surrounded Apollo and Iskender, greeting the returnee with cheerful back-slapping, taking care of Leda, unstrapping Apollo's saddlebags, comparing jocular notes on the horsemanship of the Red Army. After a few minutes a young girl pushed out of the crowd, tugged on Apollo's sleeve, standing on tiptoe to whisper in his ear. Unceremoniously, Iskender-Khan brushed her aside. Giggling, she melted back into the milling mob. Turning from his conversation, Apollo caught a glimpse of the pretty girl before she disappeared into the throng, and raising his hand in greeting, he cast a lazy wink in her direction.

Noting the exchange even as he addressed the servants about the disposal of Apollo's things, the old man remarked tartly to his great-grandson, "Someone is going to have to marry Tamara soon to save her from her own folly. A more forward young filly I have yet to see."

"Probably be a good idea," Apollo agreed with a grin.

"Interested?"

There was a ripple of general laughter and a flash of amusement from Apollo. "No, thanks. I don't have time to play nursemaid to a young sultana. In fact, I just received a very indecent proposal from her. She's going to give a husband a merry chase."

"No desire to marry?" Iskender looked directly at his great-grandson. It was a leading question. Although the patriarch of five hundred thousand Dagestanis, waiting upon ceremony for introductions, had not acknowledged Kitty, he certainly had noticed her and was wondering with considerably more than idle curiosity just how large a role she occupied in his favorite great-grandson's life.

"Well . . ." Apollo hesitated. "Not at the moment." Then in a more formal manner, he continued, "I'd like to speak with you in private, sir. But first, come and meet a young lady who means a great deal to me." Taking Iskender by the arm, he led him over to Kitty. Apollo lifted Kitty down from the saddle with a cautious tenderness, the old chieftain observed, and then turned. Holding Kitty tightly by the hand, he said, "Iskender-Khan, I'd like you to meet Countess Kitty Radachek. Kitty, this is my great-grandfather, Pushka."

The minute Iskender heard the name Radachek everything fell into place. Peotr had been a frequent visitor to the mountain aul since Apollo had first met him at the Corps de Pages, the beginning stage of their military training. Iskender first thought: Is Peotr dead? But courtesy precluded asking that. The young lady looked quite pale and drawn. Bowing in a courtly gesture, Iskender said pleasantly, "Welcome, Countess, to Dargo. Won't you come in? Rooms have been prepared for you."

"Thank you for your hospitality. It would be quite wonderful to lie down for a moment—"

"Lord, yes," Apollo broke in. "I should have thought of that myself." Bending low, he looked at her small face, concern evident in his gaze. "Do you want me to carry you? How do you feel?"

Kitty flushed a bit. "No, no, I can walk. I'm feeling well."

"Sure?"

She nodded.

Iskender stood quietly aside, conscious of a change in his profligate, undisciplined great-grandson. No longer evident was Apollo's usual careless inattention to a female. Instead, Apollo displayed thoughtful deference and for the first time Iskender witnessed something other than charming playful repartee between Apollo and a woman. Old in years and wisdom, Iskender decided the countess apparently performed more than a minor, transient part in Apollo's life. "Tembot will show you your rooms," Iskender said. "I wish to thank Karaim and Sahin for keeping you safe. I'll join you shortly for tea."

Holding Iskender's glance over Kitty's head, Apollo said, "We'll talk then."

"As soon as you're refreshed," the old chieftain said. Turning away, he strode toward Karaim, his hand outstretched in welcome.

Apollo guided Kitty up the long flight of stairs, then followed Tembot down several narrow corridors to their rooms, which opened onto a balcony overlooking a walled garden. When Tembot left to see to hot water for bathing, Kitty timidly queried, "Are we *staying* here?" Her eyes swept the richly decorated room, hung with silken tapestries. This was *her* room, apparently, for Apollo's saddlebags had been carried farther down the hall.

"Only 'til dinner."

"Oh, good." Kitty, comforted, gave a happy sigh. The thought of being alone with Apollo had sustained her for the last day of their cold, arduous journey, when the long miles had begun taking their toll on her last reserves of energy. "I'd rather be with you than alone in this room," she said softly.

"Not nearly as much, sweet, as I want to be alone with you." Apollo pulled Kitty into his arms and nuzzled the tip of her nose with his lips. "A few hours more, to say hello to Pushka. Then . . ."—his grip tightened—"to our own place. It's very nice to be home at last." He sighed deeply. "And sheer heaven to have you with me."

"You don't mind?" Kitty was still in need of assurance. She had seen the effusive welcome extended to Apollo, had seen the genuine pleasure in Apollo's face, his sense of belonging, his feeling of coming home. It wasn't easy to forget the soft women's laughter when they spoke of the Falcon, or to disregard Apollo's knowing, casual wink at the fresh-faced young girl. Although Kitty was with Apollo, the man she loved, all else was alien to her: the savage warriors; the feudal display of propriety and authority; the outward appearance of a life-style far removed from the bucolic aspects of her own Aladino. And despite her passionate love, so heady and irrational, Apollo was almost a stranger to her. She had been with him for a grand total of twelve days since first finding him in her bed last December, and the time since Stavropol had left little opportunity for conversation or intimacy.

"Mind what?" Apollo placidly inquired.

"That I came here with you." With her chin resting against his hard chest, she looked up into his mildly startled face.

"I asked you, remember? I *want* you with me."

A smile curved the full sweetness of her lips. "Then everything's all right—even your great-grandfather?"

"Of course," Apollo gruffly replied, bestowing a light kiss on her forehead. "He understands."

Kitty sighed contentedly. Considering the utter chaos of the world they lived in, she was blissfully happy.

I *hope* he understands, Apollo thought—which consideration reminded him that a private conversation with Iskender was urgent. A few moments later when Tembot returned, followed by a number of servants bearing buckets of hot water, Apollo excused himself. "I'll freshen up," he said, rubbing the golden stubble on his face, "and meet you for tea with Pushka."

# 12

Apollo's bath and toilette were completed in record time. With his hair still damp and curling on his neck, he greeted Iskender-Khan.

With his long absent great-grandson—his favorite—home again, standing deferentially before him, Iskender-Khan knew Allah had indeed been beneficent. Tall, vital, matured into a man, Apollo was both his hope for the future and a poignant reminder of his own youth. Apollo remained standing out of respect for elders, the cornerstone of tradition and of the unwritten Adat. Old age, a woman, honor, and a guest in your home were all sacred. Apollo was now lavishly dressed in expensive silk and finest leather, as befitted his station. Iskender's knowledgeable eyes scanned the smooth, tanned skin, the gilded hair, the long hands, jeweled again after months of nothing but sweat-stained leather gloves.

Apollo smiled diffidently at the scrutiny, an amused gleam in his eye. "Finally back, and all the parts are intact. Remarkable after four years of slaughter."

"Not remarkable, necessarily," Iskender replied, pride in his low voice. "Karaim said you are a heroic warrior—a real *djighit*."

Apollo smiled serenely. "Lady Luck," he said modestly, "rode with me."

"And a little skill, no doubt." The gaunt, chiseled face creased into a smile. "We've missed you, As-saqr As-saghir. Come, sit down."

They were both seated cross-legged on silk cushions, and after all the homecoming amenities were concluded and a glass

164

of pungent Khahetian brandy was before each of them, Iskender-Khan came right to the point, his tone mild and of a grave delicacy. "I understand the countess is with child."

Apollo knew Karaim and Sahin would have reported to their chief. A trace of color rose under his bronzed skin. "*My* child, Pushka," Apollo said evenly.

His great-grandfather eyed him attentively. "Karaim says she was found in Stavropol . . . a kept woman. A Red pig of a general's kept woman. The child may not be yours." Iskender spoke in a soft and savorless voice which Apollo found peculiarly uncomfortable. "You must consider that."

"The thought isn't new to me," Apollo replied, his voice empty of expression. "Nevertheless, it's mine," he said intently, not mentioning any of his own skepticism.

With the wisdom of his years, Iskender-Khan had his doubts concerning the truth of that declaration, but since Apollo was his favorite, he was inclined to indulge his fancy if need be. Time enough to decide what steps to take after one saw what the child looked like. "What about the husband? Could the babe be his?"

The answer came a trifle too fast. "No."

"I see," Iskender said composedly. "Well . . . in any case, what of Peotr? He's alive, I understand. Will he be seeking the return of his wife and . . . your child?"

"Not likely," Apollo replied curtly.

Iskender's gray eyebrows levered upward.

"As you may know"—Apollo's voice was quick and caustic—"he has a mistress and two children in Baku—as well as a decided predilection for females of every persuasion if the mood strikes him."

"Not too unusual conduct for the Russian aristocracy," his great-grandfather said dryly.

Apollo gave a curious grimace. "No, I suppose not. His marriage to Kitty wasn't so unusual, either, in society's eyes. A marriage of convenience. Very acceptable. The problem arose only when the advance of the Red Army threatened Astrakhan and was massing to march on Baku almost simultaneously." Apollo shrugged. "Peotr couldn't be in two places at once. He chose the woman most important to him. The children, of course, were significant in his decision. He asked me to see to Kitty. He was hoping she had escaped ahead of the Red advance, but barring that, he asked that I escort her to the evacuation port of Novorossiisk." Apollo looked carefully at a distant point beyond Iskender's head and picked his words. "I have no idea what Peotr's plans were, if any, should they all meet in Paris. I didn't ask him." He stirred a wine ring on the delicate inlaid table with a long slender finger. "I probably didn't want to know."

Iskender, noting Apollo's disquiet without comment, asked, "Did you kill the general?"

"No."

"You should have."

"I couldn't," Apollo said in a low voice. "We needed the extra hours he would spend sleeping off the vodka to get us into White territory. If I had slit his throat, his orderly would have sounded the alarm at dawn."

"A pity, but sensible," Iskender said briefly. "What was his name?"

"General Beriozov."

"I'll send out four men in the morning."

Apollo's voice sharpened. "I'll do it myself." He used the most sacred of all oaths. "I swear on the bread." The strain was apparent in the tersely worded statement. "Only wait until Kitty is settled—then I'll go."

"Very well, as you wish." Honor was sacred in the mountains. Iskender understood Apollo's wish to see to the general's death personally. Only then would his integrity be cleared.

The mountains were like another world where pagan mysticism, the flame of Islam, the lily of chivalry, and the trickle of blood were interwoven into sacred custom. The heart of the Caucasus had remained unchanged for hundreds of years. Iskender-Khan knew what Apollo was feeling, felt his need for vengeance, and knew as well that the countess was more than "important" to him.

"She's very beautiful."

"Yes," Apollo said simply.

"You know I don't object to her having a husband."

"I know," Apollo returned, unruffled. Having been raised in the mountains, he understood that abduction was a recognized form of courtship.

His great-grandfather was looking at him very hard. "I do object to the general, however, if the countess had a choice in the matter." He raised a prickly eyebrow. "If you can't trust her, she'll bring you unhappiness. Promiscuity is not acceptable to the woman you choose for your own."

Apollo stirred uneasily. "She was a captive, Pushka." He repressed his own niggling doubts on that matter. It served no purpose to torture himself. "The general was cruel to her; he whipped her frequently. He even had a chastity belt locked on her."

Iskender said nothing, he merely sat back in his chair, stroking his neatly trimmed beard, and stared thoughtfully at Apollo. Now why, the old man mused, would anyone need a chastity belt—because of the general's own neurotic needs, or because the lady couldn't be trusted? He would see that the countess was watched. If Apollo wanted her, he could have her, but if she dishonored him, he must be told. To punish her then would be Apollo's privilege. Not a tactless man, Iskender-Khan perceived his great-grandson's unease and stopped his inquisition. His own curiosity could wait. "In any event," Iskender said ambiguously, "the *general* can be taken care of."

"Pushka—" Apollo said sharply, but his eyes were wary, sensing the words left unsaid.

"And I hope," Iskender went on mildly, a half smile on his face, "you and the countess will be very happy."

Apollo had half risen from the silken cushions and now sank back, a warm grin appearing across his fine features. "As happy," he said softly, "as two rabbits in a clover patch."

Kitty came in for tea an hour later. She had bathed and rested before dressing. Her clothing was native garb: loose silk trousers of pristine whiteness; a knee-length tunic of forest-green surrah buttoned with a line of tiny amber buttons; and gold-embroidered velvet slippers decorated lavishly with semiprecious gems.

Rising when she entered the room, Apollo swiftly walked the length of the large hall to greet her with a kiss. "I like the clothes," he said, admiration in his voice and eyes. The sight of Kitty in the supple, fluid silk tunic and trousers . . . she seemed so much more a part of his life now. Dressed as he preferred, here in his own mountain aul, the reminders of her former life were remote. No Paris gowns, no elaborate coiffure, her heavy golden hair now falling in simple waves down her back.

"The trousers feel very strange."

"But not uncomfortable?"

"Oh, no, on the contrary."

Apollo bent to whisper into her ear.

Kitty blushed, her eyes glancing nervously in the direction of Iskender-Khan, who remained seated several paces away. "Please, Apollo—your great-grandfather." Kitty slid another sidelong look at the imperious old gentleman whose profile was as sharply chiseled as a rugged mountain landscape.

Drawing her into the circle of his arm, Apollo smiled that irresistible smile that never failed to send her heart into flutters. "Relax, darling; Pushka knows I'm *very* pleased to have you with me, and he's not too old to understand that you're damnably distracting." He winked at her still rosy flush and said, "I *hope* dinner isn't too long." And he meant it. Since walking into the general's suite in Stavropol, Apollo and Kitty hadn't had more than a few moments alone and Apollo was, indeed, looking forward to the coming night—alone with Kitty in his own home, his own bed. A surge of heated desire tore through him. Drawing himself back to the present with an effort, he said in a pleasant conversational tone that had, from tedious teatime through midnight rendezvous, charmed many a hostess, "Come now. Pushka is anxious to talk to us both. You'll enchant him."

The patriarch and leader of half a million mountain people was benign courtesy through tea and dinner. With a deference he rarely utilized, Iskender-Khan inquired into the aspects of Kitty's life politeness allowed and tactfully avoided those areas pertaining to her husband or General Beriozov. The absence of prying, moral or otherwise, was deeply appreciated by Kitty.

Tea was sumptuous, served in rare T'ang bowls; dinner more extravagant yet: gold plates, ivory flatware, eight wine-glasses at each setting, and obsequious servants by the score, while a full repertoire of Khahetian wines smoothed over any awkwardness. In addition to European fare Kitty had an op-portunity to taste the mountain delicacies: pickled lamb's tongue that seemed to melt in your mouth, leaving a sour tang; eggplant stuffed with lamb and rice; cold mountain trout; and goat cheese roasted on coals—soft and creamy inside with a crisp crust smelling a little of smoke.

As ten o'clock approached, Kitty, although she'd declined most of the wine, found herself becoming sleepy. Since her pregnancy, she lacked her usual energy, and drowsiness was all too common. Stifling the third yawn in five minutes as unobtrusively as possible, Kitty raised her eyes and met the dark discerning gaze of Iskender-Khan.

"Apollo, the countess is fatigued," he offered softly, and Apollo turned to Kitty beside him, his pale eyes instantly distraught.

"I'm sorry, darling. I wasn't thinking." Addressing his great-grandfather, he said, "Please, excuse us, sir. Kitty's go-ing to have a baby," he added unnecessarily. "It's very tiring."

"Of course."

Rising to his feet in a swift blur of black silk, Apollo lifted Kitty from the low cushions, saying, "Come, sweetheart, we'll go home. You must take care of yourself and our child."

"Maybe your child," Iskender softly reminded.

There was a tiny silence while Apollo set Kitty on her feet. The softly spoken question was uttered in a language known only to the two men—not in Dagestani, the native tongue, but in a language of princes discernible only to those privi-leged few in the mountain hierarchy.

Kitty didn't understand Iskender's mildly enunciated

words but she saw Apollo's chin jut out belligerently, saw the dangerous set to the mouth, and heard his sharp, angry retort. "Mine!" Apollo said curtly.

Iskender's eyes rested fondly on his favorite great-grandson, so light and fair, so different from the dark, hawk-visaged men of his clan, so much like his favorite daughter's husband, chosen so many years ago when he had come riding into camp from the outside world.

"As you wish," he said with gentle indulgence, exactly as he had so many decades ago to his lovely daughter Shouanete when she had demanded the baron for herself. "I won't interfere."

"See that you don't!" Apollo retorted, still in a ferment of fury, for in truth Iskender's skepticism was too near the mark for comfort and he didn't care to be reminded of the fact. "And," Apollo continued in a low, tight voice, "if Kitty *disappears* as Noenia did, I'll take this village apart brick by brick." He was almost shouting by the end, incensed by his own unanswered questions concerning the paternity of Kitty's child.

Iskender's deep, hoarse voice spoke calmly. "I understand perfectly, Apollo. I give you my word." The wily old chieftain hadn't lived more than four score years, ruling hundreds of thousands of high-strung warriors, without learning the diplomacy of retreat. In this case Iskender readily acquiesced when Apollo's temper flared—and irrevocably, honorably, he would stand by his word. But he had his private reservations. If, when the child was born, it resembled the blackguard of a general or whomever other than Apollo, well, in that case . . . the lady herself might *decide* to leave Dargo entirely on her own initiative. If that were to happen (the ways of Allah are mysterious), his given word would not be impugned.

"What was that all about?" Kitty inquired, glancing nervously at the black rage still so evident in Apollo's expression. The night air was cool—more than cool; chill—when they emerged from Iskender-Khan's tower citadel, and before long the angry flush faded from Apollo's lean face.

"Nothing," Apollo replied, lifting her onto the horse, held in readiness by a servant.

"I heard my name," Kitty continued, her words quiet but clear in the still black night.

"Mentioned in passing, nothing more," he dissembled, adjusting a stirrup before leaping lightly into his saddle.

"You won't tell me?"

He didn't answer, only reached over for the reins of her mount and, gently nudging Leda, drove her down the steep street leading away from the palace.

"Apollo—" Kitty pressed.

"Nothing to tell. A ridiculous argument I'm tired of, that's all. And I told Pushka so. Please, sweetheart, I don't want to go into it." His voice was weary and a little sad.

"If it's anything I've said or done—" Kitty apologized.

"No, it's nothing you've said. . . ." And the unfinished sentence hung in the air.

After long, awkward moments in which both wished the past few months could have been undone, all the painful memories wiped clean, Apollo halted at the crest of the trail and drew up the reins he was holding so their horses were abreast. The night wind ruffled his flaxen hair, tugged at the pale wispy tendrils framing Kitty's face. Behind them lay the mountain aul, below them the large, fruitful valley, beyond— on the distant mountain wall—a great bastion of rock, overlaid and terraced by intricacies of pale marble. Apollo's home; lights shining warm and glowing from hundreds of windows. Reaching out, Apollo's fingers cupped Kitty's chin, gently turning her face to his. "I love you, Kitty," he said very, very softly. "Nothing else matters."

Tears sparkled in Kitty's green eyes. "Just keep telling me that," she whispered, so desperately in love. She loved the fair, handsome man whose thigh intimately brushed hers, loved him with a passion and intensity that dwarfed even the soaring snow-capped mountain peaks. "Don't ever stop . . . loving me," she breathed, quietly as wing beats in a night sky. Her unshed tears spilled over in glimmering rivers.

He stretched out his arms for her and with a smooth

strength lifted her into his embrace. Kitty felt the rough shagginess of his *burkha* against her cheek, heard his powerful heart beating beneath her ear.

I tried, he thought, holding her close. I tried to stop loving you. His arms tightened, enfolding her protectively. The moon shone off his tawny head and caught at his gilded curls when he bent his head to kiss Kitty's gently curved lips. "Till the rocks melt with the sun. . . ." he murmured, their warm breath mingling. Then their lips touched and doubt, uncertainty, war, guilt, husbands, generals, daunting cynicism disappeared at the first tentative brushing caress. Hope and happiness trembled and quickened with a force so explosive they both caught their breath at the wonder of it.

Their lips and mouths tasted, blended, their tongues danced lightly in blissful exploration as they paused from time to time on the slow ride across the sleeping valley to the lighted palace on the rocky cliff. And when Apollo carried Kitty up the courtyard stairs, across the enormous entrance hall, up the divided marble stairway, and along the entire length of the second floor to his suite overlooking the distant mountain peaks, no one else existed in the entire universe, no one save themselves.

Dozens of servants had parted like waves before their master's progress upstairs, having been on the ready since afternoon to welcome the Falcon home. Not until the bedroom door opened before him did Apollo see faces in the murmuring sea of welcome. He turned at the threshold, Kitty held high in his arms, and beaming from ear to ear said, "My woman, Countess Kitty Radachek."

A flurry of greetings broke from the massed servants, to himself, to his "woman," all of which he acknowledged with his flashing white smile, a polite bow, and a few short words of heartfelt appreciation for being home. "My lady's exhausted," he went on, "so you can all tell me what I missed during the last few years—tomorrow." Half turning into the bedroom, he added, "And if anyone knocks on this door in the morning, I'll have their head." His smile belied the fierceness of the threat.

Kicking the door shut, his heelless kidskin boots padded across the peach-and-green Oushak carpet. Laying Kitty gently on the oversize tortoiseshell bed, he followed her down, poised above her, arms framing her face. His eyes gleamed possessively in the subdued light of the bedroom. His voice was roughly husky. "You're my woman, *dushka* . . . forever."

"Forever," Kitty breathed happily, lacing her arms around his neck.

Mine at last, he thought, remembering the months of unfulfilled longing. Now, his seething brain thought. "In my house, in my bed, under me," he whispered softly and reached for the tiny amber buttons.

Suddenly his hand stayed. "The baby . . . is it all right?"

Kitty nodded shyly and murmured so low he had to bend his head to catch the words, "Love me . . . love me."

"All my days," the golden-haired prince of a mountain kingdom, heir to the immodest Kuzan fortune and title, warrior, pilot, explosives expert, and lover of beautiful women gravely replied, "all my days."

Apollo's touch—warm, soft, tender against her body—slid the silk tunic from her shoulders.

"Is this real?" Kitty whispered, looking up into his eyes. "Are we really safe and together for always? Tell me it isn't a dream; tell me I won't wake up and find myself back . . ." —her voice diminished to a pained, scarcely heard breath and she shuddered a little—"back in that blood-washed land."

Strong, masculine fingers compassionately smoothed the line of her collarbone, stroked the ivory satin of her shoulders. Apollo's glance melted into hers. "This is real, *dushka*. You and I are real. . . . You're mine and I'm yours 'til eternity, and no one and nothing will ever separate us again."

Kitty's small hands lightly caressed the iron-hard muscles of his chest, poised above her. The feel of him beneath her fingers was comforting solace. "Thank you, Apollo," she murmured in a very tiny voice, her eyes large and dark like some woodland nymph, "for giving me back my life."

His hand moved up to softly brush her peach-bloom cheek.

"You're mine, you know, and no one else's. I may have given you back your life, but I want it now for myself." His voice dropped to a hoarse whisper. "It wasn't altruism alone. I want you." His pale eyes drifted over the fragile beauty that had haunted his dreams for months. "Will you marry me?"

A smile lit Kitty's face, a glow of pure happiness. "There's nothing I'd rather do."

"Princess Kuzan. . . ." He tried the words on his tongue—this man who had never thought of marriage or, if he had, had relegated it to some vague time in the distant future. Princess Kuzan. . . . He liked the feel and taste and sound of it.

Kitty's emerald eyes shone with a deep and profound joy when she heard his words. Knowing his love matched hers, she felt a blessed peace at last in the arms of Apollo, the only true husband of her heart.

"Princess Kuzan," he repeated. "I like it. My wife, my soul—marry me, little kitten?"

Kitty nodded happily, her eyes glistening with unshed tears.

"Let's see now, we have to do this right. Something old . . ." His tawny eyes searched the room in one swift glance.

"Apollo—no, it's impossible, you know that!" He was really serious, Kitty thought nervously, caught up in one of his willful, headstrong moods.

Taking off his ring, he said, serenely unperturbed, "This will have to do. Chinese Ming should be old enough, right, darling?"

"*Apollo!*"

"If you're upset about the ring and prefer a diamond, rest assured, dear, the emerald is only temporary." He smiled one of those calm, patronizing smiles and, ignoring her distraught look continued, "Now then: something new. Hmmmmm . . ." The pause was only brief before his golden eyes flashed and his hand dropped gently to the small rise of Kitty's stomach. "*That*," he said, very softly, "is the newest in the world." Kitty blushed rosy pink. "Won't it be nice to have our child at the wedding?" he went on blandly and smiled in that unutterably devastating way that always sent shivers up Kitty's spine. She smiled back in spite of herself. Bending toward her mouth, Apollo's low, deep voice quietly ordered, "Tell me three's not a crowd, but a perfect family; tell me you're happy; tell me you love me."

And as his lips brushed hers, Kitty replied in blissful delight that soared over the score of problems facing their future, "Yes, yes, yes!"

"Good" was all he said long moments later when his mind returned to the matters at hand. He lay propped on one elbow beside Kitty. "Something borrowed, next," he declared, momentarily diverted but intent on having his way. Grasping one of the numerous pillows, he effortlessly tore off the six-inch lace border and draped it gracefully around Kitty's shoulders. "I've never seen a bride yet without yards and yards of lace." He reached for the next pillow.

Laughing softly, Kitty stayed his hand. "This will do quite nicely. No need to tear up the entire bedroom."

"A woman who doesn't like frills? What am I getting myself into? Just how bizarre are you, *ma petite?*"

"Just bizarre enough to appeal to a wild man like you. And for your information, I do like frills, but under the circumstances this is enough, thank you."

"You're sure?" He was sincerely earnest. He was perfectly willing to give Kitty every scrap of lace in the palace if she wanted it.

"About the lace or your being wild?"

"The lace, of course. I *know* I'm wild. And by the way, you're right. Prim and proper people don't appeal to me."

Kitty's reserved nature, not entirely jettisoned yet, caused her to flush. "I don't exactly know how to respond to that."

"Say 'thank you.' It's a compliment."

Gathering what insouciance she had, Kitty returned the thank-you, and Apollo delighted in the naiveté that still clung to the beautiful lady at his side. Her blushes were touching in their innocence and he counted himself a very lucky man.

"No more lace," he went on then, "we're agreed on that. In that case we only have the 'something blue.' Ah . . ." he said with satisfaction, his gaze lighting on the bouquet of flowers on the bedside table. One large hand closed around a clump of miniature blue iris artfully interspersed with pale pink roses. "Flowers for my bride," he quietly said, snapping off the long stems, and one by one he laid them gently on the masses of honey-gold hair spread on the lace-covered pillow. He tucked one into a curl near Kitty's cheek. "I'm sorry they're not sweet peas. Tomorrow, *dushka*, I promise, I'll have sweet peas planted in the greenhouses. There," he said, precise, assured, satisfied. "Now there's a perfect bride."

"Oh, Apollo." Kitty sighed, smiling and crying at the same time. He loved her and she loved him, and in their own private way they were more man and wife than any couple married before a registrar, a priest, or the entire court.

Then Apollo's face became serious. As his hand brushed away Kitty's tears, she saw an unfamiliar gravity settle in the golden eyes. "Don't cry anymore, kitten, everything's going to be perfect from now on. You're my woman," he said, his fingers playing lightly over her. "For always." Then, taking both her hands in his, looming large above her, the dark centers of his eyes unusually intense, his low voice vibrating with feeling, he said in the tenderest way, "I, Apollo, take thee, Kitty, as my wife before God. . . . Say it back," he prompted when Kitty hesitated.

"I, Kitty, take thee, Apollo"—her voice was as soft as a rose petal—"with all my heart, to have and to hold, from this day forward. . . ." Kitty felt a warm enchantment, felt young and new and innocent, as if her life had only begun tonight with the man she loved. Apollo had found her, had come for her through danger and war; guards hadn't stopped him, nor generals with proprietary designs. Neither distance nor battlefields had mattered and she knew, really knew, he loved her. That knowledge filled her with a bliss so perfect and true it was as if, for her, the world was born afresh tonight.

"From this day forward. . . ." Apollo echoed, and when their lips first touched, a piercing sweetness insinuated itself like the fragrant warmth of springtime into the fullness of their hearts.

• • •

He had never been so careful in his life. His hands moved over Kitty like the whisper of fireflies in moonlight. She had been through so much; he never wanted her hurt again. And the presence of the child—so new and different—that, too, made him cautious. But before long in his own special way, he brought the small, soft woman beneath him to a blazing, wild excitement, and when her hands clung to his sinewed shoulders and tangled in his hair with a madness that wouldn't end until their flesh became one, he moved his body down over hers and very slowly gave her what she wanted, what they both wanted—the bewitching deliverance memory had kept alive since the long-ago days in December.

Lingering hours passed sleepless, playing at love, and the moon dropped low on the dawn horizon. Apollo lay sprawled on the bed, one arm gently cradling the fair woman sleeping curled against him. His eyes swept the familiar room, contentment seeping into every bone, nerve, and tissue of his body. His golden eyes swung back to gaze out the wall of windows before him, and a snow-capped panorama of mountain peaks, orchards, fields, and village lay spread before him, frosted with the tinsel of early light: all peace, rest, protected, and . . . his. Prince Apollo Kuzan, As-saqr As-saghir, the Falcon, was home.

# 13

The next two weeks were idyllic. They rarely saw anyone. Apollo politely refused several dinner invitations from Iskender-Khan and since the old chieftain had a very keen memory, recalling what young love was like, he didn't impose his will as he could have. In the course of the next fortnight, Apollo and Kitty *did* dine at the citadel occasionally and it was plain to see, the other guests remarked, the Young Falcon had found his heart's mate.

They spent long blissful hours in the tumbled disarray of the enormous tortoiseshell bed. Exquisite pleasure was exchanged, savored, experienced with a new tenderness as well as a new intensity. What he asked for, she gave. What she craved, he lovingly proffered. It was a paradise of the senses.

One morning two weeks later, Apollo excused himself for a short conference with Karaim, who had stopped by to see him. When he returned, the remainder of the day was leisurely dissipated, but that night, Kitty woke to find Apollo lying sleepless, his arms locked behind his head, his pale eyes staring unseeing at the elaborately stuccoed ceiling.

The following day, Apollo lapsed into a retrospective musing on more than one occasion, and late that night, Kitty lay and listened to the incessant whisper of Apollo's footsteps pacing the sitting room carpet.

By the third day after Karaim's appearance, Apollo's restlessness was painfully obvious. He seemed to strain like a borzoi on a leash. Later that evening he was as sociable as a Trappist monk, Kitty ruefully noted—a troubled, reticent man, his mind obviously distracted. Before retiring for the night, they lounged in front of the fire, Kitty stroking the tense muscles in Apollo's neck, bracing herself to ask the needed question. Everything had been so perfect, after literally years of unhappiness, that she had stubbornly resisted endangering such undiluted joy.

When Apollo rose abruptly and strode to the window, she finally forced herself to ask, "What did Karaim say?"

Apollo didn't turn. He leaned his forehead against the cool window pane and said flatly, "A raid's in the planning." Standing motionless, his form was lost in shadow.

"How does that concern you?"

"I'm their leader."

"Is the raid necessary?"

"It's a way of life for a mountain warrior. Their blood and upbringing guide them. Too long at home, well fed, well rested, and under exercised, they begin looking for trouble and end up fighting each other."

"Let them go without you."

"I can't," he said with an almost helpless simplicity.

"What do you mean, you can't?" Kitty countered insistently. "If you're their leader, you can do anything you want. There's—"

Apollo's voice, carrying a resonant power, cut across her words. "It's not that easy. Honor's involved. Raids, warfare, fighting are a warrior's life. The foundation for his existence, for his family's existence, for the life of the aul. If you give that up . . . you relinquish being a man."

"It sounds positively feudal."

"Maybe it is, but it's the way I've been raised. I've lived here all my life, except for the time in the Corps de Pages and during the war. I share the same blood. I'm all that they are— my great-grandfather's prejudices, my father's spirit, my mother's love. I'm Karaim's cavalry experience, the courage of my first horse, part of a brotherhood of warriors that have never been conquered. I can't tear these things from my heart."

Although Apollo had lived for a time in the aristocratic milieu of Petersburg and Paris, his spirit had always remained in the mountains, and he kept with him the tough, esoteric core of the mountain world. Society, the court, even the officers' corps were superficial accoutrements to his sense of being, his masculine ethos which had slowly and simply been instilled in him until it was as natural as breathing. And in a way, it was as important. At least, this particular raid was. Maybe later some of the others could leave without him, but this one he would command himself.

Karaim had come to tell him three days ago that General Beriozov was now resting in Sochi before moving east. They could reach him in five days of hard riding. And all Apollo could think of, the only desire filling his mind, was that of sinking his *kinjal* into the evil heart of the man who had abused and humiliated Kitty. Images of Kitty and the general overwhelmed him with a merciless, impotent rage.

Yesterday, Karaim's report had been followed by a message from Pushka informing him that horses and supplies were ready—the men only waited his decision to mount up. Now unstirring, Apollo stared out into the darkness and his lust for vengeance grew, uncurbed and violent.

Her eyes on the back of the motionless man, Kitty ran her hands nervously over her silk-trousered legs. "Please don't go, Apollo," Kitty pleaded, sensing somehow that this was no ordinary foray, trying to understand Apollo's feelings, but fighting her own terrible fear. "I know how much it means to you but please don't go. For me—for the baby. . . ."

Apollo shut his eyes briefly, his head still resting against the cool glass, his knuckles and nails yellow white with pressure on the dark windowsill. Did she think he *wanted* to leave her? Good Lord, it was the last thing he *wanted* to do. But mountain law required that an insult be avenged—and even if the Adat hadn't demanded retribution, his heart would have claimed that justice. He could not rest until that pig who had dared to penetrate *his* woman was dead, and if there was time, he promised himself the general would stay alive much longer than he wished.

Pushing away from the window, Apollo turned to Kitty, who was still sitting on the floor before the fire. She looked up at him, standing tall above her, his powerful body defined in the shadowy chiaroscuro of the flickering flames, his face restless, illuminated by the amber glare. He sighed softly, releasing some of the tension that had been building over the last three days. "Let's not argue about this anymore; it's senseless. You know I love you. I'd do anything for you." His voice was placating but cautious.

Tears were sliding down Kitty's ivory cheeks, catching the firelight in staccato sparkles. "Don't go on the raid, then."

It tore at his heart to hurt her. "Anything," he said very gently, "except that."

Hours later, after the expected accusations and recriminations, the quiet tears and heart-stricken apologies, Kitty lay asleep in Apollo's arms. He was wretched at having to leave her, understood her perplexity, but he could no more deny himself the need to punish the general than he could deny his love for Kitty.

Mountain law demanded vengeance, the chivalrous warrior code demanded it, but most of all, a savage blood lust deep inside Apollo demanded it. A dozen times a day he remembered the night in Stavropol, remembered the way Beriozov's large hand had leisurely caressed Kitty's bared breasts, remembered the towering rage that had possessed him, and remembered most of all the necessity for curbing his murderous mood. That necessity was past. Kitty was safe. He was saddened by his leaving, but finally reconciled: he'd be back soon; he had promised her.

But in case he didn't return . . . ? Even with his troop of riders, the possibility existed, Apollo knew, since General Beriozov lived behind a front line phalanx of guards and subalterns. The general lived warily, conscious of the thousands of deaths that bloodied his hands. He wouldn't be easy to get to.

Without disturbing her, Apollo shifted slightly, gently easing Kitty's head from his shoulder. Slipping a pillow under the tumble of shimmering gilt waves, he covered her and slid from the bed. Walking barefoot into the sitting room, he lit a lamp, pulled out a sheet of heavy paper from the drawer of the faded rosewood writing table, and sat down to compose a good-bye note.

He deliberated for long moments. How did one put down on a page of paper all that was in one's heart—and worst of all, how did one say good-bye to the love of one's life? If he were killed on this raid, he wanted to tell Kitty how much she meant to him, how she had brought him joy and changed his life; he wanted to try to explain again why he had to go; wanted to express his regret at not being there to help her raise the baby. And business matters should be mentioned: his will, newly revised since their return to the mountains; the European bank accounts; the homes he owned in Dagestan, Nice, Geneva, Paris, the Loire valley; the stud farm in Kent; the hunting box in Normandy—all left to her and the child in the event of his death. There was too much to say . . . and so little time. He contented himself finally with telling her of his love, his strong hand moving swiftly across the sheet, the dark scrawl rapidly filling the cream-colored surface. Turning the thick paper over, he added two more lines acknowledging the complicated financial interests by writing, "If I don't return, see Pushka. You and the child are my beneficiaries." With a quiet sigh, he finished, "I've loved you, kitten, from the first night, and always shall. Give the baby a kiss from me. All my love, Apollo."

Quickly sealing the note, he put it in a larger envelope addressed to his great-grandfather and took it to one of the servants with instructions to have it delivered immediately.

Returning to bed, he slept restlessly until daybreak.

He and Kitty said good-bye in the breakfast room.

"Don't come out," he suggested, rising from his chair. "There are too many people about to properly bid you adieu." He was trying to avoid any further hardship on her.

Kitty stood up, fighting back the terrible fear haunting her, trying to present a brave front despite her distress.

One look at her face and in three strides Apollo was at her side, drawing her into his arms. He was dressed all in black; silk *beshmet*, heavy worsted trousers, leather boots—only his sunlit hair dazzled. Against such somber hue, Kitty in her

Chinese silk robe, small, fragile, golden as a sunrise, contrasted starkly, like a rare orchid clinging to a towering, dark tree.

"Please, be careful," she whispered into the curve of his chest. Kitty was well aware of the dangers waiting outside the protected mountain valley. Reports had it that the Red Army had taken Azerbaijan and was marching on Georgia's borders.

"I'm always careful." The soft silk of her robe felt warm beneath his hands. He buried his face in the perfume of her hair.

"When will you be back?" It was no more than a hesitant murmur.

Five days down, five back, he thought, maybe one or two days to reconnoiter the general's defenses. "Probably in two weeks," Apollo said, lifting his head. "Maybe a day or two sooner." He didn't want to continue any further discussion about the raid. Hours last night had been devoted to the subject and at best a reluctant stalemate existed between them on that score. Above all, he wanted to leave without acrimony. It might be the last time he ever saw Kitty, or held her. His embrace tightened. "I love you, remember that," he said softly. "Take care of the baby."

Kitty looked up anxiously. An ominous apprehension gripped her. Apollo sounded so . . . final. "You'll really be back in two weeks?" Her voice was tinged with fear.

"I'll be back."

"Promise?" She knew it was a childish demand, but she needed the blanket assurance.

He nodded to please her. "Promise." His golden eyes took in every detail of Kitty's exquisite face, storing away the memory against an uncertain future. Then his arms dropped away. "The men are waiting. *Au revoir*." He kissed her lightly and strode from the room.

Kitty listened unmoving to the light footfall passing down the long hall and swiftly descending the stairs. With the slam of the front door she ran from the breakfast room and climbed to the high terrace affording a view of the courtyard and trail leading down into the valley. She watched Apollo, heard his familiar voice, unfamiliarly crisp, giving last-minute instructions, saw his face totally without expression, all the graceful nuances swept clean as he concentrated on details, questions, the buckling on of his arsenal. Weapons on, tack checked, all the men mounted, Apollo, in the lead, turned Leda out of the courtyard and a moment later put her to a trot down the incline. The men followed in pairs, the narrow trail accommodating no more than two horses abreast.

He rode with animal grace, his hair gleaming silver pale against the sleek black of his tunic in the spring morning light. His weapons, thoughtfully added outside to save Kitty alarm, bristled from his large body: double cartridge belts were crisscrossed over his broad shoulders; a carbine was slung behind his back; pistols were holstered on his hips; his cavalry saber lay conveniently scabbarded near his right leg. The two *kinjals* stuck into his belt didn't show from the vantage point of the terrace.

The troop's array of weapons was quite complete. Their mounts were the finest of mountain-bred horse-flesh; they were well equipped with supplies and money. Each man was hand-picked by Apollo and Iskender-Khan. The weather was pleasant. Now all they needed was an enormous amount of luck to ride five days across enemy territory, pluck out the general from his well-guarded retreat, kill him, and find their way back to safety.

At the point where sentry posts guarded the narrow pass into the valley, Iskender was waiting to bid his great-grandson good-bye.

"Do you have enough men?" he asked Apollo.

Apollo nodded. "Plenty."

"If you decide you need more, send back a messenger."

"Too many will only attract attention. Even now we might have more than we should."

"We'll watch for you after ten days."

"It'll be closer to two weeks, so don't begin to worry."

"Take care. I know you want to do this yourself, but no Red swine is worth the sacrifice of your life."

"I'll be careful, Pushka. Karaim's my voice of reason."
Apollo grinned at his companion, who was lounging in the
saddle alongside him.

Karaim only snorted through his hawklike nose. He'd ridden bodyguard to Apollo since Apollo was old enough to
mount a horse and to the best of his recollection his advice
had usually gone unheeded.

"Until a fortnight." Apollo raised his hand in casual salute.
"Good-bye, Pushka. You have my letter to Kitty?"

"I do." The old man's eyes took in the splendid, rangy form
of his great-grandson and he prayed he'd never have to
deliver it.

"Take care of her if need be . . . and the child." Their eyes
met, old and young, and understanding passed between them
like a living thing.

"She'll have the honors due your woman, and the child
those of your heir. My oath on it." Iskender lifted his hand
in benediction. "Allah travel at your side."

Apollo loosened his grip on the reins and Leda sprang forward. The riders moved out, tunics fluttering, fringes swaying, passing by their chieftain Iskender-Khan. His dark glance
swept the score of men turned out in battle array, selected for
their courage, fearlessness, and savagery. "Protect him with
your lives," he quietly said to them in passing, and each dark,
fearsome warrior nodded mutely in acknowledgment.

Kitty tried to keep herself busy after Apollo left, but the
day was endless. She paced, she tried to read, she walked up
the mountainside to a glen she and Apollo had favored. But
with nightfall her melancholy only deepened, and with it the
shattering fear, poised and menacing, crept closer.

Without Apollo her loneliness was appalling. She felt a
stranger in the mountain aul. Unfamiliar with its customs,
unused to the limited role allowed women, unaccustomed to
the language, she was painfully aware in Iskender's presence
that she was only here on his sufferance—as though he were
delaying judgment until some certification was accredited. He
was never impolite, only reserved. It was daunting to be alone

here, pregnant and alone, with Apollo on some undisclosed
raid. Alone, with no family, no friends, no other home left in
Russia; alone amidst luxury; alone in a palace staffed by hundreds.

She had been a princess in her own right, born to wealth
and privilege, had married and added to her fortune. Now
none of that remained. She was destitute, entirely dependent
on Apollo, not only for her physical existence but emotionally
dependent as well. The change in her status, in her life,
brought with it a turbulent chaos of uncertain feelings. The
adjustment from supreme independence to one of dependence
was not easily reconciled.

Still, she was bound to Apollo by more than love; she carried his child. And while the growing child gave her joy, it
had, by its existence, sapped her self-reliance. It had necessitated her subjugation to the general—a sore point still not
entirely rectified between Apollo and herself—but, more than
that, it physically limited her ability to fend for herself. When
Apollo left, she could no longer follow, and she despised the
feminine feebleness cast upon her suddenly. Forced now into
a docile waiting role, she chafed at its awful limitations.

She found herself restlessly wandering around the huge palace trying to recapture Apollo's presence: sitting in his library
for hours, picturing him lounging in the worn leather chair
near the window; walking out to the pond in the garden where
they used to lie in the sun; straightening his clothes in his
dressing room; touching his ivory-handled brushes on the
lowboy; remembering him shaving, standing tall and tanned
before the oval pedestal mirror, carefully drawing the gold
razor down his lean cheek.

She spent long hours in his mother's sitting room, surrounded by family photos scattered atop tables, desks, con-
soles, gracing the liberty print walls, arranged haphazardly on
the grand piano. She especially liked the one of Apollo as a
boy of ten, tall already, his eyes bright with youthful mischief
belying the seriousness of his face. He'd been dressed in full
mountain regalia, the rugged Caucasus range as background.
Even then a duplicate of Leda was standing beside him, the

reins held in his small gloved hands, the wind ruffling golden hair and mane alike. Apollo's father, Prince Alex, as amateur photographer had captured the barely suppressed excitement underneath the outward show of maturity. It was his first full-sized thoroughbred, Apollo had told her, the day he had left childish ponies behind. Kitty would have liked to have known him then, to have been a part of his life and memories. She knew so little about him, only fragments of his life depicted in these photos—his mother and father, his sister . . . the glorious day he bought his own airplane.

That photo Kitty had moved to her bedside table while Apollo was gone. Splendid in high leather boots, jodhpurs, and a leather aviation jacket, he stood, one hand possessively on his airplane, smiling that heart-stopping, boyish smile of his. The sunlight was caught in his hair, his eyes looking straight at the camera, and Kitty felt when she saw it that he was about to make some typical teasing remark. Between the photo and his few things scattered about the room Kitty kept the feeling of him close.

She hadn't moved the riding boots carelessly tossed half-under the chair the night before he left—and she wouldn't allow the servants to move them, either. It was silly, but who was there to notice, and it gave her the illusion of Apollo's nearness.

Please, Apollo, Kitty silently prayed during those lonely days, come back safely. She refused to even consider what would happen if he didn't return.

By the morning of the third day, Kitty decided she simply must "do" something rather than mope around. Her attempt at managing the palace met with quiet but determined resistance. The servants were quite capable of directing the palace functions and indeed had done so, with a minimum of interference, since it had been built. Apollo's father thought households ran themselves, while his mother, Princess Zena, though aware of the error in this assumption, was more interested in her husband and children's company or her newest research project than in any chatelaine duties. As a result, the entire staff was stubbornly autonomous.

With the housekeeping activities denied her, Kitty turned to the outside, to aspects of farming which truthfully were much more appealing. Luckily Apollo's steward didn't guard his prerogatives as jealously as the inside servants, and when Kitty approached him about taking a hand in some agricultural project, Edyk was more than happy to oblige the Falcon's companion. He immediately took Kitty around the acres of fields, explaining their methods, producing, and harvesting. He showed her the experimental plots for short-season wheat, the hybridized vineyard, the pear orchard where grafting was systematically producing a better, sweeter, larger pear. Kitty was instantly in her element, and while the fear and loneliness remained there were moments in the days that followed when they would be pushed aside briefly. Edyk was her savior.

Sochi was close to paradise this time of year, warm, sunny, all the semitropical vegetation in bloom.

General Beriozov relaxed on the cushions of the chaise located near the balustrade on the sunlit terrace of the mansion overlooking the sea. After the fall of South Russia and the conclusion of mopping-up operations against odd fragments of the White Army, he had taken a vacation at Sochi, a resort community formerly serving the aristocratic classes of the empire. He was occupying, and had for two weeks now, the former residence of Grand Duke Vladimir. The general was amusing himself in his usual manner with drinking and women, but since the abrupt departure of Countess Radachek he hadn't found a proper replacement. Only transient females came and went in the mansion by the sea.

Snapping his fingers for a fresh vodka, he shaded his eyes against the saffron glow of the setting sun, gazing down the endless expanse of beach lying at the foot of the steep, grassy incline running down from the many terraces of the villa. Lemon groves were planted on the distant hills; tea plantations skirted the town and the fragrance of bougainvillea attested to the semitropical nature of the climate.

The general's musing of late—and today was no exception—often dwelt on the retribution he intended to exact from a certain pseudo-Colonel Zveguintzev and Countess Radachek when they were apprehended. His patrols were out, and had been since the morning he'd awakened to discover his paramour gone. It was possible the pair had escaped on one of the numerous ships embarking for Europe, but then again . . . perhaps they hadn't. In any case, he intended to find them eventually. Escape to Europe would merely cause a delay in picking up their trail on the continent. The general was determined. *No one* had ever bested General Dmitri Beriozov and lived to tell the tale—and the ersatz Colonel Zveguintzev and devastatingly tantalizing Countess Radachek were not about to become the first. He was a patient man. It was simply a matter of time. The only fretful grievance in his rather persistent musing was the possibility that disease, starvation, or the subzero temperatures might have cheated him of the pleasure of personally killing the colonel and countess.

Memories of Kitty absorbed him. He thought of her often—too often for his own peace of mind. It wasn't just her beauty. She was more than beautiful. Beautiful women he could find anywhere. She carried about her a purity . . . there was no other word for it. Like some *jeune fille*, she had an enduring innocence, the fresh bloom of early summer roses. Perhaps it was her enormous misty green eyes, heavily lashed, framed by downy eyebrows, ragged like an urchin's. No one else had soft, drowsy eyes like that. Her straight nose, that opulent lower lip, the small, fragile curve of jaw and throat— all youth, all tender, sinless delicacy. The long golden hair falling in sinuous arabesques, even that was uncommonly chaste, like honey from hybrid white lilacs, pale, only lightly kissed by the glitter of the sun.

Each time he looked at her he had wanted her, a virginal child-woman—and she had been his. He knew the innocence had been only a physical illusion; her mind was that of a very competent young woman, and her tongue occasionally indistinguishable from that of a hardened shrew, but he wanted that physical presence, the virginal innocence, because it fired his blood like no woman before or since.

When he found her again, maybe he *wouldn't* kill her. In

the back of his mind he knew very well he wouldn't. But this time he'd bind her tighter. Make the cage stronger. This time his pale golden nymph would stay.

That evening followed a pattern that had become routine at the Black Sea villa. Several women were brought in after dinner and the general selected one or two, always mentally measuring them against Kitty—always disappointed in the results, but always making a selection nonetheless. His physical needs required attention on a daily basis, and even the countess's absence didn't transform a carnal man into a monk.

Tonight he felt like two. The rest were dismissed and the general and his companions retired to the large bedroom occupying the west wing of the seaside mansion.

To ride cross-country from Dargo to Sochi was a life-threatening feat now that the Reds were in control; to make it less risky, Apollo and his small party traveled by night, intent on avoiding large bodies of cavalry or troops. The hand-picked men rode with silence and speed, pounding northwest almost too fast for caution in their race against discovery. Twice they were spotted by patrols. The first they prudently outdistanced, since they were badly outnumbered, but they slaughtered the second. The odds were only two to one—by mountain standards, easily manageable. The fewer reports of a troop of mountain men traveling north, the better.

They entered Sochi late one night in a thick fog. By twos and threes they found accommodations for themselves, after agreeing to meet west of town the following day. The information needed was that of the location of the general's home and, if possible, some idea of the number of soldiers guarding it.

Karaim, Sahin, and Apollo arrived early at the arranged rendezvous in order to reconnoiter potential access to the beach fronting the villa requisitioned by the general. His life-style made his whereabouts common gossip in Sochi; even in an era of unprecedented license, General Beriozov's proclivities for amusement tended toward excess.

The three men were six versts northwest of the general's

retreat and had scoured the surrounding shoreline thoroughly. The land abutting the sea near Sochi was picturesque and delightful to the eye. High, jagged limestone bluffs rose majestically from the crashing sea, bordering pale beaches narrowing almost out of existence in some areas, then broadening to smooth silky ribbons rimming an ultramarine expanse of water. The general's villa was situated above a superb length of chalk-white beach extending over a mile in both directions.

Unfortunately—and the reason reconnoitering was necessary—entry to the beach was restricted to narrow stairways cut into the white limestone cliffs. The possibility of descending to the beach on horseback was, to the ordinary way of thinking, out of the question. Since it *was* considered impossible, the beach offered the only unguarded approach to the general's home. In selecting his vacation hideaway, General Beriozov had given its limited accessibility high marks.

Under a measureless sky, blue upon blue, Apollo and Karaim were standing knee deep in wild anemones on the crest of a sunlit seaside bluff, its limestone shag dipping away precipitously to a narrow strip of sand sixty feet down, the sea sparkling like tissue below them. Sahin had been sent to the rendezvous point to guide the men back to this bluff.

Apollo's tanned face was creased into a pleased smile, his tawny eyes were narrowed against the afternoon glare. A light sea breeze lifted wisps of his pale hair, streaked already by the vivid sun. "The impossible only takes a little longer, eh, Karaim?" he murmured complacently, his gaze falling on a meager ravine which flood torrents had littered with debris over the years. It was hardly more than a crevasse, but its broken path led down to the beach below and, dangerous though its vertical descent was, the surefooted mountain-bred horses—accustomed to sliding down rocky, washed-out trails on their haunches—could navigate it if led down carefully one by one. Familiar with sharply pitched inclines, lack of footing, and the general treachery of mountain terrain, none of the mounts would panic.

"And riders from the sea, As-saqr As-saghir," Karaim ironically replied. "Another impossibility, it would seem."

"Let's hope so, since we're outnumbered by his guards. It's the only thing we've got going for us." He turned to Karaim and his smile widened. "But it's enough," he said softly, meeting the pleasure in Karaim's black eyes. He swung around toward the sun. "We'll go in just before nightfall. Enough light to see by, but darkness for our way out."

Karaim nodded his agreement. "What about the servants?"

"Spare them if you can. I don't have any argument with anyone but the general . . . well, him and the Red Army . . . and the Cheka. Hell, you know what I mean. The servants aren't Bolshis; they're only trying to make a living."

"And the females . . . trying to make a living?" Karaim's voice was soft with suggestion. Karaim always had an eye for women, and the general's predilection for new women every night was a curiosity rumored widely in the streets of Sochi.

Apollo laughed lightly. "I don't think there'll be time, Karaim." One eyebrow rose. "Even for you. We'll be riding hard to stay ahead of the telegraph wires."

Simultaneously both thought, *If* we get out. But neither cared to wager money on it. The conversation turned by mutual consent to lighter things.

An hour later Sahin and the men arrived. The number of soldiers guarding the entrance to the villa was discussed; each man had something to add, their various investigations producing a profusion of detail. It was decided the bulk of the troop would swing around the front of the estate to attack the majority of posted guards once the villa was breached. Although General Beriozov was well protected by a full platoon of the Sixth Division, discipline was lax. After two weeks of leisure, any sense of alarm that may have existed had been lulled into complacency. According to Sahin, several of the guards had been boasting in the local taverns of drinking while on duty.

"Let's hope tonight is no exception," Apollo declared. "Drunken guards will be much easier to handle." It was agreed, in the usual unlicensed discussion customary to the mountain men, that they'd start down to the beach in two hours.

The troop rested in the lee of a small rise, obscured to all views except from the sea. The horses browsed, some men lounged in the sweet-smelling grass, others smoked, played dice, gossiped, ground razor edges on their sabers. Apollo napped, falling asleep almost instantly, a skill acquired during the long years of war. His dreams were of Kitty, of a pine-paneled bedroom, and of the heady fragrance of sweet peas.

When the sun was dipping low in the western sky, Karaim shook him awake. "It's time," he said.

Apollo's golden eyes flashed. "At last," he murmured, un-coiling his tall body and standing up. He shook his head once to clear away the cobwebs. Automatically, he pulled out both Mausers and checked the chambers. The pistols slid back into their well-oiled holsters. "Let's go," he said, the gleam of a zealot shining chrome bright from his eyes.

Each man carefully and quietly led his horse down the treacherous descent, and when all were assembled on the coarse, damp sand below, the order to mount up was quietly given. Weapons were checked one last time. Apollo called, "Allah direct our sabers!" And after an answering murmur, reins were laced lightly through dark-fingered hands. Every man was relaxed, ready to do his job. No frenzied excitement, no nerves. In the mountains they had been taught to be afraid of no one.

Before the signal to advance was given, standing in his stirrups, Apollo made a final statement in the soft Dagestani dialect. His voice was low, scarcely raised above a conversational tone.

"The general's mine," he said.

And each man understood what was in his heart.

# 14

They came out of the setting sun in the classic battle maneuver, precious as a jewel, and at first General Beriozov, following custom with a predinner drink on the terrace, thought his eyes were deluded by the radiant iridescence of a gilded, flame-colored sunset.

He blinked once and took another sip from his glass. A bird, no doubt, flying across his line of vision, accented against the glow of the setting sun.

But when he rose from his seat and looked again short seconds later, the dark speck moving along the base of the limestone cliffs miles away was much too low to be a bird.

Then suddenly it disappeared. Apollo and his men vanished behind a curve in the coastline, and the sky's colors, muting gently as they do at sunset, shifted from brilliant saffron flame to a graded intensity shaded with fingers of peony mauve and wisps of carnelian. A trick of the transient light, the general decided, sitting back down.

He lifted the glass to his lips twice more before a wary conscience, with the devil's own record of sins, urged him to rise from his comfortable ease.

*Riders!* The shock waves started in the toes of his finely booted feet.

By this time they were close enough to recognize. No bird or illusion of eyesight, but a score or more of men, riding hard down the ribbon of beach not more than a verst away now, sun glinting off their inlaid weapons, each dressed in black with embossed sword mounts and rifle stocks ornamented with gold niello, twinkling and catching the long rays of the dying sun. No one else affected the brio of gold scabbard and stock except—mountain men!

In the lead was a golden-haired, wide-shouldered, competent-looking warrior who had an easy, adroit way with a horse. Another streak of sunlight glittered off his yellow head. Unusual hair, the general speculated briefly. Most Circassians were black as spades.

What the hell were they doing riding at a charge on the beach west of Sochi? And even as he asked the question he knew the answer. For a fleeting instant he wondered how they had gotten down to the beach on horseback—an unthinkable feat—but the passing concern was quickly inundated by more pressing matters of survival; for he knew, as he watched for one second more, that the beauty of men and beasts galloping along the wet sands concealed in its grace a savage and imminent death.

Dropping his glass, the general ran for the house. Bellowing orders, he sped along the terrace to the bedroom where his side arms had been left carelessly on the desk. Two weeks of idleness had softened his reflexes; the end of the war had lulled him into a false sense of security.

Apollo had glimpsed the figure on the terrace, had seen it disappear. He dug his heels into Leda and she surged forward.

They took the steep grassy incline at a full charge, urging their horses up the sheer slope toward the villa at its crest, sabers unsheathed, guns at the ready, screaming war cries to Allah. The horses dug in, scrambling furiously upward, mounts and riders intent on reaching the top with all speed. Apollo and Karaim, neck and neck, were first over the terrace balustrade, surging into three soldiers attempting to carry a machine gun to the parapet. Four Mausers belched fire and the three-man crew lay dead on the marble pavement.

In seconds the terrace was a melee, Apollo's riders soaring over the terrace railing and descending like moths. A squad of running soldiers was dispatched at the turn of the first corner, and several riders careened around the east side of the mansion, intent on silencing the guards protecting the entrance to the estate.

Their work was neat and unspectacular, involving close-quarter saber and *kinjal* work and rapidly fired pistols. Their mounts were trained to an inch, curvetting, wheeling, lunging forward at the merest touch of the knees, precision appendages to the killing, slashing blades of their riders. There were fewer and fewer live Red soldiers and finally, in a startlingly short time, none at all.

At a word from Apollo, Sahin went off to cut the telephone wires to the estate. Apollo and Karaim dismounted and with several men cautiously began to search the interior of the quiet villa. The general wasn't among the dead. He must be inside.

Swiftly the rooms were explored. Guns were carefully poised at trigger action, eyes and ears were attuned and alert. The upper floors were empty. They found him eventually, barricaded in the wine cellar cut deep into the limestone cliff: General Beriozov, four soldiers, and a machine gun.

If this was his day to die, General Beriozov reflected in the security of his basement stronghold, he intended to take a good share of his enemies with him—although he had no idea who these particular enemies were.

By the time the general's lair was discovered, time was becoming a factor. Someone could drive up at any moment and give alarm; or possibly a telephone call had gone through to Sochi before the wires had been cut. Any number of unknown problems could arise before the general could be dislodged from the wine cellar.

This wasn't the moment for finesse. Time wouldn't allow for subtlety. "Shoot the bloody door down," Apollo commanded.

A machine-gun fusillade answered their rifle shots and they all dove for the floor, bullets splintering through the wine cellar door, screaming and ricocheting off the stone walls.

"Sonofabitch," Apollo swore softly, breathing in the musty smell of the stone floor. *That* was too damn close for comfort. *This* was not the place he cared to die, not after surviving four years of war, and particularly not now, when a woman he loved waited for him. "Get some grenades," he grunted, and one of the men scrambled up the stairs.

Upon his return, Apollo shouted into the stillness of the basement, "I only want Beriozov. If anyone wants to leave before I toss in this grenade, come out with your hands up." Dust from the spraying bullets settled lightly in the dimly lit room, dancing mutely from the vibrations of sound.

A rapid exchange of undecipherable conversation was followed by a scuffle of footsteps. A single shot rang out and a shriek of pain filled the air. Then silence for the count of ten before General Beriozov called out, "Who are you?"

"A friend of Countess Radachek."

The general immediately recognized Apollo's voice. "Ah," he exclaimed across the quiet, "the erstwhile Colonel Zveguintzev."

"Kuzan's the name."

"Katherine, it seems"—the intimate use of Kitty's name drove a stab of jealousy through Apollo—"has found a richer protector." The Kuzan name had been a byword for fabulous wealth and profligate luxury over a thousand years. "Even though the mines and munitions plants are gone now, I understand the family's fortune is quite safe in Europe. Send her my congratulations."

The general's remarks bitingly lashed into Apollo's mind, for self-torment of that exact nature had tortured him since Stavropol and all Kitty's remonstrances hadn't completely obliterated his corrosive unease concerning her choice. Had she only left the general because Apollo had offered a better future? A future for the child she knew she was carrying?

While the general deliberately provoked Apollo with his cold logic, underlying his premeditated nettling was a wrenching, gut-felt hatred that had been nourished and sustained for a lifetime, a hatred of the old imperial aristocracy so strong and deep and rooted in his early life that he had never escaped it, no matter how far he had traveled from the poverty of his childhood. "So then, Prince Kuzan, how is the countess?"

"None of your business," Apollo growled, his voice gray and flat.

There wasn't a chance in hell of getting out of here alive,

the general thought, unless the telephone call to Sochi he'd
ordered had gotten through. If it had, any delay would be
helpful, and if it hadn't, he wanted to take the countess's
protector with him. With these alternatives in mind he gently
goaded Apollo. "What of the countess's pregnancy?" he inquired, silkily sarcastic. "Is that none of my business, as well?"

Apollo stiffened, the words lacerating his fragile weakness.
"Damn right," he snarled, but a chill ran through him at the
query, and the fractional pause before he answered told the
general his barb had struck home. Beriozov went on to savage
the wound.

"On the contrary, Kuzan, I'm a *very* interested party." The
general had discovered shortly after capturing Kitty that she
was *enceinte*. Her monthly cycle had never disrupted his am-
orous activities, and while he had taken mental note of the
circumstance he had never questioned Kitty on the matter. It
was none of his concern whose brat she was having as long as
it didn't interfere with his pleasure. The fact that he knew of
the pregnancy, however, would perhaps be of great concern
to the prince. A prospective father, as well as a lover? If so,
another weapon at his command, Beriozov speculated briefly.
Lovers and expectant fathers were notoriously possessive
and . . . defensive.

"You lying bastard!" Apollo roared, jumping to his feet,
pistols in both hands, hate fuming from all the poisoned corridors of his mind.

The general's cool voice went on. "Why do you think I put
a chastity belt on her? To be sure that if she had·a child, it
would be mine. You can't trust women, any fool knows that.
You're a case in point. Look what happened. She took up with
the first man who came along. If that isn't proof of her fick-
leness I don't know what is. You'd better keep her chained to
the bed, Kuzan, if you want her for yourself."

"That won't be necessary," Apollo snapped, already tensing
to move.

"Good luck, then; you'll need it. By this time next year,
she'll be in someone else's bed."

The thought was insupportable and intended to be. Apollo,

never sensible about Kitty, had moved two full steps toward
the wine cellar before Karaim, deciding Apollo had put his
life in jeopardy too many times already over that woman,
heaved the grenade through the splintered door, pulling
Apollo down an instant later.

When the grenade exploded, Karaim and Apollo were
jammed against the four-foot-thick outside wall, and even
then the vibrations jarred their bodies like the kick of a horse.
Smoke billowed out of the wine cellar; the door, already
smashed by machine-gun fire, was completely gone now.

"Dammit, I wanted him myself, Karaim," Apollo hissed
angrily, resentful of the missed opportunity to personally kill
Beriozov.

"There's no time. We've got to get out of here," Karaim
replied, ever sensible, but he didn't explain his real reason.
Apollo's blood lust was too high and insensate where Kitty
was involved. Iskender-Khan was right, and everyone but
Apollo understood. One Bolshevik general, however many
times he had bedded the Young Falcon's woman, was still not
worth Apollo's own life. "Let's go. Troops could be on their
way out here from Sochi right now. The pig is dead."

And as if in answer, from the depths of Hades itself, Beriozov's harsh, grating rasp came out of the demolished wine
cellar.

"Come and get me, Kuzan."

Apollo, rising slowly, fingering the black Mausers at his
hips, smiled at Karaim. "You heard? He's still alive," he said,
as gently as a blade through butter.

Beriozov was dying, but his strong body, the stubborn body
of an ox that had survived so much since the early days in
Siberia, was not drained of life as easily as ordinary men. His
companions in the wine cellar were all dead. One had been
shot with a chill anger when the bastard had tried to leave;
the others were blown to bits by the grenade. The general,
partially protected by a large cistern, hadn't felt the full impact of the explosion, but he wouldn't live much longer and
he knew it. Both legs were useless, his left arm hung in tatters
of flesh and bone, his chest was peppered with shrapnel, and

blood seeped from hundreds of puncture wounds. Dragging himself across the floor with his right arm, he propped himself up against the wall facing the shattered doorway and leveled his handgun at the entrance.

"Leave him, Apollo. He's all but dead," Karaim advised quietly. "We've still five days of hostile country to ride through. Let's not waste any more time here."

But Karaim would never know if his advice had reached Apollo or not, because the general's voice then hissed, "Katherine's child is mine. Remember that every time you look at it."

There was a cold, lethal growl of rage and Apollo launched himself with terrifying suddenness toward the doorway. He had been trained to perfection to be a warrior in sinew, muscle, and brain, and he moved in that cool, dim basement with the instinctive coordination of a hunting panther. He lunged, rolled, fired, and behind the chill, almost inhuman gleam in his golden eyes there was not an instant's doubt his bullets would reach their destination.

He hurtled through the opening, rolling through to the left, his blazing guns flashing fire in the small chamber, his body a blur of black and gold, too elusive a target for Beriozov. And while the general emptied his automatic in a staccato pattern of death, it was Apollo's revolver that found its mark.

The murderer of thousands, ravager of hundreds, the ruthless commander of the Sixth Division's iron-fist shock troops, slumped in death.

Apollo gracefully unrolled himself from the debris. He stood broad and powerful within the frame of smashed wood and crumbled masonry, smoking pistols hanging in both hands, a primitive figure of dreadful vengeance. Standing still, scarcely breathing, all his mind and all his passion flowed into the long, searching glance of unleashed hatred he gave the dead general. Kitty's cruel captivity was avenged. "Now," he said softly, sliding the Mausers into their holsters and flexing his fingers lightly, "now we can leave."

•     •     •

The first two hours out of Sochi passed unchallenged, but by the time the lights of Nalchik were in sight, a flurry of activity at the crossroad—roadblocks being put into place, armored cars screaming out of town—indicated that the general's demise had been discovered. As indeed it had when the local procuress arrived with the evening's selection of girls. Mass hysteria by the ladies of the night had greeted the sight of the bloody remains of the general and his guard. The local Cheka was out at the villa within the hour and instantly telegraph and telephone wires relayed the news across the width and breadth of South Russia.

Very soon, Iskender-Khan heard the news as well, since he paid the spies he had posted in the garrisons bordering his territories very generously; and while he rejoiced at the reports of the general's death, he knew Apollo and his men still faced grave danger. To cross the entire width of South Russia when the alarm had been sounded was a gauntlet of treachery whose successful navigation courage alone couldn't guarantee.

Iskender's men had been held in readiness since Apollo's departure. He understood Apollo's need to accomplish this venture alone, was proud of the boy's bravery, but now with the general dead it would serve no purpose to have his favorite great-grandson lying murdered, the victim of a machine-gun ambush or a superior force of the Red Army.

Riding out himself at the head of his warriors, a position relinquished to younger commanders over a decade ago, Iskender-Khan rode through the narrow pass guarding the valley of Dargo and down from his mountain fortress to see that the odds against his beloved great-grandson were slightly evened. Iskender-Khan with six hundred riders galloped west.

Near each garrison town, one of his men would ride in to receive the current telegraph reports from his paid informers, while the small army remained concealed on the outskirts. Military messages followed Apollo's route north and east from Sochi. His troop had evaded the roadblock at Nalchik. A Red patrol outside Muri had died when they'd stumbled on the forward scouts of Apollo's band and attempted to outrace

them back to the garrison. The twenty mountain men had
been sighted briefly at Dshava, then at Ananur. The last report
put them in the vicinity of Telav and still riding hard for the
mountains.

Iskender shifted his route slightly south by southwest,
steering at a tangent for Apollo's line of escape. He had expected him to cut across the Tush and Dido region, but apparently Apollo was headed for the Bogos Ridge.

No one slept that night; they rode without rest or food,
stopping briefly only to water the horses. The six-hundred-
man army marveled at the stamina sustaining their old patriarch through hour after hour of a pace grueling even to a
man in his prime.

But more than ordinary physical or mental endurance was
fortifying Iskender-Khan through the long hours. His proud
spirit wouldn't rest until Apollo was safely returned to him,
and no Russian army, regardless of affiliation, had ever sub-
jugated either his spirit or his nation. Invading armies had
from time to time made their point, but never permanently.
He still ruled his people as he had for four score years, protecting them against any foe whether tsarist, red, or white.
The clans in his mountain nation had existed before there was
a Russia and they would continue to exist despite successive
political changes in Leningrad or Moscow.

At Kvarshi, near midnight, bad news met them. The garrison at Shanada had trapped a troop of mountain men just
before sunset.

Grim-faced, Iskender-Khan received the information. A
savage light shone briefly in his eyes. In high dudgeon, he
raised his right arm and brought his *nagaika* precisely across
the heaving rump of his horse.

The six hundred men and their indomitable leader raced
south. If Apollo is lost, Iskender thought vengefully, I'll light
fire to this country from Yalta to Baku.

They came on the site of Apollo's troop an hour after dawn.
The small band was trapped in a deep ravine several hundred
yards off the main road to Shanada. Although Apollo had
avoided roads wherever possible, the straight three-mile

stretch blasted through the mountains had been chanced to save themselves a day and a half of mountain trails. By this time their horses were hopelessly tired, nearing exhaustion.

The roadblock had appeared suddenly, looming ahead of them as they'd careened around a sharp curve in the road. Apollo, in the lead, had veered, hesitated at the sight of massed men and artillery, and then, altering course grimly, plunged into the ravine paralleling the road in hopes of circumventing the waiting ambush. Too late, he'd discovered what the local Red officer had already known: the ravine ended in a cul de sac.

Apollo and his men, at a desperate disadvantage in numbers, had been trapped, pinned down since dawn by rifle fire from every side.

With a wave of his hand Iskender deployed his men. Twin flanks of black-coated mountain warriors swung out in a wide arc a quarter mile long, three waves deep, and beautifully drawn up in serried ranks. When Iskender signaled the attack they advanced stirrup to stirrup in parade-ground style, the vibrating ground and trembling hum of the earth the first intimation of attack. Turning around, the Bolsheviks' blood froze in their veins. A now screaming wave of mountain men in a solid body were sweeping down on them, spreading fanwise, their formation bulging forward in the middle, falling back on the flanks. Three deep and seemingly endlessly wide, they encircled the Bolshevik position with a black-coated wall of approaching horseflesh and shattering rifle shot. The Red troops, having no wish to argue with an army of mountain men, immediately put to flight in a tangled rush toward Shanada.

None of them reached it. The charging men with high, wailing cries, gleaming teeth, and black eyes came in firing at a gallop and Red soldiers fell before they had run ten steps. In an instant the scene was a foot soldier's nightmare; cavalry pursuing infantry, a rhythm of flashing forearms, the clash of steel, laboring bodies and horseflesh, the Reds all dying at farther or lesser range by bullet, saber, or *kinjal*. The mountain men were invincible, battling savagely through the ranks of the Red soldiers like a flame through wax. They devastated them, broke them, and within a half hour it was over.

Apollo heard the battle cry of Iskender's army, and when his adversaries turned from their target practice in the ravine to defend themselves, Apollo and his troop mounted and rode out of the cul de sac to lend their support to the battle.

Iskender and Apollo met at the ruins of the roadblock when it was over. Apollo galloped up and about a dozen feet from Iskender reined in, Leda fairly sitting down on her hocks. He saluted—not the flashy, sharp, military salute, but a calm, courteous gesture, a manner learned from childhood.

Iskender acknowledged the salute and then embraced his great-grandson. "The *gourai* dogs had you badly outnumbered."

"My thanks, Pushka, for a timely rescue. In saving miles we damn near died. But the horses . . ." He shrugged then and stopped. It had been a calculated risk; they had almost lost.

"A marvel you made it this far, As-saqr As-saghir," Iskender observed, pride shining in his eyes. "The whole of South Russia is up in arms and out to stop you."

Apollo smiled then, absolved from what some may have considered foolhardy recklessness. "And you thought you'd even the odds," he said, his glance taking in the hundreds of massed warriors converging on the roadblock.

Iskender smiled thinly. "It's all I could muster on such short notice. The farther reaches of the nation were unable to arrive in time. A sufficient number, however, against such as these," he observed tranquilly. In the same moderate tone, oblivious to the hundreds of dead soldiers littering the landscape, he continued, "So for home now, and a peaceful future."

"For home," Apollo agreed softly, and the two tall, proud-visaged men, one so old and one so young, yet compatriots in spirit and purpose, left the treachery and perfidy of civilization and turned their horses toward the mountains.

Iskender asked no probing questions of Apollo. All he cared to know would be available from Karaim or Sahin if he was so inclined. The details didn't matter to him. In the ninth decade of his life he found that details mattered less and less to him. What mattered more, he had discovered, was a certain serenity concerning the purpose and fulfillment of one's life. And how one approached that goal—or attained it—mattered infinitely less than the personal satisfaction of achieving it. So if Apollo was satisfied with his choices in life, whether won or lost (and in the case of the White cause, the outcome, of course, had been unsuccessful), Iskender hoped they brought a moderate amount of happiness to the youth who was as dear as life to him.

He did ask Apollo a question on the following day when they parted at the base of the citadel, as Apollo was about to strike out across the valley for his own home. "Did the general's death serve its purpose?"

"It did," Apollo replied shortly.

"Are all your doubts put to rest?"

"Yes," Apollo said, but Iskender saw the flash of anger flare momentarily in his great-grandson's pale eyes, and he was sorry he had asked.

Apollo rode toward his home, home to the woman he loved, but a weary despair overlay the success of the mission. He had thought that when he killed Beriozov it would be over—the wondering, the frustration, the anger and resentment. But Beriozov was dead now, and those last taunting words echoed endlessly in his mind . . . and the worst of it was that he couldn't kill him over again.

All his life Apollo had lived with the reality of *kanly*, of blood feuds and retribution for wrongs committed. But no one had ever told him that blood vengeance couldn't rectify the original sin or destroy the memory, or, curse it, stop this abominable litany that rasped at him from the pits of Hades itself. Child is mine . . . remember that . . . Katherine's child . . . mine. . . . When it's born . . . remember that . . . remember . . . remember . . .

Kitty, in sea-green tissue silk, came running down the steps when Apollo rode into the courtyard. His heart leaped and all his black temper and misgivings were stilled; the sight of her uncontained joy and magnificent beauty conquered him anew.

She tugged at his leg, his *burkha*, even before he could dismount, smiling up at him with tears in her misty green eyes, love shining openly on her fragile face. "I was so worried—" He looked tired. It was clear in his face.

"I'm fine," he responded, pulling off his gloves.

Kitty noticed with a lurch of concern the ragged gashes across both hands. "You're hurt! Your hands—"

"It's nothing, sweetheart. Only scratches." Apollo swung out of the saddle and she threw herself at him. His arms folded fiercely around her and despair, weariness, dark cynicism were gone. Only the moment mattered. Only holding her close mattered. And having her. The future was theirs. . . . Kitty was his, only his, and nothing else bore thinking of.

"I missed you," Kitty sobbed softly into his chest. "I was afraid . . . alone."

"*Duskha*, don't cry," Apollo soothed gently. "I'm back now. I won't have to go out again."

Kitty looked up at him searchingly. "No more raids?"

"No more raids."

"What about the men?"

"Karaim can lead the next one. So dry your tears."

"Consider it done." Kitty laughed shakily, wiping her eyes with the back of her hand and sniffling softly. Her heart soared with joy. To have Apollo back after almost two weeks of not knowing whether he was alive or dead was like a wish come true, earthly paradise, and the promised land all rolled up into one. He was tall and beautiful, his hair two shades paler, his skin two shades darker after the past days on horseback.

"And how is the baby, *Mamasha*?" Apollo asked, holding her at arm's length and gazing at the now obvious bulge of her tummy. In his pleasure at seeing Kitty again and knowing she loved him, he could ask the question with a solicitude untinged by rancor. After all, he had promised many weeks ago on a cold and snowy hillside that he would be the father of her child. Now he only required the sincerity to uphold his vow.

With Kitty soft and warm in his arms, her vivid eyes alight, her lush honeysuckle lips parted in a smile of elation, upholding his vow was no hardship.

"The baby's fine and I'm fine and I love you," she said, smiling happily, "more than your great-grandfather loves his collection of paleolithic bronzes."

"A formidable encomium." Apollo grinned in return. "I only hope now I won't disappoint such adoration," he said in a roguishly husky voice.

Kitty's hand drifted up the dark silk of his *beshmet*, ran up his throat, and gently traced the curve of his upper lip. "You never have in the past," she replied in that particular breathy, teasing tone he always associated with the very happiest of his memories.

"We try," he murmured softly, lapsing comfortably into the royal pronoun, one eyelid narrowing in a sinfully delicious wink.

Prince Apollo Kuzan, bred to luxury as heir to the vast Kuzan fortune, scion to Iskender-Khan's mountain nation, young, gifted, handsome, felt himself more truly blessed by the single bounteous asset of Kitty's love than by the abundant wealth of all his other fortune.

The baby's paternity no longer signified, liabilities like husbands were effaced, bitter memories of swinish generals disappeared. It was spring in the mountains; he was home after a successful venture. Kitty declared her love in enticingly visual, verbal, and tactile ways, and just as soon as the dirt of the journey was washed away, he'd show her the fullness of his adoration. "I think we've given the servants enough to talk about. Shall we go inside? I need food, I need a bath, and I need you—not necessarily in that order." A broad smile creased his sun-bronzed cheek, and taking Kitty by the hand, he started up the entrance stairs. "I think a bath first—unless, of course," he teased, his golden eyes alight, "the smell of the stables excites you. There are women with such fetishes. . . ." His voice trailed off suggestively.

Kitty laughed in her quick, breathtaking way. "After sleep-

ing alone for two weeks," she replied with a lighthearted imp-
ishness, "I don't need a fetish to accept you any way at all."

Apollo raised one dark brow. "So it's only because you dislike sleeping alone. Will any man do?" Although he was still
teasing, the smallest sensitivity stirred deep inside.

"Any man," Kitty retorted playfully "as long as he's tall,
golden-eyed, and has wild, longish hair like a lion's mane.
*That* sort of man *desperately* attracts me."

"Desperately?" Apollo asked wolfishly. They had entered
the large foyer, decorated with Persian porcelains and carpets,
and were heading for the divided staircase leading to the living quarters.

"Absolutely desperately," Kitty whispered softly. She wondered briefly at the abandon this lovely man provoked in the
heart and soul and mind of a genteelly nurtured, reserved
young woman who had never, even in marriage, felt this way.
She had given up her latent modesty and soul's silence for
him, had given up her marriage vows and husband for him,
would willingly follow him to the ends of the earth—and the
staggering magnitude of her intemperance awed her. She had
always seen herself in practical terms, her soul nourished on
the food of reality, not a stardust; her spirit far removed from
exotic dreams of peacock gardens and romance as extravagant
as pigeon's-blood rubies. Yet Apollo had entered her life and
in three days had dashed away, without effort or intention,
her entire former existence. He had also, with tenderness, joyous spirit, and passion, made her happier than she had ever
imagined possible.

She loved him with the blithe, fragile innocence of childhood, she loved with the full-blooded ardor of womanhood,
she loved with the balmy indiscretion of a mistress and the
dissolute candor of a whore; she loved him poignantly with
the inexplicable love of a woman for the man whose child she
bears.

And he was home safe. It was all she asked.

A trail of clothes led from the bedroom door to the bed,
and the order of events was adjusted to meet the more demanding concerns of passion.

# 15

An idyllic spring and summer passed. The two young, golden-haired lovers adored each other deeply, amorously, pervasively, and the revolution-torn, chaotic outside world disappeared for them.

Occasionally, as in any Eden, brief moments of strife would appear, but reconciliation was always swift and enchantingly satisfying.

The blatantly secondary role assigned women in the tribal culture took a certain amount of getting used to. The life of a warrior contributed mightily to the concept, for men only fought or played, they did nothing else, which left all the obligatory tasks of daily living to the female population. Those prosaic duties didn't affect Kitty, since Apollo's palace staff was self-sufficient, but she took umbrage at the work burden that befell the women of the aul. The fact that the Moslem religion was nominally supported further weakened the position of females, and Kitty—having acquired a certain independence and self-reliance after years of managing Aladino—was appalled at the submissive attitude of the village women.

Apollo, raised in Dargo, was sympathetic in theory to Kitty's accusations of blatant inequality—after all, his mother was one of the more unconventional females he knew—but nevertheless he inherently possessed that pervasive air of masculine authority and certainty particular to the mountain warrior.[13]

Needless to say, such diametrically incompatible stances did create an occasional *contretemps*, but Apollo, with the in-

209

dulgent good humor of a man head over heels in love, was generally acquiescent and obliging to Kitty.

One afternoon, while basking in the sun in adjoining wicker chaises on the newly constructed terrace, the subject of women's roles came up again. Apollo courteously evaded making any overt judgments that might rankle. He was, in any event, pleasantly content and gratified. He and Kitty had just spent an enticing two hours in bed and sensual indulgence always left him amiable.

"Apollo," Kitty said, her gold hair hot on her shoulders, "when we get to France, I'd like to go back to school."

"Sounds fine," Apollo murmured agreeably, his eyes only slits against the brilliant light. He was fully aware that modern women acquired university educations. The last twenty years had seen much progress in that field. His mother, in fact, was a well-known historian, and Apollo's family had always encouraged formal education. A variety of tutors had been trekked up to the mountain retreat in his childhood and, as was the custom in the Kuzan family, he had matriculated at the Sorbonne, spending time in the study of economics. "Any special subject?" he asked cordially, enjoying the sound of Kitty's voice, inclined to consider himself the luckiest of men to have her beside him, and thinking speculatively that the study of literature or painting, or perhaps philosophy, would be a pleasant diversion for Kitty once they settled in France. After all, those unfailingly dull bridge or tea parties women were obliged to spend so much time at must be boring as hell.

"Farming," Kitty declared.

"Good God!" Apollo sat upright and looked disbelievingly at his plumply pregnant sweetheart lying next to him, her skin flushed and speckled with the sun. "Are you serious?" Apollo was more than willing to indulge his Kitty in any of her wishes, but *farming*? His own cherished notions about the qualities appropriate to the female sex tended to follow the traditional concepts of beauty, availability, grace, elegance, charm. Not that an educated wife wasn't an agreeable com-

panion, but . . . farming? Somehow farming seemed so . . .
masculine.

Kitty stared squarely back at him and inquired sweetly, *too*
sweetly, "What's wrong with farming?" She was definitely
glaring now, he decided, and when Apollo saw the flinty look
appear in those wide green eyes, he graciously reconciled himself to a wife on a tractor. "Farming sounds delightful," he
said with a crooked grin.

In a flash the basilisk look changed to a twinkle and Kitty
laughed happily, enchanted with Apollo's spontaneous about-
face. He pampered her outrageously, and after Peotr's indifference she adored Apollo's casual, unrestrained kindness.
Responding to the laughing irony in his crooked smile, Kitty
teasingly went on in mild, dulcet tones, "After all, *someone* has
to make some money while you're out spending your time on
the polo fields."

Apollo, his voice redolent with agreeableness, the droll
light of mockery shining from between his narrowed lids,
replied, "How nice. My fortune will then be intact to squan-
der on my lady friends." He ducked just in time to avoid a
morocco-bound copy of Colette's newest novel and, laughing,
bounded out of range of the next hurled volume.

In those summer days Apollo took delight in showing Kitty
the beauties of his mountain valley. They picnicked in lush
green glades that were carpeted in mountain gentian, snow-
drops, enormous tiger lilies. Apollo fished the cool, clear
streams while Kitty lazed on the grassy banks. She was awed
by glorious rose-and-coral sunsets, flaming like Renaissance
embroidery, as they viewed them from rocky ledges rising
high above the valley floor. And they loved each other amidst
the splendor of a mountain summer like two passionate adolescents allowed their first freedom, intent on exploring every
nuance and magnificent subtlety of their love. They both became golden children of the sun; Apollo deeply tanned, his
hair pale white by summer's zenith; Kitty's skin a fairer glowing peach bronze, her lemon-bright hair less inclined to bleach
to the creamy ice of Apollo's ruffled curls.

• • •

Despite the charming idleness of his summer devoted to
Kitty, Apollo was still the leader of the coterie of young, hot-
blooded warriors in camp, and he would infrequently of an
evening join them in their fellowship. *Aracq* and Khahetian
wine flowed, and talk would always turn to the next raid.

Apollo had remained behind on the last two, and while
rationally he accepted his temporary constraint, the reminiscing always brought forth a quickening of desire to mount up
and make mischief for the new Bolshevik government on the
plains below. He gracefully accepted the inevitable teasing
that ensued each time he declined a raid—in the warriors'
eyes, a woman's wishes were no reason at all to stay behind—
but he found it much more difficult to ignore the drunken
comments that had occurred alluding to Kitty's sojourn with
the general. On the two occasions when too much heated *aracq*
had inadvertently brought forth mention of the general and
Kitty, the faux pas had been immediately silenced by an
abrupt change of subject.

But one night in August, an intemperate young buck railed
at the number of women in the perimeter mountain auls bordering their nation who had been abused by Red swine, and
immediately Apollo felt himself the focus of a score of eyes.

Absolute silence descended on the room. Apollo was a
chancy bastard to cross. "I think," Apollo said, putting fifty
generations of ice into his voice, "that the subject has been
exhausted." He fixed the group with the kind of look linked
with murderous duels. There was a pause, which prolonged
itself to uncomfortable lengths. Then, unexpectedly, he
laughed. "Oh, hell." His lips twitched into a grin. "Since
when haven't women meant trouble? Pass me the damn wine
jug."

Everyone's face broke into a relieved smile and four bottles
of Khahetian wine appeared simultaneously.

That evening he was perhaps more sensitive because of the
amount of liquor he had consumed, or perhaps the approach
of Kitty's confinement brought the old distracting thoughts

into prominence once again. Whatever the reasons, Apollo rode home in a foul temper, black, angry memories of Kitty and the general sharing center stage with a very inebriated sense of affront.

Kitty should have recognized from his careful walk and gentle dishevelment that Apollo was no longer quite sober when he strolled into the sitting room. She should have noted by the dark scowl and grimly pursed lips that all was not well. But she had been absorbed in a fictionalized account of Lord Monmouth's life, and while her glance took in Apollo's surly expression, her mind was still partially occupied by the seventeenth-century tale. "How was your evening?" she asked, flipping through the remainder of the book, gauging the number of pages left to read.

"It could have been better," Apollo said in a sullen drawl, walking over to the fireplace and kicking in a loose log. Night temperatures in the mountains could be surprisingly cool even in the summer.

Kitty glanced up from the small task of marking her page in the story and for the first time noticed Apollo's brooding, dark look. Sliding her slippered feet over the side of the gray satin sofa, she sat upright and solicitously inquired, "What happened?"

"Same old thing," Apollo snapped, laying both rigid fists on the mantel. "Some impetuous young buck had too much to drink and didn't catch himself in time. He alluded to my 'dishonored paramour.' God Almighty," he said with sudden exasperation, "I can't very well kill everyone who *thinks* that."

Dishonored? Paramour? Kitty reacted angrily to the first word, feeling she had had no recourse to the general's attentions save suicide. The word *paramour*, on the other hand, caused a bit of unease, because no matter how one glossed over their situation, that's exactly what she was. And the worst of it was . . . she was Apollo's paramour by choice. Anger prevailed over the less violent emotion of unease. "What do you mean, dishonored?" she asked heatedly, her eyes almost black in her white face. "It's *your* child, after all."

"So you say," Apollo returned with heavy sarcasm, the liquor speaking at the moment. His head between his arms, he continued to look at the fire.

Kitty sat up stiff-backed, both palms flat on her lap. "What does *that* mean?"

"It only means," he drawled, taut with temper, "I should be allowed my mild skepticism. Good God," he said, straightening and turning, "I spent only three days with you in my entire life prior to March. How can you be so sure?"

"Because I was never with any other man," she protested, her small chin tipped up belligerently.

A little malicious smile crossed Apollo's face. "Don't forget the general," he said rudely.

Under the surveillance of his mocking and rather malicious gaze, Kitty tossed back hotly, "That was later."

"Later?"

"*After* I discovered I was pregnant."

"So you say," he repeated with exaggerated courtesy. "Can you prove it?"

"No! No, I can't prove it." Startlingly, she flushed.

Apollo's skeptical gaze lingered on that blush; an unnerving, cynical scrutiny, its anger barely concealed. "And yet you expect me to believe implicitly in your curious exclusivity when it comes to my fatherhood. Hell, as far as I know, anyone could be the father—certainly the general has more than a minor claim."

Flashing eye met flashing eye.

"*Damn you,*" Kitty cried. "Why should I lie?"

"Why indeed," Apollo said with silver-tongued sweetness, his flared nostrils indicative of the temper he chose not to unleash. "You'd be a fool if you didn't. You must admit, the general and I aren't on a par—"

"Sometimes," Kitty retorted tartly, momentarily exasperated with the entire arrogant masculine world, "I can't see much difference!"

"Consider, love, that there are minor differences at least," Apollo murmured dryly. "After all, I've had the decency to keep my whips for my horses." It was clear Apollo was out for trouble.

Kitty rose, so she wouldn't be at such a disadvantage, and her voice, diamond hard, took up the challenge. "Granted, you're from a much more *refined* culture. No whipping women. Your bodyguards will simply kill me when I begin to bore you." She continued with contempt, "It's so *much* more civilized when one is armed with such well-defined codes of conduct!" Kitty's eyes were glinting with outrage and her voice rose. "Maybe I should have stayed with the general," she continued recklessly. "At least there I wasn't completely *certain* I'd be killed once my usefulness was over. *Maybe* I should go back to him," she finished with a deliberate nonchalance, her stormy eyes wide and bitter.

Apollo appeared undisturbed by the threat. His golden eyes narrowing, he said in a mocking, deep voice, "You'd never get out of the palace, let alone the valley, without my permission."

"Why, you arrogant, overbearing beast!" Kitty cried, her cheeks reddening. "Do you mean to tell me you keep me here against my will?"

Apollo's pale eyes studied her impassively. Gazing down at her from his great height, he mildly replied, "I could put a leather collar on you and chain you to my bed and no one within a hundred versts would raise an eyebrow."

"You—you—primitive *savage*," she choked out, infuriated at the casualness with which he assumed his seignorial rights. "I suppose you make a practice of chaining up women, you damned feudal lord!"

He looked astonished for a moment. Did she think he needed coercive measures in dealing with a female? "I've never had to before," he said somewhat stiffly, "but your, ah, provocation imbues the notion with a decided charm." His smile was not pleasant.

"Don't you dare threaten me!" Kitty shouted, her temper flaring.

"Don't *you* challenge me," he warned in an overquiet tone. "You'll lose."

"Go to hell, *noble* and *supreme* Prince," she countered in rage. "Don't forget *I'm* a princess born and, although rarely tempted, know how to snap my fingers as well as you. Chains or no chains, if I feel like leaving, I will!"

A cruel smile curled Apollo's lips. "As far as going back to the general is concerned, I'm afraid that's impossible."

"Impossible?" she asked crossly, her breathing still rapid. "How smug. How can you be sure he wouldn't take me back?"

In the ensuing silence, Apollo's eyes were icy with malice. "Because," he said in a voice as soft as silk, "I killed him."

An appalling stillness hung between them. All the primitive blood lust, all the savage mountain ethos was contained in that simple statement. All the differences that separated their upbringing and views reverberated like violently struck timpani across the small distance.

Kitty was reminded afresh of the incomprehensible warrior's code of chivalry that guided Apollo's thinking, of the thin line—with which she could never feel quite comfortable—between justice and murder, and suddenly she felt entirely alien, alone, and insecure. Apollo was her anchor, her entire life, and in the flash of a moment he'd taken on the appearance of a stranger; a cold-blooded, impenitent killer. A ghastly sense of bewilderment and vulnerability closed over her, and Apollo saw it.

Kitty's dark, unhappy eyes lifted slowly to his searching gaze and she whispered almost inaudibly, "I don't really know you, do I?"

Her pained expression struck him forcibly and he was instantly contrite. Jesus, what a brute he was to bait and harass Kitty. Damn his temper, and damn his black cynicism, and damn the old unwinnable argument. Why take out his misgivings on Kitty? What good did it do? The child within her had grown large by now, and all the misgivings in the world wouldn't alter that fact. To continue to torment her for his own evil mood was grossly unkind, and now that his temper had peaked, he was more then ready to make amends.

Running a hand through his hair, he smiled at her gently and said in a different tone, "You know me better than anyone. Forgive me. For my stupid temper, my jealousy, for . . . all my sins." His mouth twisted ruefully. "You do that to me. I can't help it, but I'll try. Forgive me?" He smiled again, his warm, achingly sweet smile. "None of the old arguments matter, *dushka*"—and for a moment his voice lost its steadiness— "only that you're here with me."

"Are you sure?" Kitty asked hesitantly, Apollo's winning smile and apology allaying the momentary blaze of her own resentment. God help her, she loved him—savage chivalrous code, temper, and all. Nothing could change that, and now that the cold implacable fury had faded from his eyes, he resembled again the lover and friend she knew.

"Very sure." He stretched out an arm, touching Kitty's shoulder, his repentant eyes saying even more than the simple words.

Kitty moved the few steps into his embrace. Snuggling against him—or at least as close as she could, considering the baby's predisposition to take his share of space—she queried quietly, "You *do* believe me, don't you, Apollo? About the baby, I mean." She spoke with a quiet dignity that undid him.

He kissed her worried brow. "Of course, my own sweet kitten," he lied smoothly, and only he knew what it cost him to so lightly agree.

In the course of the last weeks, Iskender-Khan had been approached by some Europeans interested in drilling for oil in the vicinity of Dargo. While all of Russia was nominally under Bolshevik control, in practice, the oil companies knew if the local chieftains didn't sanction the operation, no drilling was possible. While Kitty and Apollo seldom dined with Iskender, preferring a quiet evening to themselves, Iskender wished to discuss the subject with Apollo since two of the Rothschild representatives were coming to Dargo the following morning.

Kitty and Apollo went for dinner, an informal affair, primarily family: a few cousins, aunts, and uncles. Since dinner Apollo had been deep in conversation with his great-grandfather. At first Kitty listened politely, Apollo, holding her lightly, one arm around her shoulder, including her in the conversation. But once the business arrangements were concluded, guerilla tactics became the topic of discussion. Kitty quietly excused herself. Apollo, at ease, talking earnestly with Iskender, hardly noticed.

The other female guests were intent on a card game in one corner of the large drawing room, but Kitty at the moment preferred the silence of the starlit summer night to their company. While all Apollo's relatives were pleasant, his young cousin, Tamara, had taken every opportunity to be disagreeable since her arrival. Tonight was no exception. Apollo seemed immune to Tamara's flirtatious cajoling, but this evening at dinner her remarks had been suggestive enough for Iskender to peremptorily silence her with a curt word. Since then, Tamara had sulked in a theatrical way, and to avoid being in her vicinity Kitty chose the outdoors.

Strolling out onto the balcony, Kitty lingered at the railing, the lukewarm summer night frosted with moonlight, all color drained to *grisaille*, gray on pearl on silver. The pungent perfume of climbing roses furled around her. She inhaled the sweet drifting aroma of new-mown hay, viewed with fresh wonder the tapestry of stars spilled like sequins in the limitless blue-black mountain sky.

The loveliness was disturbed suddenly by a throaty, sullen voice at her shoulder. "You're very clever to keep him interested so long, but he'll never marry you."

Reluctant to face the petulant owner of the all too familiar voice, Kitty turned around slowly and found she was being inspected with undisguised animosity. "And that would suit your plans admirably, wouldn't it?" Kitty said with a calmness she was far from feeling. Tamara always seemed able to invoke her most hidden insecurities. It didn't help, either, that the young girl was darkly beautiful, her form slender as a willow branch.

Ignoring Kitty's question, Tamara rudely remarked, "He's brought women up here before. Many times. You're not the first—and you're not the first pregnant one, either. Ask him how many brats he's sired already. Ask him."

Kitty stiffened visibly at the cruel, cutting words. "I'm not interested in Apollo's past." The tone was supposed to be dismissive, but Kitty's voice was strangely unsteady at the end, for in truth, thoughts of Apollo's previous amours always struck her particularly hard. She had chided herself about those jealous suppositions many times already, in the course of the past weeks, when Apollo had been greeted by women friends. It seemed to her that far too many of his female acquaintances in the aul were unusually friendly, although Apollo had never been more than politely civil in response. Stupidly, she had never even considered children. What a fool. Here she was, pregnant with his child—and worse, married to another man. It left the future rather uncertain; and left her prey to a terrible sensitiveness.

In the dim light, Tamara's pouting face shone eerily, framed by the blackness of her hair. "Maybe you're not interested in his past, but you might be interested in what Apollo does with his paramours"—Tamara sneered the word— "when he tires of them."

Kitty, scarlet with embarrassment, was spared the need to reply, for Apollo appeared in the entrance to the balcony. "Kitty," he called, his rangy build outlined in the open doorway, "are you out there?"

"Yes," Kitty quickly replied, overjoyed at the opportunity to terminate the unnerving conversation with Tamara. Perhaps it was cowardly, but she wasn't up to a verbal brawl with her—nor ready to cope with the painful reality of Apollo's previous lovers.

"You won't last," Tamara hissed while Apollo was still out of earshot. "Apollo likes white flesh, but he's been raised in these mountains and he'll never marry a *Giaour*. Never! I mean to have him!" Turning to leave, she tossed over her shoulder, "Ask Apollo what happened to Noenia." Then, flouncing past Apollo's approaching figure, she disappeared into the drawing room.

"My Lord," Apollo said, taking Kitty's hands in his, "you and Tamara in a tête-à-tête. What in the world did you find to talk about?"

"Very little," Kitty said.

"I should think so. Tamara's a child and flighty as a wisp in the wind. She can't have a serious thought in her head."

Far from a child, Kitty thought acerbically, but she simply said, "Oh, she has a few."

"Such as?" Apollo asked skeptically.

"Nothing important," Kitty mumbled, while in fact her mind unlocked doors of disquiet she had carefully guarded all these months.

Rather than pursue the subject, Apollo steered Kitty toward the lighted doorway. "Come and see Karaim's most recent acquisition. You'll love it." Apollo's tone was warmly animated.

Forcibly suspending any further thought of Tamara, Kitty responded to Apollo's affable expression and cheerful words.

"What will I love?" she asked, smiling.

"Two reels of film. One French and one American."

Kitty squealed in delight. The cinema, as Apollo was well aware, was an obsession with her, and for that reason he had added his request to Karaim's list on his last foray out of the village.

"And if you're very good," Apollo teased, "we'll take them home tonight to view."

"Tonight? Really? Doesn't Karaim mind?"

Apollo laughed. "He minds like hell, but I just won the throw of the dice. Tonight they're ours." Looking down at Kitty's jubilant face, his grin widened. Picking her up, he twirled her around. "Do I take care of you or do I take care of you?" he asked laughingly.

"You . . . take . . . care . . . of . . . me . . . very . . . well!" Kitty mirthfully exhaled, winging through the air.

Setting Kitty down, Apollo kissed her lightly on the cheek, then, gazing with a keen-eyed look that traveled slowly from the top of her head to her toes and back again, taking in the fullness of her blossoming pregnancy, one eyebrow shot up and he said with a lazy smile, "It seems I certainly do."

Kitty's lilting laugh floated through the room.

One slim, young girl brooding in a corner viewed this playful repartee with chillingly cold eyes.

In the course of the night, between the cinema and other pleasant activities, Tamara's vindictive words were forgotten. But in the glaring light of day, the disturbing phrases began drifting in and out of Kitty's thoughts. "He'll never marry you. . . . I mean to have him. . . . Ask him what happened to Noenia. . . ."

Apollo, seated on the window seat across the bedroom, was pulling on his boots when Kitty, ensconced in the center of the bed watching him, asked, with studied casualness, "Who's Noenia?"

Stopping in midpull, Apollo tensed for a moment, then resumed his task. Looking up, his face a bland mask, he said, "Who?"

"Noenia."

Rising, Apollo smiled at Kitty and, manlike—wanting to avoid a topic that could prove uncomfortable—replied, "Never heard the name." Walking the two steps to the door, he paused, one hand on the latch. "Hurry and dress now. I'll see you in the breakfast room in twenty minutes. I'm going to check on Leda."

Great, Kitty thought dispiritedly, watching the door close on his tall, lean form. He claims he doesn't know her. Now whom do you believe? Some snippy little hussy like Tamara, or the man you love? She recalled Peotr and all his paramours, considered Apollo and his wartime reputation, thought of the promiscuous habits of reckless young Russian aristocrats who gambled, drank, and made love lightly, expertly, and transiently, always completely charming, completely drunk, and completely irresponsible.

Some snippy little hussy, that's whom she believed. Damn, damn, damn. She fell back in bed and covered her head.

Kitty lay there thinking morosely. He says he'll marry you, but does he mean it? It's easy to say, particularly since you already have a husband. Does he really care, or are you simply another passing fancy? The last thing she needed was that conversation with Tamara last night. As if she weren't already feeling insecure enough—she hadn't been able to see her feet in three weeks.

How the hell had Kitty heard of Noenia? Apollo was uneasily speculating as he descended the stairs three at a time. Damn gossipy women. Someone evidently had mentioned Noenia.

When she'd disappeared Apollo had raised holy hell only because rumor had it Iskender had been to blame, and youthful independence had necessitated immediate affront. A year or two later he'd heard of Noenia again; she was living in Besh-Tau, the mistress of one of the grand dukes. He wished her well. If he had known at the time what Pushka intended, he could have saved Iskender the confrontation with Noenia's fiery temper as well as a tidy sum of money. Apollo had enjoyed the pretty woman's company for an unheard-of five weeks, but he'd had no more intention of marrying her than of marrying any of the other ladies he'd entertained himself with.

Thinking about it, Apollo supposed he could have explained all that to Kitty, but it had happened so long ago . . . best leave it alone. Women were always quick to read romance into past amours. His had been strictly physical. Why confuse the issue?

After breakfast they strolled to the pond in the meadow. Formerly they rode in the morning, but Apollo wouldn't permit Kitty to ride anymore. There'd been some words over that; Kitty had felt well physically and was extremely fond of an exhilarating gallop early in the morning. Apollo had been adamant, however, quoting the local midwife verbatim and very sternly remarking, "I mean to see that you do what you're told."

He was quite a bully with her health, always admonishing her with some snippet of advice from mountain lore, and later that morning while swimming lazily in the pond, Kitty reluctantly admitted to herself that she really couldn't move very rapidly anymore. Their mock tag races under the pear trees had declined recently into a slow-moving choreography with Apollo conceding her victory very early to save her from fatigue. All in all, Kitty mused, floating in the cool spring water, this wasn't a good time to be assailed with acid comments like Tamara's; she was feeling unwieldy, unlovely, and about as graceful as an unpended turtle.

After the swim, dressed again, lying in the sweet-smelling grass beneath heavily laden pear trees, the impulse to know wouldn't desist. Despite Kitty's very determined effort, Tamara's disastrous words were still not dislodged from her consciousness but danced and pirouetted vexingly, faster and faster. "Won't marry you . . . other children . . . ask about Noenia . . . many women . . . you're no different." Kitty counseled herself to silence, cautioning herself not to exaggerate another woman's personal injuries to pride, reminding herself that she had learned in the demanding school of life, over the last three years, not to expect constant felicity. In addition, it hardly ever paid to be sulky and difficult. Also, deep down, she knew Apollo's affection couldn't be faulted.

So she tried to be unruffled and calm about Tamara's disclosures. And she was, for almost ten minutes more. Then abruptly her inner struggle came to an end, defeated by a temperament too long trained to independence. "Tell me about Noenia," she blurted out. "I know you had her up here. I know she exists and you spent time with her." A rising querulousness was startlingly evident by the final word.

There was a racking silence. Apollo looked up slowly from the book he was reading. "Who told you about her?" he quietly asked.

"So you *do* remember her," Kitty said, a little too sharply, her worst fears rapidly coming to fruition. "And your children. You never told me. How many do you have besides the one growing in me?" Her voice had 'risen more than she wished. Taking a breath to calm her racing heart, she said, "If you don't mind, I'd like to know."

Apollo hadn't moved. With a quiet intake of breath he replied, "Not many."

The evasive retort ignited Kitty's warming temper. "*Not many*! God above, how insouciant the male animal can be! What the hell is *not many*?" Every slight to womankind, every difference between the sexes, trembled in the vibrating timbre of her voice.

"It means two."

"And are they here underfoot? Do you see them? Visit their mothers? Am I cramping your style? Why didn't you tell me?" She finished in a wail.

"It didn't seem very pertinent."

"But of course. Children never seem *pertinent* to libertine men!"

Apollo's voice was still gently calm. His eyes reflected a quiet sadness, rather than anger. "The reason it didn't seem pertinent," he explained patiently, "is that my children are in Europe being raised by their mother and her current husband. The lady, you see, when she discovered she was pregnant, wasn't interested in marrying a seventeen-year-old boy. At the time I found it rather heartless. But she was adamant— and her husband, when he returned from Egypt, apparently was amenable. I've only seen the twins four times since they were born."

Immediately Kitty was contrite. "I'm sorry," she said softly.

"I am too," was Apollo's murmured reply.

Kitty was momentarily nonplussed by the flash of melancholy in his pale eyes, but once begun she wanted all her questions answered. She realized Tamara's words had upset her more than she'd known. "You did know Noenia," she softly accused. "Why didn't you say so this morning?" And she wondered how many other lies and evasions she had been subjected to.

"I thought it unimportant. Now who told you?" Apollo insisted softly, setting his book aside. He didn't like to have Kitty upset, particularly over something as senseless as this.

Kitty marveled at the quiet arrogance. Didn't seem important to whom, for God's sake? Here was a man used to doing exactly as he pleased; the world, at least here in the mountains, ordered to his perfection. "Why should it matter who told me?" Kitty said defiantly, struggling to a sitting position. Apollo moved quickly to help her but she brushed his hands aside and repeated, "Tell me what happened to Noenia."

"Tell *me*," he said evenly, "who *told* you about her, and I will."

"Oh, very well," Kitty replied coolly. "It was Tamara."

"The bitch," he muttered. "I might have known."

"What's the difference how I found out?" Kitty observed petulantly. "Evidently your amours are common gossip." Her face mirrored her distaste. "And I'm just another juicy tidbit for the rumor mill."

"Look here, Kitty," Apollo said somewhat ominously, leaning on his elbows and staring directly into her eyes. "Number one, my amours are *not* common gossip; outside of little snits like Tamara, most people mind their own business. Number two, you, my sweet, have not, are not, and never will be a subject of gossip. You're the woman I love and my future wife."

"Why should I believe you? After twins you never told me about, and some mystery woman you denied knowing, not to mention all the doxies you and Peotr entertained from one end of Russia to the other, I don't know what to believe. You probably tell every woman you love her!"

Apollo choked a little at her naiveté. "Listen, Kitty," he said gravely, "if I didn't want you here, you wouldn't be here. It's as simple as that."

She stared at him and frowned. "That's not what Tamara says."

"Now, sweet," Apollo said with mild exasperation, "if Tamara knew me as well as she professes, she'd know I've mastered the art of polite good-byes very well. If I don't want a woman around, she doesn't stay—and I'm embarrassed to admit that most of the women I've known have gone out with the empty brandy bottles in the morning. The few who have lasted slightly longer"—a trace of mockery sharpened the deep voice—"simply had a wider latitude of expertise. None of them, *dushka*, ever affected my heart . . . until you."

A small flame kindled in Kitty's soul at the quiet words, and eyes that only moments before were acid green now shone with the sea-green buoyancy of sparkling waves. "So I outlasted the brandy bottle?"

"Long past." Apollo's eyebrows went up in that quick little reflex, acknowledging the remarkable fact. Almost in a musing tone he went on, "First, you outlasted that terrible time in the forenoon when the night's liquor has worn off, you're too exhausted to make love anymore, and conversation is beyond your energy. And then, after that, the expected ennui never came, nor the usual tedium. Nor the boredom, at which point I usually began to wonder exactly how to word a polite good-bye."

"You never thought, even once, about an elegantly worded adieu for me?" Kitty was teasing a little now, feeling joyous after the last disclosure.

"Well . . . the first time, I didn't have any choice. The troop was waiting to ride off to God only knew where. And after the general, on the way to Novorossiisk, that was different. I was so damned mad—no elegant words there, just sheer fury. But never once did I really want to leave you, *dushka*, my soul, and that's God's truth. It was love even then, despite Peotr, despite the general, despite everything." Rolling over, he pulled Kitty into his arms. "I love you. You're my life," he said very gently. Stroking her cheek softly, his gaze held her wide-set emerald eyes, a smile crinkled the corners of his mouth. "Satisfied?"

"Very, very satisfied. But—" Apollo's dark straight brows rose at the word *but*. Kitty impishly continued, "Don't forget Noenia."

The heavy brows dropped back into place and a lazy smile curved Apollo's mouth. "I wish you'd let me."

"But I don't intend to. I want the *whole* story."

"I don't think you do."

"Think again," said Kitty, unmoved by his evasion.

"It's boring."

"Apollo!"

He grinned. "You're too damned curious."

"Concerned," Kitty said, smiling, "only concerned. I have this impression of Noenia chained in some dungeon somewhere, and I dislike dampness. . . ."

Exhaling quietly, Apollo said, "If you must know, although this all happened so long ago . . ." He began to recount a severely edited version of his friendship with Noenia. ". . . and the last I heard of her she was living very well under the protection of Grand Duke Constantine at Besh-Tau. Knowing Noenia and her well-developed sense of self-preservation, I expect she's preceded us to Paris. Now," he repeated patiently. "Finally satisfied?"

Kitty nodded happily from within the circle of his arms. "It's just that I'm so clumsy and fat now. I can't move very well, or ride or run anymore. It's silly, I know," she admitted with a rueful smile, "but under the circumstances . . . the insecurities mount. And people like Tamara can be pretty unsettling."

"Ignore bitches like Tamara, darling," Apollo replied, even while contemplating the tongue-lashing he intended giving his little cousin. "You're as lovely as the first time I laid eyes on you, or"—he smirked roguishly—"laid hands on you. You're absolutely beautiful. Sweetheart, you're not fat, you're pregnant. It's different."

"Really?"

"Really."

"You're not just saying that to be nice?"

"Would I lie to you?"

Her green eyes met his from under half-lowered lids.

His teeth flashed in a grin. "Let me rephrase that."

Several kisses later he continued. "And, I might add, my lushly pregnant darling, I look forward with delight to the birth of . . ." He swallowed hard and smiled. "My child. Now, tell me you love me." Apollo lowered his head, his mouth tasting Kitty's again.

"Ummmm, I love you," Kitty purred happily against his lips.

"You'd better," he murmured, "because I'll never let you go."

And with those words all of Tamara's malicious goading dissipated into nothingness.

That afternoon when Kitty went as usual to survey the progress of the experimental grainfields with Edyk, Apollo begged off. In fifteen minutes he tracked down Tamara. She was in the garden behind a small white-washed villa with two of her friends, ostensibly weaving on looms set up under the walnut trees but doing more gossiping than weaving.

Apollo tramped into the high-walled garden enclosure like a bull on the rampage and with a curt, imperious gesture dismissed the two girls from their own garden. He pointed one long finger in Tamara's direction. "You, stay." His breathing was rapid, the restless motion of his *nagaika* stirred the air near his boot tops, his blazing yellow eyes followed the backs of the young girls leaving.

"Now, what the *devil*," he said, his eyes turning from the empty gateway to bayonet Tamara where she stood beside the painted loom, "do you mean by talking to Kitty about my old lovers?" Apollo's voice was thick with fury for half a dozen words and then he had it controlled. "You," he continued with a wintry smile, "have no business bringing up such topics with Kitty—or with anyone else, for that matter."

"She's not one of us," Tamara, a pampered chieftain's granddaughter, shot back with her own brand of arrogance. Her dark eyes were cold with unleashed storms.

For a moment he was still. "What has that got to do with anything?"

"She's an outsider, with no mountain blood in her veins." Pride sounded chill in her voice.

Apollo's gaze, direct and deliberate, held hers for a long moment. "Lord, Tamara, don't be so insular."

"She's married to someone else!"

That remark hit a sore point. "Not for long," Apollo replied, and his mind jogged back momentarily into the old familiar grooves etched into his brain by constant contemplation of that wretched problem.

Her breath beating in her throat, Tamara took advantage of Apollo's lapse into musing to move forward and touch him lightly. "Take me, Apollo. Let me love you. Send the blond woman away...." Her hands slowly drifted up his well-muscled chest, then, clearly experienced, began to twine around his neck.

He smoothly stepped back from the clinging fingers. "No, Tamara," he said gently.

Her anger flared at the rebuff. The same hands which only moments before had been seductively stroking now curled into tight, hard fists. "You won't have *me*," she choked out furiously, "but you'll keep a slut who slept with every Red soldier in Stavropol!"

Apollo's mind recoiled at the gallery of grotesque images that instantly ignited his imagination, but when he spoke his voice was steady. "Shut up, Tamara. You've said enough. I only came here today," he went on, carefully explanatory, "to warn you: Stay away from Countess Radachek. I won't have her upset."

"*You* won't have her upset!" Tamara screamed. "You lovesick calf." She laughed contemptuously. "You know what everyone's saying, don't you? The child isn't even yours!"

Apollo struck her with the hardened flat of his hand, the first blow he had ever directed at a woman. "If I ever hear you've repeated that," Apollo said, looking down at her, his eyes grim as death, his grip on the *nagaika* turning his knuckles pale, "I'll personally see you're eternally sorry. I mean it, Tamara," he whispered through lips bared in a feral grimace. "Don't think I won't." His gaze, even and cold, continued to hold hers until, in the end, Tamara's eyes shifted.

Turning, he stalked from the quiet walled garden.

# 16

Kitty went into labor unexpectedly, weeks earlier than she had anticipated.

They had ridden to Apollo's private mountain lake for the day. It was miles up the side of Koshtan Tau, but they had traveled slowly, cautiously, making frequent rest stops, Kitty perched on an old-fashioned pillion, well cushioned and comfortable. Maybe the ride had been too strenuous; maybe the high mountain altitude had affected her in some way; maybe fate was taking a hand and seeing to it that the baby was born in the place Apollo loved most in the world.

The clear blue mountain lake was bordered by sweet-smelling meadow grass and silver firs; the valley surrounding it was fringed with spiky pine. A rustic pavilion, scarcely more than a roof to keep out the rain, nestled in the silver firs near the lake shore.

Kitty didn't mention the pains at first, really no more than a murmuring ache. She had had some intermittent contractions earlier that morning but they had subsided, and those types of erratic cramps had occurred occasionally in the last few days with no lasting results. It was too early in any event; the baby wasn't due for some time. Kitty was familiar with the rudiments of the birthing process, having managed a large estate for years, but in fact her isolation from any close female friends had denied her the particulars of a woman's travail.

At midafternoon, just prior to their departure, Kitty rose from the fragrant bed of clover and meadow grass where she and Apollo had been lying, enjoying the heat of the sun, and suddenly a warm gush of fluid ran down her legs. Her first reaction was panic. They were miles from the mountain aul and she didn't know what was happening, or if vaguely she did know, she didn't want it to happen now, here.

Nearby Apollo was gathering their picnic things. His initial reaction to Kitty's horrified gasp was panic as well, but he instantly concealed his response when he saw the fright in Kitty's eyes. With a start he saw she was soaked, faint tinges of blood coloring the thin white silk of her loose trousers.

"Apollo . . ." Kitty faltered in a weak voice, suddenly afraid. "It's too early! What are we going to do? It's two hours back down the mountain and—"

Horrified, Apollo watched her double over, her arms curled around her stomach, pain etched like brush marks across her face. He tossed aside the picnic gear and rushed to her side. Swinging her into his arms, he strode rapidly to the pavilion, placing her gently on the Dargo-loomed rug near the coarse stone fireplace. Before he could straighten from his kneeling position, another convulsive pain wrenched across Kitty's abdomen and her arms tightened around his neck, a whimper breaking from her clenched lips.

"Try and relax, *dushka*," he whispered into her soft hair, her fingers digging into his shoulders. His large hands stroked her back, trying to soothe and comfort while his mind was numbed with a fear he had never known in four years of battle.

"It *hurts*. Oh, Apollo, it hurts," Kitty moaned quietly into his chest, everything in the world obliterated by the piercing shock of pain. Then slowly the spasm subsided; her grip on Apollo's shoulders eased and loosened.

Drawing away, he seated himself beside her, his own breath still tight in his lungs. Taking her small hands in his warm grip, he squeezed them softly. "Once the water breaks, things progress pretty rapidly, I think." He was trying to sound calm and objective even while his mind was trying to find a way out.

Kitty's brow knit worriedly. "I don't know what to do, Apollo. I mean it, I don't know! Daria knows everything; I was counting on her." She took a deep breath. "There's no choice, though," she said faintly. "You'll have to deliver the baby." Her fearful eyes searched his face anxiously, looking for the support she desperately needed.

Apollo, who thought nothing of riding hundreds of miles deep within enemy territory, who casually handled dynamite and nitroglycerine as if they were toys and playthings, knelt saying nothing, his gaze on Kitty, his temples moist as if he stood in the heat of the midday sun. He looked as horrified as he felt. I can't, he thought, ashen to the roots of his sun-bleached hair. I can't! Then another lacerating shock tore through Kitty.

"Apollo!" she wailed in urgent appeal, her stricken eyes lifted to him.

Apollo, who had never seen Kitty so frightened, was shattered. Drawing her into his arms, he cradled her against his shoulder, a cold sweat tracking down his neck and spine under his black silk tunic. Inhaling like a drowning man to steady his nerves and violently beating heart, he said with difficulty, "You can do it, Kitty. I'll help. I've seen babies born in the refugee trains the last few years." He smiled at her encouragingly, her head resting against his arm now that the contraction had passed. His voice was calm, soothing, responsible, while inside he shook with trepidation. What if something should go wrong? Any number of problems could arise. It was impossible to leave Kitty and go for aid. Lord God, he silently prayed, help us.

Although Kitty had been practicing some of the village midwife's relaxation techniques over the last few weeks, no one, she thought a trifle resentfully, had ever said it would hurt this much. With the clawing pain receding to a dull ache, her breathing became more normal. Looking up at Apollo, she attempted a small smile. "I'm sorry. I'm afraid you have two babies on your hands, me and the one about to enter the world. I'm not very good about pain. Daria never described it like this."

Not knowing if he felt like smiling or crying, Apollo said, "I don't suppose she'd dare. Who the hell would ever have a child if they knew?"

"I'll warn you now," Kitty said sheepishly. "I think I'm going to be screaming."

Apollo, his strong fingers brushing a damp curl off her cheek, replied gently, "You just scream all you want." His light touch smoothed the hair over her shoulders. "I wish," he continued quietly, "I could take the pain for you. You're too delicate . . . too small. Oh, damn!" His golden eyes glistened with unshed tears. "I don't want you to suffer."

"Just hold me," Kitty whispered, "and I'll be all right—" Already another contraction was creeping up, spreading agony slowly, corrosively. She breathed softly, trying to remember Daria's admonitions on relaxing. The tentacles of pain were tightening their grip. She cried out softly; her fingernails went through Apollo's silk beshmet, leaving half-moons in his skin.

Lifting her higher in his arms, he held her gently, afraid he might add to her pain, tensing his muscles to enfold her with infinite tenderness.

The afternoon died aflame in a crimson-washed sunset, but Kitty was unaware of nature's glorious adieu to the day. She was wrapped in a cocoon of nearly constant hurt. The breathing helped, but it didn't do more than soften the worst cutting edges of the insidious agony pulling, stretching, digging into her tender body.

When the sun went down Apollo eased away briefly to build a fire in the fireplace, then returned to cradle Kitty, soothing, crooning, kissing away her tears. Day turned into evening, evening into night, the moon dropped low in the western sky and nothing had changed. He was beginning to worry. Cautioning himself to avoid imprudent alarm, he reminded himself that a first confinement was almost always lengthy. But, he thought with inner alarm, Kitty's contractions had been so constant and intense for the last several hours he wondered how much her fragile body could take. Even though he had witnessed several births, he had no way of recognizing the signs of complications, no way of knowing how much stress Kitty's delicate body could absorb before rebelling in some dangerous way.

He reminded himself that he had seen children born under much worse conditions. The woman they found on the train platform at Orel last November had barely been alive, but they had carried her into their railway car and later that night in Apollo's bed she had given birth. A fragment of hope kindled in Apollo's fearful mind, for even under those terrible circumstances both mother and child had lived. God willing, Kitty's labor would end as successfully.

By the middle of the night, all Kitty knew was pain and fear. There was no relief from either, and between contractions she faced the thought of dying. The torturous cramps peaked one after another, but the baby didn't seem to move. If something was wrong, neither of them knew what to do. Tears of sadness mingled with the tears of pain in her eyes at the thought of leaving Apollo. Try to breathe rhythmically, she told herself through the rising curtain of clawing anguish trying to suffocate her.

In his own enormous terror, Apollo made a decision. He'd wait two more hours, and if Kitty's labor hadn't progressed, he'd start down the mountain with her. He couldn't just sit here and watch her die.

It was then that he started talking, partly in an attempt to distract Kitty, partly to drag his mind from his numbing fear. While he stroked and comforted Kitty with steady, gentle hands, he talked about their summer together; about the days fishing and the afternoons in the orchard under the pear trees; about Pushka and Karaim; about the new sun terrace they had built; about the way Leda had taken to Kitty. And when he ran out of current subjects he talked about his childhood, about school lessons and riding games and visits to Paris, about nurses and tutors and relatives.

He was unused to sustained talking and it took effort to dredge up subjects and topics and events, but he persevered, talking himself hoarse because it seemed to soothe Kitty, seemed to ease the furrows of pain on her sweat-drenched brow.

Once when miraculously she appeared to be dozing lightly, he dashed the few yards to the lake and brought back some of the cool mountain water. In the course of the long, slow hours of the night, between her contractions, he attempted to make Kitty more comfortable. Moving her closer to the fire, he carefully stripped the damp clothes from her, washed her gently, and slipped one of his silk shirts over her shoulders. He brought two more rugs from a storage chest, placing them as close to the fire as the heat would allow. Spreading a cashmere shawl on top of the rugs, he lifted Kitty onto the cushioned bed, adjusting her comfortably in his arms.

Time crept by. Kitty was exhausted from a pain so persistent and unrelenting that her cries and tears coalesced into an inhuman kind of ragged sound. The flickering firelight, the strangeness of her surroundings, the light-headedness of her battered senses made it all seem like a dream, except for the clawing monster attacking her body. She clung to Apollo, finding solace in his solid strength, feeling safe in the circle of his arms, the murmur of his deep low voice like balm on a savaged wound. Then another pain would roll over her, seizing at the raw interior of her punished body, and she would lose all sense of time, place, reason. Apollo was the only constant she could rely on, and while she clutched his arms and screamed, he held her with the greatest tenderness, whispering his love into the sweat-dampened golden curls, trying to keep from crying at his helplessness.

Finally, very near the limits Apollo had set for departure, when Kitty was existing only in some hazy dimension outside reality, a coiling spasm began to climb through her senses, even though at each nerve juncture her brain tried to hold back the intensity, cut off the control switches, sidestep the building agony. It didn't work. The inexorable demon snaked onward, ignoring her feeble defenses, until finally it broke through the misty haze that had been protecting her. Arching her back, Kitty screamed and screamed and screamed until her body took pity on her mind and she fainted.

The sound echoed through the dark valley, bouncing hideously from tree to boulder to lake. Apollo, white as paper, gripped Kitty's frail shoulders as if his physical strength and sheer willpower alone could force back the black fall of unconsciousness. Blood began welling from Kitty, soaking the cashmere shawl and dark carpet. "Kitty!" Apollo shouted, seeing her slip away, desperate to keep her with him. He prayed to every God he had ever known, offering frantically in his terrible fear whatever he thought would propitiate a vengeful deity. "Don't let her die," he sobbed.

Then, miraculously—and he viewed it as a miracle forever after—the baby's head emerged, its little face downward. Apollo reached down one hand to support the small head, gently easing Kitty onto the carpet with his other hand. The tiny shoulders came next and with one final contraction, the baby was born. Apollo had delivered his son! And *his* son it was, at first glance and no mistaking. Any chafing, murky doubts Apollo might have harbored were instantly dispelled. A tiny treasure in red and gold. Looking at him, Apollo marveled to see his own hair, his own eyes and features printed in miniature. A fine, perfect boy child, light and fair, hair pale as swansdown, lay in his father's large hands. After a brief, furious cry of complaint the child lapsed into quiet contentment, his unblinking eyes gravely surveying the jubilant golden gaze of his father.

Apollo wept then in happiness and profound relief.

Minutes later, coming back from a great distance, Kitty said in a very small voice, "It doesn't hurt anymore." For a moment her mind cleared and she saw Apollo's yellow head bent over her, tears streaming down his face. She blinked as her vision clouded over, then closed her eyes in exhaustion, a faint smile playing over her serene face. "I did it, didn't I?"

Apollo gazed down at the new scrap of humanity cradled in his palms, adoration in his eyes, and breathed softly, "You gave me a son."

While Kitty, her eyes black with fatigue, dozed in the aftermath of her strenuous labor, Apollo bathed the baby, wrapped him in a warm shawl, and then simply sat and admired his son for a long, contented time.

Kitty heard a voice, dreamlike, as a child waking from a nap hears a voice in the summer air outside his bedroom window. She recognized Apollo's quiet murmur and wondered for a vague, forgetful moment whom else he would address so tenderly. Under the soft and gentle cadence he sounded tired, but she had no energy to decipher the puzzle of words and sank comfortably back into her slumber.

Later, when Kitty's eyes opened—attentive this time—she glanced at the small bundle lying near her and inquired in a quiet, breathy murmur, "Do we have a son or a daughter?"

"A son, *dushka* . . . a very beautiful son."

Her eyes twinkled. "Is the old argument finally reconciled?"

Apollo grinned sheepishly. "Irrevocably, darling." He turned back the shawl from the baby's face so Kitty could see for herself.

Studying the features, a small, happy smile touched Kitty's mouth. Her son's hair was pale like Apollo's in the summer; his nose, remarkably un-babylike, was classically straight like his father's. And the Tartar ancestor, who had swept across the steppes from the east so long ago, left his mark once again on the youngest member of the Kuzans. Her child's feathery brows swept up like baby heron's wings over large, precious eyes, tipped exotically to catch the slanted brows. With eyes like that his patrimony could not be questioned.

"He's beautiful," she said, beaming.

"Very beautiful," Apollo agreed softly. "Like his mother."

"He has your eyes," Kitty murmured with satisfaction. Those golden eyes, Kitty thought, that can tease, cajole, amorously entreat, and make you forgive them anything.

"Do you think so?" Apollo said, too awed by the precious littleness of his son, the overwhelming babyness, to distinguish features. "Whosoever eyes, sweetheart, he's perfect. Thank you for giving him to me."

"Are you really pleased?" Kitty asked, suddenly overtaken by a terrible vulnerability. After all, she wasn't even married to Apollo, and Peotr was perhaps still alive somewhere out in the world beyond the mountains. How would Dagestani custom accept the child? Mountain law governed so much of Apollo's thinking.

Apollo's throat constricted. "More than pleased, kitten—thrilled, ecstatic, every other superlative expression." He touched the baby's cheek gently, then picked up Kitty's hand and carried it to his lips, holding it afterward in both of his own. "I can't thank you enough. It wasn't easy for you." There was a pause. "Now that it's over, I'll confess I was worried as hell. The entire night will be engraved forever on my liver. Are you all right? Is the pain gone?"

She nodded. "I've a confession, too. There were moments last night when I wanted to wring your neck for putting me into this predicament—even though I knew it wasn't particularly your fault."

"I do remember," Apollo said, smiling faintly, "that I had a role in making this son of ours, but I had my irrational moments last night, too. There were times when I wanted to shout, 'Stop! Stop all this. It isn't working out.'" His expression was humorous, but Kitty was surprised to hear his voice shake. "I'm proud of you," Apollo whispered, "and proud of the son you gave me." His adoring smile entered his golden eyes before he bent to kiss Kitty, raining caresses on her lids, and on her cheeks, and lips and hair. "I love you."

"I love you," Kitty breathed, inhaling the sweet smell of him, knowing this quixotic man, who could kill without remorse and yet be infinitely tender and protective to those he loved, was the heart and center of her life.

When the sun glowed with midmorning warmth, Apollo carried his family down the mountain, afraid that the horses' jolting might be too uneven for Kitty's present state. The horses were set out to graze; he handed the baby to Kitty, then lifted them both into his arms.

He walked slowly, holding her against his chest to keep from jarring her, careful of his precious burden, and very soon Kitty and the baby dozed. He chose his route prudently, intent on not disturbing them. His cavalryman's fluent, rolling gait never altered, nor did his breathing, although the burden was heavy. It was only when Kitty wakened and he spoke that she realized—with a shock—how much sheer willpower that smooth, even journey had required.

"We're almost to one of the summer grazing meadows," he said.

When she insisted they stop *now*, he chuckled, without much breath to do it with, and said, "You're not in a very good position . . . to give orders."

Kitty made a point of staying awake after that. From there on they stopped to rest often, to eat from the stores in the pack Apollo carried on his shoulders, or to drink from the mountain streams that rushed in miniature torrents down the mountainside. Rustic in its simplicity, blissful in its harmony, the small family was the microcosm of the universe.

Approaching the village, they immediately became the center of elated congratulations. A long procession followed them through the aul, cheering and celebrating the birth of a new heir to the nation. Apollo accepted the felicitous regards cheerfully, and the masculine jocular allusions gracefully. He was at heart more pleased and content than ever before in his life, surrounded by people he loved and who loved him and who would love his child. An heir, his son; a deep sense of satisfaction permeated his soul, and the shining happiness in his golden eyes was visible to the entire village. Although everyone knew the countess wasn't his wife, this fine boy was the Falcon's, and that was enough. Jubilation continued throughout the night and the official celebration, which began in earnest the following morning, lasted five days.

At the end of the week, when all the festivities abated and some semblance of normalcy returned to everyone's lives, Iskender and Apollo took wine together late one night.

"Have you decided on a name yet?" Iskender asked, leaning over to fill the delicate Persian cups.

"Not yet," Apollo replied with a small, crooked smile. "Kitty, as you know, has a mind of her own. We haven't been able to agree."

"He should be baptized soon."

Apollo's smile widened, and one dark brow rose. "That, I'm afraid, is another point of contention," he said agreeably.

"Humph," snorted his autocratic great-grandfather. "Times have changed since my youth. Women are becoming . . ."

"Unmanageable?" Apollo suggested cheerfully.

"Precisely," Iskender retorted, but his voice was tolerant. "I understand it's called . . . progress."

"Whatever it's called, I quite adore Kitty, Pushka."

"And your son?" Iskender's old eyes shone with pride. He had already showered the newborn babe with gifts and titles and magnificent horseflesh as befitting a mountain warrior and future khan.

"Those feelings are too deep to describe," Apollo said simply. Apollo had fallen passionately in love with his son. He played with him so much that Kitty had to coax the baby away to feed him. Apollo insisted on helping with his bath and dressing. He brought him down to the village every day, displaying him with intense delight to every pleased member of the tribe.

"He's very beautiful," Iskender declared. "And, if I might add without angering you"—his heavy lids lowered infinitesimally—"undoubtedly yours."

"As I've been telling you these many months." Apollo's smile was benign.

"Impertinent pup. As if you didn't breathe a sigh of relief as well as I."

"Perhaps a small one," Apollo admitted with a twisted grin. "Events *had* been quite chaotic, you must admit, and one's cynicism is hard to abruptly jettison."

"What of marriage?" Iskender asked.

Apollo wasn't surprised by the sudden question; he'd been anticipating it for days. It was important, although not necessarily imperative, that he marry the mother of his son. "All in limbo at the moment. I left a message at Poti months ago before we entered the mountains, asking Papa to obtain a divorce for Kitty. None of his communications have mentioned anything about it. Evidently there are problems. Under the circumstances, it's to be expected. Somehow Peotr has to either be located or declared dead. Were the emperor still alive, an imperial edict could have easily circumvented all the bureaucratic red tape, but . . ." Apollo turned his palms up.

"Your family could increase in the meantime."

"In that case, the children can all be legitimized in one fell swoop. You know the Kuzans have a tradition of irregular unions anyway. It's typical. No harm has ever come of it. Money opens all doors, Pushka, as you well know. Legitimacy or illegitimacy has never stopped a Kuzan yet. And who knows . . . Papa may have good news soon." Apollo's expression became solemn, his voice grave. "Kitty means everything to me, Pushka, and I intend to marry her as soon as possible."

"Good," his great-grandfather replied succinctly. "And as to the name and baptism, I trust you'll be able to come to an agreement soon. It's not wise, As-saqr As-saghir, to let a woman always have her way."

"Oh, I have my way on more than enough occasions to keep me satisfied. Life isn't a contest, after all. I very much *enjoy* giving Kitty what she wants and the reciprocity is . . . genial, I assure you."

"Humph," the old man said again, but his dark eyes twinkled knowingly from the harsh craggy face, for he saw that his young great-grandson was more content than ever before in his life.

In time the youngest of the Kuzans found himself with a very long name, since neither of his parents were known for their submissive temperaments. Kitty wanted him named Gregory for her father. Apollo then felt his father should be similarly honored; Alexander was added. The members of his clan had chosen their own name: Yarak, which meant a young falcon in keen hunting conditions: Custom, of course, required the patronymic. So in due time when he was baptized, the baby became Prince Gregory Alexander Yarak Apollonovich Kuzan. His parents called him the Cub.

From the day of his birth, the Cub became their joy and their focus. When he smiled for the first time they both agreed he was extremely clever. When he learned to communicate with his toes, they marveled at his dexterity. "I showed him your picture today, Apollo, and he laughed." Kitty beamed with pride. In happy accord, the young parents decided the Cub would be much more comfortable—with such keen intelligence—at the Sorbonne, rather than at Le Rosey. That warm fall, optimistic plans were made for his future in great detail, including tennis, polo, Nice, English governesses, and French châteaus. Apollo said nothing unpalatable about the savage terror called world revolution and did not mention that men, women, and children were vanishing by the thousands without a trace. He didn't say they were prisoners in their paradise. He didn't say anything because the Cub was still very small, and plans could change. For the moment, their world ended on the borders of the mountain valley, and it was perfect.

In the sunny days of the autumn of 1920, while Apollo, Kitty, and the Cub passed their time in happy companionship, reports from the outside world informed them of Wrangel's final defeat on the Crimean peninsula. While Bolshevik suzerainty encompassed all of South Russia with the exception of Georgia, Azerbaijan having fallen in April, continued uprisings and furious resistance persisted up and down the countryside.

Apollo had been chafing at the bit for several weeks now. Numerous raiding parties had been coming and going, and with the rebellion continuing so near in Azerbaijan, the opportunities to tweak Soviet noses and confiscate Soviet gold were constant.

One night in November, Apollo and Kitty were lying in bed. He was propped up on one arm, his free hand tracing languorous patterns over Kitty's naked flesh. Both were sated from lovemaking, lazy and replete.

"For a matron, *ma petite*," Apollo said very softly, "you have a most tantalizing body." His fingers lightly trailed the curves from neck to hip, his practiced touch feather-light and as delicate as a hummingbird's. "Have I told you lately how much I adore you?"

Kitty's deep green eyes, drowsy with a rich and luxurious satisfaction, languidly drifted over the broad-shouldered, athletic man sprawled beside her, and the firelight picked up a bewitching glimmer from under her heavy lashes. "You know how I despise vanity in women, but tell me again. I think it's been a minute or so since you last mentioned it."

"*Je t'adore*," he whispered against her ear, the curve of her jaw, against her neck, then his warm breath tickled one rosy nipple, and by the time Apollo had traveled his leisurely path down Kitty's voluptuous body, leaving a trail of fiery kisses, the object of his adoration was emitting soft moans of pleasure, her fingers laced in his pale satiny curls, now lying between her thighs. "No, no," she had murmured, feeling her senses were quite unable to withstand another assault no matter how deliciously tender. Then her quiet denials turned to breathy sighs as Apollo's tongue explored and his long fingers gently probed, opening the way for his lightly caressing tongue, and very soon her sighs changed to pleading entreaty. Kitty's body had been flattered, captivated, seduced to a fine frenzy of sensation so wanton that nothing would suffice but the satisfaction she craved. "Apollo, please . . ." Kitty implored softly, moistening her upper lip with her tongue. "I want to feel you." Her hands tugged gently on his shoulders.

Apollo slowly lifted his head and said very quietly, his breath stirring warm against her, "But you *are* feeling me." And he went back to his pleasant business. Kitty arched and gasped at the shock wave when his lips touched again, grew wild under the insinuating tongue that licked, nibbled, explored.

"Apollo, *chéri*, please, please . . . I'm going to die," she moaned in a low, throaty whisper. "I want you inside me."

He raised his head again. "Ahh . . . you want *that* inside you."

"Yes, yes . . . hurry—" Kitty groaned, the torrid, pulsing focus of her world beneath Apollo's mouth.

"How much do you want it?" he teased, his chin resting on the light triangle of silken hair, his lean fingers running over the smoothness of her stomach.

"Apollo—" Kitty wailed.

"One small favor . . ."

"Anything!"

Apollo's eyes were twin pools of serene, unblemished gold, chaste in their innocence. "Anything?" he teased, recklessness glinting in his formerly guileless expression. "It almost makes one greedy."

"Apollo!"

"Patience, sweet one," he said calmly, "I'm hurrying." She was tearing at his shoulders, writhing softly in an agony of desire while he drew his long body up from the foot of the bed. He hesitated on the brink of entering her. "My favor's granted?"

"Yes, yes—please. . . ." Apollo had, in his expert way, lit a flaming fire of longing that burned out of control, burned so fiercely and deeply that the only sensation Kitty was aware of was the rush of blood through her veins and skin, a heated violence so wild that nothing could breach the perimeter of her mind but her frenzied, driving need for him.

Apollo penetrated her, slowly, leisurely, making certain Kitty felt every silken centimeter of the invading hardness, and when he reached the full depth of his thrust, he lingered deep inside. Kitty arched against the exquisite, tantalizing rapture washing out in waves from the vital masculine presence inside her. She undulated, her hips moving slowly beneath his, her head thrown back, eyes closed, oblivious to all except the flaming hot climax beating into her nerve endings.

Apollo withdrew then in a languorous lifting of his lean hips and Kitty's fingers left blood on his back.

"No!" she cried wildly, her shadowy green eyes unfocused, a new strength in her hands now clutching Apollo's arms. So immersed was she in the carnal tide pouring out from the center of her being that nothing else mattered.

"Hush, *dushka*," Apollo whispered, shrugging off her hands, his thumbs gentling the soft verges of her breasts. His strong mouth curved into a lazy smile. "You're always so impatient, like a . . . European. Let me touch you again, here . . . and here . . . and here." Kitty trembled. "See how you like that?" Apollo's husky voice went on, his own sexual hunger evident in the delicate hoarseness. His dark hands slid up the length of Kitty's long, slender legs, forcing them wide, lingering, his palms warm against her inner thighs. The tips of his fingers touched her heated moistness and her shiver was breathless in its urgency. Knowing she couldn't wait much longer, his mouth lowered over hers and minutes later, her legs wrapped around him, they took each other to a singular earthly paradise.

Curled in Apollo's arms, her dizzying sensations now only a silken feeling of warmth, Kitty vaguely recalled the quietly mentioned "favor." She glanced up at the peaceful face. Apollo's eyes were closed, and a faint smile was painted across his deeply tanned face. "What did I promise you in the heat of passion?" she murmured. Her full-lipped rose mouth quirked wryly. "That *wasn't* exactly fair."

His eyes still closed, Apollo drowsily replied, "All's fair, et cetera, et cetera." Grinning quietly on the pillow, he contemplated the gratification it always gave him to see Kitty so lost to reason.

Kitty's voice, aggrieved, slid into mild reproof. "You took advantage."

Apollo's pale eyes half opened then, and he glanced down. "It's always such a pleasure to," he said agreeably. "I can't resist."

"That's not nice."

"*Nice?*" His eyes opened quite wide and Kitty watched disapprovingly as Apollo choked with laughter. "Darling, I've been called many things in my day, but have never aspired to 'nice.' "

"Well, it's rotten, then."

"Really," he drawled, his eyes crinkled, mocking her. "Was that why you were screaming . . . right before the end?" His brows rose.

Kitty had the grace to blush and knew she had lost that particular argument. That's what came from giving in to lust instead of thinking of England. "So tell me," she said in mildly theatrical affront. "*What* did I promise?"

"Not to complain when I go on a raid," he replied equably. Kitty snatched herself clear of his arm and shot upright.

Sitting straight-backed, facing him with a glare, direct and stormy, the words tumbled out in a rushing torrent, "I *never* would have agreed—"

"Under normal circumstances," he finished blandly, a smile tugging at the corners of his mouth. "I know."

"You tricked me," Kitty blurted out indignantly. Her eyes were visibly sparking and Apollo reached out to pull her close once again.

She resisted. He didn't insist, although he could have very easily.

"Sweetheart," he said gently, his hands resting lightly on her shoulders, "It was only a game. I won't hold you to such a promise. But . . . I do want to go. Consider," he continued in a softly placating tone, "I've been dutiful since last spring. That's eight months, darling, and while the men haven't understood, they've endured." Apollo rubbed one hand across the nape of his neck in a rueful gesture. "It has, on occasion, chafed at my pride. Understand, *dushka*, only because of my great love for you and the Cub have I remained docile so long." His voice was moderate, reasonable, his golden eyes sincere.

Kitty sighed softly. "Has it been so difficult?"

Apollo nodded. "I haven't minded so much. It was important to you."

"But you want to go out again."

He nodded again. "Only occasionally. Nothing risky. All of Azerbaijan and Dagestan is up in arms. The Georgian Military Road is in the hands of the Ingushians and Ossetians, who are seizing automobiles and making a collection of them. The Chechens are attacking the Terek Cossacks, who have held their land for Russia for a hundred years. Grosny's besieged. The entire Soviet Arkani field force was destroyed at Arkaz a few days ago. The whole Caucasus is in the process of self-determination. It's tempting to take part—destroy a munitions dump, or rob a Soviet payroll to help the insurgents, or just harass a Red Army garrison that's been raising havoc in the lower villages. However," he said very quietly, "if you're still adamantly against it . . ." His voice trailed off.

Kitty's breath felt constricted, but she had to ask, "You do miss all that, don't you?"

"It's been my life," he reminded her softly.

"And I've denied you that life."

Apollo shrugged, then smiled. "The compensation has been more than adequate. I'm not complaining, but—"

"It's been long enough?"

"Am I a selfish brute? I'm sorry, *dushka*. When I watch Karaim and Sahin come back, time after time . . . Oh, hell, I don't know." He ran a hand impatiently through his long bright hair and dropped back down on the pillow. "Just forget it, sweet. It was a bad idea." His arms were flung above his head.

"Where are they going this time?" Kitty inquired in a small voice, her eyes raking his powerful, rangy form.

Apollo's whole body tensed and his tawny eyes met hers cautiously. "Down to Derbent. The monthly payroll is due in three days."

"How dangerous?"

One eyebrow raised languidly. "A piece of cake."

Kitty took a deep breath, exhaled softly, and said, "Don't be gone long."

The joy in Apollo's eyes would have lit the Champs Élysées for a week. Hauling Kitty into his arms, he crushed her in an elated bear hug. "I'll be back in four days without a scratch, not a hair out of place." Apollo was like a young boy given his first taste of freedom. "Oh, kitten, do you know how much I love you?"

"Tell me," Kitty whispered, fear gripping her heart. And he did.

The troop left early the following morning, their mood festive with Apollo in command once again. Each rider had shaken his hand in welcome. It was considered a good omen to have the Young Falcon let loose.

Kitty watched Apollo canter out of the courtyard and turn with raised hand at the gates to bid her adieu. Leda caracoled

and pranced down the mountain trail, as excited as her master
to be riding out again, and when they reached the valley floor,
in sheer high spirits, Apollo loosed the curb he'd held on her
and she stretched out flat with extended rein and curbless
mouth along the valley road.

# 17

Apollo and Karaim were looking through binoculars from a point halfway up a sandstone cliff above Petrovsk.

There had already been two successful raids in less than a month, and the Red commander in Petrovsk had vowed that no mountain guerillas were going to steal *this* gold. He had enormously augmented the train's protection: machine guns were mounted at every window, door, and orifice; the entire train bristled with soldiers and rifles. The commander was quite correct, of course; the train was secure.

"That would be suicide," Apollo observed pleasantly to Karaim, his binoculars sweeping the armored train from front to back. "Good Lord, he has practically emptied the garrison."

"A shame," Karaim agreed.

Apollo smiled serenely. "And we don't have a thing to do until the gold is safely deposited in the garrison at Derbent." He let the glasses drop to hang from the leather strap around his neck. "I expect the men left at Petrovsk plan on being paid this week, eh, Karaim?"

"Assuredly, As-saqr As-saghir."

"Why settle for one payroll, then, when two would do as well?"

"Why indeed?" Karaim concurred.

"Is Madame Gautier's still on Mokhovaya?"

Karaim's voice held a scornful note. "The commissar's wives and girlfriends like silks and satins the same as everyone else, propaganda notwithstanding."

"Care to go shopping? Kitty hasn't had a new ball gown since—" He was going to say "Aladino" until he remembered the armoire full of Poirets at Stavropol. "Well . . . for a long time."

Karaim's even voice gave no indication he understood the brief hesitation. "I can always use a frivolous silk or two."

"Or three or four, with your reputation," Apollo cheerfully amended.

Karaim shrugged, his dark face bland. "Allah has been kind to me."

The Petrovsk garrison payroll was freed from Soviet hegemony late that night with a minimum of fuss and no casualties to the raiding party. The skeleton guard left behind had made their task inestimably easier. Apollo and Karaim shopped rapidly at Madame Gautier's while the remainder of the troop fidgeted impatiently outside the fashionable dressmaker's shop. In short order, Madame's stock was lessened by several gowns, paid for with Soviet gold.

When the telegraph lines were repaired the next morning and news was relayed to Derbent of the raid on Petrovsk, the protective guard started back immediately. The furious Red commander vowed to pursue the culprits until each and every one was caught. Obviously, he was new to the region. There were areas in the mountains where a man could stay hidden for a lifetime.

So while the armored train and its complement of heavily armed men rushed north, Apollo and his riders set out for Derbent. Shortly after midnight, Apollo and three of his men were lounging in the office containing the safe for the Derbent garrison. Slaughtered Red soldiers—discreetly hidden, of course—formed a trail of sorts to the walnut-paneled room. Apollo rocked in a large, padded desk chair, his eyes half-closed in relaxed scrutiny of Sahin's cousin Yazid as he intently worked on the safe's combination. The clever young man—who had spent two months as a bank teller in Baku—opened the safe in under five minutes. His expertise hadn't been acquired in the short space of two months of employment, but the skills already learned from an elderly uncle had certainly been polished to a fine gloss. The bank at Baku had been poorer by a considerable sum when Yazid retired at a young age and returned to Dargo.

"Sometimes, Karaim," Apollo said, strolling back to their horses held in readiness near the basement entry, "it makes one nervous, it's so damn easy to steal from these Bolshis. I'm afraid we're going to lose our fine edge and blunder out of boredom some fine day." He hitched the heavy saddlebag of gold higher on his muscular shoulder and pushed open the basement door.

"If they repair the telegraph lines before morning, you might have a little excitement on the way back," Karaim remarked with his usual neat restraint. "That should help keep the edge." Side by side they moved toward their horses, two tall, lean men, one fair, one as dark as Lucifer.

"You think so?" Apollo inquired, a lift in his voice. "Fifty roubles says we're clear to Gunib before they're repaired."

"Akusha; no farther."

Turning to Karaim, Apollo's pale eyes glowed with their own inner fire. "You're on." Clearly, he was hoping to lose.

A full moon shone on the troop while they swiftly divided the gold among their various saddlebags, evenly distributing it to allow each mount maximum speed. Twenty men swung up into the high-cantled, heavily padded saddles.

"To the foothills north of town and then to the Gunib plateau?" Karaim brusquely inquired, already wheeling his horse to the north.

"One short detour," Apollo declared cheerfully, his strong hand holding a curvetting Leda in the melee of men and horses.

"There's not much time. It's after midnight already, and we should be past the garrison at Madjolis before dawn."

"Ten minutes, no more. Kitty needs some jewelry for her new gowns, and Firez and Sons survived the Revolution. Do you think I still have an account there?"

"Not one that's likely to be healthy. Stop next time. We'll be back."

Apollo's hand went out to soothe Leda. "Go on ahead if you want. I'll catch up in a few minutes."

Karaim would sooner have condemned his soul to an eternity in hell than leave the Falcon's side. "Foolhardy as ever," he snorted avuncularly.

"Humor me, Karaim. I've been sage too long."

With time at a minimum, Apollo climbed the grilled fence guarding the store's rear entrance and forced the door of Firez and Sons. In less time than he would have liked, but considerably more time than Karaim deemed safe, Apollo selected several pieces of jewelry for Kitty. The gold to pay for them was discreetly placed under the senior Firez's elegant silk-cushioned divan along with a note of thanks for extending his shopping hours.

The riders passed the garrison town of Madjolis only slightly behind schedule, missing the early morning patrols by ten minutes. Although the telegraph lines north out of Derbent had been cut, the Red Army, by dint of repetition, was becoming extremely speedy with their repairs. Just north of Akusha two of Apollo's scouts came back to report that two armored cars mounted with Lewis guns were patrolling the road.

"Damned if you weren't right, Karaim. I owe you fifty roubles. Let's go down and take out those cars."

"Think of the countess, As-saqr As-saghir. They've got Lewis guns. . . ."

"I suppose you're right." Then Apollo's clear, golden eyes lit with an alternative not particularly dangerous to them. "A few lobbed grenades couldn't hurt. Think we can get ahead of them before they reach the Shura defile?"

"Don't see why not," Karaim replied with a tolerant smile.

"You're always so damned reasonable, Karaim. That's why we get along."

"We get along because I give in to all your harebrain schemes."

A flash of white teeth accompanied Apollo's winning smile. "Well, that too."

The garrison at Akusha lost two armored cars that day. The heights above the Shura defile had always been a favorite spot for target practice by the mountaineers, and the blundering Russians hadn't learned that critical fact in a hundred years.

Moving up into the high mountain trails after Akusha, Apollo and his men entered Dargo that evening. The troop dispersed to their homes; Karaim and Sahin rode to report to Iskender.

"Tell Pushka I'll talk to him tomorrow," Apollo said on parting company with his two bodyguards. A smile flickered across his face. "*Late* tomorrow."

Ascending the steep incline to his palace, Apollo felt elated, exhilarated, alive. Riding out always left him in that state; the feel of a prime horse, the outwitting of one's adversaries, the adrenaline flowing until one experienced a sense of invincibility. He must thank Kitty again for being so understanding, although the gifts piled high behind his saddle might, in small measure, express his feelings. He hoped, too, that the Cub was still awake—a little surprise for him had caught Apollo's eye during his swift inventory of the stock at Firez and Sons.

On entering the courtyard, Apollo immediately saw his hope was answered. Kitty, holding the Cub, stood waiting at the top of the stairs, illuminated by the light pouring out of the opened foyer door.

Tossing Leda's reins to a waiting servant, Apollo leaped from the saddle and bounded up the stairs. His long legs brought him to Kitty and the Cub in four gigantic strides; father, mother, and son smiled, laughed, beamed, all spoke at once within the crushing circle of Apollo's embrace.

After giving instructions for the disposal of the packages, Apollo, carrying the Cub, his free arm around Kitty's shoulders, strolled into the entrance hall. "What new trick has the Cub learned while I was away?" Apollo asked, smiling happily first at his son and then at Kitty.

"He can almost roll over by himself. You'll have to watch before he goes to bed." Kitty's emerald eyes were alight with joy. Her worst fears had evaporated on hearing the signal blast reverberating around the valley when Apollo's troop had been sighted. She'd had an hour, then, to wait until his arrival, during which she had bathed in a heady elation of bliss, delight, every other sensation of goodness and cheer. Apollo was back, as he had promised, safe and sound. At that thought, her eyes quickly repeated her earlier scrutiny. Had she missed a cut or wound or scratch?

"Do I have egg on my face?" Apollo inquired with amusement in his voice. Kitty's gaze was quite intent.

"Just looking for blood, bulletholes, things like that. . . ." Her relief at not finding any was evident in her expression.

"I told you it was a simple little raid." He made no mention of Lewis guns or armored cars or the scores of dead Bolshevik soldiers left behind. "Do I get a gold medal for effort? We're back a day early."

"Two gold medals," Kitty replied, her face wreathed in smiles. "One from each of us."

"I drove the men mercilessly, you know, and all because of my timid-hearted wife," Apollo teased.

"I just wasn't raised for it, I guess . . . didn't cut my teeth on a mountain *kinjal* and *kanly* blood lust."

Looking down at the delicately featured, golden-haired woman at his side, Apollo said softly, "However you were raised, you turned out splendidly." Nearing their suite of rooms, Apollo inquired, "Do you suppose the Cub will perform for me now?"

"He's only learning. Sometimes he's patently amazed when all the pushing and struggling works. You'll see for yourself."

Laying the small, sturdy baby—his hair as downy gold as a chick's—on the bed, Apollo gazed at him for long moments, taking in the changes that seemed to have occurred in three short days. Apollo's hair and clothes were full of dust. Reaching out a long, bronzed finger he brought a smile to the Cub's face, talking to him, tickling him softly under the pudgy little chin. He lazily continued the quiet game, unbuckling his belt with one hand. The Cub's eyes, bright as doubloons, followed his every movement. Straightening, Apollo threw belt and holsters on the bed; pulling off his boots, he slung them under a nearby chair. One more fizzing, drooling smile coaxed from his son brought an answering warm grin to Apollo's face, and Kitty stood smiling with blurred eyes at the sight of the two loves of her life.

Looking up at Kitty, Apollo said in the gentlest of voices, "I missed you both." Unbending, he turned and held open his arms. Kitty fell into them, tears of happiness glistening in her large eyes—and while his parents held each other in welcome, thanksgiving, and love, the Cub threw one tiny leg across his body and, pushing vigorously with the other, proceeded to disarm his father and mother with his infant determination. Before long, his little face rosy with the exertion, the energetic flailing and shoving was successful and—enormous baby eyes open wide in astonishment—he lay on his tummy. Both parents clapped, cheered, glowed with admiration of their very clever son.

Rummaging through the packages that had been brought up by the servants, Apollo brought out a hand-carved rocking horse, left over from imperial times, that he had wrapped in a scrap of silk. Firez and Sons had used it as a display piece. Carved from clear, dark ebony, it was embellished with gold filigree on tack and rockers, the eyes two splendid sapphires, the mane and tail of flowing horsehair; overall it didn't stand over a dozen inches. Carrying it over to the bed, he placed it beside the baby.

"It's lovely, Apollo," Kitty said, taking in the elegant toy. "But he's only three months old. He's so small. . . ."

"I know that, dear. That's why it's a very *small* rocking horse. Look, he likes it." The Cub had caught hold of the flowing tail and was testing it for flavor. A father's elation shone on Apollo's face. "He's going to be a true *djighit*."

"You mountaineers. All you think about is horses and weapons. I'm surprised you didn't bring him home a gun." Kitty's tone was teasing, but the slightest edginess could be distinguished.

"I wouldn't do that."

"I should hope not."

"Of course not. It would break Pushka's heart. He's having one made for him. It's almost finished."

"Apollo!"

"It's only a very tiny one, kitten. Just a toy." Turning his warm, utterly disarming smile on Kitty's stern face, Apollo said, "Have I turned out so wickedly, raised in these mountains?" He tipped her chin up and softly brushed his knuckles across her cheek.

"Oh, Apollo, it isn't that. . . ."

"Afraid of all the killing?"

Kitty nodded her head.

"It'll be different in France. Don't worry. Just humor Pushka for now."

"Apollo, do you think we'll ever get out?"

"Of course. I promised, didn't I?" Inwardly, he hoped he'd be able to keep that promise.

Much later that evening, after the dirt of the trail had been washed off, dinner served, and the Cub fed and put to bed, Apollo carried several packages in from his dressing room and tossed them on the bed. Kitty, seated at her boudoir table brushing her hair, turned at the commotion.

Apollo, lounging against the bedpost, indicated the objects with a quick gesture. "A few presents for you. Very few, I'm afraid, shopping being what it is now. Once we get to France, I guarantee an improvement." His black silk robe, casually tied, set off his bronzed skin and pale shiny hair in the subdued light of the bedroom.

Kitty's hand flew to her mouth in delighted, delicate surprise. "Apollo . . . how did you dare? You could have been arrested at any time, walking into a shop!"

"Not at one o'clock in the morning, love."

Setting down her brush, she half twirled to face him, her urchin eyebrows raised slightly.

"Don't go moral on me, *dushka*. It's much too late," he said in an amused tone. "Besides," he continued, pushing his hands in the robe pockets, "these are all paid for very properly."

"With Soviet gold?"

"Which used to be imperial gold, and a good share of Kuzan gold, as a matter of fact. Satisfied?"

"Oh, I wasn't questioning the morality of it. You've long since converted me to your more . . . unorthodox life-style."

"Because of my charming ways, no doubt." A slow, lazy smile curled his lips.

"That, of course, and one other thing," Kitty facetiously replied, a very bewitching smirk touching her crimson mouth.

Apollo settled his shoulders more comfortably against the carved post and the lazy smile crinkled his eyes. "Yes, I've always found the combination quite . . . well, effective."

Kitty made a pretty moue. "I don't care to hear about the 'alwayses,' if you don't mind."

"Jealous?"

"Abominably."

"I suppose," he said, his eyes guilelessly clear, "you're going to go all wifely on me and expect me to be faithful."

"Not *expect*, dear man," Kitty replied ominously. "*Insist*."

"*Insist!* Oh-ho, this sounds serious. Why don't you try on the things I bought for you, and then I guarantee, darling, I'll be entirely open to any reasonable discussion of my faithfulness." He was grinning widely.

Kitty, glaring mutinously, retorted tartly, "And if I feel the subject is *not open* to discussion?"

Pushing himself away from the bedpost, Apollo untied the belt of his dressing gown and dropped the garment to the floor. He disposed his tall, lean body in a comfortable sprawl on the bed, then stretched, clasping his hands behind his head, his powerful shoulder muscles flexing and flowing in the light of the bedlamp. "Try on the gowns, pet," he said hospitably, "then, er, 'persuade' me to drop the discussion. You know how amenable I am to your 'persuasion.'" A slow, sensuous smile took possession of his mouth and his eyes grew sultry, flame gold, hungry. "And hurry, kitten," he breathed softly. "Three days is a long time. . . ."

It was a game, a delirious, exquisite game they both delighted in.

He tossed a peridot chiffon gown at her and said, "Why don't you dress by the fire; it's warmer," then sank back against the pillows like an elegant young prince.

Kitty felt the small shivers start even before she slipped out of her blue angora robe. Even the heat from the fire, playing over her body like waves of summer, couldn't allay the tiny chills spiraling up her spine. Apollo looked so magnificently virile in his negligent sprawl, his bold eyes already taking possession of her body. She cast a sidelong look at his broad, muscled shoulders; his taut torso, whip lean and hard; his slim hips, that rode horseflesh or females with equal power and skill; his long, athletic legs, their bronzed surface dusted with golden hair, now lying casually spread to welcome her. His arousal was instant and flagrant.

"Come here if you need help dressing. I'm very good with buttons . . . and hooks. . . ." His voice was rough-soft, curling around her like licking fingers of velvet.

Kitty picked up the beaded gown and stepped into it, one shapely leg after the other. She wiggled it over her hips, the silk lining like whispers of invitation against her naked skin. Lifting the beaded bodice, shimmering in draped rivers of silver and pearl, Kitty slid the weighted fabric up and over the heavy fullness of her breasts. The pressure of the intricately massed beads, however light, lay on her sensitized flesh like the brush of a hundred kisses. As she slipped the glistening straps over her shoulders, her creamy breasts moved against the silk-lined weight of the bodice; her nipples, already peaked, rubbed across minute undulations of chiffon and beads and a searing torrent trembled downward.

Apollo saw the flush beginning, saw the tiny quiver of her hands and offered in a voice already husky with passion, "Come here, love. I'll help." When she came, he turned her around, his hands firm on her hips, and deftly he fastened the myriad hooks up the back. Taking her hand in his, he pulled Kitty to face him and, half rising from the bed, adjusted the narrow straps on her shoulders. "Lovely. . . ." he said in a low voice, his hand running up the pale smoothness of her bare arm. "I like the color . . . the fit . . ."

"I like what you're wearing better," Kitty whispered, bending forward to reach his lips. Every slowly kindling nerve in her body wanted him, but when their lips met, he drew back, his large hands gently pushing her away. Looking up into green eyes already dark with desire, he murmured in a coaxing, sensual rasp, "Try on one more. . . ."

"I don't want to," Kitty softly breathed, premonitions of ecstasy already shivering down her thighs. "Later, Apollo, I'll try them on later. Don't make me wait—"

One bronzed hand released her waist and, in a graceful movement, slid over her hip, under the peridot chiffon skirt, and up the silkiness of her inner thigh. His fingers touched a pulsing beat, heavy with readiness, shamelessly wet.

The exploring contact scorched through Kitty like an electric jolt. Primordial feelings surged through her heated blood and her hips moved impatiently against the strong, invading hand.

"One more dress," Apollo cajoled gently, his long artist's fingers, equally at home with violence or seduction, moving inside the inner softness with superlative skill. "Only one more, kitten." His voice was delicately redolent, hushed with anticipatory pleasure. He enjoyed exercising a quixotic, sensual power over her; giving her more than she felt she could support; taking her past reason, words, and hearing until nothing was left but desire and need. With his free hand gripping her chin between thumb and forefinger, he pulled her face down to his and kissed her. She kissed him back, hungrily, opening her mouth, sucking his lips, moaning in little breathless sighs.

While she trembled, he slipped the green dress off swiftly, unhooking, unfastening, his fingers hasty but sure.

Kitty's hands moved down boldly, in her aching need, to Apollo's manhood, pressed hard against his belly, but he evaded her, his hands brushing hers aside. Gently, those hands, dark as mahogany, pushed her upright, then stroked her soothingly as a trainer might calm a high-strung thoroughbred. "Try this one on," he said in a voice like liquid silver, pulling over a flimsy wisp of a gown. "Lift your arms."

Almost mesmerized, in a trance born of surging passion and blind instinct, Kitty obeyed.

The diaphanous material fell over her head and shoulders and Apollo carefully settled the midnight-blue charmeuse over her thrusting breasts. She felt his touch like heated honey on her flesh, and the resulting shock waves surged through every aching nerve. She lifted her heavy lashes, and her sea-green eyes met yellow flames that pierced to her burning core. "Apollo . . ." she implored breathlessly.

"Look at me," he said, and she knew what he meant. "Soon, kitten," he whispered, adoration in his eyes, "very soon."

She moved restlessly, her eyes on his pulsing arousal.

His hand swept over the sheer pleated tulle falling from her hips in a blue waterfall. Without an underskirt, the silhouette of long slim legs, lush thighs and hips beckoned invitingly.

"Now, Apollo, now—" Kitty quietly insisted, her breathing quick and shallow, her eyes drawn by the evidence of his desire.

Ignoring her, he swung his long legs over the side of the bed, casually unabashed by his upthrusting desire. Businesslike, he pulled Kitty between his legs, took the triangular scrap of blue silk that served as half the chemise top between his fingers, and, with the other hand, lifted the soft weight of one of Kitty's breasts until the small piece of fabric cupped the bottom curve. He gently repeated the procedure with the other side of the bodice. The minute top revealed more than it concealed, and Kitty's ivory-white, peaked breasts flared out like large globes around the tiny blue triangle of material. Satisfied, like some serious if erotic couturier, Apollo ran his hands over the pale roundness pulled extravagantly high by the dark, taut chemise straps and traced her breasts as if they were resplendent ornaments for his pleasure. "Very nice," he said in a low, smoky voice, his knuckles trailing softly over the peaked nipples outlined by dark silk. "Are you mine, little kitten?" A hoarse triumph wound through his deep, raspy murmur, like a khan mastering a new houri, as he now idly rubbed the sharply pointed crests of Kitty's breasts between stroking thumb and forefinger.

A white heat raced downward from the languidly fondling touch, and, moaning, Kitty laced her fingers into the pale shiny hair, pulling Apollo's head fiercely to her breast. Silken handfuls of hair filled her hands, slid through her fingers like silver mercury, as she held the strong hard planes of his face against her yielding softness. Apollo twisted his head out of her hands and she gasped, then cried out, a low animal sound of a carnal pleasure, frenzied, out of control. Apollo's white teeth, gently holding a damply wet, silk-encased, taut nipple, eased open enough to say, "Tell me you're mine."

It came out in a faraway whisper, the pitch of witless longing past the point of reason. "Yes, yes, I'm yours. . . ."

His mouth closed and she shuddered, then groaned, her fists closing convulsively over his thick, satiny hair. Apollo's hands roamed lower, while his teeth and lips and tongue tantalized each breast; he could feel Kitty's body quivering beneath his touch. His hands flowed over flaring hip, the dip of her stomach, the gentle rise where crisp hair prickled through filmy blue tulle, and then, deftly, with one finger, he drew a line burying the silk tulle into the moistness between her thighs. "Silk on silk," he breathed around the crested peak his tongue was caressing, his long, dark fingers still stroking her slick, sleek wetness with the pleasure of a connoisseur.

Kitty almost swooned at the intensity of feeling. She cried and sobbed, grinding herself against the teasing mouth and stroking hand. Breathlessly she gasped, "Apollo—" Pleadingly, "You're cruel, inhuman. . . ."

"Walk to the fireplace and back first. I want to see you. Then—"

"No!" Her tone was pouting, sulky.

"It's just a few steps, pet. Please?" he coaxed in nectar-sweet tones. Then his expert hands found the delicate touchstone, wrapped in filmy diaphanous tulle, and when he said, "Please?" very gently one more time, Kitty nodded her head.

Carefully spinning her around, he gave her a light push on

her shapely bottom. With a dreamy, long-legged stride, Kitty slowly moved toward the fireplace, looking, Apollo thought, utterly tantalizing, like a nymph, a primavera: her long golden hair tossed about her shoulders, young, beautiful, slimly lush, and as opulent as a lifetime of May days. "Can you feel the silk when you walk?" he asked, his tone as caressing as the tulle rubbing the secret, throbbing places between her legs.

She was past answering but turned to face him and he saw. The pleated blue tulle, billowing around her rounded hips, divided in a sharp, deep, tautly stretched juncture, and the rising mound—pale blond hair visible through the sheer blue fabric—glistened wet with pearls of moisture.

He watched her walk back; he watched her eyes and he could almost feel the rubbing silk himself.

When he touched her she thought she would die, but he undressed her slowly and she didn't die. Then, laying her on the bed, he softly asked, "Do you want me inside you?"

"Yes, yes, yes," she sobbed, her eyes closed tight against the dizziness of passion burning deep inside her.

"Open your eyes. Look at me."

Her long, dark lashes fluttered open, and as he entered her, Apollo whispered, "I want you to look at me when you come. . . ."

Sometime later, he mockingly chastised into the riot of her honey-peach hair spilling over his shoulder, "You haven't even looked at the jewelry and baubles I brought for you from Derbent."

"It's your own fault," Kitty murmured, her tongue licking soft patterns in the perspiration on Apollo's chest. "You distract me."

"Who distracts whom?" His fine white teeth flashed; his drawl was sardonic.

"An arguable point, I concede." Kitty's tongue went back to tracing the line of Apollo's fourth rib.

A suntanned finger appeared directly across the route of her tongue and blocked its passage. "Do you want to see them?"

"Of course," she amiably replied and sat up, her full breast rubbing across Apollo's jaw. The drive he thought had been sated was immediately resurrected.

Rolling over on one elbow, he reached for a brown leather drawstring pouch, then loosened the leather thong that held it closed and rummaged through its contents until he found several rings. On an open palm he offered them to Kitty. "For my lady princess. Rings for her fingers, and—paraphrasing slightly—rings for her toes. You'd rather wait on the music," he said, watching Kitty's small hand select a sapphire-and-diamond ring, "if you heard me sing."

Kitty smiled, admiring the glittering bauble on one of her shapely fingers. Looking up, she remarked, "Come to think of it, I never have heard you sing."

"A deliberate act of mercy on my part, sweet. Consider yourself lucky. Do you like them? Here, take another. I'll do the toes." He began putting an enormous ruby on her little toe.

"Apollo, you're being silly. . . ." She glanced down at the large stone incongruously perched on a very small toe.

"I can be silly if I want. I'm a prince and a Kuzan, and if that's not reason enough, my mother also spoiled me rotten. Is the ruby too large, do you think? Let's try a smaller one for the other toe. It wouldn't do to be accused of bourgeois ostentation. Never let it be said that a Kuzan can't be discreet. I'll cover your remaining toes with very small gems." Which he proceeded to do, amidst kisses, giggles from Kitty, and much teasing laughter.

"And now," he said much later, his eyes scanning Kitty's nude body, her fingers and toes ornamented with twinkling jewels, "that about does it for rings. . . ." His pale eyes narrowed for a moment; then he continued in a soft voice, "Almost." Gently pushing Kitty down on her back, he reached for two more rings, said, "Don't move," and very carefully arranged two diamond rings, one on each nipple, stones hanging down. Bending his head he softly sucked, then teased with tongue and teeth until each crest peaked stiffly hard. "There," he murmured, his eyes intent on the jeweled nipples, "now the rings will stay on." His glance drifted up to Kitty's face, rosily flushed from the exquisite ministrations only recently applied to her sensitive nipples. "Do you like your rings?" His long bronzed fingers closed on the diamonds circling the painted peaks and slowly twisted the rings around and around. Unable to speak with the stabbing pleasure curling inside her abdomen, Kitty ran her tongue over her moist lower lip and languidly nodded. "I thought you would," he said, the faintest of smiles playing across his fine mouth.

Sliding his hand under her neck, he lifted Kitty a fraction of an inch and clasped a collar of lapis and gold around her neck. It was heavy, a hybrid cross between Celtic and Egyptian design, and it lay with a cool weight halfway down the curving roundness of her white breasts. Apollo's hand smoothed the dark surface of blue and gold lightly, pressing the precious metal and gems into the plump, full softness. Kitty responded to his touch as she always did, desire leaping like a live creature within her, an irresistible need freshly sparked by the contact. Her hands came up to draw him close, but he took them between his own and kissed each finger before placing them back at her sides saying, "Wait, love, there's more." She felt the cool weight of a massive, three-strand necklace of pearls fall into place around her waist; heard the click of the snap clasp; tensed at the tactile sensation of Apollo's hand on her stomach. It lay dark-skinned and startling across the paleness of her flesh, like a watermark imprinted on the finest, most delicate parchment. He stroked her smooth, silky skin, then straightened the three strands of enormous matched pearls, which drifted down the firm hollow of her abdomen. That adjustment of the long pearl chains brought the large emerald cabochon pendant at the middle of the pearl ellipse to a most intriguing point. One of Apollo's bronzed fingers slipped down over the pendant and, testing, pressed lightly. Kitty's momentum of building passion soared in an instant; she uttered a muted sound low in her throat and, quite involuntarily, her toes curled as the shock waves reached her hidden place.

"Like that?" he murmured huskily.

"Yes—no—I mean, you shouldn't do that with . . ."

"Why not?" His slender hand was nuzzling experimentally and Kitty was having trouble thinking clearly.

"It doesn't . . ."

"Tell me how it seems, little kitten," his voice softly demanded. "I want to know," and with a delicate slowness he slid the smooth cabochon jewel into the damp softness, his eyes watching her intently. He forced it upward into the tight passage, and when his fingers nudged it deeply, Kitty melted away from the sweet agony of sensation flooding over her. His tawny eyes lazily smoldering, Apollo, with a devastating gentleness, traced the emerald along the inner surfaces, guided by a light, sure touch, and as it moved higher, lower, from side to side, slick from her ardent arousal, cool against her heated interior, Kitty arched to meet the mounting, compelling rapture.

"Does it feel good? Should I leave it in?" Huskily intimate and knowing, a half smile of pleasure tilted across his face.

She gave a breathless little "No."

"No?"

"No—yes—I don't know. Lord, Apollo, don't ask me . . . now. . . ." Each word was wrenched from a mind obsessed with other things.

"Do you want me to stop?" It was a sensuous murmur, provocative, as his lean hand moved the pendant slightly higher.

Kitty stirred against the smothering ecstasy and he had his answer.

He continued to stroke languidly inside the heated woman, who was softly writhing under his feathered touch, and his deep voice lazily caressed her senses like the August sun. "I could unhook the pendant from the pearls and leave it inside you, as the Oriental women do. Then every time you moved, you'd feel it. Every shift and rustle of your body would make you ready for love, ready for me. You'd feel it when you walked, when you sat down to luncheon; you could feel it when you bent over to pick up your shoes or reached for a frock from your armoire." The sound of his voice was a sensual whisper that curled through her heated mind like pale wisps of fog. "I'd have to stay close to you . . . to keep you satisfied. . . . Maybe you could stay in the bedroom and I'd come to you when you wanted more. Should I leave it in for a day or so?"

He could always control her so easily with his adept expertise, with his touch that had known so many women, and a small corner of Kitty's mind fought at that terrible loss of independence. "No, no, I don't want to," she cried through the blood pounding in her ears.

He gave a very small smile as he gazed at the flushed, passionate woman. In that familiar, self-assured tone he said, "What if I say you do? You'll like it, I know."

A tiny spark of resentment surfaced through the sexual haze inundating her. "How do you know what I'd like?"

"I just do," he said, and instinctively Kitty knew he was talking about women from his past.

She fought against the peaking crescendo and tried to struggle free. "In that case, *I* definitely won't—"

One sun-darkened hand held her shoulder with an effortless casualness and the other hand shifted, two fingers going where one had been, and Kitty's last words were lost in a soft, shivering whimper.

"When I have you here like this, I can make you do anything, *chérie*. You know it and I know it. Your luscious body is quite insatiable. Am I right?"

She was being very stubborn. "No."

"Am I right, kitten?" he purred, and his mouth closed over the hardened peak of one rosy nipple, lifting it lightly.

Instantly beyond reason or mundane resentment, Kitty sobbed wildly, "Yes—yes . . . Apollo, save me!"

He knew she couldn't wait for him; it was too late already, so he let her go without him and Kitty crested beneath his hands in shuddering, convulsive waves. "*Je t'adore*," he whispered against her warm cheek as she stilled in his arms. He did adore her, her open sensuality so fresh and pure; her vixenish impatience he hadn't been able to curb; most of all, her demanding desire for him, and that, he happily mused, would, with luck, never be curbed.

Kitty floated back to reality, sinfully pleasured, sinfully

happy, in the arms of the man who imprisoned her senses, who could, at his merest touch, suddenly make all else illusion. She heard a metallic click, felt the pearls fall away, the emerald glide wetly from her body, and then her deep green eyes focused on the male-hard body poised above her. The sensation of warm legs easing hers farther apart tingled up her thighs, a hardness penetrated her yielding softness, filling her slowly so she felt each persuasive sliding pressure, and as hip met hip she rose to meet the man who made her complete.

Sometime later, stripped of all her jewels which Apollo had casually tossed aside like yesterday's croissants, Kitty lay across his chest, pouting a little. "It isn't fair, when you stroke me, thus and so—" Her hands flew lightly over his shoulders and down delineated pectorals. "I'll do anything for you."

"It's the same for me, sweetheart, often, every day. All I have to do is look at you and I want you." He smiled into the waves of her hair resting beneath his chin. "You don't know how many times I've damned the number of servants we have underfoot."

"You're always so much in control—or so it seems, curse your conceited hide." The opulent curve of Kitty's lower lip was distractingly petulant, like ripe fruit, and now that she had looked up, it was simply willing him to take a bite. He rigorously forced his gaze away. She was the most distracting female he'd ever known and he proceeded to explain that to her.

"On the contrary, pet, look at me sometime, even in the midst of company. You'll come walking into the room looking delicious and I'll have to sit down immediately and cross my legs to avoid being indiscreet. You have me in a slavery of love, *madame*. There is nothing one-sided about this relationship."

The little pout had eased and a faint smile had taken its place. "I'll have to look next time."

"Please don't. It'll only make the obvious more obvious. Think how embarrassed our guests will be."

Kitty laughed then, the delectable, throaty peal that was

distinctly hers. "It's marvelous to know I have such power over you."

"I knew I never should have told you," Apollo replied with an amiable twitch of his lips. "It leaves my libido vulnerable to all sorts of blackmail."

Kitty giggled delightfully and teasingly purred, her face very close to Apollo's, "The next time we're at a party, I'll have to walk up to you as you're seated sedately in your chair and say, 'Apollo, will you get me some more champagne?' "

"And I'll say, 'Have the servants get you some.' "

"Then I'll simply have to coax you up to, say, meet one of the new guests."

"If you do that, little vixen, I'll call your hand and do you one better. When standing, my arousal will be patently clear to all, and I guarantee you, with or without polite excuses, you will be carried upstairs right before everyone's titillated eyes."

"You wouldn't!" The green eyes registered hesitant disbelief.

"I would—and you know it, hussy." He grinned. "Be warned."

Kitty's long lashes lowered coquettishly and one bare foot laced itself around Apollo's leg. "It might be amusing to call your bluff sometime. What would your parents say if you were to do something like that in Paris?"

Apollo chuckled and Kitty felt the soft motion of his body. "Papa would say it was a marvelous way to duck another tedious evening party, and Maman would continue her conversation as though nothing had happened. And if anyone would be so bold as to call her attention to my behavior, she would simply shrug and reply that her boys were always so unpredictable . . . like their father. You see, you're simply going to have to learn to do what you're told. I always win," he said with a grin, and only just in time caught the leg aimed at his groin.

The playful tussle that ensued was not unlike that of a puppy battling a benign wolfhound.

Much later Apollo drew away and, reaching down to the

foot of the bed, pulled up the remaining packages, saying, "Now that we've both caught our breath, see if any of this strikes your fancy."

Kitty unwrapped three more dresses and two tea gowns in pale lace. The third package yielded an extravagant chinese brocade in shades of black and silver, very theatrical and resplendent. "Everything's magnificent! The Revolution hasn't diminished the couturier's trade, it seems."

"Apparently not. Karaim says the commissars' wives and mistresses are quite insatiable when it comes to extravagant living."

"And the jewelry—" Kitty ran her hands over the pile of pearls, rubies, emeralds, diamonds, and lapis that Apollo had tossed in a heap on one side of the large bed. "So much, Apollo, and all so lovely. It wasn't necessary," she whispered.

"But I wanted to. When we finally reach Europe, I'll be able to buy you so much more. I miss being able to buy you trinkets."

Kitty's head was bent, but she was silently fingering the modest fortune in lustrous jewelry.

When she remained quiet for several seconds, Apollo looked at her more closely. The firelight glistened off a tiny trail of tears, and when he reached for her, Kitty brushed them away in embarrassment. "Sweetheart, what's the matter? Did I say something?" He tipped his golden head to look into her face, his dark brows furrowed in concern. "*Dushka*, if you're worried about my fidelity, don't. I was only teasing you. I've quite reformed. My word on it."

"It's not that." Kitty shook her head, reaching up to intercept two more tears racing down her cheek.

"What's wrong then, kitten?" Apollo inquired gently and, casually shoving aside the treasure in jewels, he gathered her into his arms. Lifting her into his lap, he sat cross-legged on the bed, holding her close, his hands stroking her soothingly. "Don't cry. I didn't mean to hurt you."

"You didn't hurt me," Kitty softly replied.

"Then why the tears?"

Kitty looked up into Apollo's pale eyes, now filled with

love and anxiety. "Peotr never bought me a present in all our years of marriage."

Apollo knew his self-centered friend well enough not to be surprised at this, but he still wasn't reassured about the source of Kitty's tears. "And you're crying about that?" he asked with a certain perplexity—and, if he was honest with himself, a certain twinge of jealousy.

"No, I'm happy," Kitty said, which didn't help his perplexity at all, although it neatly quashed the jealousy.

"So, you're crying. . . ." he said slowly.

"Tears of happiness, dummy." A quivering smile appeared.

Although Apollo's expertise with women covered certain areas in depth, this was his first experience with this particular cliché. "Ah. . . ." he said in apparent understanding, accepting Kitty's explanation, but still prone to a vague uneasiness. "So you're actually happy?"

"Very happy."

"And you like the gowns and jewelry?"

"Immensely."

"In that case, *dushka*," he said with a wicked grin, "I'll have to go on another shopping expedition very soon."

"Don't you dare!" Kitty squealed, her pummeling fist accenting the exclamation, melancholy wiped clean from her fragile features.

He rolled onto his back in mock affright, laughing softly as she followed him down, her fists bouncing off the hard muscles of his chest. Tears made him nervous, especially poignant tears about her past. He much preferred his independent, autocratic, vixenish Kitty, and, rolling away from her, he lightly leaped from the bed, raised his hands in a lazy gesture of surrender, and said, "You're the boss, ma'am." Splendidly naked, he stood there, just out of reach. "I'm resigned to life with a malapert shrew."

"A shrew! You beast! You incorrigible—" Scrambling across the bed, she lunged for him, and effortlessly he caught her. Slowly he slid her down his body as she continued the heated description of his character, until suddenly her downward progress halted and Kitty uttered a tiny, "Oh."

She looked up quickly and met warm golden eyes. "As I said, *madame*," Apollo murmured softly, "I'm your slave. . . ."

Whether slave or master of his fate, no further raids ensued, for a greater force held sway. The winter storms came howling down the rugged Caucasus range, and the mountain passes were either closed or barely passable. The village of Dargo settled into its winter hermitage. Word came through occasionally; the most ominous those concerning Georgia to their south, the only nation remaining independent in what had been old Russia's borders. Although the Soviet government had signed a treaty with Georgia recognizing its independence, now, through the winter months, they were disputing a thousand and one diplomatic technicalities with the small nation. The fall of Armenia in December should have served warning to Georgia, but its politicians existed in a vacuum of diverse and warring political ideologies, so while the diplomats busily negotiated over trivial, minute changes in commercial treaties or railroad right-of-ways and the political parties in Georgia's parliament scrapped over power, Soviet troops massed on the borders of Georgia and the Russian Eleventh Army prepared for a full-scale attack. Georgia's independence was ticking away; it was only a matter of time before the last remaining sovereign nation would be "welcomed" into the Soviet Union of Socialist States.

In fact, on the same day—February 25, 1921—the first foreign minister of Georgia, Chkhenkeli, was presenting his credentials to the president of the French Republic in Paris, hundreds of Georgian soldiers fell on snow-covered battlefields defending their country against attack. On that day, Red Army troops captured the capital of Tiflis. Commander Orjonikidze telegraphed Moscow, "The red banner of the Soviet regime is aloft in Tiflis. Long live Soviet Georgia!"

# 18

During the last week in March, the Cub fell ill.

Apollo and Kitty had been carrying him for three days. He was so sick that it was the only way he would sleep. He would hold on to their thumb, and if they'd hold their hand very still he'd sleep. But the minute they'd move their thumb he'd wake right up. He could swallow only ice, so the kitchen staff delivered fresh fruit ices and sherbets every hour 'round the clock. On the fourth day of the fever his breathing became raspy and difficult, his little face turning blue at times from the effort to breathe. Kitty was terrified, and Apollo's alarm mounted at the Cub's labored struggles. All the village remedies and folk medicines had failed to help in any way.

By late morning, fearful for his son's life, Apollo abruptly declared, "I'm going to Shura for a doctor."

"Send someone, Apollo, please," Kitty pleaded. "Don't go yourself. Since Georgia fell there's no safe haven, and they're still killing any White officers they find. Please, Apollo, don't! You're *known* in Shura," she cried in fear. "Someone might recognize you!"

"He's my son." And as if that were explanation enough, Apollo handed the Cub to Kitty, walked into his dressing room, and began to buckle on his holster. Kitty's face was contorted, her eyes wide with anguish—was she to lose both those she loved most in the world?

Seeing the panic, Apollo returned and took Kitty and the Cub gently in his arms. "Sweetheart, now listen to me. The doctor won't come up here unless I fetch him. You know that. No one in Shura trusts the mountain men. And I can't sit here and watch my son die without help. Just take care of the Cub until I return."

"But Apollo, if you're recognized . . ."

He bent to kiss her gently on the forehead. "It'll be dark by the time we reach Shura." Placing a light hand on the Cub's cheek, his fingers touched the feverishly hot skin. "Damn," he muttered worriedly. The Cub was burning. "I'll be back as soon as I can; eight hours at best." With a light, brushing kiss into Kitty's hair, Apollo turned on his heel and ran from the room, shouting orders as he raced down the wide stairway. Maybe if they tried the Erpeli-Gimri pass they could be in Shura earlier. Last week the snow was still too deep, but a week of warm weather in March could make a difference. It was worth the risk.

Before Apollo was completely dressed in *papakha* and *burkha*, Leda was being led from the stables and Karaim had appeared in the foyer. Immediately out the door and down the steps, both were in the saddle before the horses were completely packed with gear, Apollo impatiently brushing aside the additional equipment. He didn't have time. Apollo dug in his heels and Leda lunged down the mountain trail. Bending forward, Apollo spoke softly into the mare's ear. Straightening, he gave her her head and she plunged and skidded down the narrow track. At the valley floor, the golden Karabagh sprang forward like a released crossbow. Understanding the tone of urgency, the panic in her master's voice, Leda responded with strength and heart.

"I hope you're ready for a hard ride," Apollo shouted to Karaim across the brisk and windy mountain air.

"I'll stay with you," Karaim shouted back, and side by side they rode like madmen.

They entered Shura four hours later, their horses lathered. The city was drifting into early winter twilight, the streets busy with workers on their way home. Avoiding the main thoroughfares they arrived at the doctor's house undetected. Waiting in the back with the horses, Karaim kept guard while Apollo went inside to persuade the doctor to venture out on the dangerous ride up the mountains. The gold Apollo carried was his most persuasive argument, although he was perfectly willing to use the pistols strapped to his hips if necessary. He fingered them impatiently while the doctor hesitated fractionally, and whether the gold or the threat of death proved more effective, the doctor went for his bag and coat.

After leaving the doctor's residence the trio skirted the busy areas of town, keeping to the quiet side streets. They were nearly to the outskirts when one of the newly formed people's security units suddenly appeared from between a livery stable and a tumbled-down tavern.

"Stop!" a heavyset, bearded man at the head of the group demanded. "Your papers!"

In a split second a score of alternatives and probabilties tumbled through Apollo's mind, but the revolutionary fervor of these police squads was well known, and the possibility of successful debate with them was negligible. "One never escapes bureaucracy," Apollo said, a faint, grim smile on his lips, and for a second a living flash of bereavement and farewell passed from his golden eyes to Karaim. Then his *nagaika* came down brutally on the flanks of the doctor's mount and he screamed, "Ride, Karaim!"

In a swift, fluid motion only a lifetime in the saddle could achieve, Karaim stretched out on one stirrup, grabbed the bridle of the doctor's horse, and, savagely manhandling the frightened animal, spurred his own mount. The two men careened at a gallop toward the deserted stretch of road ahead.

Apollo turned to fight.

He swung his horse frantically and went crashing into the rabble, firing both Mausers. Leda responded to Apollo's commands, plunging, rearing, flailing out with lethal hoofs. When his pistols were empty, he laid on heads, faces, shoulders, backs with his sword and *nagaika*, managing to wreak disaster on the group before the squad's sheer numbers overwhelmed him and he was hauled from Leda's back. He fought every foot of the way down the street to the security commissar's office; he fought when they dragged him down the hallway; he kicked and cursed when they unbolted the cell door. Then, their prisoner secure, the ruffian band jabbed at him with sticks and rifle butts, lashed out with booted feet and clenched fists. A powerful blow collided with Apollo's golden head, and halfway into unconsciousness he cursed the end of four years of phenomenal luck.

For days he lay in jail while the newly created commissars argued about the particular manner of executing him, several schools of manslaughter strident in their preferences. The hierarchy of authority was still very muddy and chaotic in the new Soviet Union, and control was frequently directly related to the loudness of one's voice. The noisy, clamorous uproar was eventually resolved by a perspicacious new commissar who had the good sense to understand that supreme power still resided in the capital. He wired to Tiflis regarding the captured White officer and received an immediate reply: DO NOT STOP REPEAT STOP DO NOT STOP EXECUTE APOLLO KUZAN STOP SEND TO TIFLIS STOP. It was necessary to emphasize the negative since the utter dissolution of civil tribunals had resulted in every tree and lamppost becoming an instant courtroom, and Tiflis was very anxious to hang Captain Prince Apollo Kuzan with as much fanfare and publicity as possible. The execution might serve as an object lesson to the Dagestanis, who had been very slow—in fact, completely disinterested—in recognizing the new Soviet government. The reluctance of the Dagestanis to surrender themselves and their lands to the benevolence of Bolshevism was causing problems in Moscow. They must be made to understand who their masters were, and with the execution of their prince perhaps the point would be more readily taken.

The argumentative commissars in Shura did as they were told, and as it happened, on the day Apollo left for Tiflis, the train to the capital carried an inordinate number of Dagestani warriors.

When Karaim arrived back at Dargo without Apollo, Kitty's heart almost stopped. Light-headed with despair, she asked for details. Karaim assured her men were even now retracing the route to Shura; shortly, they would know what had befallen the Falcon. Whether to follow Apollo's orders or to stay with him and chance the Cub's life was the hardest decision of Karaim's life. Unyielding devotion to his prince's orders had prevailed over his own personal inclinations. He tried to reassure Kitty in his taciturn way, but his spare phrases did little to comfort the shrieking terror echoing through Kitty's numbed brain. Apollo gone? Captured? Maybe dead? How was she supposed to survive a loss like that? To have her happiness suddenly snatched away after only just finding it? Huge tears welled into her eyes and Karaim, in an uncharacteristic gesture, took both her hands in his dark leathery palms, saying gruffly, "We'll get As-saqr As-saghir back for you, Countess. That I promise. But now . . . the Falcon's son. Please. He needs you. He must live."

Into the awkward silence, Kitty replied a little shakily, "Yes . . . of course," her confused mind still dazed with the enormity of her loss.

"Go with the doctor," Karaim said gently, pushing her toward the stairs, "and we'll find the Falcon. I'll return later with news."

Kitty turned back. "Oh, yes, please. Come any time, Karaim. I'll be up and waiting." Her eyes were dark with fear.

"Sleep if you can. The Cub needs his mother in good health."

Kitty knew Karaim was right, and while she grieved for her son in his illness, a part of her would die if she were to lose Apollo. "Have me wakened, then, Karaim, when you return with news. Anytime, please!" And Kitty took a deep breath to forestall the tears threatening to burst forth.

"As soon as I know anything, Countess."

Early the next morning, Karaim returned with the information: Apollo was being held in the jail at Shura, but rumor indicated a possibility he was to be transferred to Tiflis.

"Why, Karaim?" Kitty anxiously cried. "Are they going to spare him? Is it possible, since they haven't killed him yet?" The flare of desperate hope was pathetic in its intensity.

"I don't know, Countess. We must wait and see," Karaim carefully replied, not wishing to inspire any unrealistic expectations. "If he's taken to Tiflis, we'll follow and see if he can be freed at some point in the journey, or possibly later in Tiflis."

"If you go, Karaim, I'm going, too." Her voice was coldly determined.

Karaim was momentarily startled; he could never get used to the countess's lack of understanding of the most elementary principles. Regaining his composure, he quietly remonstrated. "Impossible. The Falcon would never allow you to be exposed to such danger."

"Say what you will, Karaim." Kitty set her shoulders resolutely. "I'll not stay behind and wait for tidings of Apollo's . . . death." Her lips quivered but she lifted her chin high. "Don't think I don't know why they want to transfer him to Tiflis. Bolshevik feeling against former White officers runs gallows high. It'll be a circus, won't it? A high-ranking White officer—a Kuzan and Iskender-Khan's heir—being hanged. Like a public spectacle."

"I don't know, Countess," Karaim said noncommitally, but he resolved to lead his rescue troop out of Dargo in the greatest secrecy. Neither Iskender-Khan nor Apollo would allow the countess to put herself in such a vulnerable and dangerous position.

Meanwhile, with the doctor's drugs, the Cub rallied, and within days he was well on the way to recovery. But his mother had been unable to smile, despite the gratifying improvement. She felt, disconsolately, that Apollo's life was too high a price to pay.

Two days after Apollo's capture, nearly riding three horses to death, Sahin had reached Poti and dispatched a telegram through the underground route. The message was received in a grand château on the outskirts of Paris. The cryptic wire stated only: THE FALCON IS CAGED, but endless wheels were immediately set into motion. Markers were called in, gold exchanged hands where it would do the most good; influence was pushed to its limits. Even a beautiful woman in the Crimea decided it was definitely worth her while to encourage the advances of a fat little commissar from Tiflis, who only hours before had filled her with loathing.

So Apollo languished in Metekhi Prison at Tiflis awaiting the convenience of the chief commissar currently on holiday near Yalta. The prince was ignorant of the fact that the date of his execution hung on the merest whim of frivolous fate and on the degree of erotic pleasure the commissar's stunning new girlfriend could evoke.

Apollo wondered at the delay, but however abhorrent the incarceration, his will to survive valued each new dawn that arrived. He knew if it were humanly possible, Iskender would find a means to rescue him. The move from Shura to Tiflis, however, had been orchestrated in such a way that any attempt would have been suicidal as well as unsuccessful. A single armored car had been attached directly behind the engine and Apollo had traveled in that heavily guarded car. The remainder of the train had been armed with soldiers inside and atop the cars, machine guns at the ready. Should there be an attack, the cars behind the armored one were to be uncoupled immediately while the engine and Apollo's vault were to speed to Tiflis alone.

Coincidentally, on the same day Apollo was escorted to Tiflis, the golden Karabagh mare disappeared from the police chief's stable at Shura. "She was never meant for that worm, anyway," a dark Dagestani warrior spat on a moonlit mountain trail. "She wouldn't let him on her back." Behind him, Leda shone silver gilt in the light of a new moon.

The police chief had mistakenly assumed the egalitarian principles of the Revolution included thoroughbred Karabaghs as well. But Karabaghs were bred only for princes, and if the police chief had forgotten that fact in the rush of revolutionary fervor, Leda had not. His pedigree was not to her liking.

Apollo had been in Tiflis now for almost ten days, and while he appreciated each day of life, he knew the possibilities of being liberated from the Metekhi were slim. The prison, formerly used for tsarist political prisoners, was completely inaccessible on three sides, built on a jutting precipice high above the Kura River. The Cheka guard, who came occasionally to make his life miserable, had gloated that no successful escape had occurred from Metekhi since 1822. Well, once each century, Apollo had thought optimistically, and then he had forced his mind to concentrate on pleasant memories of Kitty to evade the excruciating pain of the rubber whip striking his body with searing monotony. Flogging with the stiff rubber lash was one of the Cheka's favorite torture devices, for it caused internal injuries and bleeding without external evidence.

Luckily the second in command at the Metekhi while the commissar was vacationing in Yalta regarded the Cheka as an inhuman aberration, and strict orders had been given—preceded by a curt telegram from Lenin himself—that the prisoner was not to be visibly maltreated. On the day of Apollo's "trial" and public hanging, the Soviets wanted no broken, tortured ruin of humanity to appear before the people of Tiflis. Too many stories of torture and atrocities were finding their way out of the country, contributing to an unsuitable image abroad.

So the Cheka monsters who came irregularly to Apollo's cell kept their hand in with forms of torture that wouldn't break a man, only make his life grimly oppressive.

Apollo was now very white and only his fingers unobtrusively linked behind the chair back held him erect. His chest and arms were a bruised pulp, the feeling in his legs had disappeared an hour ago. While stubbornly proud, he wasn't foolish. He knew he couldn't last much longer; he was existing on willpower alone. With a kind of brutal persistence he braced himself for the next blow, his face set like iron. Father, Pushka, get me out of here, Apollo prayed for the thousandth time since noon.

The Cheka torturer heated another small iron rod.

"Hasn't this game gone on long enough today?" Apollo said in a faint, gasping breath. "You can't seriously think they're going to want a charred corpse for trial. Think how unhappy Lenin will be." For days Apollo had been trying to get some response from the brute. The goading distracted his mind, however briefly, from the pain.

The hulking monster was coming toward him with the red-hot iron.

"Try that once too often and you won't have a guinea pig left," Apollo whispered, his head flung back, the last shreds of strength ebbing away. His hair was dark with sweat and his fingers cramped, resisting the raw agony.

"You hang soon, anyway," the guard said, applying the iron with emotionless eyes.

And just before the darkness engulfed him, a wisp of a grin crossed Apollo's mouth. By God, he gloated, he'd finally made the bastard talk.

Kitty discovered two days after the fact that Karaim had departed with his men. In a frenzy she confronted Iskender-Khan. "I wanted to go to Tiflis!" she screamed, quite unconcerned with the row she was making in front of several visitors he was entertaining.

"Ah, Kitty, my dear," the old chieftain replied calmly, rising to meet her and murmuring quiet apologies to his guests as he moved to the doorway where Kitty stood.

Indifferent to tradition and protocol, Kitty shouted, "I'm *not* sitting here, waiting—I'm leaving!" Her voice blasted through the hushed room like an anarchist's bomb.

Taking her arm, Iskender turned Kitty aside. "It's too dangerous." His voice was moderate, reasonable.

"I don't care," Kitty cried, her hands clenched into fists at her side.

"It's no place for a woman." A placating attempt at chivalry. He touched her shoulder gently and she shook him off.

"Don't you dare say that!" Kitty retorted through gritted teeth, fed up with mountain tenets of what a woman could and could not do.

"Apollo wouldn't approve if I let you go," Iskender patiently explained. It was true.

That touched off the explosion. Kitty was nearly hysterical, and this was not the time to bring up male prerogatives. She rounded on him. Her face, appallingly white within the framing mass of honey-apricot hair, was unflinching. "I don't care!" she hissed and, in a whirl of silk, left.

"I'm sorry," Iskender apologized, turning back to his guests. "As-saqr As-saghir's woman is distraught. His capture, following their son's illness, has taken its toll on her nerves. Now, as we were discussing: Ali, could you see that the streets are clear between Krasilnava and Bebutovskaya on the morning of April twelfth? And Shirez, about the touring car . . ." Kitty's female hysteria was dismissed from his mind as plans went apace for Apollo's rescue.

Frustrated in her efforts to convince Karaim to take her along and irritated by Iskender's patronizing behavior, Kitty finally lost her temper completely and decided to take matters into her own hands. Something she should have done a long time ago, she thought. The months with Apollo had made her soft. Good Lord, she'd run her own affairs for years with no help from anyone. It was about time she broke out of the cushioned confines love had woven around her.

Several hours before dawn the following morning, Kitty and the Cub were passing through the last sentry post guarding the mountain aul. Mother and son, dressed in dark peasant garb, sat atop a mountain pony packed high with Kurdistan carpets and went unnoticed in the lengthy caravan of burdened horses leaving Dargo in the train of an Armenian rug dealer.

The Armenian, whom Kitty had approached the previous evening, was richer by a ruby-and-diamond necklace valued in the range of two years' income. Only for such an extravagant price would he have even considered spiriting As-saqr As-saghir's woman and child out of the village. If Iskender-Khan were to discover his part in her flight, his life would be worthless—less than worthless, for he would be hounded from one end of the earth to the other. Patting the heavy necklace, he prayed to all the gods he knew.

At Shura, Kitty and the caravan parted company. Purchasing a ticket for herself, she and the Cub boarded the train for Tiflis. She wasn't certain what she would do when they

reached Tiflis, but she had to be near Apollo. She had plans
and would begin by looking up the only acquaintance she
knew there: her former music teacher, Professor Pashkov.

The interior of the car she entered was a mass of humanity.
Since the Revolution, privacy was almost impossible unless
one was high in the party ranks. Compartment walls had been
torn up for firewood along with doors and woodwork. The
cushioned seats had been ripped apart, broken windows haphazardly boarded up, the floors littered with refuse.

Kitty and the Cub found a corner among a group of mountain villagers traveling with their stock of newly made rifles
they were going to sell in Tiflis. The journey passed safely
until the outskirts of Tiflis when two guards came into the
car checking identity papers. When a hand was held out to
receive hers, Kitty replied she had lost them. Two calculating
eyes studied her. Behind the black, voluminous peasant garb
was a startlingly attractive blond woman.

"An Ossete?" the soldier brusquely asked. That mountain
tribe was almost wholly blond, distinctive in the Caucasus
where dark-haired, dark-eyed coloring prevailed.

"Yes," Kitty quickly replied, and hoped he didn't know
the language.

"A little out of your territory, aren't you?"

"My late husband's from Dagestan. I'm returning home to
my people."

"Your husband's dead?" A familiar gleam Kitty had seen
so often in Stavropol lit in his eyes.

Uneasily, she answered, "Yes." The guard's scrutiny now
became attentive, taking her in from head to toe, dwelling at
length on the Cub sleeping in her arms.

"No papers, hmmm?" There was no mistaking the lust
kindling behind his small, inset eyes. He patted the pistol on
his hip. "Come with me. I'll have to . . ." The pause was deliberate. "Interrogate you."

Kitty followed him, with a pounding heart, through three
railroad cars, everyone glancing away prudently from the by
now familiar sight of an arrested individual. Though fear
seized her, deep down she was determined to suffer no further

indignities at the hands of a Bolshevik. Her hand slipped down into the folds of the blanket wrapped around the Cub and eased the *kinjal* handle slightly from its sheath. Apollo had insisted she learn to wield the mountain dagger, and for the first time since the endless lessons, she was thankful for his insistence. She could almost hear him quietly saying, "Slide it in between the second and third ribs. No, no, you're too high; down there. . . . Didn't I tell you it was easy?" And when she had become fast and expert he'd teased her into performing for Iskender one night. She'd never forget the glowing pride in Apollo's voice when she had gotten under Iskender's practiced guard and touched him lightly exactly over his heart. "What did I tell you, Pushka," Apollo said, excitement warming his voice. "You have to admit she's good."

The guard was motioning her into a small compartment at the far end of the car, the third in a row of rooms in a once plush sleeping car. She followed him in and he shut the door. The click of the lock left her in no doubt of his intentions.

"Women without papers, or at least the pretty ones, spread their legs for me in payment." He uttered the blunt statement matter-of-factly, as one might mention the price of the morning newspaper. Evidently familiar with the procedure, he was already reaching for Kitty.

Backing away until her legs met the cushions of the padded seat, Kitty nervously said, "The baby. Let me lay him down on the floor."

"Get rid of the brat anywhere. Just hurry—we'll be into the station at Tiflis in minutes."

Turning away from him, Kitty bent to set the Cub in the corner of the compartment and slid the *kinjal* into her hand during the apparent adjustment of his blanket.

She came up from the floor in one smooth crouching lunge, up and under the guard's arms, by now half raised in astonishment. Even before the surprise fully registered on the crude, unshaven face, her gold-hilted *kinjal* neatly slid between the ribs Apollo had pointed out to her time and time again. One short, sharp cry, and the guard's ruptured heart failed to beat again. Kitty jumped back from his towering bulk crashing downward.

Filled with horror, Kitty looked for a frozen moment at the still twitching body. Realizing suddenly that the train would be pulling into Tiflis at any moment, she started to roll the guard's body behind the door. He was very heavy, but—pushing, shoving, and heaving—she made progress. She had to keep the murder from being discovered until she was safely away. Losing precious seconds, she gave the body a final pull, then turned and seized the Cub.

Moments later the train was pulling into the station, and the commotion was sufficient to hide anyone wanting to melt into the crowd. The Cub chose that time to wake up and complain noisily, but in the turmoil of chattering passengers intent on leaving the train no one noticed a young blond woman and a lustily squalling baby.

Praying that Professor Pashkov still lived at the address Kitty remembered, she set off on foot to find him. An hour later, Kitty was able to relax for the first time since stealing out of Dargo. The Cub had been fed and bathed, she had washed away the dust of the journey, and Professor Pashkov's quietly efficient wife, Grunia, had put together a wholesome, if modest, tea.

"I can't thank you enough," Kitty was saying for the tenth time since her sudden arrival.

"Stay as long as you wish."

"I don't *have* much time," she confessed, and went on to relate the story of Apollo's capture and her precipitous journey south to attempt . . . something. "I brought my jewels with me, hoping maybe to bribe someone. I thought I'd try to petition the prison commander."

"It's extremely uncertain of success, Countess." The professor went on to explain that he had become a musical commodity much in demand by the high-ranking army officers for their entertaining. His reputation as a violinist was well known, and at least he was able to keep from starving. He was too old to emigrate, he explained to Kitty when she asked the obvious question; his whole life had been spent in Russia, and with so few years left he didn't care to spend them in a foreign land. Soon it was decided that Kitty would go as his accompanist that evening to Colonel Ismailovich's; the commander of the Metekhi was often in attendance. He would be easier to approach informally this way than within the confines of the prison.

A gown and shoes were purchased with a small sapphire ring, the Cub was left in the tender care of Madame Pashkov, and Kitty and the professor entered the colonel's home shortly before ten.

"I should discourage you in this madness." Professor Pashkov sighed, carefully arranging his music on the stand of cherrywood. "Won't you reconsider, Countess?" His bushy white eyebrows came together in a worried frown.

Kitty looked up from the music she was vigorously pushing around above the ivory keys of the grand piano and met the professor's eyes. "Just point out the commander to me when he walks in," she replied in a tight, quiet voice. Then a small smile touched her lush lips, and her tone changed, permeated by a delicate sadness. "I have to try. If I didn't, I could never live with myself."

The professor sighed again. "Very well. He's short, dark, and affects a cavalry mustache. I'll let you know the minute he enters the room."

"And then, God willing, we'll see what half a million roubles' worth of jewelry buys," Kitty uttered with a nervous exhalation.

As it turned out, there was no need for the professor to point out the commander of the Metekhi when he entered. The moment Commander General Tergukasov came to the drawing room, his eyes were drawn to the vision in blue playing the piano. The woman with blond curls and bare shoulders was the most stunning female he had ever seen. For a count of ten he stood arrested in the archway and then, bold by nature—an asset in a military man—he strode in a straight line across the room to the slightly elevated dais. He took the two shallow steps in one light leap and his graceful hand came down on Kitty's fingers. The small, dark-haired man smiled winningly and said, "Mademoiselle . . . no one as lovely as you should have to work for a living." His hand dropped away from Kitty's, his heels clicked together in the old imperial manner, and he bowed slightly, the smile lighting up his black eyes. "Please, golden angel, be my guest tonight."

Kitty's wide green eyes, surprised and faintly alarmed, lifted to his, and the impact of those splendid eyes stopped the words in his throat. Her eyes were delicious, vulnerable, luminously green, framed in heavy lacy lashes. It was unheard of for General Tergukasov to be at a loss for words; an apt turn of phrase was his forte. Wrenching his glance from the lure and spell of those enormous eyes that seemed to offer unknown promises even while they retreated in fear, he turned his head briskly to Professor Pashkov and said curtly, "The *mademoiselle* is through at the piano."

"But sir," Kitty interjected nervously before the professor could speak, "Colonel Ismailovich has engaged us for the entire evening." She didn't want to give up her opportunity to meet the commander of Metekhi prison, and if this stranger insisted on monopolizing her all night, what chance would she have to make his acquaintance?

Violin tucked under his arm, Professor Pashkov said in carefully enunciated tones, "I'm sure, Katherine, Colonel Ismailovich will understand. After all, General Tergukasov is the guest of honor."

The general missed the involuntary clenching of Kitty's small hands. Smoothing the crushed peau de soie, Kitty replied in a breathy, slightly brittle voice, "General Tergukasov, how nice of you to interrupt a working girl's tedium."

"From this moment, *mademoiselle*, consider your working career over."

"Oh, really, sir, you're too kind . . . and it's *madame*."

Dark brows moved up a fraction. "Is your husband here tonight?"

"No. My husband was lost in the war."

Sharp black eyes looked at her in a straightforward way. "I should say I'm sorry, but I'm not. Children?"

"One. A son." Kitty had never encountered such directness, and while blunt, it wasn't unkind.

"Hmmmm" was all he said for a long moment and then, apparently tabulating all the answers in some form satisfactory to his whims, he took Kitty's hand in his and pulled her up from the piano bench. "Come, *madame* . . ." He paused and looked at her inquiringly.

Kitty gave her maiden name. Radachek could be notorious after Stavropol.

"Come then, Madame Kurminen. I hope you like champagne—and I trust before the evening is over we'll be on a first-name basis."

He was solicitous and eager. Charming and eager. Gallant and eager. He was offering the sun, moon, and stars to her as partial payment for sharing his apartment with him. With a sinking feeling Kitty wondered if he had sufficient money to find her offer of jewelry a bagatelle. She sidestepped, evaded, demurred, all politely and all coquettishly, promising him she would give some answer tomorrow.

"Marvelous. I'll take you to the Botanical Gardens for a picnic. I'm sure we can reach some agreement amenable to us both."

When the general and Kitty left Colonel Ismailovich's late that night, a Dagestani warrior watching from the shadows across the street nudged his elbow into his companion and pointed. Within the hour Karaim had news of Kitty's presence in Tiflis. After he finished swearing, he asked for details. No, she wasn't with General Tergukasov; he had only given her a ride home. Where was home? She was staying with a Professor Pashkov near the inner city. Good Lord, that female had nerve, Karaim mused, and if they hadn't had watchers on General Tergukasov twenty-four hours a day, he never would have known that she had come down from Dargo—at least, not in time.

"She's at the professor's now?"

"Yes."

"And the general went back to his apartment?"

Another affirmative.

Karaim sighed. "Good. She'll be safe 'til morning then. Send two men for her before noon. Even the general, however ardent a suitor, shouldn't be back before then."

And there, you see, is where varying degrees of ardor can punch a hole in the most logical assumptions.


The two men Karaim dispatched shortly before ten the next morning arrived at Professor Pashkov's just in time to see the general's Benz touring car disappear down the narrow street. Fortunately the old part of the city consisted of narrow, convoluted streets barely wide enough for the splendid Benz to inch through. Two men on foot were capable of keeping the car in sight. And, doubly fortunate, General Tergukasov was of a romantic bent. Exiting on one of the main thoroughfares, he had his driver stop at the first florist shop they passed. Politely excusing himself, he went inside to purchase some exotic flower for the marvelous woman he had dreamed about all night.

Kitty sat in the car's luxurious leather interior, uneasily wondering exactly how she was going to broach the discussion of the most important prisoner Metekhi Prison currently held, and what bribe would release him. A score of opening sentences came to mind and were promptly discarded as unsuitable, illogical, inane. She knew what the general wanted, and her turmoil of indecision centered not so much around whether or not she would make the sacrifice—Apollo's life was worth any sacrifice. It was more a question of whether the general could be trusted to keep his word, if she was the only bribe he would consider. Too many stories had circulated in the last few years of wives willing to buy their husbands' lives at any price, only to find they had given themselves for nothing. Their husbands had been executed by their ravagers.[14] What to do? She had so little time to weigh all the ramifications.

Then, before her startled eyes, the driver's door was wrenched open, the passenger door opened, the driver was pulled out and thrown to the pavement, two men slid into the front seat, and the car roared away from the curb. The man on her right turned back, smiled briefly, and said, "Keep your head down, Countess."

Kitty stared, aghast. "Sahin! No! You have to take me back—I'm going to talk to the general about Apollo!" She clutched at his shoulder, frantic, seeing all hope dashed in a few short seconds. "Turn around—drop me off. I've got to get back there!"

"We're taking As-saqr As-saghir out in two days."

Kitty sank back into the soft upholstery as the news registered in her mind. "Thank God," she whispered over and over again, tears streaming down her face.

Short minutes later Kitty was facing Karaim, and when she heard the plans, she felt for the first time in weeks a blazing hope.

With time at a premium, the Cub was fetched and the professor and his wife were relocated. The general was bound to backtrack eventually if he was intent on finding the enchanting blond female kidnapped along with his car. Apologizing for the danger she had brought upon them, Kitty was assured by both the professor and his wife that their last apartment had been only one in a long line of domiciles they'd inhabited since the Revolution had disrupted their lives—and the gold Karaim gave them ensured their comfort even if the professor's musical income was curtailed until General Tergukasov moved on to another post.

# 19

One day later, just before evening turned into night, while pale gray shadows hid much from sight, Prince Alexander Kuzan's yacht dropped anchor in a secluded cove twelve miles north of Poti. The four waiting men wrapped in *burkhas*, squatting around a small fire on the sandy shore, rose to greet their old friend. Apollo's father had arrived with men and supplies to collect his only son from Metekhi Prison.

A second telegram from Sahin, received in Constantinople, had relayed the critical news that Apollo still lived. Several containers of dynamite and four land mines were unloaded from the yacht to assist in the deliverance of Prince Alexander's son. For a fortnight Alex had launched himself and all his substantial possessions, brains, power, money, and charm in a singleminded assault on authority. Everyone who could possibly aid in the escape had felt the impact of the prince's determination and it was only a matter of hours now before it would be known whether all the effort would be successful or not.

Prince Alex waded ashore from the small boat. He was dressed in mountain garb—black tunic, trousers, soft boots—and his tall, broad-shouldered frame still possessed a youthful vigor. Although nearing fifty, he was still lean and fit, his dark hair only faintly touched with gray, his handsome, chiseled face tanned dark from hours spent on the polo fields. In bearing, appearance, form, in all aspects he belied his age.

Reaching out, he grasped Karaim's hand firmly. "How are you, Karaim, after these long years of war?"

"Fine, Sasha."

"You look fit. And Apollo? Any more news?"

"Still alive, as of this afternoon."

Alex's golden eyes softened in relief. "Pray God keeps him through one more night. That's all we need. And how are Kitty and my new grandson?" he inquired on a more cheerful note. News of the Cub's birth had been received by Zena and Alex with pride and joy.

"See for yourself," Karaim replied, grimacing ruefully.

Golden eyes registered surprise briefly, but as quickly concealed it when Kitty, carrying the Cub, came forward from the darkening shadows. She was greeted warmly and graciously by Apollo's father; the Cub was given a kiss on one chubby cheek. Gazing at the sturdy baby in Kitty's arms took Alex back two decades or more, and he saw his son in the child before him. The same pale hair and golden eyes, the same strong, robust baby form and dimpled smile. "He's quite like Apollo at that age," Alex said softly, and his mind raced back to the fair-haired baby born in Nice when the century and old traditions were moving into a new millennium. "You must be as proud of him as Zena and I were of our firstborn."

"Very proud, Prince Kuzan," Kitty replied quietly. "He's his father's son in every way."

Alex looked up at the baby's pretty mother and said with a grin, "He has a bit of his mother, too, I think."

"Perhaps . . . but in temperament, definitely Apollo." She smiled. "He likes to have his own way."

Alex laughed. "A Kuzan trait. Quite incorrigible, I'm afraid. But please, since you're one of the family, call me Sasha. I'm sorry there's so little time to visit, but later . . . Right now, we must be off immediately for Tiflis." Taking Kitty gently by the shoulder, he began leading her to the small boat pulled up on the shore. "My men will see you to the yacht." Alex's voice, though pleasant, was dismissive, allowing no argument. "Be assured, Kitty, we'll be back with Apollo before midnight two days hence." Or we'll all be dead, he thought but refrained from saying. "The men have orders to make for Ilori and wait for us there. *Au revoir*," he said, bending to kiss his grandson.

"Godspeed," Kitty whispered, knowing that the fate of Apollo depended upon the smooth operation of each step of the plan.

Alex and his companions reached Tiflis by morning and were disconcerted to discover the execution had been rescheduled for one day earlier. Perhaps fear of reprisals had prompted the decision, or perhaps the hanging had been advanced to discourage rescue attempts. Whatever the reason, it meant no one slept that night. Everyone worked frantically through the all-too-short hours of darkness. Charges and land mines were set and concealed at both exits of the narrow street servicing the prison gate Apollo would pass through when he was transferred to the vehicle that would carry him to the execution.

A Turkish merchant and childhood friend of Alex's—who had found it as profitable to trade with the Red commissars as with the old nobility—was enlisted to aid in the rescue. He resided in an elegant townhouse near the scene of the hanging: the city square.

In the last hour before the sun rose, all was in readiness. While the men rested for the brief time before the plan was set in motion, Alex and Krym Seid Bey sprawled on opposite divans in the elegant drawing room facing the square and sipped cognac.

Alex let out a breath. "Good Lord, Krym, that was close." He lifted the glass to his lips and after swallowing a fortifying two inches of dark liquor continued. "One less hour last night and we wouldn't have made it. Whatever possessed them to advance the execution by a day?"

Krym moved his bulk—evidence of too many self-indulgent years—and sighed softly. "According to high-placed rumor, lust is the reason . . . one of the cardinal vices, after all. It seems"—and his brow lifted sardonically—"the commissar misses Lola and must be off to Yalta again."

"Christ!" Alex exploded quietly. "I asked her to do a good job for me, but apparently she has exceeded requirements."

Seid Bey eyed his old friend, now slouched low on the down-cushioned sofa. Alex was long, lean, handsome, no dissipation evident in face or form, no evidence of too much hedonistic living, and Krym ruefully resolved to give up a few of his vices starting tomorrow. "Now, Sasha," Seid Bey reminded him wryly, "you know damn well Lola would do anything for you. She's always been hungry for you, even though she knew you had eyes only for your wife and wouldn't give her a tumble. Of course she'd do a good job. Don't go coy on me."

Alex looked up over the rim of the glass and didn't insult either of their intelligences by pretending not to understand. Alex's experience with the gentle sex had been wide and varied, and he knew very well when a woman wanted him. The "wanting" had never diminished over the years—his dark good looks still attracted constant attention. But shortly after his marriage many years ago, the wide and varied part of his experience had abruptly ceased. When Alex found the love of his life, females like Lola had been forced to repine without his attentions. "Lola's intentions, despite the unexpected results, were of the best, I'm sure—"

"Indeed," Seid Bey interrupted with a smirk.

Alex grinned in acknowledgment and continued conversationally, "but her unquestionable allure—"

"You've noticed, then." Another interruption, accompanied by another smirk.

"I happen to be in love with my wife, Krym. However, I'm not blind. Now, if you're through being lascivious," he said calmly, "I'll finish." Alex looked squarely at Krym and after a five-second pause went on. "Her unquestionable allure for Tiflis's little commissar made us all work our tails off tonight. Fortunately, all was accomplished in time, and we only await the rising sun. Lola meant well, despite the abrupt change in plans, and she'll be abundantly rewarded for her efforts. She kept my son alive for ten extra days, and for *that* she can name her price."

"A *personal* gift, Sasha?" Seid Bey asked with a decided leer.

The solemn look vanished and Alex chuckled softly. "Jesus, Krym, you're in a mood tonight. Is your harem on your mind after a solid night of unaccustomed physical labor with dynamite and land mines?" He grinned, then, setting his glass down, said, "And no, not a *personal* gift. You know me better than that."

The finality of Alex's tone reminded Seid Bey of all the times before the war when he and Alex had spent entire nights at Lola's in Yalta, gambling and drinking. While everyone else would invariably retire upstairs with some accommodating female guest, Alex had always politely declined. Just like tonight, that same softly spoken yet ineffably firm "no." "Still, Sasha?" Seid Bey asked wistfully, feeling in that somber hour before dawn a sense of deprivation, an obscure bereavement that his life, perhaps, had been misspent and frittered away. "Still only Zena after all these years?"

"She's all I've ever wanted, Krym," Alex quietly replied.

Within the half hour, activity was in full swing once again. Red Army uniforms had been obtained—Seid Bey had more connections than a younger son of a sultan—and those uniforms allowed a very smooth and relatively undisputed requisitioning of the truck appointed to convey Apollo to his hanging. The original guards in the truck, of course, were replaced by substitute Bolsheviks bearing a very distinctive Dagestani countenance and physique. The newly requisitioned truck and its imitation guards sped through the streets of Tiflis, then climbed slowly up the narrow streets of the old quarter toward Metekhi Prison.

Apollo was sleeping, his head buried in his bare arms, when they came to wake him before daybreak, leaving him a change of clothes and the dismal fare they called breakfast. "So you look respectable for your execution," he was told with a light note of hilarity. The derisive words filtered past the throbbing ache in his brain. And suddenly the thought of dying made Apollo more angry than sad.

Christ Almighty, he had a hell of a lot to live for, and he didn't feel like docilely giving up his life. He wanted Kitty, and he wanted to watch his son grow up. It didn't make much sense now, in this maze of cells and corridors floors below the street, but once he saw daylight again—damn! He was at least going to make a bid for freedom. Better to die with a bullet in the back than be so much sacrificial meat dangling and turning purple on the end of a rope.

Without very high hopes, but with a driving need to try, Apollo made some swift, if limited, contingency plans. It was more of a gesture for life than anything else. He stirred then, marshaling his depleted strength. He would have to walk, think, act. Stiffly he rolled over and sat up, taking his time. He felt like hell. He hauled himself upright and started dressing.

He was brought up from the subbasement of the prison and escorted through a spiderweb of corridors, stairways, turning hallways, and guardrooms. The long walk took its toll on his fragile stamina. Prison had sapped his strength. He had lost considerable weight, and every part of his body now rebelled at the strain put on it. His tall frame looked even taller because of the prison leanness; the pale hair lay in long curls at the nape of his neck; his dark, heavy brows, golden feverish eyes, and stark cheekbones gave him the dangerous look of a bird of prey.

Calling on his reserves, he managed to walk the long distance unaided, drawing strength from necessity.

One last chance, he thought, seeing the glimmer of daylight coming through the doorway at the end of the long corridor before him. One last chance before the ride to the scaffold. For perhaps the first time in his life, Apollo was stretched to the limit, his concentration essential. There would be no second chances today.

As Apollo emerged into the sunlight of the courtyard, the bold light caught his overlong, untidy fair hair, defined the shadows and hollows of ill health, and lit his brilliant yellow eyes. He looked singularly high-strung. Momentarily blinded by the radiant morning sunshine, he stumbled on the low step, falling against the escorting guard to his left. With instincts of survival nurtured in the mountains and honed to a fine pitch by years of war, he took his slender chance. In a single blur of movement he pulled the pistol from the guard's holster and fired point-blank even before it was completely free of the leather. With an animal-like twist he spun around, firing at the guard on his right—once between the eyes. A neat, rather largish hole at this close range, his brain abstractly noted. Recovering himself, he poised to leap forward just as a Cheka guard came running up from behind. A leather-coated arm jerked up viciously and a rifle butt slammed into Apollo's head.

The force of the blow drove Apollo to his knees, and, flinging his head up, he turned half-around with the violence of the impact. For one second—two—he clung to consciousness, defying darkness and death, until with surprise and fury he realized he was falling. His knees gave way and he dropped like a stone, stunned and helpless.

"Give me some help with this bastard!" the Cheka guard snapped at the soldiers in the truck that had drawn up to the doorway, already dragging Apollo's semiconscious form forward. "He's still alive, and he's going to hang a damn long time before he dies."

Everyone in the truck had viewed the few swift seconds of gunfire, but they had stayed their hands, reluctant to bring out the entire contingent of guards inside with the sound of full-scale firing. When it had become apparent that the third guard was going to be a problem, fingers had tightened on triggers and guns had trained on the Cheka. If he made a move toward killing Apollo outright . . . with a terrible leisure they had watched Apollo go down.

In response to the snapped order, two Red soldiers jumped out of the back of the truck and lifted Apollo. Carrying him back, they placed him on the bed of the truck, then lightly vaulted back in to join the two guards already seated in the dim interior.

Thrusting his head into the covered truck, the Cheka guard's gaze swung around the benches lining the walls. "Where's Georgi?" he inquired curtly. "He's supposed to be on duty today."

In a monstrously mangled articulation of the Russian syntax, a voice replied, "Georgi feel no good, yes."

To Apollo, on the floor, the sound of a choir of angels could not have been lovelier as he dimly recognized the familiar voice.

With considerable effort, Apollo turned his head toward the sound.

His heavy lids laboriously lifted, and a dim circle of dark and blurred faces refused to come into focus. Apollo shut his eyes, then tried again. This time his dazed golden eyes met the amused gaze of Karaim.

"Stay here and wait for me," the Cheka guard commanded. "I have to notify the prison of the death of these two guards. I'll be right back." He turned.

"Yes, to please Your Honor," Karaim murmured softly, and the Cheka guard spun around at the deliberate, clearly enunciated aristocratic formula. Karaim gut-shot him.

Sahin had already given the command to drive, and before the body hit the cobblestones the truck was thirty feet across the courtyard.

"Jesus." Apollo grinned, speaking with the least possible expenditure of effort. "I'd just about given up on you. Next time don't call it so close. I was already trying to remember my prayers."

"We were waiting for Sasha," Karaim explained.

"Papa's here?" Apollo struggled a little unsteadily to a seated position in the swiftly moving vehicle.

"Driving."

Apollo leaned back against the truck wall and exhaled a great sigh. Suddenly the world took on a rosy glow.

Seconds after the truck exited the courtyard and narrow street that fronted the Metekhi, both outlets to the Krasilnava exploded in a fiery blast. Windows were shattered for blocks. Several hairpin turns later, down steep, narrow streets, the truck squealed on two wheels onto the Bebutovskaya, proceeded for six blocks at high speed, turned right onto Ganovskays, and after a block and a half turned left again into Seid Bey's spacious garage, a mere five hundred yards from Erivansk Square, the site of Apollo's scheduled hanging.

For the remainder of the day while the city crawled with

troops and police and Cheka conducting a door-to-door search for Apollo, the men enjoyed the hospitality of Krym Seid Bey within the confines of his harem. Once, late in the morning, Krym was summoned by servants and left to guide the party of Cheka in black leather coats through his elegant abode—but even the brash, disreputable security troops of the Red Army knew better than to disturb the sanctity of a man's harem. Every Moslem from the Manchurian steppes to Constantinople would have risen in rebellion at the affront.

Seid Bey returned two hours later. "The search didn't take long," he explained to his assembled guests disposed on divans in one of the larger chambers, "but drinking to Lenin's health from my private stock required a nicety of timing and sincerity. It would never do to rush the amenities."

"How is the search coming?" Alex asked with a wide smile.

"I detected a note of frustration," Seid Bey replied, a faint smile quirking his mouth. "It seems the Metekhi is considered escape-proof."

"Once every hundred years," Apollo murmured from the pile of silk cushions on which he was half dozing. His face held a distinct smile although his eyes were closed.

"Really?" Seid Bey inquired. "A fitting occasion, then, to celebrate." He clapped his pudgy hands sharply and within minutes his orders were being carried out. Champagne came first, followed shortly after by food served by a score of exquisite harem females. The rest of the day passed in pleasant idleness.

Apollo ate heartily, drank moderately, eschewed the women with grave politeness, and slept the evening hours away. Having received a bath and clothes immediately upon arriving within the confines of Seid Bey's sprawling home, Apollo's much maligned body was now clean, fed, bandaged, freshly dressed, and convalescing with the remarkable recuperative energies of youth.

As the night drew toward its zenith, Alex extended his heartfelt thanks for the last time to his old friend, offered the sanctuary of one of his several homes on the continent should the need arise for Krym to discontinue doing business in Tiflis, and then woke his son for the last leg of their journey to the yacht and . . . freedom.

Shortly after midnight, on a black night with no moon, a sleek Pierce-Arrow slid out of a garage near the Erivansk Square and, taking a circuitous route out of Tiflis, purred down the road to a quiet cove ninety miles west of the capital.

After the initial exuberant greetings between father and son and friends early that morning, and after he had been given three weeks worth of news in swift detail, Apollo had been calm, composed, almost indolent; resting, sleeping, talking very little. Now as they approached the Ilori area, Apollo became alert, sitting upright, staring intently out the window into the blackness.

"She might be sleeping," Alex said, understanding what was going through his son's mind.

"I know."

"She came down out of the mountains herself with the child, looking to rescue you. Did you know that?"

"Sahin told me."

"A very brave woman."

"And more." It was impossible to adequately express what she meant to him.

Alex smiled, a smile of contentment and reminiscence. "The Cub is the spit of you at six months."

Apollo's head turned from the window. "I'm very lucky," he said, and there was a wealth of meaning in those three simple words.

"So I understand. Would you have wanted her, had the child borne the stamp of another man?"

"I told myself I wouldn't, but I think I knew I was always lying to myself about that." Even before the mountains he had known.

"She hasn't had an easy time these last few years."

"I intend to spend the rest of my life remedying that."

"If you and Kitty can be as happy as your mother and I have been, a man can't ask for more."

"God willing," Apollo said softly and turned back to the window, his golden eyes searching the darkness for the shimmer of dancing light that meant the *Southern Star*—and his wife and son, whom he had expected never to see again.

"By the way, Leda's on the *Southern Star*."

Apollo's head twisted around, his face lit from within. "From Shura? You got her from Shura?"

"Sahin did."

"I owe him a helluva favor." He laughed softly. "I bet she didn't let anyone in Shura ride her."

"So the rumor went, but they wanted her back nonetheless. Since there are only a dozen Karabaghs in all of the Caucasus, she was dyed to disguise the color and brought down three days ago."

"You were so sure of my release?"

"Of course."

"Such confidence?" One brow arched slightly.

"Not confidence, necessarily, but determination. I would have died trying. And many besides me."

"Thank you," said Apollo simply. "And thank you for remembering Leda. We've been through a lot together. On more than one occasion she brought me out of a battle on her own."

Kitty was rocking her son in the master stateroom of the *Southern Star* when Apollo walked in. The Cub had been restless through the night, perhaps sensing the tenseness in his mother, and he had just fallen back to sleep.

He had the familiar, elegant presence, but he seemed quieter, less dynamic than she remembered. Apollo came only a few paces into the room, then stopped and smiled. His burnished head glistened in the dim light, his large tawny eyes were shadowed underneath with blue. He was leaner, Kitty noted. He had been mistreated—the signs were all there—but he walked steadily and he was very much alive.

Apollo's voice was pleasant, unchanged. "*Bon soir, dushka,*" he said softly, the smile feathering his eyes and grooving his cheeks in well-remembered, achingly familiar lines. "Tell me, does the Cub have any new tricks for his papa? I've thought about you both during these many days."

Joy, relief, overwhelming love swept over Kitty like a tidal wave. Her misty eyes reflected the great happiness that inundated her senses. "I've showed him your picture every day," she said, her mouth trembling, her eyes clinging to him shamelessly, "and he always smiles."

Her heart bled at the slight limp when he crossed the short expanse of pale blue carpet. Apollo lifted his sleeping son from Kitty's lap, kissed him softly, and placed him in his cradle. "In the morning he'll show me his smile." Turning back, he reached for Kitty and pulled her fiercely into his arms. "God, I've missed you," he whispered, his arms like iron vises. Only that morning he had contemplated never seeing her again. Tears glittered on Kitty's lashes. They clung to each other. Their lips met in an aching kiss. Time stood still as their hands and lips said all the things they felt.

The soft bed whispered under their weight and for a time only the sounds of love sighed in the stillness of the room. She heard him swear once as pressure was put on some of his burns, but nothing so mundane could stop him. Urgent mouths tasted, tempted, tantalized; urgent hands and limbs touched and twined, growing wildly impatient until the burning, covetous craving was satisfied in a savage ecstasy.

And then, in the poignant afterhush of release, Kitty gently stroked the scars, the old whippings, the freshly mutilated skin, sorrowing for every painful degradation. Her touch was infinitely tender. "So much suffering. It must have been terrible."

"But I lived," Apollo breathed quietly, an inexpressible thanksgiving in his heart. His expression pensive, he added, "And so many haven't." Then his muscled body tensed almost imperceptibly and he deliberately changed the subject. "Papa tells me you were bent on some reckless heroic path. How did you slip Pushka's guard?" He alternately marveled and lovingly chastised Kitty as she related her harrowing experiences. "It doesn't seem," he chided mockingly at the end of the narrative, "that you are inclined to be a stay-at-home, docile female."

"Is that what you really want?" Kitty inquired in a low,

throaty voice, her hands rediscovering the contours of his face, the bones too prominent now, the hollows too deep.

"Well . . ." Apollo said slowly, taking her small hand in his and pressing the palm to his lips. "Perhaps occasionally."

"I'm amenable. I'm sure we can work out some arrangement," Kitty purred.

"I'm sure we can," Apollo retorted lazily, his hand drifting down to capture her chin. His mouth lowered to hers. "Now show me again," he murmured, his fingers smoothing her waist suggestively, "just how amenable you are."

Much later Apollo opened the door to the passageway and, standing casually naked in the doorway, shouted down the corridor, "Call the captain! I'm getting married in five minutes!"

"Are you mad?" Kitty gasped from the rumpled disarray of the bed. "It's impossible!"

"Nothing is impossible for my father," Apollo replied, coming back to the bed and seating himself. "Allow me to be the first to congratulate you on your divorce, which was finalized three weeks ago."

"Good Lord—how?"

"I had a telegram sent to Papa as we were leaving Batum for the mountains, asking him to find Peotr and expedite a divorce. I was hoping we could be married before the Cub was born, but Papa said all attempts to locate Peotr failed until he arrived in Paris a month ago. He, Suata, and the children had been delayed leaving Baku, and then spent weeks traveling through Persia and Turkey to the coast—only to lose several more weeks interred on a quarantined ship unable to embark from Constantinople."

Kitty raised inquiring, bewildered eyes. "Suata and the children?"

"His family. A mistress in Baku, and a boy and a girl. My explanation regarding Peotr's decision to head east was so damned weak, I thought you must have suspected something."

"A family?" Kitty was still dazed. "Really? A family?"

"I'm sorry," Apollo said softly. "Do you mind terribly? Papa says Peotr's horribly guilt-ridden about leaving you behind."

Kitty looked at the concerned tawny eyes searching her face and she lifted a finger to lightly trace the furrow on his brow. She smiled then. "How can I mind?" she said tremblingly, love shining in her eyes. "If not for Suata, I never would have seen you again."

"Good," Apollo said, exhaling the breath he had been holding. "The wedding, then, and the sooner the better. If you want one with all the fuss, we'll be married again at Chambord."

"Married?" Kitty said the word softly, as if it were a new taste to get used to.

"Of course, married. What did you expect?"

"I don't know. . . ." It had always been Kitty's fondest wish. But deep down she had never really thought it would come true, with the revolutionary turmoil, and a husband already, and, if the truth be told, with Apollo's track record with women. None of those things had strongly presaged the real possibility of marriage. "Married?" she repeated.

"Why should it seem so strange?" Taking Kitty into his arms, his face only inches away, Apollo whispered, "I love you. You're the mother of my son."

Kitty's face closed in an instant. "And that's why—"

"No, no. Oh, God. I didn't mean that." He shook her then, furious with himself for his unsuitable phrasing, furious with her unwarranted assumption. "Dammit," he said grimly, "we're getting married, whether you like it or not. Jesus God Almighty, we're not going to argue about *that*!"

"And you intend to have your way as usual," she chided, half-provoked, half-teasing.

"Damn right, as usual." But his mouth twitched into a faint smile. He pulled her close in his arms and they both felt an emotion deep and strong, of joy, of gladness, of spinning lightly above the earth's mundane realms.

"This is unbelievable," Kitty whispered, happiness possessing her soul.

"This is love," Apollo whispered back, his arms tightening around her. "And I intend to take my duties as husband very seriously," he breathed softly into her hair.

Suddenly laughing lightly, that low, delightful sound Apollo knew so well, Kitty asked with gentle whimsy, "Will you think it shabby, marrying a dishonored woman? Are you sure you really want to?"

"If you'll have me," he said in the tenderest of voices.

"Oh, I'll have you, with pleasure," Kitty murmured contentedly, wrapping her arms around his neck. "And if I begin to bore you?" she teased lightheartedly. "Will Karaim and Sahin neatly solve your problem?"

"I won't be needing Karaim and Sahin," Apollo replied huskily, smiling sardonically, an indiscreet, reckless gleam shining from his golden eyes. "I know one or two ways to keep boredom away."

# EPILOGUE

In a world tired of war, intent on forgetting sorrow and hardship after "the war to end all wars" had taken the brightest and best of every nation and snuffed out their young lives, Apollo, Kitty, the Cub, and a new baby brother and sister lived quietly happy on a thousand acres of green, green valley. Only occasionally did they venture to the bright lights and feverish pace of the French capital.

Kitty farmed as she vowed she would, and was an adoring wife and mother, as well as best friend to the golden-haired prince at her side.

Apollo played polo with a passion formerly devoted to war, looked after his business interests, cherished his wife, and contentedly watched his children grow.

Both parents were an integral part of their children's lives, not subscribing to the traditional mode of handing offspring over to the care of servants, nannies, and governesses. Apollo became as adept at changing nappies and partaking of nursery fare and games as he'd been at handling a *kinjal* and Mauser in an earlier time.

Leda grew sleek in retirement, but periodically when Apollo rode her she sensed, with the special kinship between them, the restlessness of his mood, and on those days she stretched her long, muscled legs in a wild, reckless gallop through the serene countryside, helping as only she could to chase the demons away. The marches were over, the thundering charges and sounds of battle gone, but the memories were there for both of them.

Infrequently, messages quietly relayed to Apollo from the

émigré committees in Paris brought a crease to his brow and
necessitated a brief trip to the capital. He mostly kept these
activities from Kitty, for she wouldn't approve, and never had
reconciled herself completely to the vengeance of the Adat.
But Kitty was more aware than Apollo suspected of his émigré
affairs, for she had her own friends among those transplanted
from the old Russia. And whenever new reports and rumors
came out of the Soviet Union, a nameless fear would surface
to mar the perfection of Kitty's life, for she knew Apollo was
not, by nature, the kind of man who could sit passively by
and watch events unfold without him.

Apollo helped the émigrés where he could with money,
strategy, and influence, and so far that had been enough. He
loved Kitty too much and his children were too young; he
had told his colleagues from the beginning that he wasn't
available for trips into Russia—at least, not until the children
were older.

# NOTES

[1] "Piter" translates as "St. Pete," an affectionate nickname for St. Petersburg. To eliminate the Germanic sound, the name of the city was changed to Petrograd in August 1914, but many people continued to use the old name. (In 1924, Petrograd was given its modern name, Leningrad.)

[2] Mamontov had under his command eight thousand selected cavalrymen on the best horses the Don region could provide. Besides wreaking havoc behind Red lines, Mamontov narrowly missed capturing Trotsky in Tambov, an event that would have significantly changed the course of the war. In addition, at Kozlov during the same raid the entire Red Army HQ just escaped capture at the very last moment. These two incidents underline the fine balance between victory and defeat in the long years of the Russian Civil War.

[3] Thoroughbreds were an affectation of many of the young officers who wanted secondhand "racers" for chargers, but these mounts could be dangerous unless the rider could handle his horse. An incident that took place during World War I illustrates the risk involved for an inexperienced horseman: Four subalterns had gotten themselves horses from the Moscow track and were very proud of them. One day the whole regiment charged. When in full run, they met terrific machine-gun fire and had to turn back—all but the four subalterns. The four thoroughbreds raced each other straight into the arms of the Germans. Miraculously, neither riders nor horses got so much as a scratch. The next day a German airplane dropped a message that read, "Lieutenant Count Rebinder won by two lengths, in case you had any bets on the gentlemen."

[4] In mid-October of 1919, the Reds had 160,000 infantry, 26,000 cavalry, and 4,500 machine guns. The Whites had 63,000 infantry, 48,000 cavalry, and 2,300 machine guns. The chief advantage of the Whites had always been their excellent cavalry, but by the second half of 1919 they had been greatly weakened by constant fighting.

[5] The rules of dueling were prescribed by the mountain Adat: Should one man mortally offend another man, they shall each pick a trusted friend. These two shall do their utmost to bring about peace, for it is said that there is more courage in confessing an error than in fighting over it. However, should all peaceful efforts fail, at the appointed time a cloak of black felt—the *burkha*—shall be spread on the ground. The combatants

shall stand and fight on the *burkha*. Shame and disgrace to the one who, retreating, steps off the felt. The combat shall continue until death or mortal injury ensues.

[6] The *tachanka* was developed during the Russian Civil War and immediately became the most lethal weapon on the battlefield. In 1917, an ex-convict by the name of Nestor Makhno founded a gang of guerillas in the Ukraine, and it was his wont to ride about the plains of southern Russia under the black banner of anarchy, plundering and slaughtering noblemen, Jews, Communists, priests, and anyone else who incurred his displeasure. His safety lay in his mobility. His long trots, followed by a sudden appearance where he was least expected, became legendary, as did his equally rapid disappearance after one night of orgiastic drunkenness and slaughter. Makhno's problem was how to combine the heavy rapid-fire power of a machine gun with his mobility. His idea was to mount all his machine guns on the backs of light carriages or buggies, and the result was the *tachanka*. With it one could gallop up to the enemy, turn around, open fire, and then gallop away, still firing, if the enemy retaliated. The *tachanka* was fast, light, unobtrusive, and perfectly lethal, and it soon became the main support arm of both the Red and White cavalries.

[7] Due to the utter lack of passable roads, war was waged on or near the railway lines, and both armies used thousands of railway carriages for shelter.

[8] "I can see you are new to the country," said a friend to British journalist C. E. Bechhofer when he visited Russia in 1919. "For the last two years nobody worries about what will happen to him tomorrow. These are not like the old days, when you and I used to meet in Petrograd and even made appointments two or three days in advance. Never mind, you will soon get used to it. Wait 'til you have lived under the Bolshevists, as I have! I tell you that until you have experienced Bolshevism, you don't know what the world really contains. Fancy thinking about what will happen tomorrow! What a strange idea!" This sense of transience and fugitive morality is evoked time and time again in the memoirs and diaries of the period; between war, typhus, the bitter cold, and lack of food and water, one's existence tomorrow was gravely uncertain.

[9] There were no titles, as such, in the Red Army, and people were addressed by the rank they held at the given moment. In the interest of ease in reading, Beriozov will be designated as the general.

[10] Before the October Revolution the Bolsheviks had systematically destroyed the old Imperial Army by undermining every aspect of military servitude. Once in power, they tried to confine their needs to small Red Guard units, but owing to the unreliability of these and to the rising tide of counterrevolution, they called for a new Red Army of volunteers, bringing in mainly adventurers and cutthroats of the worst variety. Therefore, Trotsky cast aside doctrine in favor of expediency. He reintroduced call-up, abolished elective command, and decided to use former officers from the Imperial Army. Amid ideological and indignant protests from within

the party, he reinstated 48,409 of these "specialists" in the field and another 10,339 in administration over the next two years. By the spring of 1920, over 80 percent of the Red Army's commissions were held by ex-Imperial Army officers. The measure had its problems, and many of the professional officers who came forward at the beginning simply waited for the opportunity to take their units over to the Whites. The practice was soon remedied by strict surveillance—as well as by keeping tabs on relatives and families who could be contacted in case of desertion or treason.

[11] Only a very small proportion of the urban proletariat could ride, and an even smaller proportion were accepted by the Cossacks and mountain warriors, whose allegiance to the party remained grudging at the best of times. Their loyalty was to their clans or commanders, not necessarily to either Russian army. Cavalry units did desert and change sides *en masse*, so the post of commisar to a squadron of Cossacks or Circassians was not, needless to say, one of the favorites.

[12] *Inogorodnie*—"people from other towns"—was the name given to the peasants who had moved into the rich agricultural areas of the Cossack territories in the nineteenth century but who could not become members of the Cossack estate or even acquire permanent residence. They remained much poorer than the Cossacks and had to be satisfied with renting land or working as hired hands. In 1917 this nascent class struggle was exacerbated by an increased hostility between the two halves of the population, and thus the *inogorodnie* were ripe for Bolshevism.

[13] The mountain men were reared to be warriors and nothing else. All other activities of daily existence in the mountain auls were seen to by servants or women. Owing to their extraordinary skills and bravery, even as privates in the Russian Army they did nothing but fight—they refused to be servants, drivers, or any sort of noncombatant. The only menial task they would perform was to take care of the officers' horses. They were addressed as "riders," not "troopers," and in a military organization based on a tradition of corporeal punishment, no officer was allowed to raise his hand to a mountain man. Their personal sense of worth, the honor and dignity adhering to the role of warrior in the Caucasus, was carried by them everywhere. They did not bend to authority.

[14] The Bolsheviks' practice of coercing pretty women into becoming their mistresses by arresting their husbands or nearest male relatives and sentencing them to death was so common as to hardly elicit remark. When the woman interceded, she would be told that unless she cooperated, her relatives would be lost. After she cooperated, her relatives would be shot as if no agreement had been made. The outrages against women during the Russian Civil War were systematic, inclusive, and unlimited by any political or moral restraints. Women's predators were everywhere; their sanctuaries were few.

# ABOUT THE AUTHOR

Susan Johnson, award-winning author of nationally bestselling novels, lives in the country near North Branch, Minnesota. A former art historian, she considers the life of a writer the best of all possible worlds.

Researching her novels takes her to past and distant places, and bringing characters to life allows her imagination full rein, while the creative process offers occasional fascinating glimpses into complicated machinery of the mind.

But perhaps most important . . . writing stories is fun.

Thrill to Susan Johnson's
next historical romance

# Wicked

available from Bantam Books
in December 1996

*Here's a sneak peek at this sizzling love story
from the acclaimed mistress of the erotic
historical romance. . . .*

When he first heard the soft footfall in the passageway outside his stateroom, he glanced at the clock mounted on the ship's overhead beam as if to substantiate the odd sound to the moment.

Two o'clock.

He came fully awake.

A woman was on board his yacht.

He immediately recognized the tiptoeing gait as female but then Beau St. Jules had vast experience with tiptoeing rendezvous in the middle of the night. As he had with women of every nuance and description, his amours rivaled—some said surpassed—his father's distinguished record. The Duke of Seth's eldest son wasn't called Glory by all the seductive ladies in London for the beauty of his smile alone.

That celebrated smile suddenly appeared on his starkly handsome face as he threw his legs over the side of his bed and reached for his breeches.

A female stowaway on his yacht. How serendipitous.

Entertainment perhaps, for his voyage to Naples.


Creeping down the dimly lit passage, Serena hardly dared breathe. She'd waited until all sounds of activity had ceased on the yacht save for the night crew above decks. And if she hadn't been famished she wouldn't have risked leaving her hiding place in the small closet filled with female attire, the scented fabrics reminding her poignantly of her mother's fine gowns.

Long ago . . . before her mother's death.

Before her father's spiral into drink and gambling.

Before her own servitude as governess to the despicable Tothams.

A small sigh escaped her as she moved toward the galley she'd seen when she'd stolen aboard the yacht at Dover late last night. How far removed she was from that distant childhood—without funds, in flight from England aboard a stranger's yacht, hoping to reach Florence by the grace of God and her own wits.

Her stomach growled as the delicious scent of food from the galley drifted toward her. She eased open the door and the more urgent need to eat drove away any remnants of nostalgia or self-pity.

She was adding a crusty loaf of bread to the cheese and pears she held in the scooped fold of her skirt when a voice behind her gently said, "Would you like me to wake my cook and have him make you something more substantial?"

She whirled around to find a gentleman lounging against the door jamb. His smile flashed white in the subdued light, mitigating the terror his voice had engendered although his state of undress, clothed as he was in only breeches, gave rise to another kind of fear. He was powerfully built, the light from a small oil lamp casting his muscular body in shadow and plane, his virility intense at close range.

"Have we met before?" he softly asked, wondering if he should know the young lady. The blur of women in his life occasionally made it difficult to recall specific females.

"Not precisely," Serena replied, hesitant, not certain of his mood despite his soft voice. "I saw you in the parlor of The Pelican last night."

"Really," he said with genuine surprise, shifting slightly in his stance. He rarely overlooked women of such striking good looks. She had glorious golden hair, huge dark eyes, a slender, voluptuous form and a sensuous mouth he was definitely interested in tasting. "I must have been very drunk," he added, half to himself.

"You may have been," she said, repressing an odd flutter induced by the graphic display of rippling muscle as he moved. "You didn't come aboard till almost dawn."

"Really," he said again, his voice mild. "Are we sailing mates then?"

"I'd be happy to *pay* for my passage."

His gaze raked her swiftly, pausing for a fraction of a second on the food gathered in her skirt. "But you prefer not taking conventional routes."

"My ship left without me after I'd already paid for my passage." Her eyes suddenly filled with tears.

"Please don't cry," he quickly said. "You're more than welcome aboard the *Siren*." He was uncomfortable with distrait women and she was obviously without funds if she was reduced to stealing aboard his vessel.

"I can . . . reimburse you for my passage," she said, swallowing hard to stem her tears. "Once we reach Italy." The tuition money she'd sent to Florence should cover her fare.

"Nonsense," he murmured. "I'm sailing there anyway." He smiled briefly. "How much can you eat, after all." Easing away from the jamb he stood upright, his height suddenly formidable to her upturned gaze. But his voice was bland when he said, "Why don't I find you some better accommodations and real food. Do you eat beefsteak?"

"Oh, yes." Serena salivated at the thought, her last meal a frugal breakfast in London two days ago. "Yes, definitely."

"Why don't you make yourself comfortable," Beau suggested. "The second door on the right should do," he quietly added, moving back into the passageway to allow her egress from the galley. "I'll join you directly once I get my cook awake."


He didn't reappear for some time. Instead a young lad with hot water and towels appeared in his stateroom, followed shortly by another servant with a decanter of tokay and cookies. He was allowing his beautiful passenger time to wash and refresh herself while he gave directions for a sumptuous meal to his French chef he'd cajoled out of bed with a sweet smile and a lavish bribe.

Some sauteed scallops first, he'd requested while the young Frenchman had sulkily rolled out of bed. "She's very beautiful, Remy, and not quite sure she can trust me."

"Nor should she," the slender young man muttered

standing motionless beside his bed for a moment, still half-asleep.

"But your luscious food will set her mind at ease."

"So I'm supposed to help you seduce her," the Frenchman grumbled, his chestnut hair falling into his eyes as he bent to pick up his trousers from a nearby chair.

"Now, Remy, since when do I need help there," Beau murmured, his grin roguish. "I just want her happy."

"Then maybe you should serve her oysters first," Remy said with an answering grin as he stepped into his trousers. "And save the scallops for lunch for tomorrow when her passions are sated."

"She wants beefsteak too."

Remy groaned. "You English have no subtlety. Served bloody, I suppose."

"With your mushroom and wine sauce, *s'il vous plait,*" Beau pleasantly added, "and I'll add another fifty guineas to my offer."

"Make it sixty and I'll give her floating islands for dessert as well. Women adore them."

"You're a treasure, Remy. How would I survive without you?"

"You'd be skin and bone with all your fucking, no mistake."

"And I'm deeply grateful." Beau's voice was amused.

"I suppose you need this all within the hour so you don't have to wait too long to make love to this female you've found."

The young Earl of Rochefort grinned. "After all these years you read my mind, Remy darling. An hour would be perfect."

But he gave no indication of his designs when he entered his stateroom a few minutes later. "My cook is grumbling, but up," Beau said with a smile, walking over to a built-in bureau and pulling out a crisply starched shirt from the drawer. "So food should arrive shortly. Are you comfortable?" he politely queried, slipping the shirt over his head.

"Yes, thank you," Serena looked up at him from the depths of a soft, upholstered chair she'd almost fallen asleep in. "The cookies were delicious . . . and the wine."

"Good." Glancing at the crumbs remaining on the plate, he gauged the amount of wine remaining in the decanter with an assessing eye.

"I'd like to thank you very much for your hospitality." The lanterns had been lit by his servants and Serena's fairness was even more delectable bathed in a golden light. And her eyes weren't dark but aquamarine, like the Mediterranean.

"My pleasure," he casually said, dropping into a chair opposite her. My *distinct* pleasure, he more covetously thought as he gauged her lush beauty tantalizing. How would she respond, he wondered, to his first kiss? "Where had you booked passage?" he asked instead, gracious and well-behaved. "Perhaps I could see that your money is returned."

"Do you think you could?" She sat forward, her eyes alight with hope.

And for the briefest moment Beau St. Jules questioned his callous pursuit of pleasure, her poverty so obvious. But in the next flashing moment he soothed his momentary twinge of conscience by deciding a generous settlement once they reached Italy would more than compensate for his dishonorable intentions. And who knew, he considered in a more practical frame of mind, she might not be so innocent despite her enchanting delicacy. She'd stowed away after all—not exactly the act of a proper young lady.

"I'm sure I could. How much did you lose?"

"Fifty pounds," she said. "I'd been saving for years."

Good God, he thought, briefly startled. He gambled thousands on the turn of a card. "Let me reimburse you in the interim," he suggested, reaching for a wallet lying on his desk.

"Oh, no, I couldn't possibly take money from you."

He looked up from the purse he was opening, not because of her words but her tone. A small reserve had entered her voice and her eyes, he noted, held a distinct apprehension. "Consider it a loan," he calmly replied, gazing more critically at her, trying to properly place her in the hierarchy of female stowaways—a novel category for him.

Her navy serge gown was worn but well-cut, her shoes equally worn but impeccably polished; her exquisite face and radiant hair couldn't be improved on in the highest ranks of society. Was she some runaway noble wife dressed in her servant's clothes or someone's beautiful mistress fallen on hard times?

"I'm a governess," she deliberately said.

"Forgive me. Was I staring?" His smile was cordial as he counted out a hundred pounds. "Here," he said, leaning across the distance separating them, placing the bills in a neat stack on a small table beside her chair. "Pay me back when you can. I've plenty. Do you care to divulge your name?" he went on, noting her necessitous gaze, willing her to pick up the money, wanting the distrust in her voice to disappear.

"Why?" Her blue-green gaze rising to his was cool, guarded.

"No reason." He shrugged—a small lazy movement, deprecating, indulgent. "I was just making conversation. I have no intention of hurting you," he softly added.

Her expression visibly relaxed. "My name's Serena Blythe."

Definitely an actress, he thought. She couldn't be a governess with a name and face and opulent body like that. "Have you been a governess long?" he casually asked, waiting to decipher the fabrications in her reply.

"Four years. When my father Viscount Amberson died I was forced to make a living."

He felt his stomach tighten. A *viscount's* daughter? Did she have relatives? he instantly wondered, the kind who would exert all the conventional pressures? And then as instantly he decided any young lady so destitute must be on her own. "I'm very sorry."

She sat very still for a moment, thoughts of her father always painful, and then taking a small breath she said in a controlled tone, "Papa gambled his money away. He wasn't very good at cards after his first bottle."

"Most men aren't."

She glanced at the bills and then at him and he could almost feel that small spark of elation he suddenly saw in her eyes.

"Are *you*?" she mildly inquired.

"Best hand wins the hundred pounds?" he softly suggested, one dark brow raised in query. "Although I warn you, I'm sober."

"It would legitimize my taking the money." She smiled for the first time, a lush yet curiously girlish smile, enigmatic like her.


Twenty minutes later when the first course of oysters arrived, she was five hundred pounds richer, the tokay decanter was empty, an easy bantering rapport had been established and Beau had only deliberately let her win two hands. The rest she'd won on her own. She was either very good or very lucky. But she was definitely beautiful, he cheerfully noted, lounging in a comfortable sprawl across from her, his cards balanced on his chest, his gaze over the colorful fanned rims, gratified.

As was his mood.

The chill in her voice had disappeared, the guarded expression in her eyes replaced with animation. And when she smiled at him after a winning hand, he found it increasingly difficult to refrain from touching her.

She ate the oysters with relish.

She drank more wine when another decanter arrived and she said, "Thank you" so sweetly and gracefully when only the empty oyster shells remained on her plate, he almost considered giving up his plans to bed her.

But then she leisurely stretched and smiled at him. And

all he could think of was the plump fullness of her soft breasts raised high for that slow lingering moment with her arms flexed above her head. Even the plain navy serge couldn't disguise their delectable bounty.

"Did you make your gown?" he inquired to mask his overlong gaze with politesse. "I like the lace trimmed collar."

Leaning back against her chair, she delicately touched the white lace. "It was my mother's. I outgrew all of mine."

He swallowed before he answered, the thought of her outgrowing her girlish gowns having a profound effect on him after just having observed the voluptuous swell of her breasts.

"We could probably find you some additional dresses on board."

"Like the ones in the closet under the stairwell?"

"You were hiding there?"

She nodded. "The scent was luscious. Very French."

"I'll have my steward put together a wardrobe tomorrow," he blandly said, not about to discuss French scents or the reason they were there.

"Whose gowns are they?"

He gazed at her for a brief moment, gauging the degree of inquisition in her query but her expression was open, innocent of challenge.

"I'm not sure," he evasively answered. "Probably my mother's or sisters'. Which meant the more garish gowns would have to be culled out before offering the lady her choice. His light of loves had a penchant for seductive finery.

"I often wished I had siblings. Do you see your family often?"

He spoke of his family then in edited phrases, of their passion for racing and their winning horses, of their stud in the north, how his younger brother and sisters were all first class riders, offering charming anecdotal information that brought a smile to her face.

"Your life sounds idyllic. Unlike mine of late," Serena

said with a fleeting grimace. "But I intend to change that."

Frantic warning bells went off in Beau's consciousness. Had she *deliberately* come on board? Were her designing relatives even now in hot pursuit? Or were they explaining the ruinous details to his father instead? "How exactly," he softly inquired, his dark eyes wary, "do you plan on facilitating those changes?"

"Don't be alarmed," she said, suddenly grinning. "I have no designs on you."

He laughed, his good spirits instantly restored. "Candid women have always appealed to me."

"While men with yachts are out of my league." Her smile was dazzling. "But why don't you deal us another hand," she cheerfully said, "and I'll see what I can do about mending my fortunes."

She was either completely ingenuous or the most skillful coquette. But he had more than enough money to indulge her and she amused him immensely.

He dealt the cards.

And when the beefsteaks arrived some time later, the cards were put away and they both tucked into the succulent meat with gusto.

She ate with a kind of quiet intensity, absorbed in the food and the act of eating. It made him consider his casual acceptance of all the privileges in his life with a new regard. But only briefly because he was very young, very wealthy, too handsome for complete humility and beset by intense carnal impulses that were profoundly immune to principle.

He'd simply offer her a liberal settlement when the *Siren* docked in Naples, he thought, discarding any further moral scruples.

He glanced at the clock.

Three thirty.

They'd be making love in the golden light of dawn . . . or sooner perhaps, he thought with a faint smile, reaching across the small table to refill her wine glass.

"This must be heaven or very near . . ." Serena murmured, looking up from cutting another portion of beefsteak. "I can't thank you enough."

"Remy deserves all the credit."

"You're very disarming. And kind."

"You're very beautiful, Miss Blythe. And a damned good card player."

"Papa practiced with me. He was an accomplished player when he wasn't drinking."

"Have you thought of making your fortune in the gaming rooms instead of wasting your time as an underpaid governess?"

"No," she softly said, her gaze direct.

"Forgive me. I meant no rudeness. But the demimonde is not without its charm."

"I'm sure it is for a man," she said, taking a squarely cut piece of steak off her fork with perfect white teeth. "However, I'm going to art school in Florence," she went on, beginning to chew. "And I shall make my living painting."

"Painting what?"

She chewed a moment more, savoring the flavors, then swallowed. "Portraits, of course. Where the money is. I shall be flattering in the extreme. I'm very good, you know."

"I'm sure you are." And he intended to find out how good she was in other ways as well. "Why don't I give you your first commission?" He'd stopped eating but he'd not stopped drinking and he gazed at her over the rim of his wine glass.

"I don't have my paints. They're on the *Betty Lee* with my luggage."

"We could put ashore in Portugal and buy you some. How much do you charge?"

Her gaze shifted from her plate. "Nothing for you. You've been generous in the extreme. I'd be honored to paint you"—she paused and smiled—"whoever you are."

"Beau St. Jules."

"*The* Beau St. Jules?" She put her flatware down and

openly studied him. "The darling of the broadsheets . . . London's premier rake who's outsinned his father, The Saint?" A note of teasing had entered her voice, a familiar, intimate reflection occasioned by the numerous glasses of wine she'd drunk. "Should I be alarmed?"

He shook his head, amusement in his eyes. "I'm very ordinary," he modestly said, this man who stood stud to all the London beauties. "You needn't be alarmed."

He wasn't ordinary of course, not in any way. He was the gold standard, she didn't doubt, by which male beauty was judged. His perfect features and artfully cropped black hair reminded her of classic Greek sculpture; his overt masculinity however, was much less the refined cultural ideal. He was startlingly male.

"Aren't rakes older? You're very young," she declared. And gorgeous as a young god, she decided, although the cachet of his notorious reputation probably wasn't based on his beauty alone. He was very charming.

He shrugged at her comment on his age. He'd begun his carnal amusements very young he could have said but circumspect, asked instead, "How old are *you*?" His smile was warm, personal. "Out in the world on your own?"

"Twenty-three." Her voice held a small defiance; a single lady of three and twenty was deemed a spinster in any society.

"A very nice age," he pleasantly noted, his dark eyes lazily half-lidded. "Do you like floating islands?"

She looked at him blankly.

"The dessert."

"Oh, yes, of course." She smiled. "I should save room then."

By all means, he licentiously thought, nodding a smiling approval, filling their wine glasses once more. *Save room for me—because I'm coming in. . . .*

When the dishes were cleared away by the servants and coffee and fruit left, they moved to a small settee to enjoy the last course. She poured him coffee; he added his own brandy and leaning back, took pleasure in watching her slice a pear and leisurely eat each succulent piece.

"Your employers didn't feed you enough, did they?"

She turned to look at him, all languid grace and beauty. "You wouldn't understand."

His lashes lowered fractionally. "Tell me anyway."

"I don't want to," she retorted, suddenly disquieted, all the misery still too fresh. "I don't want to remember anything about those four years with the Tothams." And despite her best intentions, her eyes grew shiny with tears.

Quickly setting his cup down, he took the dessert knife from her grasp and the remains of the pear, wiped her fingers on a lavender scented napkin and holding her small hands in his, softly said, "It's over. You don't have to go back."

When a tear slid down her cheek, he gently drew her into his arms and held her close. "Don't cry, darling," he murmured. "By the time we get to Naples, you'll have won a fortune from me. And then the Tothams can go to hell."

She giggled into his chest.

"And I'll see that the portrait you paint of me is seen at the Royal Academy. Should I pose nude as Mars? That should draw attention."

She giggled again and pushing slightly away from him, gazed up into his smiling face. "You're incredibly kind," she whispered.

Her lips were half parted and only inches away. It took all his willpower to resist the temptation; her sweet vulnerability, her sadness affected even his disreputable soul.

"May I kiss you?" she whispered, her feelings in turmoil, the warmth and affection he offered inexpressibly welcome after so many years of emotional deprivation, the feel of his arms around her a balm to her lonely heart.

"You probably shouldn't." He was trying to be honorable. She perhaps didn't understand what a kiss would do to him.

"I'm not an innocent." She'd been kissed before although against her will, by the Tothams' repulsive son when he'd dared transgress his mother's commands apropos servants. It was immensely satisfying to offer a kiss of her own accord.

Beau shut his eyes briefly, her few simple words permission for all he wished to do. And when he opened his eyes, he murmured, heated and low, "Let *me* kiss *you* . . ."

She was lost then, a true innocent despite what she'd said, her notion of a kiss eons distant from Beau St. Jules's kisses.

He made her feel lusciously heated, melting, his mouth delicate at first, offering butterfly kisses on her lips and cheeks, on her earlobes and temples, on the warm pulse of her throat. And then his mouth drifted lower, following his fingers as he unbuttoned the top three buttons at her neckline, drew her collar open and kissed her soft pale skin.

She kissed him back after that and a new tremulous feeling flared deep in the pit of her stomach. Pleasure inundated her senses, her heated blood, the warming surface of her skin and most of all, gloriously in her spirit where she felt overwhelmingly happy. "You make me feel wonderful," she whispered, too long in the wasteland to want to forego such blissful sensations.

"You make me feel . . . impatient," he murmured, lifting her into her arms, moving toward his bed, his mouth covering hers again, eating her tantalizing sweetness.

"Maybe I shouldn't," she breathed moments later when he lowered her gently to the bed.

"I know," he murmured, brushing his mouth over hers. "I shouldn't undo these buttons," he whispered, unclasping another pearl button at her neckline. "Tell me I shouldn't."

"It's highly improper," she gently teased, touching his strong jaw with a trailing fingertip, smiling up at him.

"But I have this powerful carnal urge." His voice was deep, low, rich with promise.

"Should I be frightened?" Her heart was racing, her senses in tumult.

"Are you usually?" he silkily inquired, amused at how well Miss Blythe played the game.

She didn't know what to say for a moment. "No," she finally replied, trembling, eager for his touch. "I'm not."

And then the man known by salacious repute as Glory lived up to his name.